IN
FULL BLOOM

IN
FULL BLOOM

Caroline Hwang

DUTTON

DUTTON
Published by the Penguin Group
Penguin Putnam Inc., 375 Hudson Street, New York, New York 10014, U.S.A.
Penguin Books Ltd, 80 Strand, London WC2R 0RL, England
Penguin Books Australia Ltd, 250 Camberwell Road, Camberwell, Victoria 3124, Australia
Penguin Books Canada Ltd, 10 Alcorn Avenue, Toronto, Ontario, Canada M4V 3B2
Penguin Books (N.Z.) Ltd, 182–190 Wairau Road, Auckland 10, New Zealand

Penguin Books Ltd, Registered Offices: Harmondsworth, Middlesex, England

Published by Dutton, a member of Penguin Putnam Inc.

First printing, March 2003
10 9 8 7 6 5 4 3 2 1

LIBRARY OF CONGRESS CATALOGING-IN-PUBLICATION DATA

Hwang, Caroline.
    In full bloom / Caroline Hwang.
      p. cm.
    ISBN 0-525-94711-6 (acid-free paper)
    1. Korean American families—Fiction. 2. Korean American women—Fiction. 3.
Mothers and daughters—Fiction. 4. New York (N.Y.)—Fiction. 5. Single women—
Fiction. 6. Young women—Fiction. I. Title.

PS3608.W36 I52000
813'.6—dc21

                                                                    2002075703

Printed in the United States of America
Set in Goudy
Designed by Eve L. Kirch

PUBLISHER'S NOTE
This book is a work of fiction. Names, characters, places, and incidents are either the product of the author's imagination or are used fictitiously, and any resemblance to actual per-
sons, living or dead, business establishments, events, or locales is entirely coincidental.

IN
FULL BLOOM

CHAPTER 1

≈◯≈

"Ginger, you there!"

Even for my mother this was a strange way to start a conversation. The ringing telephone had cut my shower short. I secured the towel wrapped around me. "Where else would I be Monday at eight-thirty in the morning?" A mere fashion assistant at *À la Mode* magazine, I was supposed to be at work in half an hour. But my boss was my best friend from college, and Sam wouldn't be in until eleven.

"Then why you don't answer the phone quickly? I rang and rang! I worry nobody home!" My mother was still shouting. I thought I heard traffic in the background—the same rapid-fire honks that were coming in through the open window. Why was she calling from the street? What was she doing on my street? I spun toward the window, my wet hair whipping me in the face. There, directly below on the sidewalk, was her black head and bright green Chanel suit.

"Mom? Why aren't you in Milwaukee? Did something happen? Is something wrong?"

"Nothing not wrong in Milwaukee."

"Then what are you doing in New York?" I asked, somewhat relieved.

"I come to fix your life."

I laughed in surprise. "And how are you going to do that?"

"I gonna find you a good Korean husband."

"What?" I said, not because I didn't hear her but because I couldn't believe the inevitable had arrived already.

It is a truth universally acknowledged that a Korean mother in possession of a single adult daughter is in want of a professional Korean son-in-law. This maxim is so incontrovertible, this proclivity so genetically hardwired, it was a veritable miracle I'd made it this far, to my twenty-seventh year, unhitched.

"Open the door," she said.

The inevitable wasn't my succumbing to her matrimonial wishes—I needed a husband like Gloria Steinem needed a name tag—but my mother's attempting to fix me up. She'd tried when I was in graduate school, but I'd fended her off by claiming to be too busy to think about men. Not an entire lie. Though, instead of studying, I was occupied coming up with excuses to give my dissertation adviser, eluding chatty freshmen who wanted to discuss the papers they were writing for me, and cursing the admissions people who believed me when I said in my application that I wanted to be an English professor. I'd also managed to bat down a bachelor she lobbed at me several months after I left Madison. But now I had no excuse, no protection. Almost a year in Manhattan, fourteen months since I'd abandoned my dissertation on unpublished subversive female texts, I still didn't have Life Plan B. My job, a stopgap measure, was anything but demanding, and my mother knew that my evenings and weekends were free.

I dropped the phone, and tempted though I was not to let her into the building, I held down the button on the wall that would release the lock on the door downstairs. I scanned the walk-in closet that passed for my apartment. Boxes of books stood against the wall where the movers had stacked them. The bed was a jumble of pillows and twisted sheets. Clothes, shoes, and magazines carpeted the wood floor and adorned the secondhand couch. Beer bottles, some upright and others on their sides, occupied the kitchen counter like a small army on furlough the morning after. The slovenliness wouldn't have surprised my mother, but the beer bottles stoppered with cigarette butts would.

I didn't have a lot of time. It was a fourth-floor walk-up, and my mother was fifty-nine, but she was in great shape. I grabbed a shopping bag, and with my arm swiped everything on the counter into it. The sound of shattering glass was sort of exhilarating. I was trying to pluck out a plate from the bag, when the phone rang again.

"Ginger, you are what apartment? That why I call in first place."

I gave her the number, but instead of going to the buzzer, I ran with the Saks bag to the door, down the hallway, and to the garbage chute. I hated contributing perfectly recyclable bottles to a land-fill, but apparently, when things came down to the wire, I cared more about saving my butt than the environment. My mother didn't approve of drinking or smoking, and I didn't want to discuss my unladylike behavior. It was better that she continued living in the dark.

A policy I generally adhered to.

"Mom, did it work?" I asked into the intercom, wiping the sweat on my brow with the back of my hand. Through the curtainless window, the summer sun was doing its best to make the studio unbear-able.

"I still wait for the buzzer."

"Huh, that's strange. I'll try again."

I'd managed to turn the fan around so it was blowing the stale air out the window when she knocked.

I opened the door wide. She was flushed from the climb up, but she looked fine, the same as always. From her short, puffed-out hair that made her head look disproportionately big to her bone-thin, impeccably dressed body, she was, to my mind, the Korean Nancy Reagan. I took her suitcase from her and reeled backward from the unexpected weight.

"I have to go to work," I said by way of greeting.

"I happy to see you too." She stood on her toes—even with heels on, she was a half-foot shorter than me—and pecked me on the cheek. Regretting my brusqueness, I started to wrap my arms around her, but she shrugged them off. "You wet." She walked around me and into the apartment.

Readjusting my slipping towel, I followed her to the couch but remained standing. I shifted my weight from foot to foot, unsure of what to say or do. I certainly wasn't going to bring up the husband thing. Her relentless drive to get me to the altar was mortifying, and her requirement that this hypothetical husband be Korean put me in a particular pickle, as I had never met an Asian man I wanted to date, let alone spend the rest of my life with. She didn't know about my discriminatory taste, just as she didn't know about the non-Korean men I'd mamboed with in the past. (I didn't dance with them for long—and I made sure they understood I was not long-waltz material.)

I couldn't tell her. When my older brother, George, defied her and married a white woman, my mother made me promise she wouldn't lose me the same way. Granted, I was only fourteen when I made this vow, hardly a legally binding age. But I was all she had. My father left us when I was four.

She waved me out of the way. Sitting in an elongated triangle of light coming in from the window, she surveyed the apartment. It was the first time she was seeing it; I'd insisted on moving without her help. The sun made her squint and brought out the wrinkles around her eyes. She looked tired, stooped a little, the way she had after I dropped out of school and she hustled me out of Madison and temporarily into her house. I'd been planning on staying longer on campus, treading water until I figured out my next step, but she and the movers appeared at my door the first Saturday after I formally bailed from my program.

Slowly, she shook her head and clucked her tongue. "What a dump," she pronounced. A real estate agent, she was probably thinking of the house I could buy in Milwaukee, paying the same monthly mortgage as I was paying rent. "You can do better."

"Not on my salary." As it was, she was helping me with the rent, along with food, utilities, and miscellaneous extravagances. Fashion assistants earned well below the median income of college graduates, and perforce lived beyond their means.

"No, never on your salary." She got to her feet and tugged on my cheek. It hurt. "But with doctor salary, yes." She smiled.

Here we go, I thought, rubbing my face.

"I got a good doctor for you," she said with the bravado of a car salesman. It was the same tone she'd used pitching the bachelor ten months earlier. Though back then, I hadn't been surprised. I'd known she would spring into action as soon as I left grad school, which was one reason I'd loitered for as long as I did.

That time it was over the phone. "Ginger, I don't ask you to walk to Ohio," she'd cooed. "I pay for plane ticket. Just let him meet you. I buy you new dress." Meeting me, of course, was to fall in love with me. "He good-looking, he engineer, and he second son."

My father was a first son.

"I don't care about birth order," I said, stalling for time. Telling her I was feeling too down to meet anyone would have been too unprecedented an admission. She knew, though, that I was struggling. I always tried to put a positive spin on things, mustering a cheerful front for her, but she called me weekly, at unpredictable times, catching me hungover, sleeping, or moved by a tampon commercial. As hard as I tried to contain my bewilderment at the lack of achievement in my life, sometimes the truth leaked out.

"You don't care? You should. First son has to live with parents. You think I only care what he does for living. But Mommy think of everything." I could imagine her tapping her finger against her head. "That why you should trust me. I get you only the best."

"But he lives in Ohio!" I blurted out, thankful for the escape clause. Homing in on the fact that her network of Korean acquaintances with eligible sons was limited to the Midwest, I added, "I'm not going to move. I just got to New York. So what's the point in meeting him?"

To my astonishment, she gave in without putting up more of a fight, and canceled the plane ticket. I thought she relented not out of kindness or fair play, but to give me time to get back on my feet, so I could score an accomplishment, become someone a Korean mother would consider "only the best" to marry her son.

I was wrong. Or maybe I was just taking too long, because here she was in my crowded studio. I looked heavenward for succor.

"You don't say something?"

"Like what?" I asked reluctantly.

She shrugged, still smiling. "How about thank you?"

"I haven't even met him."

"So you want to?"

"Let's discuss this later. I have to get to work."

She frowned. "But your bloom is almost over."

"In the next eight hours?" As often as I'd heard that Korean saying, the English translation now stung. I couldn't pretend, as I usually did, that I was missing a cultural nuance. At the magazine, I was the oldest assistant in the fashion department by four years. Everyone my age, like Sam, was an editor.

"Don't break up my heart," she said, furrowing her brow.

"You came at a bad time. You should have consulted me first."

"If I do that, you tell me not to come, you busy."

She had a point. "But why did you take such an early flight?"

She wrinkled her nose and twisted her mouth to one side. "I didn't. I came yesterday."

"You did? Where did you stay?" As aggravated as I was, I couldn't help but feel hurt that she'd flown all this way and not seen me first.

"Mrs. Oh," she answered. "She moved to New Jersey when you little girl. We always do parknic together. You remember her?"

I nodded. Mrs. Oh talked loudly and laughed a lot. Her husband and my father had been in the same Ph.D. program. The Ohs had a son. "Isn't their boy's name Bob?" My brother and I used to get a kick out of saying his name. Bob Oh. *Bah-bo* means fool in Korean.

My mother vigorously nodded. "Bob. Bobby. That right. He medical doctor now. Lives here. Handsome like his father."

"He's the good doctor you just mentioned?"

She nodded. She must have recently reconnected with the Ohs; otherwise she would have tried to set me up with Bob instead of the guy in Ohio. There was nothing like a single daughter to motivate you to hunt down old friends. I shuddered to think how many others she'd looked up.

"I think you wasted your money flying out here. I doubt we'll like each other."

"Don't say that. You don't know."

The summer my father left and my mother started working, I occasionally spent afternoons at the Ohs' house. I didn't mind playing with Bob when no one else was around, but he was always after my dolls. He also picked his nose.

"I know."

She opened her mouth, then closed it, thinking better of whatever she was going to say. Wagging her head, she instead said, "Even so, it not wasted trip. I stay until I get you a husband."

I waited for her to laugh, wink, give some sign she was only joshing.

It didn't come. I looked back at her suitcase. She was her own boss at the real estate company; she could stay indefinitely.

I closed my jaw to speak. "How many men do you have lined up?"

She refused to look me in the eye.

"Mother?"

"Let's talk later. Like you said, you gotta go to work." She put an arm around my waist and bussed me on a spot just below my shoulder—that was where she came up to on me.

"No, let's talk now."

"No, later. You have to get ready." She started to push me in the back, steering me toward the bathroom. I tried to resist her, but she was stronger, and then she started to tickle me. She knew all my soft spots.

CHAPTER 2

⁓❧⁓

Wearing a long black Narcisco Rodriguez number that was more appropriate for a dinner party than the office, I arrived at work only an hour late. All the assistants overdressed. It made us feel interesting, if not important, while riding public transportation to our meaningless jobs. The receptionist was comfortably installed at her desk, busy transferring callers to the wrong extensions. It would be another hour before Sam and the other senior editors meandered in.

A better name for the magazine would have been *Waste*, as in the brainpower, time, and trees that were squandered within its office walls. The flagship of Glossy Publishing, Inc., *À la Mode* was historically the waiting room of young society women playing at having careers until their husbands-to-be came into their trusts. Now the Junior Leaguers had been replaced by their granddaughters—Ivy Leaguers hell-bent on using their talents and educations to help other women dress and do their hair to seduce a man. In other words, a half century after the women's movement, the staff was better equipped to do their jobs, but the jobs hadn't changed.

Though perhaps guilty by association, I didn't consider myself a defector. Aside from the few ideas I gave to Sam here and there—I had nothing to do but read the trade dailies and page through European editions—I made no contribution to the content of the magazine. I wasn't even on the masthead.

I turned onto the fashion corridor and immediately felt an unusual energy in the air. The Monday-morning kaffee klatsches seemed to be talking about something more exciting than their weekends. A copywriter bumped into me and almost made eye contact when she mumbled excuse me. Like most everyone else, she was blond and pencil-thin, but I knew who she was—the lone fashion person who snagged assignments from the features department. Paige also regularly had questions about the clothes she was writing up and Sam sent me to her office to answer them. Paige was too harried to read the reports I typed for her.

I hurried down the hall to the windowless, doorless space I shared with Dakota West. An assistant for nearly two years at the time that I started, she'd been frosty at first. Now that she understood I wasn't her competition, and what good friends I was with Sam, a senior market editor on the rise, we were office buddies. Though we weren't so close that I would tell her about my mother's sneak visit or turn to her for help. Dakota and I went to sample sales together, and she stood with Sam and me at the monthly parties thrown in the conference room to toast birthdays, engagements, and, once, an adoption of a Chinese shar-pei.

The phone to her ear, Dakota hushed me with a finger to her lips before I could say hello. She listened a few more minutes and then carefully placed the receiver in its cradle. The red light on one of her boss's lines stayed lit.

Dakota's enduring promotionless state wasn't due to lack of effort—or even daring. Today she was wearing a purple and white checkered vintage Trigère suit, red knee-high socks, and patent leather Mary Janes. Model-tall and -thin with self-peroxided cropped hair, she could pull it, or any getup, off. Her unending assistantship was due to the dumb luck of having a boss who despised her, who treated her not as an apprentice but as a coffee fetcher, Xerox maker, and all-around slave. Chantal Lewis was a senior sittings editor, but Dakota had never been on a photo shoot.

"Nan's been fired," Dakota said at bedroom volume, her eyes bugged out. Nan was the fashion director. "And I think the evil one is getting her job." She pointed her head at Chantal's closed door. "She was here when I got in."

Sam was going to wig out when she heard that her masthead equal—they were on the same line—had been promoted over her. Though Sam covered the market, going to shows and showrooms, while Chantal styled models, dressing them up for the camera, they were archrivals. It had bothered Sam so much that Chantal came first on the line they shared on the masthead, she had considered legally changing her name from Starre to Cooper, her mother's maiden name. If she had, Dakota was going to accompany her to city hall to change her name to AAA. Dakota had been a chess champion in high school.

I ran to my desk to call Sam. She should be warned before she even approached the building. Someone from our floor might be outside, smoking. Actually, a brigade was probably down there, licking their chops. Schadenfreude, real journalists have commented, was one of the most overused words in the pages of the magazines owned by Glossy Publishing, but its frequent appearance was understandable to anyone who worked there.

I looked up at the clock on the wall to see if I should try Sam at home or on her cell. Just then Sam appeared through the glass wall, the force of her strides making her flaxen ponytail swing from side to side. She was scowling. I was too late.

The only child of the ninth richest man in America, Sam wasn't used to disappointment. Her father, Graham Starre, was the S in SDM, one of the biggest venture capital funds in the country. But she wasn't spoiled or obnoxious, as I had feared the summer before college when I received her letter embossed with her monogram. We were roommates all four years at Madison, spending more time together than with any other person, including her serial boyfriends. She took after her father, the son of a dairy farmer, though she got her looks from her mother, her father's second wife and former secretary. Sam wouldn't be taking this defeat lying down.

"What are you doing here?" I asked, wondering who had beaten me to the phone.

"Um, I work here?" She was facing me but looking past my ear.

I turned to see Chantal had crawled out of her cave. I'd had minimal interaction with her; I doubt we'd said more than seven words at a time, combined—the longest exchange being, "Have you seen my worthless assistant?" "No." Chantal was out of the office on photo shoots more than she was in, and when she was in, she kept her door closed. So everything I knew about her was from Sam and Dakota. Sam said that when Chantal first arrived at the magazine, already an editor, she had a French accent, which she dropped when Dakota, newly hired, forwarded to everyone in the department a voice-mail message from her mother out on Long Island. Dakota swore to Chantal it was an accident, but their relationship never recovered. Now Dakota was fond of telling people that Chantal was a lesbian, not a slur per se, but a rumor that could hurt a fashion editor on the make, the thinking going that a woman who dresses for women doesn't know how to dress for a man.

"Hey there," Sam called over, mustering a cheerful tone.

Chantal acknowledged the hello with a nod as she tossed a stack of files on Dakota's desk. Readjusting the pile of dishwater-blond curls on top of her head, she sauntered back into her office. She left the door open.

Sam's smile cracked. She quickly recovered and crooked her neck in the direction of her office. I nodded, but Dakota, her back to Chantal's open door, gave us an aggrieved look, the one she often made while picking at her tossed salad as I bit into a hamburger or pastrami sandwich. She probably was hungry, since she always was, but it was more likely the anguish of not being able to join our conversation that was behind her long face. Sam mouthed, "Later."

"Isn't this great?" Sam asked before I'd taken my seat across from her desk. "Chantal's so insecure, she can barely be civil to me."

"Great? But she's the new . . ." Sam didn't know. It was better that she find out in the privacy of her office, from me. We saw less of each other on the weekends and at night—partly as a consequence of our spending almost all day together, partly because I found her child-hood pals pretentious and unbearable—but I would always be more than just a work friend to her. "I have to tell you something." I got to my feet to close the door.

"Where are you—?"

"Just a second," I said over my shoulder. As close as Sam and Dakota were getting, I was sure Sam didn't want her to hear her cries of indignation and pain.

I was glad for this opportunity, small as it was, to repay Sam, to hold her hand for a change. These days her primary role seemed to be playing my fairy godsister, whisking me from my dropout doldrums, bringing me to New York, a city I otherwise would have taken years to make it to, even cosigning my lease when the landlord insisted on a guarantor in the tristate area. I was grateful but a little uncomfortable with, or maybe not used to, our unequal footing. In college, the assis-tance had gone both ways. My gift for writing papers had comple-mented her aptitude for locating and getting into the best parties. She'd taught me the value of studying and not cramming, of befriend-ing professors and going to their office hours, while I explained foot-ball and procured for her the driver's license of a high school classmate's older sister when the bars near campus stopped accepting out-of-state IDs.

Okay, I was getting a little tired of being Sam's project, her under-ling, when we were the same age—when I had gone further in aca-demia.

Sam had taken out her cigarettes. Smoking wasn't allowed in the building, but when people complained about the smell traveling through the vents, she just denied it was her. No one dared to go to Helena Boyle, the editor in chief.

"Chantal," I said, shaking my head at the proffered pack, "is your new boss. It happened this morning."

Sam choked on her smoke. She rolled away from the desk and

bent over. Her shoulders shook. But she wasn't hyperventilating. She was laughing. "I'm sorry," she said, gasping for air. "I wasn't expecting that."

"I'm not kidding, Sam."

"The way you closed the door, I thought you were going to announce you were pregnant."

I arched an eyebrow at her. Unless she believed in spontaneous conception, I didn't know how she could have thought that. I hadn't gone out with a man since leaving Madison. "Nan Bran's been fired," I said.

Sam lost her smile. "No, she hasn't," she said, stubbing out her cigarette. "She quit." She pushed the *Post*, open to the gossip column, at me. "When she read this."

It took me a while to find what she was referring to; the blind item was so small. It said: "Which Glossy fashion director is this close to getting a pink slip? (And we're not talking underpinnings.) Our inside source gave the rhyme but not the reason."

"Yeesh," I said, putting the paper down. "I can't believe Nan took the bait." Hothead though she was, she must have known that by quitting she was doing exactly what Helena wanted—forfeiting her severance package. "It doesn't even give a reason."

"O'Henry was given the reason. Falling newsstand sales." The art director chose the cover models, but the fashion director styled them. "It just didn't make for such good copy."

"How do you?"

She licked her lips delicately before answering, "Chantal is acting co–fashion director."

I held Sam's gaze until her face broke into a grin. "Ohmigod! Congratulations!" I leapt to my feet.

"Hell's giving us a month to prove who's best cut out for the job." Everyone called the head honcho that, but Sam was the only one who said it to her face. "She says she has to give Chantal a shot to be fair, but it's all a waste of my time if you ask me."

"What's a month? Let me give you a hug." I squeezed her hard. She had said she was going to make editor in chief by the time she was thirty, the age her father was when he banked his first million, and she was well on her way. She was moving up in the world.

While I was still casting about for a career. As successful as my mother was, I didn't compare myself to her, because real estate, which she entered after my father left, was a livelihood, not an identity. She'd gone to college, but her broken English lowered the expectations—and gave her fewer options. She wound up working in an office, but she would have been able to hold her head up among Koreans if she'd toiled in a store backroom or restaurant kitchen— that she owned, of course.

But Sam was my peer. The ground I had lost from grad school was only increasing. And my mother's crazy husband-hunt made matters all the more urgent.

"Okay, we got to get to work," Sam said, taking out a pad of paper. "Hell's holding an ideas meeting—"

"Not to be self-involved," I cut in. "But how does this move affect me?"

Sam jiggled her wristwatch. "In half an hour."

"I mean, if Hell fills your spot with someone on staff, will I move up to associate?"

"Associate?" Sam put her pen down. "Since when do you want that?"

"Since my mother arrived," I exhaled loudly, "to spear me a husband."

Sam pushed the notepad to the side. She knew about my bind when it came to my mother's expectations and my feelings about Korean men.

I recounted my morning. Sharing it with my old best friend was cathartic and made me feel like less of a freak. I mentally took back everything I'd been thinking earlier about her help.

"It sounds like it's time to come clean with her," Sam said, leaning back in her chair.

"You know I can't do that. I can't hurt—"

"Maybe if she knew, she'd give in."

"She won't." Marrying a non-Korean was to my mother what marrying someone beneath one's station was to Jane Austen—blasphemy.

"Or tell her you're not ready."

"It won't do any good. She thinks she knows better." She had said grad school was a mistake. Her exact words: "Who hires Korean to teach English in America?"

"But what's the rush?"

"My bloom is fading."

Sam stared incredulously at me.

"She's not a total throwback," I said, defending my mother despite myself. "I mean, if I told her I wanted to go further in my career first, she would back off. That's why I need this promotion."

Sam grimaced. She reached again for her Marlboro lights and held them out. I took one. I probably already reeked of secondhand smoke.

"I'm not asking you to hand me the job. I'll work for it. Just teach me the business."

"It's not that," Sam said. "I'm concerned that you're just grabbing for the nearest thing. You'd be taking a promotion away from someone whose passion really is fashion."

"Dakota is younger. She can wait."

Sam's mouth twitched. "I agree that you've been my assistant for too long. This is the prime time of our careers and you've been pissing it away."

"Thanks."

"But you should set your sights on an industry you're actually interested in. I have connections everywhere. I could hook you up."

"This is what I want to do." Not a total lie. Just a bit of an overstatement. I felt I could do many things, and these past months I'd been savoring the vista of possibilities as well as licking my wounds. But the time for self-indulgent dawdling was over. "I may not have shown interest, but I've shown aptitude."

"You do have good taste and ideas."

"And I have the big picture. Fashion isn't just trendy clothes. It's a mode of self-expression, an art. It's like architecture, where form meets function."

"I had no idea you thought so highly of what I do."

"Editors are critics, purveyors of—"

"Enough," Sam laughed. "You're starting to sound like Chantal."

"—culture. It's a worthwhile profession as long as seduction isn't the only objective. And it wouldn't be mine."

Her steepled fingers pressed against her lips, she looked at me in silence.

"Please, Sam. I'll give five hundred percent. Just give me—"

She tossed her ponytail. "I don't care about natural talent or hard work. They don't really matter here—or anywhere, really. What I'm concerned about is dedication."

"You've got it."

"Which means total submission. I'll need you to do everything I say."

I felt uneasy but I said okay.

"I mean it. No questions. No guff."

"No nada."

"Even with my coaching, it may not happen right away."

"That's all right. If I can show my mother I'm busy, she'll go home. I may have to go on the dates she's lined up, but I can deflect them—she can't have that many."

"You'll be competing against assistants who are pretty hungry."

"Anorexic, more like it."

"I wouldn't underestimate them."

"I don't. But they don't have you."

"Like Dad says, work is war."

"I can handle it. Ph.D. candidates aren't exactly kittens. They used to intentionally mis-shelve library books."

Sam looked hard at me. I stared back. Satisfied, she said, "Okay."

Grinning, I slouched back in my chair. Now that she was on board, my ship seemed less at risk of sinking. I could relax; she didn't have any showroom appointments scheduled for the day.

"Sit up. Let's get started."

"With what?"

"Either we do it my way or no way."

"Your way," I said hurriedly, pulling myself up. No wonder she'd advanced as quickly as she had. Perhaps if we'd stayed in touch the years I was toiling in my library-stack wasteland, I would have finished my degree or left sooner. "Where are we going?"

"Nowhere." She tossed her pad of paper and pen at me. "First we've got to cover some basic tenets of office warfare."

"Are you serious?"

"Ginger—"

"Okay." I picked up her Mont Blanc and held it ready.

She took a minute, pulling together her thoughts. She cleared her throat. "Number one, always put yourself first. Before you do anything, know what's in it for you. Number two, never let people—"

I held my hand up.

"You don't have to do that."

"I wasn't sure," I said, pulling it down. "I have a question."

"What happened to—never mind. What is it?"

"Have I been breaking the first rule all this time I've been giving you story ideas?"

Sam cocked her head to one side, considering the question. "No," she said, straightening her neck. "By helping me you were helping yourself. Now, where was I?"

"Number two, never let people," I prompted.

"Oh, right. Never let people see you sweat. Everything you do should seem effortless. It makes dumb people think you're untouchable and it makes smart people underestimate you."

She paused, but I held my tongue, scribbling down what she'd said. Her father, a former marine, was a shrewd man.

"Number three, don't discuss your plans or deeds. Word always leaks."

I looked up. "*That's* why you've never told me how you moved up? You could've trusted—"

"Four, scrap loyalty. It has no place in the office."

"Even between us?" I persisted.

"Scrap best friends. There are no real friends in business." She pointed to my pen. "Write it down."

I bent my head and did as she said. While I was piqued that she'd included me in her don't-trust-anyone policy, I was surprised, and not a little pleased, to hear she still considered me her best friend.

"So I should keep secrets from you," I said, jotting the last period with a flourish, "and back-stab you at the next opportunity?"

"Yes, but under my direction." She smiled at the nonsense of what she'd just said. "I mean, the point is that you shouldn't trust anyone the way you trust me."

"That's obvious."

"Not that obvious. You're so indoctrinated, you don't realize that snakes come in both genders."

I looked c'mon at Sam. Most of the missing books in the library at Madison had been feminist texts.

"If you're going to be this difficult—"

The phone interrupted her. The caller ID said it was Hell.

"Shit, the meeting. And we haven't even brainstormed for ideas." Sam jumped up. I rose with her. She grabbed her notepad and tore off the paper I'd written on. "Quick, give me one."

"Uh . . ." Folding my notes, I looked at her black Ungaro sundress, then down at myself. "Narcisco?"

"No, I need story ideas, not market news."

Her sharp tone triggered an idea. "Arresting looks," I said. "It could be models in various scenes of being arrested. You know, up against the wall with their legs spread. Stepping out of a squad car. Being handcuffed."

"With cops in uniforms. And hunky FBI agents. You're brilliant!" She turned back at the door. "I just thought of something."

The last time I'd seen that particular gleam in her eye, she'd proposed going to Harlem to score some coke. I'd begged off, stunned to hear she'd taken up drugs.

"What?"

"I'm going to tell Hell you helped me on this one."

CHAPTER 3

Sam spent the rest of the day in Hell's office, not even coming back for lunch. Chantal was in and out, suddenly having the cover shoot to prepare for. I filled Dakota in on the maneuverings afoot, mindful to keep mine to myself, and plied the afternoon combing through Sam's magazines, looking for ideas. My mother called several times, but I let the voice mail pick up to impress upon her how busy and unavailable I was.

Having this new image to uphold, I took the long way home, zigzagging across Fifth Avenue and strolling through my favorite stores. I loved New York for its noise and bustle, how its distractions crowded out thoughts and introspection, how you could be nowhere and yet you were always somewhere. Walking the packed, prosperous streets never failed to fill me with hope.

My outlook didn't dim on my entering my apartment. My mother had cleaned. I could now see the floor and secondhand orange couch, the only piece of furniture to make the trip from Madison. The boxes were in the hall, partially covered by one of her colorful Hermès scarves. By the door, my shoes were neatly mated and lined up in parallel rows, like couples primly sitting in church pews. Before walking farther into the apartment, I kicked off my shoes, something I didn't usually do here in my home but did because she would holler.

She was freshly showered and dressed in a pink silk Chanel dress with big shoulder pads and gold C-embossed buttons running down her arms. As long as little Korean women populated the earth, the eighties would never die. Their fondness for big shoulder pads and gold buttons was preternatural. I kissed my mother on the cheek.

"There you are. I worried you miss dinner." She was now folding my clothes and putting them in shopping bags. They needed to be dry-cleaned.

"Of course I wouldn't leave you to eat dinner alone. I just got stuck at the office." I smiled at the effortlessness of the fib and quickly hid my mouth behind my hand.

"Don't touch your face. That why you have zips," my mother scolded. "You should tell me when you come home. You didn't call me back."

If we were going to reenact my teen years, we would need a much bigger apartment, one with doors to slam. She continued to fold my clothes.

"I don't have zits." I dropped my hand down to my side. Rising fashionistas didn't have flawed skin.

"You had in school. That why you stayed home, no?"

"You knew I didn't go to school?"

"Of course I know." She clucked. "I know everything."

"Not everything," I said.

"You don't think so? Tell me something I don't know," she playfully challenged.

My new career plans could wait until dinner. "You don't know that you don't need to fold clothes before you take them to the dry cleaner. They're just going to throw them in a heap."

My mother smiled. "Silly Ginger, I don't dry-clean before I give these away. If I have to dry-clean, I just throw them out."

"What?" I jumped back. "You're giving away my clothes?"

"Some of your skirts are too short. Some shirts go down too low. Not becoming for a lady."

"What's wrong with this?" I asked, pulling a Diane von Furstenberg wraparound dress out of one of the bags.

"That just ugly."

"Mommm," I said, starting to feel like there wasn't enough air to breathe.

"Whaaaaaat?" she asked, imitating the tone of my voice. "You have so many clothes, there no room in your closet."

"That's not the clothes' fault," I replied, throwing the black dress back into the bag. "It's the closet's fault for being so small."

"I need another shopping bag," my mother said, ignoring me.

She'd been doing things like this my whole life. All resistance was futile. At least she wasn't going through my underwear drawer. "There are probably more where you found the first two."

My mother shot me a look and then went to the kitchen. I walked over to the closet and looked for something that didn't smell of smoke to wear to dinner. My mother may not have treated me like an adult with a budding career in couture, but at least I had the wardrobe for it. It was nice to be able to shift the hangers from one side to the other.

I had selected a blue gingham cotton shift, when my mother returned.

"You can't wear that. You need something more expensive," she said, opening the paper bag by whipping it through the air.

"This is Calvin Klein. It wasn't cheap."

"I know you pay a lot. But you need to wear something also looks expensive."

I put it back in the closet and pulled out a vintage Lilly Pulitzer. "Why do I have to look so nice? Are we going to a fancy restaurant?"

My mother rubbed the fabric between her finger and thumb. "It good material. But it old. It looks like you got at garbage sale."

I had bought it at a garage sale in Madison. I put the yellowing white dress back and sifted through the hangers again. I held out a plaid cotton number, unmistakably Burberry. She nodded her approval.

"You have to look nice because we gonna have dinner with Dr. and Mrs. Oh. They excited to see you after so many years."

"We are?"

My mother gave the ceiling a why-me? look. "I told you this already."

"No, you didn't," I said. "But that's okay." I patted her on the arm. "Your brain cells are aging."

"I did," she insisted. "I said on office answering machine."

I shrugged. I hadn't listened to her messages.

"I also told you Bobby gonna be there too."

I raised my eyebrows in alarm. I'd expected a discussion, an opportunity to declare my new vocation and point out the difficulties of scheduling, set down some ground rules. But she was pushing forward like a runaway train.

Before I could say anything, the phone rang.

"That Mrs. Oh with the restaurant," my mother said, reaching for the phone. Her face broke into a smile. She held the receiver away from her ear; Mrs. Oh was still loud. My mother motioned with her free hand for a pen and paper. I gave them to her and read the restaurant name and address over her shoulder.

My mother shooed me toward the bathroom. She pointed to her watch to indicate we didn't have a lot of time. I didn't move. I thought I would wait for her to get off the phone. They couldn't talk for long, they were about to see each other in person.

Using both hands now, my mother frantically gestured for me to get ready. Just as adamantly, I waved her off. She talked in Korean while I stood there, trying to pick out a word or two to get the gist of her conversation. My comprehension was limited to the informal phrasing and commands that a parent used with her child. But Mrs. Oh was doing all the talking. My mother said an occasional *ne, ne,* meaning right, right, and once she said the name Ann. I was surprised; I'd never known her to call a friend by her English name. About fifteen minutes later, my mother finally hung up.

"What was all that about?" I asked.

"Nothing."

"It didn't sound like nothing."

"We don't see each other for over twenty years. We have a lot to say."

"Well, tell her that now that you're in a neighboring state, she doesn't have to shout to be heard."

My mother took my hand and led me to the bathroom. "Get ready. We have to be there in hour."

I was always up for a Korean meal, especially one ordered by Korean speakers. Restaurants seemed to serve watered-down, bottom-of-the-barrel food to Americans and people like me. And I was curious to see the Ohs. With them and my mother in attendance, I could pretend that this setup was just a dinner among old friends and their hungry adult children.

CHAPTER 4
❧

We took a cab to Koreatown, a rundown patch of mostly wholesale stores anchored, surprisingly, by the Empire State Building. When I first saw the American landmark, I took it for an impostor like all the fake Gucci and Fendi bags in the crowded shop windows. Now I thought of it as a hostage. The restaurant, Secret Garden, was in the heart of the area, in the middle, actually, of a daunting block of shuttered storefronts and indecipherable signs. The streetlamps, which seemed unnecessary under the glare of neon, had just come on.

"We might be overdressed," I said, holding the glass door open for my mother. I wiped my hand on my shift.

The place wasn't shabby, but it was definitely broken in. Korean barbecue was thick in the air and on surfaces. My stomach rumbled, happy for all the shoulder-to-shoulder people jabbering Korean—testament to the authenticity and quality of the food. My mother pushed to the front; I followed in her wake and caught the spray of dirty looks.

The young woman standing at the podium bowed low to my mother. They exchanged words, both shouting to be heard over the din of talk and laughter and the hiss and sizzle of cooking meat. The hostess then led us past the tables with charcoal grills built into the center of them, the plates of colorful food off to the sides, stacked like cannonballs. We walked to the back, where three steps led up to a wall made of rice paper and framed with bamboo. She slid the wall to the left, opening the way to a small private room.

Mrs. Oh, sitting on the floor, jumped to her feet. In a frilly red frock with big shoulder pads, she was also doing her part keeping the eighties' look alive. My mother slipped out of her shoes and ran in her stocking feet to Mrs. Oh's outstretched arms. While they hugged and squealed like schoolgirls, I stood still, not sure what to do. My feet would be bare if I took off my sandals.

An Asian-style table with midget legs stood in the middle of the room. Ingeniously, a square had been cut out of the raised floor so that people sitting at the table could dangle their legs down instead of crossing them lotus-style the whole meal. A thin man with white hair, Dr. Oh, I presumed, and his son rose to their feet. Like me, both were tall for Koreans; the father maybe five nine if he straightened his stooped back and Bob a couple of inches taller.

A woman with short brown hair, her yellow-jacketed back to me, also stood up.

Clearly, my mother needed a primer on what made a bachelor eligible.

The brunette turned to face me. She was American.

The waitress shooed me in so she could slide the door closed. Though the wall was made only of rice paper, it shut out the noise.

"Ginger, come over here," my mother said, one arm around Mrs. Oh's waist. Though a little meatier than Nancy Reagan, Mrs. Oh could have passed for my mother's sister with their similarly saloned hair, designer clothes, and lunatic grins.

I smiled but didn't move.

"What wrong?"

Everyone was looking at me, Bob rubbing his flat abdomen. He had to do more than play golf to have a physique like that. Mrs. Oh nodded in understanding and kindly pointed to slippers lining the wall. Trusting previous wearers had the foresight and good hygiene to wear socks, I slid into a pair.

"Ginger, you remember Dr. and Mrs. Oh and their son, Bobby, don't you?" asked my mother when I'd reached the table.

I shot the American a questioning look before politely nodding and shaking hands with Dr. Oh. Just as I recalled, he was very sparing with his words. He said hello and that was it. I turned to Mrs. Oh. She grabbed ahold of my hand and yanked me to her.

"What you do shake my hand?" she asked, squeezing my shoulders. Her English was more broken than my mother's, probably from not having to work outside the home. She was clearly the life of the Oh household. The table at our feet hindered the rest of our bodies from touching. "You like daughter. The daughter I never have."

Bob groaned, rolling his eyes. His mother shot him a look, then released me. I awkwardly stood leaning over the table, then righted myself.

"You grow so beautiful," she said to me. "Bobby, can you believe how beautiful Ginger is?"

Bob ignored her question and instead bowed to my mother and

said hello to me. Putting his arm around the American's shoulders, he then introduced us to Ann Miller.

Ann? I shot my mother a look. Although she had said that name on the phone in my presence, she pretended to look surprised.

"My fiancée."

My head spun back to my mother. Fiancée? Not a last-minute guest. Not a girlfriend. But a fiancée! What could my mother have been thinking? She refused to make eye contact with me.

Mrs. Oh instructed us to sit down. Her husband and son took their former seats across from each other. Bob motioned for Ann to sit next to him, and my mother sat next to Mrs. Oh. Uneasily, I took the empty fourth side of the square.

Bob, Ann, and I remained quiet while the parents discussed the menu and ordered. It sounded like a lot of spicy dishes. My mouth watered despite the awkwardness of the situation. I hadn't had Korean food since I'd been home for Christmas.

"Ginger," Mrs. Oh unnecessarily shouted from across the table, "you remember play my Bobby? You play house each other."

Warily, I nodded. I could see where she was headed. I also didn't have revisionist memories of Bob. Those afternoons when I came over, he always wanted to stay indoors, unless his mother was doing yard work. I used to have to lure him out of the kitchen with my dolls, and then snatch them back to get him to chase me.

I looked at the grown Bob's face. There was no trace of the mama's boy I had known. The little jaw was now square, the thin brows bushy, the big and round eyes hard and obstinate. Aesthetically, he wasn't bad-looking.

"My Bobby always try kiss you. But you run away. Too bad."

"I don't remember that," Bob said.

"You did," his mother informed him. "You like Ginger so much. You always ask when she come to our house again."

Even my mother raised a skeptical eyebrow.

Bob took his arm away from Ann's shoulders so he could gesture with both hands. "I was an only kid. I had no one to play with."

Mrs. Oh dismissed his words with the wave of her hand. "Don't tell me that, Bobby. You love Ginger back then. I and Mrs. Lee"—she took my mother's hand and squeezed it—"always hope you and Ginger to marry."

I cringed. Mrs. Oh clearly wasn't taking the engagement lying down. It dawned on me that she told my mother to bring me, that my mother had gone straight to the Ohs last night to plan for tonight. To Dr. and Mrs. Oh, I wasn't a single woman pathetically trying to meet their son. I was there to somehow break up the lovebirds, show Ann what she was lacking, how she was unacceptable. My mother probably wished she'd had a patsy like me when my brother curtailed our celebration of his graduating from Harvard with the announcement that he was marrying. I watched Mrs. Oh and Bob stare at each other. I had no intention of actively participating in the parents' scheme, but I felt more easy now that I understood the purpose my presence was meant to serve. I started to relax. I could enjoy myself. I wasn't in the hot seat.

When the waitress came back with the bon-chon, about a dozen little appetizers, mostly vegetables, Ann surprised me by asking for a scotch, neat, and a glass of water. The waitress, still bent over, with her hand holding the small of her back, bobbed her head twice to signal she heard the request. I licked my lips and decided right then and there to take the plunge and order a beer. Dr. and Mrs. Oh would probably disapprove as much as my mother—young ladies didn't drink—but at this point it didn't seem to matter. Nothing I did mattered. I was there just to be there, to not be Ann, who had just ordered hard liquor. The chatter and chewing stopped.

"Large bottle or small?" the waitress asked, straightening her back and looking amused.

I glanced at my mom, trying to gauge how far I could push the situation. Bob answered for me, ordering a large and two glasses. Dr. Oh piped in to make it three glasses. Mrs. Oh said to bring OB for the whole table.

The beer and Ann's Glenlivet arrived. All the Koreans, including myself, downed their drink in one take. The two mothers burped and daintily wiped their mouths with the knuckles of their bent index fingers. Dr. Oh filled everyone's glass a second time; I handed him the ones he couldn't reach. He ordered another round of bottles before the waitress left the room.

She came back with the main courses, two busboys helping her bring them all. I had been right about the spicy food. In fact, there seemed to be a preponderance of dishes made of kimchi—sliced Chinese cabbage, radishes, cucumbers, or even apples, seasoned with salt, red pepper, and garlic, fermented to a sour piquancy and stench. Until I was eight, my mother had to rinse it in water for me; now I would bring it into my apartment only in the last-ditch hope that the odor could kill cockroaches. There was raw kimchi, fried kimchi, pancakes with kimchi, kimchi casserole, kimchi dumplings, and kimchi soup. And the dishes that weren't kimchi based were hard-core—raw octopus, sea cucumbers, tripe. It was strange that my mother hadn't ordered any of the foods I liked, like short ribs marinated in garlic and soy sauce, shrimp eggrolls, glass noodles with julienned vegetables. I looked at the mothers. They were occupied watching Ann.

I shifted my gaze and saw the last bit of color drain from Ann's face. Mrs. Oh had sent the most intimidating of the dishes in Ann's direction. I reached for my beer, though what I really could have used was Ann's scotch. Only a thumbnail of amber liquid remained in her glass. Gulping my drink, I used my free hand to get the waitress's attention and point to Ann's glass and the empty OB bottles.

"This looks like a feast!" Ann said bravely.

Mrs. Oh smiled broadly. "Yes, it feast for Korean king. These traditional delicacies." She waved her hand over the food. "Please to help yourself."

Bob scowled. "Everything here is kimchi! Ann can't eat th—"

Ann stopped him, placing her hand on his shoulder. She didn't have a ring yet.

"Honey, I'll be fine. I want to try your mother's favorite dishes."

"They not my favorite," said Mrs. Oh with a worried look on her face. "They Dr. Oh favorite."

Before Dr. Oh could pass the favorite dishes on to someone else, Ann started to put food on her plate. She took a little of everything. Her plate was a study in red.

The spicy food as well as the additional alcohol loosened everyone's tongue, Dr. Oh's particularly. I didn't know what he was saying in Korean, but whatever it was, he had my mother and his wife in stitches. I was stuck making small talk with Ann and Bob.

It turned out that they knew each other from Berkeley. They'd lost track of each other after graduation but had reconnected a couple of years ago at the hospital where they both worked. He was a cosmetic surgeon and she was a nurse in the emergency room. This was the first time she was meeting Bob's parents, who had been informed of the engagement right before my mother and I arrived.

That explained why Ann hadn't known better than to order liquor in front of the Ohs. I was surprised Bob hadn't coached her. It also meant my mother's startled response when Ann was introduced to us as Bob's fiancée had been genuine, to some degree. I would cut her some slack, but she wasn't entirely off the hook.

"Have you set a wedding date?" I asked to be polite.

The room was suddenly completely quiet. Mrs. Oh harrumphed and then tried to disguise it as a cough. She overacted, but my mother played along and pushed a glass of water to her, then lightly patted her on the back.

"Not yet," Ann said. "The engagement is open-ended."

Mrs. Oh leaned over her uneaten plate of food. "Really?"

"But it's soon," Bob quickly interjected. He put his chopsticks down and put his arm back on Ann's shoulders. He certainly touched her a lot.

"It open-ended, huh?"

"It's open-ended as to when exactly, but it'll be soon."

Mrs. Oh said something in Korean that made her husband and my mother chuckle. They returned to their conversation, though with less animation than before. Ann and I spent the rest of the meal taking desultory stabs at talking and eating—though she more pushed the food around her plate than brought it up to her lips. Bob sat still and in silence.

Outside, a round of thanks and good-byes went around. Mrs. Oh hugged me tightly. "You bring your mama to New Jersey. I make you nice dinner."

I ran to the curb to hail a cab, more than glad to be getting away. I felt both for Bob and for his parents. It was an impossible situation. My mother came up to me and pushed my arm down, saying she wanted to stretch her legs a little. She walked backward, bowing and waving to the Ohs. I held her left arm to pull her forward.

CHAPTER 5

"You should've told me what you and the Ohs were up to," I said as we crossed the street, both of us facing forward now, arm in arm. "I felt like a fool when I saw Ann."

My mother smiled, probably happy she wouldn't have to feign shock over the unannounced dinner guest. "If I tell you, you say you busy and don't come."

"But how did you know I would stay?"

The answer was obvious, my mother's silence said.

"Well, you're just lucky I was hungry, though that meal was barely worth sticking around for."

My mother laughed. "The kimchi was Dr. Oh's idea. Mrs. Oh and

I knew it not gonna work. That why we talk on the telephone earlier."

I pulled her arm to stop her from walking in front of an oncoming car. "Yeah, Ann ate more food than the Ohs. She's not going anywhere no matter what they dish up."

"They don't marry. They don't love each other."

"They certainly looked in love."

"Ginger, you know nothing about love."

I wondered whose fault that was.

"They don't love each other," my mother repeated. "People who do don't wait until engagement to tell parents."

Her son had, but I didn't point that out. He hadn't even given much notice of his nuptials, shotgunning to the altar a month after he dropped his bomb. He'd probably been afraid she was going to try to stop him.

We continued to walk, now holding hands.

"Bobby told Mrs. Oh about Ann only two weeks ago when she asked him if he wanna meet you. Mrs. Oh thinks they don't date for long. Bobby too busy to date. He don't even have time to come home on weekends."

"Maybe that's because he's spending them with Ann."

My mother weighed the possibility. "No," she said, shaking her head, "I don't think so. They not serious. She don't have ring. What kind of engagement that is?"

Ann hadn't discussed her politics, but she probably thought, as I did, that a diamond ring was a smartened-up patriarchy's latter-day form of branding, pain-free and decorative. My mother wouldn't understand, so I said the ring was probably being sized.

"That engagement made to be broken." She gave my hand a squeeze.

"Spoken by a true messenger of love."

My mother pointed a questioning finger to herself.

"Yes, you."

She smiled. She really didn't get irony. "Did you see how good dresser Bobby is? You like that, I know."

"He did have on a nice suit. Italian, I think." I could give her that, knowing he wasn't an eligible bachelor. One down, hopefully I would be dispatching as easily with the rest.

"You always underestimate your mommy."

"I certainly did this time."

"You mean it?"

I made a mental note to stop being sarcastic around her. "Mother, he's not available. Despite what the Mormons do, polygamy is against the law."

"He won't marry her. He not gonna do like George." Her tone hardened with her utterance of my brother's name, making me glance over at her. "Especially if I help Mrs. Oh." Her face was set with determination.

"What do you have in mind? You can tell me. It's not like I'm going to blab."

"No, you not good at hiding what you know."

She was wrong, but it was better that she continued in her ignorance. As long as she thought I was transparent, she wouldn't suspect there was a side to my life she didn't know about.

Not that there were any relationships to keep from her anymore. Though extricating myself from the last one—with Julian in Madison—hadn't been extraordinarily unpleasant, the experience had made me give up on dating entirely. It just seemed meaningless. I couldn't marry the men I was attracted to, couldn't even get close to them to find out if I wanted to. The prospect of small advances and repeated retreats for the rest of my life made me feel empty and bleak. It was easier on the heart not to get involved with anyone. It was easier not to want ever to marry.

If my mother only knew that her drive for her kind of connubial bliss was pushing me into the life of a monk, or perhaps of someone in the closet. At school there'd been a lesbian medievalist, also all-but-dissertation, who, like me, was hiding her personal life from her family. But at least she could live with her lover under the cover that they were friends. She also had the emotional, social, and political support of an entire community. As far as I knew, there was no organization for disowned, American-dating daughters of Koreans.

We walked a block in silence, our connected arms swinging. I looked down and saw we were stepping in sync. Left, right, left. It made me think of when we used to walk together to my grade school or through the mall. Without telling her what I was doing, I would try to match my stride with hers, and she would change her step to foil me. Now I skipped on one foot, trying to get out of her cadence.

"That meal really disgusted. I thought I gonna toss up."

I looked up at her. She was watching me out of the corner of her eye, smiling. "Me too," I said, laughing. "I don't know what I would have done without the beer."

"Yes, the beer," my mother said, all mirth draining from her tone, "I want to talk to you about the beer."

CHAPTER 6

I woke to a thump, the sound, I groggily realized, of my body hitting the floor. My mother, sprawled spread-eagle across the queen-size mattress, had pushed me out of bed. Seeing the first pink of dawn through the window, I tried to climb back in, but she wouldn't budge. At that early hour, I had a glimmer of an insight into why my father left.

That was glib; I knew full well why my father deserted us—to return to his first family, the wife he never divorced and the children he never forgot.

I moved to the sofa and tried to fall back asleep. But I was too hot and bothered, though my mother had turned on the air conditioner last night, telling me that life was too short to be sweating the electricity bill. No, what was keeping me awake was the thought of my brother, memories of him kicked up by seeing the Ohs, by encountering his selfishness repeated or reenacted by Bob.

Lying there on the scratchy old couch, inert but alert, I was reminded of the summer between high school and college, when I would also wake too early and lie in bed, waiting for a decent hour to get up. But back then it was hope for the future, not remorse for the past, that kept sleep at bay. It was the anticipation of living out from under my mother's roof for the first time, being on the verge of liberation. I wasn't going far; I wasn't even leaving the state. But I was going away, the leash was being let out. There was so much for me to conquer and I couldn't wait. The days couldn't come quickly enough.

Whiling away the predawn hours, I would imagine the great person I was going to become. I didn't have specific plans or a particular career in mind. I had plenty of time to pick, to discover my passion. I was just imagining the feeling of success, the flush of accomplishment that must come on the heels of what was bound to be a brilliant, though undetermined, college career. Depending on what was on TV the night before, I would give the feeling a setting—the Oscars, the Kennedy Center salutes, the Miss Universe pageant, the State of the Union address. I didn't want to be an actor, or a musician, or a beauty queen, or the president. I just needed a stage, the limelight, applause. And the law and medical professions—one of which, in the back of my mind, I expected to enter—didn't provide them, at least not a televised version, and so not any version in my formulation of the world.

These daydreams predating my enlightenment, there was always a man, a husband, standing in the wings, sitting in the front row, waiting backstage. He wasn't a crucial character in my drama—just a prop, like the golden statuette I would have to hold with two hands or the freestanding microphone I would have to adjust. I didn't even know him. He wasn't a boy I had a crush on or a man who really existed, though he did often bear a striking resemblance to Andrew McCarthy. He was just good-looking and successful, my peer. And so, in my media-created reality, he was white.

I imagined myself with someone white. This, despite the promise I made to my mother. But it was just daydreaming, I thought, and when I started dating white boys in college, I was living wholly in the present, not thinking about the future. I didn't know then that dreams, though always changing, were a blueprint, and that you couldn't be more, do more, do anything other than what you had sketched in your mind.

Once I became immersed in campus life, the fanciful thinking and early rising gradually gave way to course work, late nights, ideology, and the tedium of striving. Now, or at least until this morning, I rarely woke up before I needed to. When I was seventeen, I counted on the march of time. Ten years later, it cruelly wouldn't brake.

Since going back to sleep was an exercise in futility, I tried to project myself into the future, imagine the fabulous career I was going to construct with Sam's help. But at my age, it seemed silly, pathetic, to have so few of the baby steps behind me.

My prime was passing, my bloom was fading, before I'd gone anywhere with my life. I'd lost my way when I lost my brother. I'd always had his lead to follow, and so when he got married and disappeared, I didn't have the habit of looking at road signs, didn't know the drill of details, hadn't learned how to chart a course. The only specific goal I'd set was to do whatever he did—better. He scored 1500 on the SATs; I pulled in a 1560. He made it to state semifinals in cross-country; I went to finals. He got into Harvard; I got in early action.

My going was never even discussed. I applied only to see if I could get in. My mother blamed losing her son on Harvard, on letting him go so far away. To her mind, she'd sent a good boy to Cambridge, and in return for her four years of tuition money gotten an independent-minded, disobedient, defiant son. She hadn't known that his rebellion had begun in her home.

I had, and I'd kept quiet. For my misplaced loyalty, I'd had to live in a house filled with his absence, a photo negative of a happier existence. I bore the guilt of my silence and the burden of reparations, as well as the duty he had shirked. I had to be everything when I had once been just half, or even one third. Her firstborn, her son, the male who loved her unconditionally, he was more to her than I have ever been or could essay to be. To think I used to envy him.

The morning his wedding banns in *The Boston Globe* arrived in the mail, anonymously sent, my mother swept through the house, stripping it of every trace of him, slamming every picture, trophy, and framed news article into the aluminum trash can she was dragging around with her. Fourteen at the time, I shadowed her in my pajamas; the racket she was making had roused me out of bed. She looked so furious, I didn't dare try to stop her.

I thought she'd lost her mind, and slunk back to my room. When I heard her drive away, to take his clothes and books to the Goodwill I later learned, I slipped downstairs and found the *Globe* clipping on the kitchen counter. We hadn't spoken to my brother in a month, not since he'd announced his engagement, and the news of his wedding, it being a fait accompli, literally knocked me off my feet. My legs simply crumbled beneath me. I'd stopped crying at the age of seven—"you ruin your face," my mother used to scold—so I sat on the cold tile floor, dry-faced and silently heaving. My mother had threatened she would disown my brother if he went through with the wedding, and I knew then, though I didn't know before her rampage, that she meant it. I'd seen her rip up photos of him that couldn't be replaced; she hadn't even done that to pictures of my father.

Of course, she had been acting out of shock and anger, and several years later, while ransacking her bureau for a sweater I wanted to borrow, I came across the pictures, Scotch-taped together, in the bottom of a drawer. The discovery wasn't a surprise, as at that point she'd made his room her study and taken to spending entire evenings in there, falling asleep on the sofa with his old comforter. She'd been unable to excise her feelings for him, but she'd never relented, never reached out to him, never tried to mend the breach. She was stubborn and hard that way.

I looked over at the TV, longing for its mindless chatter. It would waken my mother though. A book would have been good, but since leaving my doctoral program, I hadn't been able to bring myself to crack one open. I couldn't spare the energy, the mental effort—I didn't have the stillness—a novel required. I was too unsettled, baffled, harassed. I needed noise and people and facile interaction.

I got up to go to work. I would be ridiculously early for someone with nothing to do, but it was movement, action, however in vain, and the office was the site of my future. Going there was better than dwelling in the past.

Chapter 7

"Your enthusiasm for the job get the better of you?"

I had been sitting at my desk in the dark, trying to convince my limbs that getting up for a cup of coffee would be worth the effort. From the stiffness of my neck, I must have been there like that for a while.

Chantal stood in the doorway of her office, her purse strung over her shoulder. "If you need something to do, I can help you out."

Was she trying to win me over to her side? She must have seen the ground Sam had on her. But her underestimation of either my intelligence or loyalty was insulting. She didn't even know Sam's position on best friends in the office.

"Whacha got?"

Chantal barely managed to suppress her smile. "The fashion

closet. Hang on a second." She disappeared into the black hole of her office.

Of course I wouldn't do anything behind Sam's back. I couldn't even imagine what I could do to help Chantal.

"It's getting so cluttered in there," she said, returning with the fashion closet key, "with all the stuff that was never returned, that I thought—"

"You want me to clean the closet?"

"—that it would be a worthwhile project for someone to sort through the clothes and shoes and organize a sale for the staff. It's not all junk, and the proceeds could go to charity."

That wasn't such a bad idea. "What kind of charity?" I asked. Editorial pay was so measly in comparison to the lifestyle and wardrobe the magazine promoted that she might have considered herself a needy case.

"It's up to you or whoever takes charge of the project. I bet we could get at least five hundred dollars."

"Could it go to a women's group?"

"What do you have in mind?"

"I don't know. Maybe a shelter for battered women or something like that."

She twirled the red ribbon attached to the key around her finger and then unwound it. "Sure. Why not?"

"Okay, then." I jumped to my feet. "Lead the way."

Chantal flipped the light switches we passed on our way down the hall. After fiddling with the lock, she opened the door. The closet was actually more of a room, I was surprised to see. Dakota consulted the scale in here obsessively, but I'd had no reason to come before. It looked like someone had tried to cram the inventory of a small store into it. Sleeves, boas, and belts dangled from boxes stacked to the ceiling; shoes, boots, and purses spilled off their shelves and onto the floor; a kiddie swimming pool, rolled-up rugs, and even an old-style bike with a white basket leaned precariously against the walls.

Chantal pointed to the racks of clothes standing in the middle of the floor, an oasis of order. "Those are for upcoming shoots and off-limits." She waved at the rest of the room. "Everything else is fair game."

"You want me to go through all this by myself?" My back and shoulders ached just taking it all in.

"It just looks like a lot because it's in such a mess."

"You're not going to send Dakota down?" I persisted.

"Do you really want to share the credit?"

"We're not going to raise that much money."

Chantal wandered to the shelves of shoes and pulled out a pair of black, pointy-toed ankle boots. They were ugly but they were Prada. "You know, years ago I did something like this on my own initiative," she said to the shoes. "It was how I got my first promotion." She put the boots back and sauntered back to me.

"You don't have to do it all in one day. Do what you can here and there, when Sam doesn't need you."

I shook my head. Maybe at a second-tier magazine cleaning the closet by yourself would earn you a promotion, but there were more important things to do at À la Mode. Anyway, Sam was going to be fashion director and I didn't need to impress her with my industriousness. "I want help."

She studied me, her arms crossed over her chest and one hand covering her mouth. It was the pose she probably struck when appraising models. "Well, how about you start and decide how you're going to run and organize things first."

It was my turn to scrutinize her. I'd never noticed the acne scars before. I'd also never had so much face time with her. Perhaps she liked me, or sensed that unlike Dakota, I wouldn't take the best of the clothes for myself—or use the unsupervised time to leave.

"I can manage by myself. But it's going to take some time."

Chantal smiled. I'd clearly said what she wanted to hear.

"So maybe we can hold the sale next Monday, a week from yesterday."

"I'll send an e-mail to the floor." She turned on her heel and left me to my work.

I came back to my desk for lunch. Technically, we could expense meals we worked through, and since leafing through magazines and talking about clothes and movies and It celebrities counted as work, we always charged lunch to the company. With most people eating like Dakota, Glossy wasn't in any danger of going bust.

At some point in the morning I'd called Sam from the closet to tell her where I was, blowing out her eardrum with my excitement. If we charged $20 for each article of designer clothing, $10 for shoes, and $5 to $3 for everything else, we could easily beat Chantal's estimate. The money, I had decided, would go to Hand-Me-Ups, a nonprofit that dressed and prepared publicly assisted women for job interviews. Sam had sounded oddly harried, but she did take the time to commend me on my fitting choice.

I poked my head into Sam's office, to find Dakota sitting in my usual seat. Empty takeout containers sat on the desk.

"You didn't wait for me?"

Sam looked up, still laughing at whatever joke they'd been sharing. "Sorry, but it's nearly two o'clock. And Dakota here was kind enough to add my sandwich to her salad and Chantal's sludge shake." She motioned with her head for the useless assistant to scoot into the other chair.

It was just as well. My mother was probably slaving in the kitchen, making a big dinner of food I actually liked. I reached over for a cigarette. Dakota hated smoking and usually thought of something she had to do when we lit up.

"It was nothing," Dakota said, picking up Sam's lighter. She held the flame out to me. "Easy compared to tracking down designers to ask them to guest-edit the next issue."

"Hell thought of it," Sam said in answer to my questioning eyebrow. "She called me at five this morning."

"That doesn't sound so hard to do," I said, looking at Dakota. "We've got the phone numbers of everyone's PR person."

Sam shook her head. "They take too long. Hell needed to give a name to the promotions department ASAP."

"So we've got everyone's private number too." I knew this for a fact; my first task as Sam's assistant had been to replace all of the handwritten cards in her fat Rolodex with typed ones.

"I did have them," Sam said. "My Rolodex is MIA."

"That's strange." I tried to remember the last time I'd seen it.

"More than strange," Dakota said. "I'd say it's downright sinister."

"Chantal?" I said incredulously. "But how would she know you needed it urgently this morning?"

"Hell must have called her after she got my answering machine. She knows I'm the person who has the contacts, but she probably wanted to hear someone praise her brilliant idea."

"But I was here early."

"And so the evil one got you out of the way with that ridiculous closet project. She outed you by putting you in the closet." Dakota giggled. "She's such a closet case."

"You think it's ridiculous?" I asked Sam.

"No," Sam said after too long a pause.

"It's for a good cause," I said, my heart no longer in it. "I guess it'll help somebody."

"And you."

"It'll help you hone your cleaning skills," Dakota said, folding her arms across her chest.

"Isn't there a phone call you have to make?" Sam widened her eyes and glared at her.

"Oh, right. I can't believe I forgot." She stood up.

"But I let you down," I said, unable to wait for her to leave. "I didn't stop her from stealing your Rolodex and I wasn't here to help you find those phone numbers."

"Maybe next time you won't be so quick to do her bidding,"

Dakota said. "I'm paid to assist her and I do as little as I can get away with."

"Dakota," Sam said. She jerked her head at the door.

Dakota grabbed a sheet of paper from the desk and ran out.

"Really, Ginger, don't worry about it. I got a guest editor, and I'm sure my Rolodex will magically turn up this afternoon."

"But I missed this chance to do something substantive, and now Dakota's going to share the credit."

"Hmm, it is the kind of thing that'll raise a person's profile," Sam agreed. "But maybe the closet sale will put you on Hell's radar screen."

"But you said—"

"If not, the next project to fall on my plate is yours." She smiled. "I promise."

Good ol' dependable Sam. She was the kind of person who bought panhandlers food instead of giving them change. It was a bit paternalistic of her not to trust they would use the money wisely, but at least she asked them what they wanted to eat. She also took in strays, no matter how feral or mangy they looked.

At Madison, when we were first getting to know each other, I had been surprised she wanted to be my friend. In high school, I'd been sufficiently popular in the way anyone with a nice car and clothes was, but the two of us were totally different. Aside from coming from New York and being used to a faster crowd, she was the most unabashed, unembarrassed person I'd ever met. She told me everything about herself and her family, from her first sexual experience at the age of fifteen, to her mother's humble origins, to her father's predilection for women half his age. Her candidness was contagious, and I found myself telling her things about my family the first month of our acquaintance that I'd never told people I'd known for most of my life.

My confidante, my touchstone, my consigliere, she'd immediately offered her help and support the day I reached out to her from my mother's den, two months after dropping out of grad school.

"You did the right thing," she said on the phone. "I hate to say it, but I always had a bad feeling about this Ph.D. thing."

"You never told me."

"You weren't even listening to your mother."

I would have listened to Sam. Since the first day I walked into our dorm room and watched her carry on a conversation with my mother, charming her no less, while sprawled out on her bed, hiding the sleeping man under the lumpy covers, I'd admired her smarts—and sophistication.

"Still, dropping out, that's rough. I know how much that degree meant. You must be crushed."

I'd only claimed to want a Ph.D., fooling even myself for several years. But originally it had been inertia that kept me at Madison. Getting into the grad program hadn't been hard.

"Anything you need, Ginger. I'm here."

"Thanks."

"I mean it. Do you want me to fly up there? I could this weekend. We could go to Madison and hang out at our old haunts. You sound like you could use a little binge."

"Not Madison. I'm never going there again."

"Right." After a pause, "Why don't you come here? I've got a perfume launch party Friday night, Saturday I'm going to the ballet, Sunday there's brunch in Connecticut with Dad and his new girlfriend. I guess this weekend wouldn't have been good for me to go away. But you can still come. I could get you into the party and Dad would love to see you—he's always asking after you. I could use help making the gold digger know she's not welcome. The ballet though. Maybe Tatiana won't mind if I—"

"That's all right."

"Or maybe we could find you a ticket. You'll probably have to sit in the nosebleed section."

"Really, Sam, that's okay. I don't have the money for a plane ticket."

"I could pay for it."

"I couldn't." The offer was so like her, and it made me realize how much I missed her.

"I've still got Dad's credit card. Consider it a combined present for all the birthdays I missed. I missed quite a few."

"So did I—of yours." The invitations had come in the mail, and I had been sorry to skip them—her birthday bacchanalias would have put Roman emperors to shame. But her birthday was in October, and I always had a paper to write, an exam to prepare for, a crisis of confidence to tend to.

"Well, think about it. This weekend's not so great, but give me a week's notice and we'll plan a fun-soaked, man-filled time."

She called a month later with the job. Her assistant had gone to lunch and never come back, and she was left in such a lurch, she'd already gotten Hell's approval to hire me. It was sweet of her to present her act of kindness as though I were the one doing her the favor, especially knowing, as I now did, the amount of work her assistant did. But she needn't have bothered. At that point, I would have leapt at the offer of cleaning toilets at Grand Central Station. I accepted on the spot and booked the plane ticket before my mother came home. Perhaps because the silence at dinner had been growing even louder, my mother didn't raise a single objection.

It occurred to me how tiresome, how much of a drag I'd been to Sam since coming here. But she'd never complained, never said a harsh word, until yesterday, when signs of the old Ginger had resurfaced, the Ginger who could take a kick in the butt.

I sat up. Yesterday's minute of brainstorming popped into my head. "Say, how'd my idea go over?"

Sam pushed her closed lips up to her nose. "It didn't. Hell said it was impractical. The FBI and police and firemen would never get on board, and any uniforms we could get to put on models would look fake."

"Sorry. I should have thought of that." That was the first idea of mine that hadn't been approved. It just confirmed my theory that wanting things was bad luck.

"It was a good idea. We'll probably return to it someday. Hell was just totally in love with some idea of Chantal's. Some hyphenated-American story with ethnic models."

"*Hell* loved it?" Despite all the reader letters we received, she refused to put minorities on the cover or feature them in fashion and beauty spreads. She insisted that people of color didn't sell magazines.

Sam smirked. "Not after I dissected it. Or, rather, only after I made improvements." She leaned forward. "Chantal pitched . . ."

I was about to interrupt and explain what I meant by my question, but changed my mind. Sam was spilling, breaking her sacred code of secrecy. I was back. We were real partners again.

". . . at a state fair and at other middle-America scenes where minorities are rarely pictured. But I said that then we would have to dress the models in jeans and sneakers. High couture would look ludicrous in that setting. The clothes would stick out."

"But isn't that the point of a fashion story?"

"I know it sounds weak now, but in the heat of the battle it made sense." Sam settled back in her chair. "Hell thought so. She decided that an urban milieu was more realistic. Chantal argued that that defeated the whole idea. So Hell compromised and now it's being shot in the Hamptons. My suggestion."

It was a shame that Sam had had to fiddle with the story. At least she hadn't killed it entirely.

"Chantal must have been furious."

"What do you think?" Sam looked pointedly at where her Rolodex used to be.

"Are you going to tell Hell?" What Sam had done in the meeting was within the accepted rules of engagement. Chantal had committed an act of larceny.

"I can settle the score on my own."

I was sure she would do more than that. We would be shifting directly to DEFCON 4.

"Do you have something in mind?"

Sam cracked her knuckles. "All I can say now is that she's going to regret she started this shit. She made a big mistake underestimating who she's dealing with."

"The kid gloves are off," I said.

"You got it."

CHAPTER 8

"Reading the phone book again?" I asked my mother, looking over her shoulder. She was so engrossed in the White Pages, she hadn't heard me walk in and come up behind her. "I thought you put it down last time because the plot was too predictable."

My mother slammed the book shut. I had already seen, though, where she'd been looking.

"Kim?" I asked. It was one of the most common surnames in Korea, the equivalent of Smith or Jones. "Who are you looking up?"

I walked around the kitchen counter to look at the stove. There were no pots simmering. Perhaps my mother hadn't expected me home so early; it was only five o'clock. Sam had had appointments the rest of the afternoon. Chantal had left for the cover shoot in Los Angeles, on her way out handing me Sam's Rolodex with the disingenuous comment that she hoped her borrowing it hadn't inconvenienced anyone. Dakota had departed shortly after her, and I had called it a day a half hour before closing time.

"Nobody," my mother said breezily. "I wonder how many Koreans in New York. There three pages of Kims, even more Lees."

I'd also looked up my father and brother as soon as I'd arrived in

New York. I'd done it on the Internet, though, and searched all five boroughs, Westchester, and New Jersey. There were no Sung-pil Lees, but eight George Lees.

"Well, don't forget Lee is also an American and Chinese name," I pointed out. I used to tell the kids who slanted their eyes and told me to go back to Chinkland that I was a direct descendant of Robert E. Lee, giving me more right to live in this country than they had. If they had known anything about the principles this nation was founded on, they would have told me that no one had more right—and they would have pointed out that he fought for the wrong side. But they didn't. They were, after all, just kids.

"You wear that to work?" my mother asked, looking me up and down.

"Yes, I'm fashion forward without being a slave to trends," I said, pulling down my Versace tank top and smoothing my old Ralph Lauren pencil skirt. That had been Chantal's pronouncement right after returning the Rolodex. Dakota and I had sat in stunned silence. A compliment from a fashion editor, thief that she may be, was something an assistant could put on her résumé, if not her gravestone. Dakota and I had both seen through Chantal's comment, but I couldn't help feeling proud—that I was in the right business.

"But it all black, like burglar."

"I don't want to argue about this." Style mavens, I was sure, didn't fight with their mothers over their clothes. She'd already given away a third of my closet. I turned my back on her to look in the fridge for something to spoil my appetite before dinner.

"You need color at your age. Your bloom—"

"Mother."

"Your dress last night was pretty. Mrs. Oh say too. It flatter your figure."

"That was nice of her." I put the chocolate pudding back on the shelf.

"She said she don't notice your big legs. So much."

This was why I stayed away from Koreans. I hated the way they felt perfectly entitled to comment on your looks. Usually they voiced their unsolicited opinion to your face, regardless of whether they'd just met you. Even people of my generation engaged in this peculiar pastime. I didn't know if they thought they were being helpful or if they just didn't care about a person's feelings. My only consolation was that they weren't being sexist; they did this to men and women alike.

Anyway, my calves were hardly too big. They were muscular from being a former high school long-distance runner.

"Let me tell you about my day," I said to change the subject. It was high time she knew that I had settled on a career in fashion, that I was back in the gunner's seat.

"Don't make enemy with Sharon," my mother pronounced when I was finished. "You never know. She might be director."

"Only if Sam has a heart attack and drops dead."

"If Sam so great, why she not director already?"

"I explained that Hell had to give Chantal a chance."

"Why?"

"Because," I said, wishing I'd given her the short version of events, as was my custom. "It's office politics. Trust me."

"I know office politics. I work in office for twenty-three years."

"But this is different."

"It not different. It same everyplace. I don't say betray Sam. I just say be nice to both. Let both help you."

Chantal had volunteered how she got her first promotion, while my career coach had yet to. My mother's suggestion sounded like a play right out of Sam's game book. It was funny how they had such different backgrounds and yet they thought so similarly. "You mean work them both to my advantage."

"Right. Double your chance." My mother looked at the clock on the microwave and frowned.

"Do you have to be somewhere?" I wanted to talk more about strategy.

"Mrs. Oh's house in New Jersey."

"Again?"

She walked behind me, patting my back as she passed, on her way to the refrigerator. She brought bread, cheese, and mustard to the counter. "She has big problem."

I swallowed my disappointment. "But you're not even very good friends. You haven't talked in years." My mother blamed the breach on the distance between Wisconsin and New Jersey, but I knew better. Still, for my mother's sake, I was glad the Ohs had gotten over their bourgeois sanctimony and reconnected with her.

"I know, but she couldn't tell her friends, so she called me. She so sad and I still have airplane ticket from Ohio, so I said I come help her."

"That's how you're here?" I felt a glimmer of hope. Maybe she wasn't serious about staying until she'd married me off. I handed her a knife and cutting board. "You didn't come for me?"

She looked up from unwrapping the cheese. "I did. I come for both." She started to slice the cheddar. "I help at same time. Maybe I do at same time."

I groaned. She hadn't given up on Bob and me.

"I kill two birds with one rock."

"You're killing me all right."

"Come on, you exaggerate."

"Who's bachelor number two, or should I say bachelor number one?" I asked pointedly. "When do I meet him? I need notice, you know." I wanted to rush through this parade of men, going on a date every night, or even double-decking them, to be finished that much quicker.

She waved my questions away. "Me and Mrs. Oh gonna take care of Ann. That why I go for dinner, so we make plan." She saw me glance at the bread in her hand. "This for you."

"You mean plot, not plan."

My mother shrugged. "We have no choice. Ann said she gonna marry Bobby no matter what." She put the two slices of wheat bread in the toaster and jammed the button down hard. "She hurt Mrs. Oh terribly."

"To most people, marrying their son isn't seen as hurting them."

My mother shook her head. "No, Ann told Mrs. Oh she selfish and horrible mother and she lucky that Bobby so nice because if she was her mother, she tell her to go to hell!"

"When? Where?"

"After we left. They made big scene. Mrs. Oh begged Ann not to marry Bobby. She cried and she begged."

"On the street?"

My mother sadly nodded.

I raised an eyebrow. "Sounds like we missed the best part of the evening."

"Don't be that way. This not joking matter."

We both jumped at the sound of the toaster popping.

"I don't know why she so stubborn," she continued bitterly. "I don't know why American wants Korean husband. They just bossy and lazy and ask where dinner is."

"And yet you want one for me."

My mother smiled sheepishly. "I just talking. I just upset at Ann."

"So what was Dr. Oh doing during this?"

"Nothing. He always leave the dirty work to Mrs. Oh."

"What about Bob?"

"He good boy. He separated them and said he gonna call his mom. Then he pushed Ann into a cab and they left."

"He's not exactly a good boy. He's marrying Ann as much as she's marrying him."

"He not innocent, but he not the driver. Men are stupid."

The toast was hotter than my mother expected, and she threw it at the plate with so much force that it slid off the plate, off the counter, onto the floor. She cursed in Korean, bending down to retrieve the slice. Clearly, she was tapping into her own anger and experience. She couldn't have felt so strongly about Ann or even for Mrs. Oh.

I took the remaining piece of toast and slapped mustard and cheese on it.

"Ann not gonna listen to Mrs. Oh, so I want you to talk to her."

I held my sandwich in midair. "Why me? Why not you?"

"Because I have broken English like Mrs. Oh."

I didn't know how to break it to her that it was what they were saying and not how they were saying it that was behind Ann's resistance.

"Mrs. Oh wants you to tell Ann to leave your man alone."

"What?" I choked.

My mother got me a glass of water, walking it around the counter so she was standing next to me. She stroked my hair the way she used to when I was a kid and she wanted me to rub her feet.

"Please do this for Mommy," she cooed. "It nothing. Just meet her and tell her Bobby is your man and she better leave him alone or else."

"Or else what? You want me to flash a knife or something?"

"Of course not. Just offer her money."

"Mother!"

"What?" she asked, looking as though she'd merely asked me to pass the mustard she was closing.

"I can't. . . . This is—" What could I say? "No."

"No? What you mean no?"

"I mean no. I won't do it."

She looked at me in surprise, taking a bite of the toast that had been on the floor.

"Anyway, I'm sure it would take more money than the Ohs have."

My mother's jaw worked as she mulled that over. She swallowed. "That probably true. All right, I tell Mrs. Oh to go back to the drawer."

CHAPTER 9

❦

Chantal's temporary kidnapping of the Rolodex proved to be a real waste of deviousness. News came down the next morning from the corner office that Hell, in consultation with the publisher, had changed her mind about the guest editor being a designer. It was too much publicity for one advertiser and would needlessly piss off the others. The entertainment editor was now scrambling to find a hot actress known for her style. Sam seemed to take the setback in stride, having Dakota call the designer they'd gotten and explain she'd contacted her without the knowledge of the magazine. Dakota was in tears by the time she hung up. Sam promised she wouldn't lose her job and that she'd make it up to her.

Despite my fears, easily attributable to my mother, the taken-away project didn't appear to be a sign of Hell's diminished confidence in Sam. Perhaps to make amends, Hell tied Sam up for the next two days, calling her into non-fashion-related meetings, taking her to a luncheon, even bringing her to her penthouse to get her opinion on swatches. To be sure, Sam wasn't squandering the increased access, and I, now grateful for having been lured into the closet, was productively using the time she was out of the office. I was determined to make something of the sale.

I also intended to be Sam's primary aide—and abettor. I thought she should take advantage of Chantal's being out of town. But the little time Sam was at her desk, she wasn't interested in strategizing, preferring instead to revert to our old chatter about men and her social life or to be alone to make plans for her weekend.

"You know, I was thinking that I could go on these dates for you," she said Thursday afternoon. I had just come back from the closet, and seeing her off the phone, had marched in and blurted out that she should be stepping up her efforts against Chantal.

"Forget about men for five minutes. What about your promotion?" I asked, ignoring her offer, as generous as it was.

"What about it?" She marked her place in her cookbook before closing it; she read them like they were Emily Dickinson, seemingly prosaic works of actual beauty worth returning to over and over again. "There's nothing to do but be here when Hell wants me. I'm not going to make busywork for myself."

"But Chantal is shooting the cover, while you haven't done anything."

"At my level, it's not about the work you do, it's about the people you're in good with. Anyway, the next ideas meeting isn't until next week."

I didn't understand her sudden slothfulness, but she knew the business better than I did. Silently, I watched her light up a cigarette. She leaned back and made smoke rings. She'd tried to teach me many times, but I couldn't make them. I had a theory that you had to be exposed at an early age to master them. Sam's mother's boyfriend had taught her when she was eight.

"I was serious before," she finally said, "about going on your dates for you. I have nothing against Korean guys."

She had nothing against any guy who was good-looking and wanted just to have fun. In college we'd had that in common, though she'd been less successful staying out of relationships. She got addicted to the regular sex, she'd claim after each breakup. Now, however, she was determined to save monogamy for retirement; both of her parents, in their fifties, were never in want of a companion. Sam wanted to look back on her life and feel that she'd lived it fully.

A desire I totally shared with her. I, though, took it one step further, and didn't want children to clutter even my less active years. Sam didn't think her father's hard-earned wealth should go to strangers or a lesser strand of Starre DNA. She had no problem having a kid out of wedlock, but given her past proclivity to fall in love and her feelings about being raised in a broken home, I was mentally prepared for the day when she would say yes to the man she wanted to father her children.

"You feeling a dry spell coming on?" I joked.

"Me? Didn't I mention I had a date last night?" She put her feet up on her desk. "I just hate to see a single man go wasted."

"Sorry, Sam. But if these men are letting their mothers arrange their dates, they'll probably be shocked if you turn up instead of me."

"You never know. Maybe they're like you and Bob and prefer Americans."

"I'm sure you won't want to have anything to do with them." For a Korean man to be fixed up, he either had something wrong with him or an overbearing mother. Traditional Koreans, what I called Korean-y people, joined the Korean association in college and paired up there. Assimilated second-generationers held their mothers at bay until they'd fallen beyond the point of no return, as Bob and my brother had done, or forever, as was my intention.

"Who was your date with?" I asked to derail Sam.

"Some guy named Walker. He came to Dad with a business plan and Dad thought we should meet." Her father, as well as her mother in Scottsdale, was always sending men her way. They had their requirements—white and professional—and they certainly hoped that more than a fling would come of the dates, and yet their setups didn't make them seem backward or old-fashioned. And Sam's agreeing to them didn't seem weird or pathetic. I supposed it was because their bachelors weren't being thrown out as life preservers.

"How'd it go?"

"He was all right. He made publisher three years ago, when he was our age."

"Sounds like you two have a lot in common."

"Some golf magazine. People rise faster at small titles."

"No news flash there. That's what Chantal did."

Sam wasn't listening, lost in her thoughts. "He's really sharp. Dad thinks his proposal has promise."

"Are you going to see him again? Sam?" I snapped my fingers to get her attention.

She came back to me. "What?"

I repeated my question.

"Perhaps," she said, looking away from me again.

Now her reduced thirst for Chantal's blood made sense. The worst imaginable thing had happened to her career—and mine. She'd met a man she wasn't prepared to admit she liked. I didn't doubt her commitment to her profession; plenty of women high on the masthead had boyfriends and even husbands. But now was not the time to be distracted.

Sam's vulnerability both frustrated me and thrilled me. I may have had a lot of catching up to do, but I saw the one strength I had that she and probably my competition didn't. My immunity to love, my inability to feel passionate about someone, wasn't just a regretful consequence of being my mother's daughter. In the realm of work, it was an asset.

CHAPTER 10

I came home that evening to an empty apartment. For the third night in a row, my mother was in New Jersey, busy with Mrs. Oh. Left to my own devices, I'd reverted to my old routine of going for a run, eating a frozen dinner, and eventually falling asleep in front of the TV. The only change was that I didn't have to drag myself off the couch, since it was doubling as my bed, our solution to my mother's inability to stick to her side of the mattress. At some point she came home and woke me to wash my feet.

The man-hunting, advancement-seeking barracuda I had become led a life as eventful as the one I'd just left as an aimless, sleepy grad-school dropout.

I was wondering when the dates were going to begin, when my mother called from Mrs. Oh's house. I could barely hear her for the crying in the background.

"Can you lower the volume on the TV?" I said, turning off the news for my part.

My mother mumbled something in Korean and the noise died. "Sorry, that Mrs. Oh. She very unhappy."

"So I heard."

"That why I call—"

"I'm not going to call Ann and threaten her life," I cut in.

"I know."

"Or offer her money."

"I know. I know," my mother said impatiently. The wailing was creeping up to its former decibel level. "I want you go to Bobby's apartment."

"To do what?" I sat up and moved the pan of Rice Krispie treats from my stomach to the coffee table.

"Mrs. Oh call Bobby all week, five maybe ten times every night. But the answering machine just pick up."

So that's what my mother had been doing instead of being with me—helping her friend crank-call her son. "Can you blame him?"

My mother ignored me. "Now Mrs. Oh worries that something happened to him. He don't return her calls at his office either. So I want you go to his apartment and make sure he okay."

"But if he won't talk to his mom, why would he talk to me? He'll just tell the doorman not to let me up to his apartment. Bob's a cosmetic surgeon, he must live in a luxury high-rise with a brigade of doormen."

My mother hushed Mrs. Oh and told her what I had said. "Uh,

no, don't stop for the doorman. Just go to the elevator like you live there."

"What if the doormen stop me?"

"They not gonna do that. Just walk natural. You can do it."

She always had faith in me for the wrong things—for things I didn't want to do and knew I couldn't do—putting her judgment in doubt. Like when I was in college, trying to pick my major. She wanted me to be pre-med when I'd recently discovered I had no real affinity for science.

On the phone long ago she'd said, "Don't be silly. Of course you like science. You Korean, aren't you?"

"I'm Korean American."

"Same thing."

"But there are some Korean Americans who aren't good at science."

"My daughter is good for anything she tries. I have confidence in you." If we'd been talking in person instead of on the phone, she would have slapped me on the back.

"I appreciate your unconditional support, but, Mom, this time it's unwarranted. If I become pre-med, I promise you I will flunk out of college."

"Your brother was pre-med," she taunted.

"And what happened to him?" It was a low blow. At that point, she hadn't spoken to him for three years. We assumed he'd gone to medical school after Harvard, but we didn't actually know.

"Don't break up my heart. Listen to your mother."

I took a biology class and intentionally got a C; still, she didn't cave until she found out from her friends that law schools accepted English majors.

She was persisting now with this nocturnal visit to Bob. "Just talk to him," she said. "Tell him he do like your brother. Talk to him like same-generation friend."

"He won't listen. I'm nobody to him." I still wasn't convinced I could get past the doormen. I could imagine the headline in tomorrow's paper: Brute Doormen Relish Asian Takeout.

"Please," my mother entreated, "do this for me. Think about how sad I am when your brother married."

"Do you think I ever forget?" I mumbled.

"Good. So wear my shoes, and know how Mrs. Oh feels. She don't even have a nice daughter to help her."

On cue, Mrs. Oh let out a long, pitiful wail.

"All right. Where do I go?" As much as I knew my mother was playing me like the concert pianist she had once trained to be, after three nights of waiting around for her, I was in the mood for some face-to-face interaction, awkward as it may be.

"You go?"

"I just said I would."

"Mrs. Oh!" My mother told her the good news. Mrs. Oh shouted that I was a good daughter, that my mother was lucky to have me. My mother told her not to go overboard. She returned to me. "I know you gonna do it. I know you don't take me down."

"So where do I go?" I repeated.

Half an hour later I found myself in Bob's dimly lit lobby. He lived only a ten-minute walk away, but I'd taken some time changing out of my pajamas. What does one wear to an occasion like this? On a mission to tell a practical stranger to call his mother and give up his fiancée? The fashion magazines were strangely mum on the issue. I'd settled on a crisp white blouse and beige linen Katayone Adeli pants, ignoring the suggestion my mother hurriedly tossed out before hanging up that I put on a colorful dress and some lipstick. I looked casual but not sloppy.

I'd been right about his living in a luxury building, though it wasn't a high-rise. The white stone building was on Fifth Avenue, along the park, and was only fourteen stories high. The lobby whispered of old money, with its white-gloved doormen, understated decor, and fresh flowers. The people who lived here owned their apartments. I wondered how many face-lifts Bob had had to do at a discount to get past the co-op board.

I made a beeline for the elevators seemingly a football field across the lobby, tripping a little on my pants. I usually wore them with heels. I'd made it all the way to pressing the button, when the doorman I'd passed on my way in caught up to me.

"Can I help you, miss?" I discerned an Irish lilt. He had a white mustache and beard, a red nose and cheeks, twinkling eyes, and a large belly. In any other context he wouldn't have seemed menacing. "Whom are you here to see?"

"Whom?" I echoed, my mind scampering for an answer. I could give a fake name and hope the elevator came while he was looking it up, but chances were he knew every occupant by name, face, and occupation.

He sighed. "Another non-English-speaker? Your people are smart, but you have to put time into learning the language here." He cleared his throat, then repeated his question in Japanese, I assumed. He bowed from the waist, almost losing his cap.

If my mother had been there, she would have very indignantly, and rudely, informed him of his mistake. I, of course, didn't feel any of the old animosity toward the Japanese, though, and was just impressed by his cultural sensitivity. Most doormen, in my experience, would have just talked louder at me. Once when I was bringing a bag of Chinese takeout to Sam's, her doorman had even pointed me to the delivery entrance.

I was still trying to decide how to answer his question, when the elevator doors opened. We both jumped back in surprise.

"Ginger? What are you doing here?" Chantal was talking with such animation, you'd think we were more than work acquaintances.

The doorman silently tipped his hat and returned to his post.

"Visiting a friend," I said, taking a few more steps in retreat. She walked me backward, to the far wall, then pirouetted around me so that she faced the elevators and I had my back to them. It was a strange dance, but given my purpose for being there, who was I to judge strange?

"You know someone who lives here? Who?"

Again, I was stumped for an answer.

"I'm sorry. That was nosy. I'm not thinking straight. We were shooting to the last minute and I just got off the plane. It's weird to see you in my lobby. I was just thinking about the office, and poof, here you are!"

"I'm almost finished with the closet. It'll be ready by Monday."

She took a moment to remember what I was talking about. "That's fine. But that's not actually what I was thinking about. I just checked my messages." She rubbed her temples. "The Asian model for the multi-culti story we're rushing in backed out."

"That's strange." Minority models were hardly in high demand.

"Yeah, I don't get it. Annabelle can't get a replacement. The only explanation I can come up with is that someone else is doing a big 'otherness' feature."

That seemed unlikely.

"We'll have to kill our story if we don't get an Asian to complete the mix."

Sam. The sudden cancellation and unheard-of unavailability of models couldn't be mere coincidence. Chantal must have come to the same realization. She was staring at me like she was wanted to cook and serve me.

"Hey—"

"I don't even know which agencies represent Asian models," I cut in.

She gave me a confused look. "I don't want you to call them. Annabelle already did. I want you to *be* a model."

I couldn't speak for several minutes. Like a good feminist, I'd stopped basing my worth on my looks years ago, though I knew I could do this pretty much because I was attractive. Not gorgeous or a knockout. Just an Asian with a nice, symmetrical face. But Chantal's offer was too flattering to feign indifference. She was an expert on beauty, after all. I couldn't wait to tell my mother. She'd be pleased, if only because everyone was always saying I looked like her.

"I don't have any experience," I finally faltered.

Chantal smiled. "Don't worry. Modeling is easy. I bet you're a natural."

I felt foolish, but I blushed. My mother had been right. There were advantages to being caught between Chantal and Sam.

"So you'll do it?"

I collected myself. Sam would not be pleased. But she had said—no, commanded me—to look out for my own interests. "Sure, why not?"

"Great."

"When's the shoot?" I asked, wondering if I'd be able to lose ten pounds in time. Didn't the camera put on that much weight? Chantal didn't respond right away. She was looking at something over my shoulder. I started to turn, but her eyes darted back to me, pinning me in place. She smiled again.

"What'd you say?"

"I asked when the shoot was."

"Thursday, a week from today. It'll be fun. We're shooting all over the Hamptons. Sam got us the Chase estate. Do you know Tatiana?"

I knew her, though she never seemed able to remember me. She'd even come to the office once to print invitations, a real hassle, as the toner cartridge had run out midway through her list and I'd had to find out how to replace it. She hadn't even had the manners to invite me to her party after all my trouble. I made a face, but Chantal didn't see it. She was looking behind me again. I wondered if there was someone famous standing there. She was being kind of rude, the way she was with Dakota.

Did I want to tangle with her? "Thursday, did you say? Actually, I should check with Sam," I backpedaled. "You know, make sure she can manage without me."

"Of course," Chantal said cheerfully. She knew as well as I did that I could order lunch from any phone—or Dakota could. She started to inch away. "I'm running late. Just let me know."

I watched her bound through the door held open by the doorman, into a waiting car. To lead such a pampered life. How much did it take? Her salary couldn't have bankrolled it. She must come from money or be living with someone who had it. I knew nothing about her private life. But something about her, her style, her detached elegance, cool fire, made me think that if she was living with a man, he was foreign.

Thinking of men, I was reminded of the one I was there to harangue. An elevator was conveniently waiting and the doorman was still outside. I slipped past the closing doors and hit the button for the seventh floor.

Bob answered his door immediately, saying, "Back already?" His face fell when he saw it was me. "I thought you were someone else. Ann, actually." He looked me over from head to toe, then scratched his head, trying to figure out what I was doing there.

He was impeccably dressed again, this time in a French-blue dress shirt and neatly creased black trousers. Sam would have liked him. Too bad he was taken.

I waited for him to invite me in, but when he didn't, I started to explain that despite appearances, I wasn't a stalker.

"I figured my mother sent you," he interrupted. "She and your mother have been calling every night. I'd unplug the telephone, but I can't in case my service calls."

"I know. That's why I'm here. They're convinced that something has happened to you, and they've sent me to make sure you're alive. To be harassed to death."

Bob chuckled. He was cute when he wasn't scowling. "Do you always do what your mother asks you to do?" He leaned his upper body against the doorjamb and crossed his arms over his chest, tucking his hands under his armpits.

I shrugged. "It's the path of least resistance. You've been getting her calls. You've experienced what she's like."

"Like my mom." He looked at me the way he must scrutinize his patients, identifying the flaws he could correct. "You know, you're puzzling. You do your mother's bidding and yet you talk like you're cool. I can't tell if you are or aren't like the women my mother's tried to fix me up with."

"I've never been set up," I huffed.

"You know what I mean. Traditional, docile, coy. Women who watch you from under their eyelashes." He leaned forward, getting into his description. "And they don't look at you when they're talking to you—or eat. They never eat."

"At least they're cheap dates," I cracked, trying to cover up my growing mortification that he couldn't tell I wasn't one of those Korean-y women. I knew my actions sometimes contradicted who I was inside, but I trusted that people who weren't my mother could see or sense the real me. The feminist, independently minded, hiply dressed me.

"No, they're actually not. They always pick expensive restaurants and order full-course meals they never touch. It's really annoying."

"I'll have to remember that for the next arranged date." I'd planned to tell crude jokes, make bitter remarks about people around us, talk incessantly about myself. Generally behave the way Sam's friends did. But now I had a proven sabotage strategy. Though my feelings had been hurt, talking to Bob had its benefits.

"The next arranged date? I thought you've never been fixed—"

"I haven't," I cut in, rushing to clarify, to keep my cool status intact. "By next, I meant after you."

"Me?" he asked, jerking his thumb at himself.

"But I don't think Monday's dinner counts as a setup," I said weakly.

His eyes narrowed. "So you were in on the plot too."

"No," I said emphatically. "I had no idea you were engaged."

"So you came to be fixed up with me."

"Only to make my mother happy. Path of least resistance, remember?"

"Right." He didn't look convinced.

"Look, I am not Korean-y."

Bob raised an uncomprehending eyebrow.

"Korean Americans who are more Korean than American," I explained. "Like the women you described, who were always on the arms of loud and bossy men in college." I'd steered clear of them, ignoring my mother's advice, feeling that Koreans who hung out with Koreans should go back to Korea. I waited for him to signal his understanding, then continued with my defense. "My mother is here, threatening not to leave until I'm married. I'm just going along with her until she gives up." I really needed him to believe me. "I mean, I ordered that beer Monday night."

"You did," he said, nodding thoughtfully. He smiled and looked at me. "You think we're loud and bossy?"

I returned the smile, happy with the turn we'd made. "Well, Korean-y men are."

"But aren't I sort of Korean-y? I've gone on arranged dates. Aren't you? Isn't the underlying difference between Koreans and Americans that we can't tell our controlling mothers where to go?"

"Maybe we both have Korean-y tendencies. But we're not Korean-y."

"You think? How'd you spend your Friday nights as a teenager? Studying or going to the movies?"

"Going to the movies."

Bob frowned. "Okay, then what was your favorite class? Gym or math?"

"English."

"What'd you get on the SATs?"

"Seven ninety verbal, seven seventy math."

"Aha!" He pointed his finger at me.

"Aha, what? Americans aren't smart?"

"No, but you were awfully fast with that answer for someone who took the test ten years ago."

He had me. I laughed. "Hey, it's a good score. I worked hard for it."

"It's a great score," he said with true Korean awe and admiration. "My dad gave me extra math homework—he said my school was teaching me the math Korean schools taught girls—and I still didn't do as well as you."

I knew I didn't like his father. "Make sure he knows how well I did."

"It won't change his opinion. He's a typical Korean male. He'll say your brother coached you."

"Hardly. My brother was long gone by the time I was prepping for college boards." It occurred to me, as my words echoed back, that my flip attitude toward my brother's estrangement flew in the face of the errand I was there to do.

"Oh, yeah." Bobby shifted uncomfortably. "I heard from your mom's messages what happened with him. What's his name? You and your mother never say it."

"George," I said, now sober, the fun of communing with a fellow second-generationer gone as quickly as it came. "As in George Washington, the man who could not tell a lie."

"That's a myth, you know."

"I know," I said.

We shared a moment of rueful silence.

"We have a lot in common," Bobby finally said. "We should get together and compare notes, over lunch or dinner sometime."

I agreed. I was about to suggest he and Ann meet me for drinks tomorrow, when his stereo suddenly became audible. "Do you have guests? You should've told me."

"It's okay. It's just Ann."

Something wasn't right. "You thought I was Ann when I rang the bell."

"I mean it's Ann's friend. Ann went out for beer and food. The friend's still here. I should get back to him. I'll call you. Are you listed?"

I told him I was. He hurriedly said good-bye and closed the door.

I came home to a message on the machine from my mother and five hang-ups, also, I presumed, from my mother. She wanted me to phone as soon I got back, but since she seemed to be on a ten-minute calling schedule, I decided to wait for her to ring me.

Back in my T-shirt and boxers, I puttered around the apartment, tidying up, straightening the scarf covering the boxes in the hall. I threw away the leftover Rice Krispie treats. I didn't want to be the largest Korean American woman Bobby knew. I also had ten pounds to lose by Thursday. Still waiting for the call, I sifted through my closet, pondering what I would wear the next time I saw Bobby. Moving the hangers took arm strength again, since my mother had hung up her clothes.

I finally turned on the TV and made my bed on the lumpy couch. At some point I heard my mother come in, turn off the TV, and hover over me, trying to see, I imagined, whether my feet were clean. They weren't, but that was the trade-off for making me go shoeless in the apartment. She kindly let me sleep.

CHAPTER 11

The summer I turned five, my mother took an eight-week training program to earn her broker's license. I accompanied her because she didn't want to impose on Mrs. Oh too often and my mother didn't yet trust George, who was thirteen, to look after me. She said those were the reasons, but even back then I sensed it was also because she wanted me there. I was a buffer, her excuse for turning down all the American women who invited her to join them for lunch or coffee after class.

They still tried to befriend her, engage her in conversation. They would tell her about their latest decorating schemes, a shocking article they'd read pronouncing television a poor substitute for a babysitter, another article recommending hanging your children's artwork on the refrigerator to boost their self-esteem. My mother would listen, smile, and make polite noises, too shy to disagree or tell them what she thought of their child-rearing tips—I gave her a drawing once and she put it in a drawer, saying it didn't look like our family.

One parenting practice she did like and adopted, however, was the emphasis put on starting the day with a big, hot American breakfast. That summer our family was introduced to pancakes, French toast, omelets, waffles, bacon, sausage, and every other breakfast food on the menu of a greasy diner. I didn't know if it was to compensate for the rushed leftovers-warmed-over affair dinner had become or if it was because breakfast was by far the easiest meal to do and do well, but she took to breakfast like a religious convert. She kept the large breakfasts going even when she was working overtime as a junior real estate broker and my brother and I were in school. (She added a year to my age to put me in the first grade so I'd be let out after George was home.) They continued even after my brother went to college, and until I turned fifteen and decided that breakfast was fattening.

I hadn't thought of those big breakfasts in years, but I woke up Friday morning not only thinking about them, I was salivating for them. Then I realized why. My mother was in the kitchen, making pancakes, eggs, and sausage.

"You wake just on time," she said, sliding two pancakes onto a plate. She was humming. She loaded it with eggs and sausage and put it down on the counter in front of me. I pulled up a stool and picked up a fork.

Halfway through the stack of pancakes, I noticed the humming had stopped. I thought about looking up to make eye contact with my mother but decided against it. That would be an invitation to start talking, and I didn't want to know what she was up to until I'd finished eating. I didn't want to have to walk away from such fluffy eggs, juicy sausage, and buttery pancakes. If the real estate market ever bottomed out, she could always make it as a short-order cook.

I quickened my pace, shoveling food into my mouth, nervous that she'd tire of waiting and start talking without a signal from me. It wasn't long before I started to feel full and a little sick. I put down my fork and reached for the mug of coffee she'd put next to my plate. I looked up. My mother was staring at me. Her food was untouched.

"You really hungry this morning. Good thing Mommy made breakfast for you."

"Mmm," I said, still sipping my coffee. "Thank you. It was delicious. If you're going to be cooking, I may never let you go."

My mother smiled, obviously pleased. "No, I don't cook every morning. You gonna get fat." I winced, remembering my vow to lose ten pounds. "Today is special occasion. We eat now and skip lunch. We got a lot of shopping to do."

With the breakfast just enjoyed and now the shopping in the offing, it was clear my mother was rewarding me for last night's efforts. So far, Bobby Oh had been a boon to my life. In the time since we'd reconnected, I'd had a free restaurant meal, a modeling offer made in his lobby, and soon new clothes. But as delighted as I was to go shopping, it was going to have to wait. I did have a job, after all.

I mentioned this pesky fact. "Sorry," I said, really meaning it. "But what about tomorrow? Tomorrow's Saturday."

My mother shook her head. "No, we have to go today. You can miss one day. Tell them you sick."

Unlike Dakota, I hadn't taken any mental health days since coming to the magazine. I knew that taking them would be like opening a bottle of Valium: Once I started, I'd never feel good enough not to take another.

"Mother!" I tried to sound outraged. "I can't call in sick because I have better things to do."

"Why not? You play hockey in high school all the time."

"But I have actual work to do. The closet."

"You still not finished?"

I didn't answer. I supposed I could come in on the weekend to finish up. "But what's the rush? Why can't we go tomorrow?"

"I can't. I promised Mrs. Oh I gonna help cook for her party. That why we have to shop today, to find nice dress for you."

"What party?"

"I didn't tell you? No? Saturday night is Dr. Oh's birthday party. He gonna turn sixty. In Korea, sixty is a big year. You get a big party and your children give you nice presents, like a Rolex watch and Cadillac car. Don't look so scared. You still got half-year before Mommy gonna be that old. Anyway, you don't got to toss me big party or buy a present. Just name my first grandchild after me." She smiled at her magnanimity.

I smiled with her. It was really something how in less than a week she'd leapt from coercing me to look for her future son-in-law to saying she wanted a namesake. Such great strides in so little time. It was a shame she wasn't involved in a greater, less hopeless cause than her daughter, like world hunger or female illiteracy.

I smiled again. "At the rate you're going, you'll be lucky if you get a phone call from me."

She leaned over and tousled my hair. "What you mean at the rate I going? I take you shopping today if you can tear yourself from your job. I the best mommy there is."

"You are buying me a dress," I agreed. The party sounded like a good eating opportunity. I doubted she'd be doing any matchmaking. All the guests would be her and the Ohs' age.

"You my favorite daughter."

"I'm your only daughter."

"And Bobby gonna be there. He gonna see you in a pretty party dress."

I groaned. When had my mother become such a silly romantic? Unless she knew where to buy some magical stardust, a beautiful gown wasn't going to transform me into Bobby's dream mate and make him fall in love with me. Seeing me with ruddy cheeks or in an unguarded moment wasn't going to do it either. She was getting soft and sappy in her old age. She'd been watching too many movies or looking at too many ads.

"Why you groan?" my mother asked.

I pointed to my stomach. As much as I wanted to train a bazooka on the fairy-tale fantasies dancing in her head, I didn't want to lose my expensive new dress.

"Bobby's coming to the party?" I asked, steering the conversation toward safer waters.

"Sure, I told you sixty is big deal. He can't shame his father and not come. Everyone know he lives only forty-five-minute drive away. He a good boy."

"But what about Ann?"

My mother made a face. "I didn't say he perfect boy. But he come about. Dr. and Mrs. Oh raised him well. They sent him to private boarding school, UC Berkeley, Columbia medical school. They paid for everything. He has nothing to complain."

"No, I mean, what about the Ohs' opposition to Ann? Is she coming to the birthday party?"

"They wish they break the engagement before the party. That why I try to help Mrs. Oh all week. But now they have to break them after the party. I don't know if Ann gonna come. I don't know if Bobby gonna bring her."

Shaking my head, I stood up to clear the counter of our plates. "I think you give Bobby too much credit. I don't think he's going to be there Saturday."

"You think he lied to his mommy? He said he gonna come. Why he lie?" My mother sounded puzzled, as though she were trying for the first time to wrap her mind around the concept of a grown child lying to his parent.

"Well, probably at the time that he said he was coming, he didn't know there would be all this tension over Ann. When did he say he was coming?"

"Last night. He called Mrs. Oh last night. He said you convinced him." That was why my mother hadn't called again or woken me.

"I didn't realize that. He didn't tell me he was going to call. I guess he is going to be there." I wondered if he was thinking of the party as a coming-out occasion for him and Ann. Once the engagement was announced, and his parents' friends were sufficiently disappointed that another medical doctor had gotten away—and relieved that they hadn't foisted their daughters onto such a disobedient son, he'd be as good as married.

My mother reached over and patted my hand. "Bobby listens to you. He gonna be a good husband."

I groaned again. Optimism was just a nice word for stubbornness.

She took the plates away from me. "Call your office. I clean up here—you take too long. We have only the day for shopping."

CHAPTER 12

It turned out that we didn't need even half the time my mother thought we would. Because finding a dress for her was easy, we did it first to get it out of the way. The cab ride to the Chanel boutique through morning traffic was the most arduous part of the task. As soon as we walked in, the saleswomen swarmed around us, mistaking us for Japanese tourists, I was sure. With all of their aid, my mother was able to sail through the store, try on her choices, select the winner, and leave in under twenty minutes with a navy silk dress with a long pleated skirt.

That was what we had expected to happen. The surprise was that we found my dress also at the first store we tried. By eleven o'clock that morning, we'd agreed on a floral pink and green spaghetti-strapped, flowing dress. It was flashier than my taste, but my mother insisted on getting it, back on her crusade to suffuse me with color.

"You always wear black like you going to funeral," my mother remonstrated to my reflection in the fitting room at Bergdorf Goodman. I had just put on the dress. "What wrong with red? What wrong with purple? For once, why you can't wear pretty color dress? People will think, 'What a pretty young lady' instead of 'What a sad widow.' They don't notice any other women in the room."

"That's because they'll be blinded by the garish colors." I knew it was as silly to have something against color as it was to say blue was boyish and pink was girlish. But gender programming was hard to undo. I spun a full revolution on my toes. On top of the color, the cut and flounce of the dress were very slimming and girlish. I felt diminished. I felt feminine. I felt exposed. "You don't think I'm showing too much skin?" I pinched the straps above my shoulders, lifting the dress two inches on my chest.

"It fine. You look good. Bobby gonna like it." She swatted at my hands. The dress fell back in place, revealing the beginning slope of my chest. She fussed with the plunging neckline. "Maybe we pin it like this."

It was an Oscar de la Renta, and I let her buy it, having never owned one of his dresses. With all the saved time, I thought we might look around and see what else there was to buy. My mother agreed, though her idea was to start at the top floor, where the bridal gowns were.

"I would die if someone I know sees me," I protested. Wedding dresses with their pure whiteness and virginal veils were bad enough. But there was something very sad and pathetic about a woman looking at them when she wasn't even engaged.

"Nobody gonna see you," my mother dismissed. "Everybody at work now." With that, a bell chimed and the elevator doors opened to the time-warped world of crinoline and corsets. Even the saleswoman who immediately accosted us looked antebellum.

On feet like gossamer, she floated toward us, straightening dresses and fluffing skirts along her path. I stuck my fingers in my ears to unclog them. The quiet on the floor was unnatural, as though it were being piped through hidden stereo speakers. Or maybe it was just unnerving. It was the hush of hospital corridors and funeral wakes. "Which one of you is the lucky bride?" the saleswoman whispered.

Wrinkling her brow, my mother scanned the floor, probably look-ing to see if smarter help was available. The dress racks were so high, though, that all you could see were towering white gowns. I felt as though I were in a house of mirrors.

The salesclerk stood stone still, waiting for an answer, her hands politely folded in front of her. She had a blank look on her face and reminded me of computer screens that go dark when their keyboards haven't been touched for several minutes. Maybe that was how she'd managed to live for so long, by conserving energy at every possible moment. I wanted to see how long she could hold the pose, but my mother spoke, breaking the spell.

"This is my daughter." She pointed to me. "I the mother." She pointed to herself. She spoke slowly and gently, the way people did to well-dressed children.

The saleswoman was due for a tune-up. Her response mechanism was slightly off. After a pause, she smiled. "You must be proud."

I knew she was just trying to be pleasant, speaking platitudes pro-grammed on her hard drive, but her comment irked me. What must my mother be proud of? That her daughter was pretty enough or wily enough to snare herself a husband? Was a married daughter some-thing to be more proud of than a single one? I was a washout now, but Lord help me if I died and marriage was my only accomplish-ment.

"Mother, I have to go back to work," I said, turning to her. "I just remembered I was supposed to meet with Chantal today. She wants me to be in a photo shoot." Modeling wasn't an achievement that was going to bag me a Nobel Prize, but it was a start. It was a rope out of the abyss. Okay, it was twine. But it was something.

"Photo shoot? She wants you to take the pictures? What hap-pened to the photographer?"

"No, she wants me to be in the pictures with the other models. I'm hardly qualified to be a professional photographer."

"I know. I gonna ask if she ever saw your photos."

Before I could defend my picture-taking skills, the saleswoman flicked back on. "You have to go? Would you like to reschedule your appointment, then?" A trace of emotion flickered under the mask of pleasantness. Was it relief at the prospect of a break from the ghastliness of dressing single women in their satin shrouds, of costuming grown women's foolish fantasies of playing princess for a day, of being midwife to the creation of a bride?

"Appointment?" my mother echoed. "We don't need appointment. We just wanna look. My daughter gonna be engaged soon."

"Mother," I muttered, feeling my cheeks redden. "I really have to go."

"You don't have an appointment? You're not the Quinns?"

"The Quinns?" She really did need a tune-up.

"Edith and Ashley Quinn. I have them down for eleven o'clock. If you're not them, where are they? I have to find them." She seemed suddenly very unhinged, jerking her neck and limbs haphazardly. I thought she might short-circuit.

"Maybe they late," my mother offered.

"They can't be late. We have a very tight schedule. I have Mrs. Potts Dixon and Ms. Potts at twelve-thirty, and I can't help someone find the dress of her dreams in less than ninety minutes. No one knows what she wants until she sees it. Well, no one sees it until she's seen everything. Ninety minutes is the baseline minimum. I've been telling the booker she's got to space the appointments at least two hours apart, but we're understaffed since Marion retired and Sheila broke her hip, and the brides-to-be just keep calling—or, worse, just showing up." She paused and gave us a look.

"I'm letting someone try on dresses without an appointment right now, but only because she's with someone in the fashion industry, and I trust they'll treat the dresses with care. Brides are getting older and smarter, the newscaster said on TV, but you could've fooled me.

The other day, someone wanted a dress that sparkled but didn't have sequins or glass beads. Can you believe it? I asked her what she thought would sparkle—her personality shining through the dress? I suggested that if that was the case, she go naked so her guests would at least have something to blink at."

While she caught her breath, my mother and I tittered. I didn't know what this antique spitfire was doing in this job, but I liked her. She should have been in education, where her head-on-her-shoulders attitude would have done some girls some good.

The appearance of a woman in a wedding dress stopped my thoughts short. It was Chantal walking as briskly toward us as she could without tripping on her train. That was twice in less than twenty-four hours that we'd bumped into each other in unexpected places. She recognized me, slowing down a couple of feet away from us. She looked behind her shoulder as though seeking an escape route. I took an involuntary step behind my mother—the woman who had said it would be okay to take a day off from work, who'd promised me no one I knew would catch me in this most mortifying of places.

"Ginger?"

"Chantal?"

"What are you doing here?" we asked at the same time. "It's not what it looks like," we again said simultaneously. We laughed. We both waited for the other to speak.

Unfortunately, my mother was good at taking awkward situations and making them worse. "You gonna marry in that dress? It don't look so good."

"Mother!" I said, horrified, and yet glad for something to say. "She didn't ask for your opinion. This is Chantal Lewis from the magazine. She's the person I told you, er, who wants me in that photo shoot."

My mother gave her the once-over. "Really? Now I understand."

"Mother!" I said again, wondering if it had been a mistake to mention the photo shoot. Maybe Chantal would withdraw the offer.

"I agree with your mother," the saleswoman said. "The dress is beautiful, but it doesn't flatter your figure. The dress looks best on curvy women. You should consider something less clingy."

I looked more carefully at Chantal's dress. The bottom half was form-fitting and covered with white sequins. She looked like a mermaid minus the fin. I wondered that she would even put the dress on. It just proved my budding theory that becoming a bride made a woman forfeit her senses.

"I'm not buying this dress," Chantal said, blushing. "I'm not buying any dress. I just wanted to see what it would look like on me. I came out here to ask you to unzip me." She turned around and offered her back, lifting her hair.

The saleswoman frowned. "Does this mean your friend is also trying on dresses for experimental purposes?" She gave the zipper a hard tug.

Chantal remained standing with her back to us. She held her dress closed with her hand. "My friend?"

"Yes, the one you came with." The edge in the saleswoman's voice could have sliced carrots.

The friend that Chantal was having a hard time remembering called out from the dressing room. "Chantal, what's taking so long? Does she have the dress in a bigger size?" The voice was familiar, though I couldn't place it. Was it someone else from the office? Soon the mystery was solved; the friend appeared in the flesh, or, to be more precise, in a white terry-cloth robe. It was Ann.

My mother was the first to collect her wits and speak. "Such small world," she said. "Ginger's boss is friend with Bobby's fiancée."

"You know each other?" Chantal looked at Ann and me.

"We met earlier this week, at dinner with Bob and his parents," Ann answered.

"You're that Korean woman?"

I smiled weakly. I would explain later, when my mother wasn't present to contradict me, that I was an unwitting participant.

"Sure, we were there," my mother said. "Bobby and Ginger know each other long time. Ann, that was a good meal. Now you know kimchi. Koreans love kimchi. We eat at every meal."

For once, I wished my mother spoke worse English.

"I know kimchi. I've eaten it before with Bob."

My mother frowned. "So you buy dress now? You picked the wedding day?"

"Ah, so we do have a bride among us," the saleswoman said.

"No, there isn't a wedding date and she's not buying a dress yet," Chantal said sharply. "Ann and I just had some time to kill."

"You're not seriously looking for a wedding dress?" the saleswoman asked.

"No," Chantal said.

"No," Ann said less harshly. "Not now, but later I will. I may. I might."

"What about you?" the saleswoman said to me. "Are you looking for a dress?"

"No, I'm not," I said.

My mother nudged me in the arm with her elbow. "Not now," she corrected me. "But later she will. Soon she will."

I nudged my mother back, but a little harder. "Not soon. Later, much later. There isn't even a groom in sight."

The saleswoman sighed. "You'd think today's young women would have something better to do than moon over bridal gowns. You spend all this time dreaming about the perfect dress to get married in, but I have something to tell you. It's not worth it. You wear the dress for only one day. Not even the whole day. Maybe five hours, because you won't want to ruin it with sweat stains.

"You all seem like smart women. Why don't you get jobs instead of wasting your time here? Looking at wedding dresses when you're not even engaged. I can't think of a bigger waste of time, and I'm not just saying that because it's my time too. And you," she said, turning to my mother, "you shouldn't be indulging your daughter. She's young. There's plenty of time for a husband and kids."

My mother looked stunned. She'd never been scolded before—at least not in my presence. "She has a job," my mother said. "This woman Sharon is her boss."

"Chantal," I corrected her.

"I'm glad to hear they have jobs. But if they have them, what are they doing here on a Friday morning?"

I cringed. I was hoping the fact I was playing hooky would go unmentioned. Chantal seemed to be wincing as well.

"I haven't told the office I'm back from Los Angeles." She was looking at the saleswoman, but it was obvious she was talking for my benefit, since I was the only person who had any idea what she was talking about. "I wasn't going to tell, actually." She shifted her gaze back to me.

Since she was free to come and go as she pleased, skipping one day was no big deal. She must have been mortified at being caught here, in that bridal gown. With the Rolodex incident, that made two bits of dirt I had on her. But now she had something on me as well.

"I'll forget I saw you today," she said.

I glanced at my mother. "I'll do the same," I said, not specifying when I'd have the bout of amnesia. It could be after I told Sam.

"That makes three of us," the saleswoman said. "I'm going to eat my lunch before the next appointment arrives. I trust you ladies will hang those dresses correctly when you take them off right now." She gave Chantal and Ann stern looks and walked away.

"Right, we should be going," Chantal said.

"I'll see you Monday," I said to her back. "At the closet sale. It'll be ready. I'm coming in Sunday." She was already heading for the dressing room. She waved the back of her hand at me. "Ann, I guess we'll be seeing you tomorrow night."

"You will?"

"At Dr. Oh's birthday party?" I started to think I'd blundered. Maybe Bobby wasn't bringing her.

"Right, Dr. Oh's party. I didn't realize you were going."

My mother lifted my hand holding the shopping bags and waggled it. "She gonna be there all right. She don't miss for her life."

I grabbed back possession of my hand, causing the paper bags to make noise like thunder. "Only to be respectful on Dr. Oh's sixtieth birthday," I said.

"Yes, Dr. Oh is old family friend, just like Bobby. Bobby is old, close friend to Ginger. They used to play together when they were little."

"Yes, I heard all about it Monday." Ann said good-bye and scurried after Chantal.

"Mother," I said as soon as she was out of earshot. "I don't believe you."

"You don't believe me? I don't believe Ann. She pretends not to buy a dress. I wonder why. Maybe they gonna marry sooner than they say." She dug in her purse. "Where my cell phone? I have to call Mrs. Oh."

CHAPTER 13

That evening, while I was watching the news, my mother brought me the phone. "It for you," she said, coming from the kitchen.

I must have been more immersed in the weather forecast than I realized; I hadn't heard it ring. She'd been talking to Mrs. Oh, though. Maybe it clicked during their conversation.

"Hello? Hello?" a small voice squawked.

"Who is it?" I mouthed. My mother shrugged.

"Hello?" I said into the phone.

"Who is this?"

I knew the voice. "Chantal?"

"Yes? Who is this?" A strange way to start a conversation she had initiated.

I looked over at my mother. She was replacing the White Pages on the bookshelf. Was she trying to make amends for my getting caught shopping when I was supposed to be at work? But if she thought there was something more I could say to Chantal, she should have prepped me before placing the call. "It's Ginger Lee."

"Ginger? What can I do for you?" Her tone thawed only a little.

I looked at my mother again. She was walking toward me, mouthing something. What? I voicelessly said to her.

"Ask her—"

I pushed my hands down to signal her to lower her voice. "I'm sorry to be calling so late, but I had a question." What, I mouthed again, covering the phone with my hand.

"Ask her when she elope with Bobby."

She must have called Ann and Chantal answered her phone for her. I gritted my teeth and glared at my mother. How was I ever going to stop her from thrusting me into her schemes? It was too late to hang up.

"Ask her—"

I shook my head so hard, my ponytail whipped me in the face.

"What is it?" Chantal asked.

I turned away from my mother, who was remonstrating with her hands. "The photo shoot," I said. "I was wondering about the photo shoot."

"Yes?"

"I was wondering what you thought about . . . if it would be okay . . . ." My heart pounded as my mind raced for a plausible question. "Whether it would be okay if I waxed my eyebrows."

"Who is it?" my mother whispered, trying to put her ear up to the phone. I tried to push her away, but she was like a gob of sticky rice that wouldn't come off the spoon.

"So you spoke to Sam. I knew it wouldn't be—"

"Actually, not yet. But . . . I have an appointment tomorrow, and since I'm probably going to model, I thought I should check with you." For my mother's benefit, I added, "You being Chantal, the senior style, er, acting co–fashion director of the magazine."

My mother furrowed her brow, then nodded her understanding.

Chantal laughed. "Whatever you do should be fine. Just don't get them too narrow or too arched."

My mother tugged my arm. "Ask for Ann," she whispered loudly. "I called Ann." I put my hand over her mouth to stop her from saying more.

"Ann? Did you say you want Ann?" Her voice was cool again. "She's not home."

"Oh, okay. Since I was talking to you already, I just thought I'd quickly talk to her. . . ." I pressed harder on my mother's mouth. "About the other night. I felt sorry about it all. I had nothing to do with it, of course. But you know parents these days. You can't control them." Mine was squirming to be free.

"I'll pass on the sentiments."

"Thanks. I'll see you Monday."

I hung up and released my mother's mouth. "How could you?"

"What I do?"

"What did you do?" I stomped my foot. "That was Chantal! I work with her."

My mother waved her hand in a dismissive manner. "She don't care."

"Mother, you may get away with odd behavior. But I'm not a foreigner. Are you intentionally trying to humiliate and destroy me?"

"Calm down. I didn't know Sharon gonna answer."

"But you did know she and Ann are friends. You can't involve me like this. You can't treat Ann however you want without it coming back to me."

"Sharon not mad. She don't want Ann to marry Bobby either."

"What? She was helping her look at dresses."

"Yes," my mother said, wagging her finger at me, "but didn't you hear her shout no when the saleswoman asked if Ann gonna buy a dress?"

"You're just projecting your feelings onto her. Why would she oppose the wedding?"

"Maybe she don't like Koreans."

"Can you blame her?"

My mother swatted me on the head. "Or maybe she don't want to lose her roommate."

I waited for her to explain how she'd leapt to that conclusion.

"She answered Ann's phone. I called Ann's number."

It seemed unlikely that Chantal had a roommate. I was just an assistant, and I didn't have one. She was even several years older than me. But then, I didn't live on Fifth Avenue—and from the way she'd been so excited about the Hamptons, I didn't think she was wealthy like Sam.

Still, I couldn't believe she'd put her interest over her friend's happiness. "Normal people do not interfere in other people's lives like that."

My mother didn't respond. She took the phone and called the Ohs to report back.

CHAPTER 14

My mother spent Saturday in New Jersey helping Mrs. Oh cook and prepare for the party. She rushed back to the city to dress and get me. We were supposed to return before the first guests arrived to help with any last-minute things, but I dawdled, thinking I could use her need for me to hurry as leverage. I wanted to know what the anti-

Ann conspirators had planned. I couldn't stop them from trying to oust Ann, but now that their actions were against Chantal's friend, I could not afford to be their patsy again.

"What take so long?" my mother shouted through the locked bathroom door.

"I'm shaving my legs." My hair wet, I sat in a towel on the lid of the toilet, paging through a magazine.

"Let me in. I have to use the bathroom."

I looked at the clock and saw twenty minutes had passed since I'd showered. I slipped the *TV Guide* into the cabinet under the sink and opened the door.

The hot rollers were gone from her hair and she was wearing a pale yellow Chanel suit similar to the one she arrived in on Monday. She looked like she was going to work instead of a birthday party. On her lapel-less jacket, inches below the neckline, was pinned the emerald and diamond frog brooch I had given her nine years ago for her fiftieth birthday. I'd bought it, of course, with her credit card.

"What happened to your new dress?"

"I changed my mind. It too young for me."

The knee-length silk dress wasn't any more youthful than the ones in her closet back home, and I told her so. "It's pretty. You should wear it."

She shook her head impatiently. "I don't feel like it. Anyway, don't worry about me. Look at you. Your hair not even dry. Hurry up, we have to go."

I reached out and touched the frog between its diamond eyes. I had debated between it and a pair of much less expensive pearl earrings. She'd never expressed or shown a fondness for amphibious creatures, but I thought the brooch would make her happy, make her think of the good old days with my brother, maybe even make her miss him so much, she'd try to contact him. He'd had a pet toad named Todd. She'd said the gift was nice and put it in her jewelry box. At least she didn't return it to the store, though she did take away her MasterCard when she got the bill.

"I haven't seen this in years," I said.

"No? I wear my Todd each time I show a house and go to church."

"Since when?"

"Since you gave to me. You already in college, so you never saw. I tell everyone my daughter gave this to me." She stuck out her chest. "When Mrs. Oh saw it last week, she said, 'I wish I had daughter instead of my terrible son.'"

"Bobby doesn't give her nice presents? He's a medical doctor."

"He buys her pearls and gold jewelry. Nothing personal. She gives it all back if he breaks the engagement with Ann."

"Speaking of Ann, what are you and the Ohs going to do to her tonight? I want to be as far away as possible." I walked around her to the dresser against the wall. I motioned for her to move so I could open the top drawer and get a pair of underwear. My dress was so skimpy, I wouldn't be able to wear a bra.

My mother stepped into the bathroom to get out of my way. I heard her turn on the faucet. "Nothing in the store for Ann," she said over the sound of running water.

I used the moment of privacy to slip into the thong. "Nothing? They're not going to give her birthday cake with kimchi in it or confront her somehow? You have to tell me. I'm not coming unless you do." I was now standing in the doorway. My mother was brushing her teeth.

She spit. "Kimchi cake? No such thing. Believe me. Dr. and Mrs. Oh didn't even know Ann comes until you ask yesterday at the store. They not doing nothing. They have to think about their guests."

She put toothpaste on my toothbrush and held it out. I looked at it.

"They don't want another big scene."

I took the toothbrush. She reached for the hair dryer, holding it ready while I brushed my teeth and washed my face.

"Mrs. Oh called Bobby this afternoon. They have a truce, like North and South Korea. They gonna be polite to Ann, and Bobby not gonna spoil his father's birthday. He not gonna announce his engagement."

She handed me the blow dryer and left the bathroom. I bent over and started drying the hair near my neck, going over everything she'd just said. She'd mentioned before that Mrs. Oh had called her because she couldn't turn to her friends, who, I'd assumed, didn't have firsthand experience the way my mother did. It hadn't occurred to me that the Ohs didn't want their friends to know what they'd been up to. I thought all Korean parents would understand. I straightened and finished drying the rest of my hair. As I combed through the tangles, I thought of a loophole.

"But what about you? Are your actions covered by this pact or are you a free agent?"

My mother came back with my dress off the hanger. "Me? Why I do something? Bobby not my son. I only help the Ohs." She put her hands inside the flimsy material.

I was glad to hear that she had her limits, that she didn't consider the Ohs such good friends that she was willing to do their dirty work for them.

"So I'm not going to be put in any awkward situation?"

She steered the double layers of silk over my hands, cuffing me. "No way," my mother scoffed as though I'd just said the preposterous. "You don't do nothing. I told Mrs. Oh you can't risk make enemy with Ann, and it better if you friend with Bobby."

So she had been listening last night. I let her put the dress over my head. Once I surfaced, I raised my arms and let her pull the dress down over my body.

"If you his friend, he gonna confide to you and you can tell his plans to Mommy."

"You want me to double-deal like that?" Using Chantal to further my career was one thing, but now my mother was sponsoring duplicity in my private life. She'd been spending too much time with Mrs. Oh.

"You do with Sam."

"How? I'm not spilling any of her secrets." I wasn't even in on her schemes, it occurred to me.

"You help Sharon with photo shooting."

"You told me to take advantage of the situation!"

"And now I tell you to take advantage of Bobby."

She adjusted my dress, tugging it here and there. I batted her hand away.

"I'm not hurting Sam. Not really."

My mother looked at her hand. "No," she said slowly. "But you not completely helping her. You can't. You have to put yourself first." She looked up at me, smiling. "Same with Bobby."

"Breaking his engagement is your and Mrs. Oh's agenda, not mine."

"What difference?"

Shaking my head, I shooed her out of the bathroom ahead of me. I would always cover her back, but I wasn't sure I wanted her to have mine.

CHAPTER 15

My mother parked her rented black Mercedes behind the other cars skirting the Ohs' estate. We had ridden in silence, she focused on the road, me on our last conversation. I should have called Sam, told her about the modeling offer. I would turn it down Monday if she wanted me to. As curious as I was to experience a photo shoot, her promotion was more important. At least by leading Chantal to think I was interested, I had cost her a day.

On account of traffic, we were much later than even I had anticipated, arriving a couple of hours after the promised time. Who would have guessed so many people wanted to go to New Jersey? From the laughter and voices reaching us from yards away, the party sounded to be in full swing.

My mother checked her makeup in the rearview mirror. I grabbed Dr. Oh's present, a Gucci leather billfold, and reached for the door handle. I heard the sound of the power locks. The door wouldn't open. I turned back to her.

"Wrong way," I said. "You locked the door."

"I know. We gotta talk before we go in there."

I waited, impatient to get on with the evening. Normal people's families weren't so weird, didn't make such odd demands, demands you would die if the world heard about them. I longed to be like Sam, who had no disconnects in her life.

"Mrs. Oh invited many of Dr. Oh's students to the party."

A house full of graduate students—Dante could have put them in the first ring of hell. My mother was concerned about my feelings. But Dr. Oh taught engineering, not English. "Thanks for the heads-up. I think I'll be all right."

"No, listen. Most students are men, but some are women and some sisters and friends. Mrs. Oh told everyone to bring all the young women they know to meet Bobby."

I should have known the tireless mothers wouldn't miss an opportunity. I should have been suspicious when she mentioned the pact between the two Koreas. Technically, they were still at war.

"Why are you telling me this? It means something only to Bobby and Ann."

"I don't want you to think the Ohs don't like you no more. Mrs. Oh says she invited everyone before she knew we come."

"That's what you're worried about? For the last time, Mother, I'm not interested in Bobby. He's engaged. Ann is the one you should be saying this to."

"You right, Ann has a lot to worry about, so many pretty Korean ladies. You know, I look at her at the store yesterday, and she not so good-looking."

"Mother! That's not what I was saying. There's more to a woman than her looks. I'm sure she's very smart and fun and interesting to talk to." It was humiliating to have her as my mother.

"Why you think that?"

"Because Bobby wouldn't defy his parents for anyone. She must be very special."

"She must be rich."

"Whatever," I said, shaking my head. I had wondered the same thing about Ann's appeal, but I wasn't going to admit—or discuss—it now. "Can we get this over with?"

"I not finished. As long as there gonna be so many eligible Korean men at the party, you should talk to them. Don't be snob because they don't have nice clothes. They student now, but one day they work and make good money."

"Does Mrs. Oh know you want me to hit on her husband's students?"

"What she don't know not gonna hurt her."

I smirked. My credo in her words.

"Don't take me wrong. Bobby is still my first choice, but we should take advantage of the opportunity. As you said, Bobby is engaging."

Hope reared its cobwebbed head. I'd been thinking Bobby was the only setup she had for me. She'd been here a week and not mentioned any others. But I knew her too well to be lulled into a false sense of security. Now, however, I wondered again. "You mean you don't have any more men to introduce me to?"

My mother ignored my question. "So be nice. Don't eat too much. Don't talk loud. Be a lady."

I looked askance at her.

"I serious. Since you go to college and become a feminine-ist, you act kinda strange. Sometime you act opposite of what natural."

Acting like a lady was hardly natural. "I behaved at the restaurant."

"That right, you did for most part. But I sat across from you the whole time. Please, act right. Act like me. Whenever you want to say or do something, ask yourself, 'Mommy would do this?' Okay?"

She would live to regret her words, I was sure. I shrugged, committing to nothing.

"One more thing."

I groaned. If this was the windup, I feared for the actual pitch. "Yes?"

My mother drummed the steering wheel with her index fingers. Usually, she just plowed ahead, tossing up words until she hit her meaning. I shifted in my seat.

"Some of Dr. Oh's friends knew your father at Seoul University or at UW Milwaukee. Maybe they ask you how he is. Maybe they still talk to him and don't ask. But if they do, just say everyone is fine. You don't need to tell them our family business."

I looked down at my hands in my lap. There were people still in Milwaukee who knew my father, of course, but I had no contact with them. After he left, my mother stopped going to their friends' gatherings or inviting them to our house. Mrs. Oh had been the only exception, but she moved at the end of that summer. My mother also stopped taking my brother and me to the one church we had attended as a family, and went to the four other churches alone, alternating each week, to widen her base of potential Korean clients. She started to host little get-togethers when I still lived at home, but the guests were usually newcomers to the area who didn't know my father, and I stayed in my room anyway.

To my mind, going to Korea was the same as dying. He had never called or written. The thought that he still lived in people's memories, or that he actually was present in some of their lives, was a shock. I wondered who these friends were that they were important enough for him to stay in touch with.

"Of course, Mrs. Oh gossips so much, everyone already know about your father and brother. Maybe it was mistake to bring you. But there so many single men here, it shame not to meet them. If you want, just don't go near to the people my age."

She looked nervously at me, the way I had occasionally caught her looking at me right before I moved to New York. I would stare back and she would go back to reading her paper or making dinner without saying anything. I pushed away thoughts of my father and mustered up a smile. "So talk to the young men, stay away from the old."

"Especially Bobby. Talk to Bobby."

She hesitated, then unlocked the doors.

Although the summer sun had started its descent hours before, the air was still warm. While passing the train of cars and their still-ticking engines, I took in the Ohs' house. With its white stone facade, flowerpots, and archways, it looked like an old Italian villa. The Ohs had come a long way from Milwaukee, where they lived in a small yellow house with a green roof. My mother had mentioned the other night that Dr. Oh owned the patents on several widely used surgical instruments.

The stone pathway made for treacherous walking. The front door was open. Immediately, we were bombarded by loud chatter and the smell of Korean food cooking. The bouquet of garlic, ginger, sesame oil, and meat made me salivate, and it, along with the noise, brought me back to my childhood, when my parents were either entertaining or taking me to their friends' houses. I used to hang out with a gang of girls, and when we weren't having burping contests or pillow fights, we were sneaking dumplings, rice cakes, and orange slices from the kitchen. It was easier to slip by the adults than by Bobby, who was often skulking outside the bedroom door. My brother and the other boys stayed away from the girls, playing Ping-Pong in the garage or watching sports in the basement.

A table in the Ohs' front foyer was spilling over with presents. In my mother's house, real estate brochures and her business cards occupied the same place. Before her potential clients arrived, she could be found standing at the table, rearranging the red and black pamphlets, fanning them out, stacking them, laying them out like magazines in a waiting room. I never knew why she bothered, since she stuffed the brochures in the bags of leftover food she gave them.

I added our gift to a pile on the floor.

My mother tugged on her jacket and put on a smile. With that small movement, she transformed from the husbandless wife and son-less mother into the biggest Korean broker in the greater Milwaukee area. I understood now why she had gone with the suit.

This wasn't going to be an easy stroll down memory lane for her, seeing these old acquaintances who knew our "family business." It would be more like a walk along the 38th parallel, through the demilitarized zone. And as misguided as her motivation was, she was doing it for me. I decided to talk to some men, even when she wasn't looking.

We followed the noise and smells to the back of the house, where a large kitchen opened into an airy and spacious living room. Glass doors with arched tops lined an entire wall. The space was filled with so many people that I couldn't see the furniture. The men, dressed in button-downs and khakis, occupied the living room, the older men at the farthest end, and the women, wearing silk blouses and skirts or conservative dresses, had taken over the kitchen and dining room on the other side. Except for the young men and women along the invisible line separating the genders, no one was standing next to a member of the opposite sex.

As far as I could see, I was the only one wearing a revealing couture party frock. I adjusted an errant strap.

"I gonna put my purse upstairs and find Mrs. Oh," my mother shouted.

I wanted to follow her but stayed where I was. Light brown crowns bobbed in the sea of black heads, but they were dye jobs. None of them was Ann. Bobby was also nowhere in sight. I noticed a couple of young men were looking my way. For my mother, I walked over to them and introduced myself.

They both bowed, almost knocking heads. One of them greeted

me in Korean and said their names. Bum-young and Dung-hae, I thought I heard.

"How do you know Dr. Oh? Are you his students?"

They looked at each other and then at me. The one who had spoken cleared his throat. "You student?"

"No, I'm not. Are you?"

"You Dr. Oh?"

"Never mind. It was nice meeting you." I waved and pushed on past more men speaking Korean. Some nodded, but no one made way for me to join his circle. I kept on squeezing myself forward and soon found myself among the pepper-and-salt or entirely gray set. I turned around to go toward the kitchen. Someone tapped me on the shoulder.

"Are you Dr. Oh's niece?" Finally, someone with American manners.

"No, I'm just a friend of the family."

"Could you get me a plate of ribs?"

I smiled and stepped on his foot as I continued breast-stroking through the crowd. Even Americanized Korean men couldn't undo years of having their mothers and sisters wait on them. Finally, I made it to the border, where the men and women were less densely packed and still not talking to each other. It was no wonder their mothers had to arrange their marriages.

That chore was finished. I had tried.

The women in front of me would be more friendly; I was one of them at least. But they were also there to meet Bobby. I wasn't ready to join them just yet. Not seeing my mother anywhere, I headed through one of the archways for fresh air. It was dark now, and I almost stepped on a woman sitting just outside the doorway, talking on her cell phone. I apologized and continued walking, steering for an empty bench.

"Hey, you in the fabulous dress! Come back."

I turned around. She closed her phone and moved over to make room on her step. I liked her black suit. It was Dolce & Gabbana.

She appraised my low-cut, ridiculously frilly neckline. I looked down at myself and saw my breasts behind the silk drapery, waiting like actors to pop out from behind the curtain. My mother had forgotten to pin it. I crossed my arms over my chest.

"Are you going to a party in the city after this? Want to share a cab? I have to cut out of here soon."

I would have loved to leave, but I couldn't desert my mother. "I just got here with my mother. It's because of her that I'm dressed like this." I felt silly for blaming her, but it was the truth. The woman was Korean; she'd understand. "I think I'm in for a long night."

"Have some food. It'll brighten your outlook. I'd stay, but that was the hospital on the phone. There was a big pileup on some interstate and there might be a liver match for one of my patients."

So she was a doctor. Smart, chic, and put-together, she looked like one. I wondered what she was doing at the party—and what I must look like to her.

She offered her hand. "I'm June Chung, by the way."

I shook it, adjusting a strap again. "Ginger Lee." I felt the need to convince her I wasn't one of the ladies in the kitchen hoping to be chosen by the prince. "I really don't normally dress like this."

"No? You look great."

"Thanks. It's a bit flashy for me."

"Showing a little cleavage never hurt anyone."

"It's not the sexiness factor. More the girlish frills." I flicked them.

"Feminine is in this season   or so my friend who works in fashion says. She hates my suits."

"Well, I work for a fashion magazine and I like them—at least the one you're wearing."

"You work for a fashion book? Maybe you know my friend—"

"I doubt it. I started only a year ago." June widened her eyes. "I know, I'm too old to be an assistant. My mother says I don't have long before I lose my bloom."

"I wasn't going to say you were too old. I was going to say you're too expensively dressed to be in it for only a year. I know how little magazines pay."

"I have a generous mother."

"I'd say. I know you got it at a sample sale, but still, it must have set her back several hundred dollars."

"Actually, we got it retail." I usually refrained from talking about the cost of my clothes, embarrassed that I hadn't paid for them myself, but with her it didn't seem crass.

"Wow." June slowly shook her head. "Too bad you have to put up with the horrible things she says to you."

"My fading bloom? Doesn't yours say the same thing?"

She leaned away from me. "I may be thirty-one, but I'm not losing any bloom."

"That's not what I meant. I thought all Korean mothers talked about fading blooms. I thought it was a Korean saying."

"If it is, I never heard it. But then, my mother is dead and my father would never say anything like that to me."

"I'm sorry," I said, not knowing what else to say about her deceased mother. I thought of things people said to me when I mentioned that my father left us, but "I didn't know Korean people did that" or "Did you lose complete contact?" didn't seem right.

"Thanks, but it happened when I was a baby. I don't even remember her."

"That's like with my dad. He went back to Korea, never to be heard from again."

June just nodded, it being her turn not to know what to say. I looked at her pretty face, her flawless skin, nice clothes, confident style. I'd never thought this about anyone before, but she reminded me of myself. She was like that device in fiction, a doppelganger, the person I would have been if I'd only taken the beaten path and gone to med school, as was my prescribed lot as a second-generation Korean American.

June's cell phone rang and I watched her talk. "That was the hospital," she said, hanging up. "The liver is a match. I should say bye to Bob. Have you seen him?"

So she was Bob's friend. I told her that the front of the house seemed empty and suggested she look in the dining room or upstairs.

"Thanks," she said. We both stood up. "We should continue this conversation, get together some time. Maybe I could connect you with my friend. Do you have a pen?"

I watched her tailored back disappear in the crowd. Maybe she and all these other women here were better off doing what was expected of them. Our parents had come to these shores to dig their heels in; our job was to make the foothold firmer. Inroads were for future generations—as were revolts. But while I was at this house to appease my mother, these women, having co-opted their parents' expectations, were here to appease themselves. In the end, we were at the same party, but they were having fun.

I came inside and meandered through the distaff half of the party, looking for a conversation to join. Some were in English, at least. From the snippets I heard, it sounded as though a large contingent of computer techies and scientists was present. Many had canceled their plans to come. Apparently, Mrs. Oh was renowned for her cooking.

Unsuccessful in my attempt to latch on to a group, I soon found myself in the dining room, next to a table of steaming, savory food. This was the mother lode of Korean cuisine, the gold pot at the end of the rainbow, the Shangri-La of destinies. Kalbi, barbecue ribs; jhapchae, glass noodles with vegetables; pajun, pancakes made of scallions and mung bean; mandu, beef and pork dumplings; ojingo, cooked octopus; doeraji, a rare mountain root preserved in red pepper and garlic; sautéed spinach; vegetable tempura; fried oysters; five kinds of kimchi, and potato salad. It all looked so good; my stomach rumbled its agreement.

I hadn't eaten all day so I would fit into my dress. The sacrifice for looking good. I also had that photo shoot next week. I put the dinner plate back on the stack and picked up a smaller one. I thought of Dakota and her endless salads, and newly appreciated her willpower.

With a helping of spinach and dumplings, I snaked through the pockets of women. My mother was still nowhere in sight. If she wasn't going to mingle, I wasn't going to either. I went back to the empty step where I'd been sitting with June.

I was in the dark, debating whether I should refill my plate, when I heard my name spoken. I was about to say hello, that I was down on the step, outside, when I realized I was being talked about.

"Is Ginger here yet?" a woman's voice asked. It sounded like Ann.

"I haven't seen her, but I know her mother's here," Bobby answered. "I think she came. Several people were talking about a woman in a hard-to-ignore dress."

"That must be the dress she and her mother bought yesterday at Bergdorf's. What rotten luck to have bumped into them like that. Chantal had a panic attack."

"She's overreacting. Ginger's not going to connect the dots. I bet she was too flustered even to pick up on them. She *was* skipping out on work."

"To drool over wedding dresses, no less."

They both laughed. I felt a stab in my chest like heartburn. I should have walked away or alerted them to my presence, but the masochist in me refused to move or speak up.

"Chantal says the office is full of silly, superficial women. She can't stand talking to them. She just wants to shake them. Her assistant Wyoming . . ."

I'd heard enough. I quietly put down my plate and chopsticks and crept into the black night.

CHAPTER 16

I found my way to the front of the house and down to the road. Some cars had left, and the empty gaps in the otherwise regular and compact row of cars bordering the lawn made me think of punched-out teeth. I continued walking, pounding down so hard and fast that the high heels of my sandals were bending and my insteps were touching the asphalt. I was ruining the only pair of Manolo Blahniks I owned, but I didn't care.

Now beyond the cars and the light cast by the porch sconces, I was in pitch blackness. There wasn't a star or moon in the sky. It made me think of the months leading up to my dropping out of school. They had been the darkest I had known.

Admitting I didn't belong there had been hard. But not unbearable. Steinem and Bouvier, the feminist thinking that had come as a revelation to me as an undergraduate, had devolved into Cixous and Irigaray, theory that had no practical applications or meaning. Accepting that I wasn't going to finish something for the first time had been painful. But not intolerably so. I knew I had the wherewithal to write and even defend my dissertation; I just didn't have the inclination to give any more time to texts that had never been published. The world beyond academia's doors was beckoning me. Editing books, representing them as a literary agent, writing advertising copy, being a war correspondent—I felt I could do any of those things.

But that was how it had been with English literature. My entire life, my all-around competency had been a plus, had gotten me through. Dilettantism even had a nice ring to it—denoting intellectual curiosity and versatility. Now, however, it seemed a crutch, a decorative word, a euphemism for someone who lacked focus, passion. Even after five years of being stuck in a rut, there was nothing that quickened my pulse, filled me with anticipation, sent me soaring. My heart was wet wood, resistant to fire.

That was the unbearable, intolerable difficulty. The blot on the sun. The cause of my crisis, my terror and despair.

A person was her wants, and I wanted nothing. Or I didn't want anything I couldn't have, which was the same but worse. Having to straddle two worlds, I was not free to jump, both feet, be reckless and wild. And having lived my life sticking to the shores, the edges, the surface, always making compromises, suppressing, holding out, I had lost the feel for passion; whatever potential for intensity I possessed had dwindled, dried up from neglect. The last time I could remember wanting something badly was as a child. A Korean dance troupe of orphan girls had come to town. They wore beautiful gowns that went down to the floor, and twirled and waved sleeves of flowing white silk. I had desperately wanted to be one of them, even after what it meant to be an orphan was explained to me.

In books, orphans were the protagonists who were free to do as they pleased.

My doom, the lot, I feared, of a second-generationer was an existence of self-abnegation and contradiction, of a will eternally struggling, churning, grinding. I was a woman in search of a husband she didn't want, a careerist without a calling, a feminist who couldn't disobey her mother. My mother was worried about my bloom when nipped buds didn't flower.

She had raised me without her language, detached me from her community, given me only herself as a link to my ancestry and culture. I didn't fault her for it. Not speaking with an accent, not feeling ill at ease in white society, not feeling Korean—they were to help me get ahead in this country, advance past her. But not being associated with Koreans wasn't the same as being American, and being held back by your family because you can't disappoint or desert them was more wrenching than being rebuffed or stymied by a society that couldn't understand you or your ways.

I wasn't vehement American Ginger and I wasn't traditional Korean Lee. I was the collision of the names—the accidental adverb resulting from the clash of two worlds, gingerly, how I was meant to go through life. I was the space in between the names. I occupied the short pause between them, the breach between the two states, like a ghost who was neither alive nor sufficiently dead.

I came to a halt along the side of the road and listened to the silent night.

I felt so small, so alone. And yet, if allowed, I felt I could fill the galaxy with my being, my yearning. The void of desire turned in on itself, inflating my chest with want, indeterminate, expansive, rapturous. The absence of something was the presence of its absence. Surely a person could be someone she wasn't.

I put my hand on my heart and felt the soft hardness, the clothed looseness, of my breast. Oxymora, dualities, paradoxes—they were everywhere.

CHAPTER 17

The second I stepped foot into the house, the irrepressible Mrs. Oh, decked out in a pale pink cocktail dress and pearls, pounced. "Ginger!" she shouted, squeezing the breath out of me. "I look all night for you." She released my ribs. "What beautiful dress! You see Bobby?" She motioned for me to come with her. "I need your help."

I had no choice but to oblige. Of the young female guests, I was the closest to being family. I followed her to the now-empty kitchen. The people who'd been standing there earlier had migrated, pushed out by the Pisa towers of dirty dishes, no doubt. I didn't mind lending a hand in the kitchen, but I really detested washing dishes. As a child, I'd purposefully dropped several fine china plates in one night. It had worked; to this day my mother wouldn't let me handle her dishes.

"Where's my mother?" I asked. I hadn't seen her on our way there.

Mrs. Oh frowned. "She no feel good. She lay down upstairs."

"Should I check on her?" My mother was like a tank. I wondered if seeing my father's friends had been too much for her.

Mrs. Oh put a reassuring hand on my arm. "She okay. She need rest."

"What's wrong with her?"

Mrs. Oh pondered my question, moving her hand to her forehead. "I think she have headache." Brightly, she said, "She have migraine. She be fine. No worry."

My mother didn't have migraines. "I should go to her," I said.

"You cannot."

"I can't?"

Mrs. Oh opened the refrigerator and took out a large white box, holding it by the sides. From where I was standing, I could see that the bottom was about to fall out. I ran to her, put my hands on the underside of the box, and together we shuffled to the counter.

"Thank you, dear," she said. She opened the lid to reveal a long sheet cake covered with white frosting. In red lettering it said, "Happy Birthday, Doctorow." The baker must be a reader. I helped her slide the box out from under the cake.

"Why can't I see my mother?"

"Why what?" Mrs. Oh brought three little boxes of candles to the counter. "Oh, your mother. Why can't you see her? Because she sleep. You no disturb. Check later, after cake. I need you put these candle on cake. Sixty of them." She nodded as though I'd just exclaimed with bulging eyes, Sixty!

"You so talent and artist," she continued, "I know you do beautiful job." I sank three candles in the frosting. "No, straight line," she said. She took the candles out and put them back in. She continued the row, six across, and made a column, ten down. "There, follow line. I be right back."

I would get my mother after I was done here. Just as I planted the last candle, Mrs. Oh returned with Bobby in tow.

"It looks like Ginger has everything in hand."

I acknowledged his presence with a slight nod. He bowed back.

"Yes," Mrs. Oh said happily. "Look at wonderful work she do. It work of art." She leaned over and fixed several candles. I'd never seen anyone be so fussy about candles that were going to be taken out anyway.

The two of them admired my handiwork as I stared at Bobby's white, gauzy, untucked shirt.

Bobby leaned over and pointed to the candles. "You know, this would look better if it were ten across, six down. Or you should have spaced them out more."

"I know. It look better, but then Daddy have hard time blow them out, and then he no get his wish."

His wish didn't need to be articulated.

"My work looks done here," I said.

Mrs. Oh disengaged her eyes and turned her lasers on me. "No, no, we take cake now. People wait so they can leave. You two light candle and I get camera."

It wasn't with a little difficulty that we got all sixty candles lit. Focused on the flames, we kept on bumping arms. I had to be careful when leaning over that my ruffles didn't catch fire. I held them to my chest, reminded again of my bralessness. Mrs. Oh was of no assistance, snapping pictures of us the whole time.

"Okay, let's go before the candles melt down," Bobby said. He slid

his hands beneath the cake and lifted it. He held the roaring confla-
gration at arm's length. Sixty candles were a lot of candles.

Mrs. Oh handed me a basket of forks and napkins and a pitcher of
lemonade. I fell into line between the two of them.

Bobby looked back at me. "Can you go ahead of me and get the
lights?"

"No, leave light on," Mrs. Oh said over my shoulder. She rested a
hand on my other shoulder. "You gonna trip."

His neck still twisted toward us, he nodded. Sweat trickled down
his forehead.

"You okay?" I asked.

"I'm fine, but now that you mention it, could you wipe my eyes?"

With Mrs. Oh's hand still on my shoulder, I dabbed Bobby's brow
with a napkin from the basket. Despite the fire raging in front of him,
it was an oddly peaceful moment. To an outsider, the three of us must
have looked like the picture of tender domesticity.

I jerked my hand away. "Wait! What about Ann?"

Mrs. Oh released my shoulder. "Ann? No time for Ann. We go."

"Yeah, this cake is getting heavy." Bobby started moving forward,
and with Mrs. Oh pushing behind me, I helplessly followed.

As we walked in procession toward Dr. Oh at the back of the living room, the crowd parted like the Red Sea. I realized too late that I
should have walked in front of Bobby. Flickers were shooting to the
left and right of him. Once we reached Dr. Oh, the room burst into a
rousing "Happy Birthday," Mrs. Oh's falsetto hanging above us. The
Ohs and I stood in an arc, with Mrs. Oh on one side of her husband,
snapping pictures, and Bobby and the cake on the other side. I stood
next to Bobby.

It was hot at the center of attention with everyone looking at me,
probably wondering who I was. I looked down the front of my dress to
make sure I hadn't popped out of it, when out of the corner of my eye
I saw the cake was slipping. Bobby, holding it away from his body, was
losing his grip.

I threw down the basket and pitched the lemonade at the candles. Bobby jumped back and dropped the cake.

The singing stopped. The pile of smoldering white frosting and yellow cake with candles and china shards looked like a snowman that had come to a violent end.

"Why you do that?" Mrs. Oh finally asked.

"Fire" was all I could say. I gesticulated, miming the wildly danc-ing flames.

"It was a birthday cake," Dr. Oh remonstrated. "My birthday cake."

"I'm sorry," I mumbled, feeling my cheeks burn. "I thought . . ." I looked at Bobby pleadingly.

Understanding replaced the perplexity on his face. He shifted his weight and cleared his throat. "Dad, the candles were out of control. They almost burned me."

"You burned?" His mother ran to him and pulled up his shirt.

"I'm okay," he said, brushing her hands away.

"No, I see." She lifted his shirt again, exposing his chiseled torso. Dr. Oh stepped toward him, obstructing my view.

Ann, in a manly pinstriped suit, rushed up to us. She held a bowl of ice and a dish towel. "I was in the bathroom," she said, out of breath.

"You're fine," Mrs. Oh said in Korean, slapping Bobby's stomach.

"What a bunch of nonsense," Dr. Oh grumbled, withdrawing from the family huddle. "Hey, let's have some brandy," he said to the near-est group of men.

"Do you need this?" Ann held up the compress she'd made.

Mrs. Oh, who had been watching Ann, put her hands on her hips and made a loud sound of derision, blowing air between her closed lips. "Too late. Everything over." She walked over to me and put her arm around my waist. "Ginger save his life."

"It was nothing," I said, my cheeks heating up again.

"Now Bobby owe you." She pointed her finger at him. "You owe her."

"*I* owe her," Bobby said, looking at me.

"Yes, you," she clucked. She grinned. "You should make her dinner each day for rest of life. Dinner, lunch, and breakfast."

"That's okay," I said.

"Bobby great cook," Mrs. Oh taunted. "He went French cooking school."

"Only for eight weeks," Bobby said. "The summer before med school."

I looked at him. I hadn't known, but I wasn't surprised.

"Don't be modest, Bobby." Ann put an arm around his shoulders. "He makes a mean bouillabaisse."

Mrs. Oh frowned. "His chicken better."

"No disrespect, but his bouillabaisse is his pièce de résistance."

"What that mean?"

"It means that she thinks it's really good," Bobby explained. "You're both right."

"I no think so."

Ann clenched her teeth. "I think so."

"Bouillabaisse no big deal. I can make it."

"I doubt that. Do you even know what it is?"

Mrs. Oh took a menacing step toward Ann, dropping her arm from my waist. I held her in place, now putting my arm around her waist. I didn't plan on making a habit of being Mrs. Oh's keeper, but someone had to restrain her. I was never going to change Chantal's opinion of me if I let Ann go home to her with a fat lip.

"Sure, I know. It fish soup. He make for me in front he make for you."

"What? I can't even make sense out of that."

I gasped, then quickly covered my mouth.

Mrs. Oh turned to me. "What she say?"

I didn't want to escalate the argument, but Ann's ridicule of Mrs. Oh's English couldn't go without reprimand. I knew Ann had already lashed out at Mrs. Oh, using even angrier words, but telling someone in the heat of passion she should go to hell wasn't like making fun of someone's English. In all my years of contention with my mother, I had never sunk that low. Even as a child.

To Bobby's credit, he looked as appalled as I felt. "This is silly, fighting over my cooking. We'll have to let Ginger decide." He looked at me. "You'll have to be my guest some night, my and Ann's guest."

Ann relaxed her stance and nodded, probably ashamed she'd gone so far.

Mrs. Oh smiled victoriously. "When Ginger come over?"

Bobby looked at Ann uncertainly.

"Tomorrow night?" Mrs. Oh chirped.

"You just never let u—"

"Not tomorrow," Bobby spoke over Ann. "I'll call Ginger."

Ann held her tongue. Given how she was being treated, I had to hand it to her. At least she was making an effort, not forcing Bobby to choose between her and his family.

"Ginger, give Bobby your number."

"I have it already."

"You do?" Mrs. Oh's smile was as wide as her face.

"Where did you say my mother was?" I nudged Mrs. Oh to lead me.

Mrs. Oh's feet stayed firmly planted. "You such good daughter, care for your mama. We talk more. We have such good time."

We all looked at one another, unable to think of anything more to say.

Ann broke the silence. Looking at her watch, she said, "It's getting late."

"Yeah, we should get going." Bobby reached into his pocket and jangled his keys.

"You go?" Mrs. Oh worried her lip. "You say you spend night and clean tomorrow morning."

Bobby and Ann exchanged looks. "I know I did, but there's been a change in plans. Ann has to fill in for someone at the hospital tomorrow. I have to take her home."

"She take your car. You sleep here."

"How am I going to get home then?"

"Mrs. Lee drive you. After we breakfast big family." She knitted her eyebrows. "Eat," she said triumphantly. "After we eat big family breakfast."

"I'm spending the night?" I asked.

She nodded. "No wake your mama." She threw her arms out as though she'd just had a eureka moment. "Tomorrow we eat big family breakfast." Her hands hung in the air. She pulled them down, a dubious look on her own face.

An improv actor she wasn't. She should have prepared for the unexpected or maybe even said her lines in Korean, because it was obvious that this sudden turn of events was not spontaneous.

My mother. Technically, she hadn't lied. She hadn't made any promises about what was going to happen after the party.

"I can't let Ann drive alone this late. I'll clean up now and then we'll go."

Ann put her hand on Bobby's arm. "No, honey, I'll be fine. Stay here with your family and old friends." She held her hand out for his keys.

Bobby hesitated, staring into her eyes, then dropped the keys into her palm.

"Wonderful," Mrs. Oh said. "Ann, I get your handbag." She bolted for the stairs.

I looked around, and was surprised to see that the party was leaving. There was a bottleneck in the front hall, where Dr. Oh stood, shaking hands and bowing. The lights seemed brighter, though they probably hadn't been touched.

"You don't really have to make me dinner," I said now that Mrs. Oh was gone.

"I insist," Bobby said. "It's the least I can do to thank you for saving my life." He smiled.

"I really thought the cake was about to slip and start a fire."

"Don't worry about it. You did us all a favor. The party was never going to end."

"Your dad hates me."

"Join the club," Ann said. "At least his mom adores you."

"It's more of a curse than a blessing."

We all chuckled.

"We should have dinner together," Ann said. "Chantal will want to come if Bobby's making bouillabaisse." She tossed the keys high in the air and snatched them mid-descent with the snap of her wrist. "It's far better than his coq au vin."

I started to see what Bobby saw in Ann—a little of his mother. I took a step back and half held my hands up in surrender. "I believe you already."

Ann laughed. "Sorry. I'm not normally like this. She does it to me."

I smiled uncomfortably. It was one thing for me to speak facetiously about Koreans, another for her to. "I'm going to check on my mother."

CHAPTER 18
✦

I didn't feel right opening the closed doors in the upstairs hall, so waiting for Mrs. Oh to come out of one of the rooms, I looked at the family photographs on the wall. On closer inspection, I realized it was a gallery of Bobby portraits. I gazed at him on his first birthday wearing traditional Korean garments next to a bowl of fruit. My mother had similar pictures of my brother and me stashed in her bedroom closet. The next two photos were of Bobby at Disney World between Mickey and Minnie Mouse, looking like the boy I once knew, and as an adolescent with braces and longish hair. He had been a late bloomer. As a teenager, in his tennis whites holding a trophy over his head and at the prom, and even as a college graduate in cap and gown, he was skinny and looked more pretty than handsome. I couldn't tell when it was that he transformed into a full-grown man with jowls and bulked-up shoulders; the next and last photo was a fairly recent one taken in Paris in front of the Eiffel Tower.

I wondered if the Ohs would remove the pictures after Bobby married Ann. All the framed photos in my mother's house postdated my brother's departure. Anyone looking at them would think I was an only child—and that I had come into being with pimples and permed hair. It was just my luck that my brother had to get married before my awkward, experimental period.

The opening of a door jerked me back to the bright hallway. Mrs. Oh, loaded down with purses, jumped at the unexpected sight of me. She slammed the door behind her, but not before I glimpsed the soft bluish light of a television set.

"Ginger, I surprise see you," she said loud enough for my mother to hear. The volume of the TV went up for a second and then went quiet with a hard zap. "Why you here? Bobby leave?"

"No, I think he's still downstairs with Ann. Isn't she waiting for her purse?" I pointed to the handbags.

"Right." She hitched the straps higher on her shoulders. "My Bobby handsome, no?" She came closer to the picture of him in Paris.

"He takes after his mom."

Pleased, Mrs. Oh covered her cheeks with her hands. "I just old lady. Everyone say he look like his dad."

I didn't point out that Dr. Oh was just as old.

"*Yo-bo!*" Dr. Oh shouted from the bottom of the stairs. In Korean, he yelled for her to come down with the purses.

"*Ah-da-so!*" she hollered back. She took a step in his direction, then paused. "You go check your mom?" she asked loudly again.

"I won't wake her," I said truthfully. Mrs. Oh smiled and headed for the stairs. I reached for the doorknob.

The light from the hall shone on my mother lying on her stomach, her head turned to the drapes. The remote control peeked out from under a pillow. I closed the door behind me, and walking with my arms out as feelers, I confirmed on my way past the TV on the dresser that it was warm. I plopped down on the mattress, making the whole bed shake.

"Mother, I know you're awake."

Her response was a snore. I leaned over, turned on a reading lamp, and waited.

My mother's eyes snapped open. She knew the jig was up and smiled. "Everyone gone?"

"They're leaving now."

"Good." She sat up and palmed her hair into place. "I thought they never go."

"You don't have to pretend you were hiding from them." I folded my arms across my chest. "I know what you and Mrs. Oh are up to. You might as well come clean."

"Who pretend? I really didn't wanna see them. I thought I could face your father's friends, but I was wrong. I couldn't stand them then. . . ." She looked down at her left hand and started tracing the liver spots with her right index finger. "So I came up here."

Though she'd had a fairly easy evening, lying on the bed, watching TV, she looked knackered, all of her fifty-nine years. I believed her. Her plan to play sick had, luckily for her, dovetailed with her need to skip the party.

"You meet some nice men tonight?" she asked hopefully.

I was sorry her sacrifice, or near sacrifice, had been in vain. "Ah, no, I didn't. All the men were speaking Korean and ignored me."

"They did?" She shook her head. "They don't matter. Dr. Oh likes only the rude and arrogant people. Forget about them." She reached over and stroked my arm. "How about Bobby? You have nice talk with him?"

"If you're asking whether he bared his soul to me, the answer is no. And I don't think he will at breakfast either."

"You can't expect it right away. Friendship take time."

"So let's go home. I have to go to the office tomorrow."

"We can't. Mrs. Oh counts on us."

"But you're not even very good friends."

"We were."

I watched her as she stared ahead, seeing, from the look on her face, something other than the blue flowers in the yellow wallpaper. I was about to relent when she, nodding to herself, leaned over the edge of the bed and reached for her purse. She put car keys in my hand.

"We're going home now?"

"No, go to the trunk and get my overnight bag. You be home by noon." Before I could say okay, she added, "Just do me this one favor. I pay you back."

"How?"

"Trust me. I don't forget my debt."

CHAPTER 19

The cawing of a lonely crow was getting on my nerves. I couldn't see it through the windows; even if I'd gotten out of the bed, I still probably wouldn't have seen it, perched, I imagined, on a telephone wire miles away. That's where they'd been when I was young, sitting in the backseat, watching the poles go by. The backseat was where I always sat as a child. Ever since I could remember, and until my brother left for Harvard, George was the designated direction giver, my mother's right hand.

It was probably the cawing that had woken me. The sun on the other side of the house, the room was cast in shadow. I was in a well-appointed room, with an oak sleigh bed, matching dresser and desk, and heavy forest-green drapes. Mrs. Oh had fine taste. It was a shame Sam wasn't Korean; she would have made the perfect daughter-in-law to Mrs. Oh. They would spend all day rushing to appointments with swatches in hand. What a strange thought—to think it was a shame not to be Korean.

Especially after seeing the discomfort the Koreans caused my mother last night. The potential for their snubs would never dry up as long as my mother associated with Koreans, but over the years, it had gone deeper underground as she built up her business, accumulated wealth, and rose in stature. In Milwaukee, her social circle was made up of relative newcomers to the area who probably knew about her sham marriage but didn't have her loss of face blazed in their brains the way people who'd been around when my father decamped for his first family did. The scandal was too cold to do real damage to her new friends' opinion of her.

Being protective of her was a knee-jerk reaction with me, as it probably was with most children of immigrants who act as their parents' translators, communicators, negotiators. I supposed it was a self-protective reflex in the sense that when you're a kid, everything that affects your parents trickles down to you. George used to get so angry when people talked down to our mother or tried to take advantage of her because of her broken English, which was far worse when my father first left.

A lot of the responsibility for our smaller family unit, in which the only parent was struggling to make a career, fell to George, a teenager at the time. The transfer happened overnight and it must have been hard on him. I was too young to remember really what life was like when our father was around, but George must have felt the difference acutely, going from pampered only boy of the family to careworn only male of the house. Suddenly he had to come home straight from school to watch me, he had to accompany her to the supermarket, he had to call the plumber when the sump pump broke.

On top of that, our mother's personality had changed. She was hard, brusque, and strict, and she stayed that way for the first several years. From him she tolerated no arguments, no rebellions. She never said it, but dissension was disloyalty, proof that he and I also didn't love her.

George accepted the new stern rule without a complaint or an argument, keeping his resentments and rebellions to himself. For the most part, he and I behaved ourselves, bound with her in solidarity in our shared feelings of rejection and shame. The circumstances of my father's abandonment of us were so weird, uncommon—and I still thought as an adult, Korean.

My father's parents had lied to the matchmaker. He was not, as they presented him, a never-married man when he was introduced to my mother's family. He wasn't even single. But his wealthy, bourgeois parents had disapproved of his wife, a student activist on scholarship he met in college near the north, and they forced him to forsake her, their children, and his communist leanings. They brought him back to Seoul and entered him into a false marriage with my mother, the daughter of a cash-poor but old and respectable family and the niece of a high-ranking general in the army. George, eight years older than me and witness to many fights, claimed that my father had confessed the truth to her in Korea. But my brother and I were already born and it was too late to undo the union. Her family confronted his family, whose solution was to send us here. They bought my father's cooperation with the promise they would set him up handsomely, and they paid school officials to give him a spot in a graduate exchange program.

But the ocean and half a continent didn't protect my family; the distance didn't weaken the pull of the family my father truly loved.

My mother had wanted to go back to Seoul, but her father wouldn't let her, wanting to keep his shame on the other side of the globe. Her mother secretly sent her black-market dollars until my mother started earning enough to support us on her own. Once she became successful, she sent checks to her father, not to pay him back, but to show him up, drown him in the largesse he failed to extend to her. George once told me that if it weren't for him and me, she could have returned. Without children, she would have been able to pretend she'd never been married, as my father had done. In a small Korean city, she could have started all over again.

America was my mother's prison, while it was her children's land of opportunity. That was her trump card, though she'd never played it, never even alluded to it. She didn't need to.

George was the person who explained everything to me. He also informed me when my tour of duty was to begin—that conversation was like a dog-eared page in my mind. I remembered the day vividly. It was the day he received his acceptance letter from Harvard, the happiest day of our family's life.

I'd come home from school—I was in the sixth grade—to the sound of Pink Floyd blaring as usual. He was probably smoking a joint with one of his hooligan friends, I thought, banging on his closed door to let him know I was home. Despite the front he put up for our mother, he was no Eagle Scout. I went on to my room to change out of my school clothes, and had just taken off my Ralph Lauren Polo shirt, when George came barging through the door.

"Hey! Do you mind?" I screamed, holding a pillow up to my chest. I'd just started wearing bras and was self-conscious about it.

"Sorry! Sorry!" George backed out of the room, pulling the door closed with him. "Hurry up!" he shouted.

I took my time. He probably just wanted to hit me up for another loan. Our mother wouldn't let him get a part-time job, insisting he devote all of his time to studying while looking after me. "You have plenty of years ahead to work," she'd say every time he brought it up. She gave him $100 a week, the amount she'd have to pay a babysitter. I got ten percent of that money for keeping my mouth shut about the pot, fifteen percent if he had guests.

I hung up my clothes, put on some lip gloss, sharpened a couple of pencils, unpacked my book bag, and did a math problem before finally opening my door. To my surprise, he was still waiting.

"Geesh, tinsel-teeth, took you long enough. What were you doing in there? Hiding a boy?" He pushed his way past me, laughing, but looked under the bed nonetheless.

"What's it to you?" I hated my braces and hated being made fun of for them, and ran to the closet and pretended to guard the door.

"You're such a runt. I know you don't have a boy in that closet. You think boys have cooties or something."

"Go ahead and think that," I challenged, remaining in front of the closet.

He laughed again but not so confidently.

"So what do you want?" I asked, looking at my nails.

"Want?" He scratched his head. "Oh, yeah, I wanted to tell you the awesome news. I got into Harvard." He gave me the letter but looked at the closet while I read it.

"Congratulations. I guess that means I won't be able to use the phone once Mom comes home and starts calling everyone." For the past year, all she and he talked about was Harvard, what his chances were, whether he should write to them about winning another math meet, what it meant that it was already the fourth day in April and still no word. I knew getting in was an accomplishment, but as his little sister I felt it was my duty not to show how proud I was of him. I tossed the letter back.

"That's it? Don't I get a hug or at least a handshake?"

I gave him my hand, and he did a wrestling move on me, throwing me onto the bed. His path clear now, he jerked the closet door open.

"You're such a sucker." I laughed, lying on my back. "And a hypocrite."

"That's a big word for a little girl. I bet you don't even know what it means."

"Yes, I do. It means telling me I can't have a boy in my room, not that I ever would, when you sneak girls in yours all the time."

"You know about that?" He grinned despite himself. He got control of his face and squinted at me. "Have you been spying on me again?"

"No, the walls are thin. I can hear them giggle. Personally, I don't know what you see in Katie Farrow."

He leapt at me, but I rolled to the side, avoiding him. I tried to get away, but he tackled me, and grabbing my hands with one hand, he started to tickle me.

"Stop . . . don't . . . stop," I said, laughing and squirming, my legs pinned between his knees.

"Which is it? Stop or don't stop, railroad mouth?"

I finally freed a leg and kneed him in the zipper of his pants.

"Ugh," he grunted, sitting back and releasing me. Tears leaked down his cheek—he was such a wimp, unable to hold them back.

After several minutes of his hard breathing: "You didn't have to hit me so hard."

"Sorry." I straightened my T-shirt. "I was just demonstrating how I can take care of myself. You don't have to worry about me around boys."

"Point taken. Point driven home." He reached over and mussed up my hair. "But let's be serious and talk." He scooted to the middle of the bed and folded his legs beneath him. He motioned for me to copy him. He was freaking me out giving me his undivided attention, and I busied myself trying to bring my feet on top of my thighs, lotus-style.

"Cut that out," he said, cuffing me in the head. "Listen to me."

The sudden solemnity of his tone made me look up at him.

"Getting into Harvard means I'm not going to be here anymore."

"Thank God," I cracked.

"Stop being a wise guy and listen to me. I'm trying to talk to you like an adult."

I folded my arms across my chest and waited.

"So I'm not going to be here to keep you out of tr—"

"Hey, you're the one who does drugs and has people over when you're not supposed to," I interjected.

"And I don't want you to think you can copy me. I'm eight years older."

"So when I'm eighteen I can smoke pot and have boys in my room?"

"No, you can't ever do drugs and you can't have a boyfriend until . . . you're twenty-five."

"Hypocrite."

"Maybe, but the point I'm trying to make is that without me here, you're going to have to grow up and—"

"I'm mature. In health class, Mrs. Robertson said girls mature faster than—"

"And look after Mom."

I gave him a what-are-you-talking-about? look.

"Hang around the house more and keep her company. It won't kill you. And help her when she needs to, say, argue with the car mechanic like she did the other day, or needs something translated. Also, stop whining all the time about wanting to eat hamburgers and pizza or not understanding why you can't wear shoes in the house when all your friends do in theirs."

I fiddled with my toes, embarrassed that he'd overheard me. I purposely had my temper tantrums when he was out of the room and unable to take our mother's side.

"You know, it's not easy for her to be raising us alone. We're really lucky she figured out that Koreans needed a real estate broker and that she's so good at it. Otherwise, who knows how poor we'd be."

"I know."

"So try to be less of a pain in the butt, and stop trying to take advantage of her not knowing which movies are R-rated or that most of your friends don't have Polo shirts."

"You just said we're not poor."

"We're not, but even Mom's bank account has its limits. Plus, Harvard's not cheap, and Mom makes too much for me to get financial aid."

"So go to Madison—and come home on the weekends. I don't see why I have to cut back on clothes and time with my friends so you can go to Harvard."

"I know that you don't mean that."

He was right. Harvard was vindication. It was proof we were better people than all the stupid Koreans who looked down on us for not having a father.

"And in your own way you're trying to say you're going to miss me."

"That's news to me," I said stubbornly.

"You are, because not only have I been looking out for Mom, I've also been running interference for you, like I did when she wouldn't let you wear jeans with holes in them. And I help you in ways Mom can't, like with your school papers. So I want you to know that even though I won't be here, you can always turn to me. I'll just be a phone call away."

"Will you *write* my papers?" I had to lighten the mood. It was getting too corny.

"No, I won't write them. But I can read them and edit them, like always. You'll just have to do them sooner to give the mail time to reach me."

"You won't be too busy? Harvard is going to be pretty hard."

"Well, we have to get you into Harvard too, so we'll be two for two—to show people my getting in isn't a fluke."

"You think I'm smart enough to get in?" I knew I was, but I was fishing for a compliment.

"It's seven years away, and by then, with my help, you should have some brains."

I was about to point out that I already was a year ahead of him, since I'd started school when I was four, when our mother shouted from downstairs.

"Hello? Where is my Harvard boy?"

"What's she doing home?" I asked, disappointed that our talk was being cut short. "It's not even three o'clock."

Not bothering to answer, George scrambled off the bed and out the door. I followed him. Our mother stood at the bottom of the stairs, her arms loaded with bags.

"What's all this?" George asked, taking the grocery bags from her.

"This for you. I come home early to make all your favorite food—chajungmyun, duangjang kuk, ojingo, and abalone. It not each day my son gets into Harvard." Even though the menu she had just described was going to take a lot of work, she looked excited—instead of tired and harried as she usually looked at the end of the day. I wasn't crazy about his favorites, and I would have to help peeling, slicing, and stirring while he watched TV, but I kept my feelings to myself.

"Ginger, go to the car. There more in the backseat."

I dragged my feet going outside, but my mood lifted when I saw a pizza box and an ice cream cake. I quickly carried the precious cargo into the kitchen, where my mother was looking at the letter and other forms from Harvard while George unpacked the bags.

"George! Look at what else Mom got!" I put the boxes on the counter, and had my fingers under the pizza lid when George snatched my wrist.

"Wait for dinner, piggy."

"Let go. I can have a slice now. It won't be as good later. Right, Mom?" We both turned to her.

"Hmm?" She looked up from the papers. "Yeah, sure, Ginger, go ahead. It not good cold. But just one piece."

I gave George a told-you-so look and he released my hand. Even though I was going to have to spend more time with her, I wasn't going to miss being bossed around by him. It was a good thing he'd be finished with Harvard by the time I got there; otherwise I'd have to go to Yale.

"Wash your hands first," he ordered.

Begrudgingly, I did in the kitchen sink. She wouldn't take my side on this point.

"So many papers. I gonna read later." She put them in a drawer. "Let's cook."

To my surprise, George hung around, keeping us company. They talked about the classes he would take, the shopping they would have to do, what people he knew from his high school who were already there. I kept my mouth shut, just happy to be listening.

"I don't know yet if any guys from my class got in. But I know this girl Katie Farrow is going. She did the early-decision application. She's known since December."

"Katie Farrow? Who she?" George went to an all boys' school. My mother carried a pot of cooked noodles to the sink and dumped them into a strainer.

George shot me a warning look behind her back. "She's just a girl I know from Latin tournaments and math meets. She goes to our sister school."

I helped myself to another slice of pizza and took a bite, challenging George with my eyes to say something. He merely looked away.

"That nice. You should get to know her. It good to know somebody in your class. You gonna be far away from home."

"That's a good idea. Maybe I'll call her and invite her over some afternoon after school. We could hang out and talk and watch TV."

"In the living room," my mother stipulated, pointing a handful of noodles at him.

"Where else?"

I cleared my throat just to let him know he wasn't pulling the wool over the eyes of everyone in the room.

"Tell me when she gonna come so I can buy some snacks."

Of course, back then, there was no way I could have known that getting permission to invite Katie Farrow over would lead to his thinking that white girls were okay. At that point, our mother hadn't said anything about who we could and could not marry.

Dinner was soon ready, and throughout the meal my mother talked about who she was going to tell in person to see their faces, and who she was going to tell so word would quickly get around, and how she was going to say it so it wouldn't sound like she was boasting. She wanted the ministers of all five Korean churches to make announcements, and she wanted George to be present for them. Of course, she'd have to make big contributions to the offering plate, but it would be worth it. They'd have to go shopping for a new suit for him and a new dress for her. Or maybe she'd throw a party. She also had to call her parents in Korea.

Every now and then she would stop to catch her breath and just beam at George. This was her shining moment, and George and I let her bask in it, listening while shoveling food in our mouths. She was so happy. It made me impatient for the seven years to pass so I could make her that happy.

Of course, when my time came and I got into Harvard too, she didn't even tell anyone. She didn't want to have to explain why I wasn't going.

That was the slightest of the consequences I paid for keeping George's secrets. I wished I had told my mother about Katie so that she could have stamped out then any notion of marrying an American. I should have brought at least one of his many rebel acts to light so that his first and only public act of defiance wouldn't have been so shocking and enormous—and the response wouldn't have been so resoundingly final.

CHAPTER 20

My mother hadn't brought a change of clothes for me, so back in my dress, even more ridiculous in the morning, I went downstairs to the kitchen, toward the sound and smell of coffee brewing. I closed my eyes against the bright sun.

"Just in time for the first pot of coffee," said Bobby, brimming with more cheer and energy than was natural for someone who hadn't been caffeinated yet.

I partly opened my eyes, and through fluttering eyelashes, peered at him. He stood directly in front of me, blocking out the light. Rays shot out from behind his head and bare shoulders. Modest about his body he wasn't.

He laughed. "Good impersonation of a Korean-y woman."

"What?" I opened my eyes all the way and looked down at myself. "The dress?" I plucked the fabric away from my skin.

"No, the thing you were just doing with your eyes. Looking at me through your eyelashes. Remember? We were talking about it the other night."

I gave him a quick upturn of my lips.

"Come outside with me while I work on my tan." He got two mugs from the cupboard and walked to the counter where the coffeemaker had just stopped percolating. Following him with my eyes, I noticed that all the dirty dishes were gone. I turned to the left, toward the living room. It, too, showed no sign of last night's festivities. Even the rug where the cake had fallen was gone. He must have been up for hours.

"I took the rug to the cleaner's. I couldn't sleep."

I turned back to him, startled by the way he'd been following my unspoken thoughts.

"I figured I might as well clean up."

Stop that, I thought. Stop reading my mind. Just give me my coffee. I like it black.

"Milk?" He held the pitcher tilted above my mug, just degrees from pouring.

Thank you.

"Milk?" he asked again.

"Oh, no thanks." I stepped forward to take my mug from him.

He smiled. "Come."

I took one last look around the kitchen, looking for I don't know what, and followed.

Outside, Bobby led me to a patio I hadn't noticed the night before. A large black cast-iron table and chairs stood in the middle of the concrete slab, unprotected by the house or even an umbrella. The table was already set for breakfast.

A lawn sprawled before us for as far as the eye could see. It looked groomed but unfinished compared to the landscaped front of the house. There were no trees, flowers, or pathways. Minimum effort had been put into the view.

Scraping metal against concrete, Bobby pulled out two chairs. He motioned for me to sit next to him, but I took a seat one over. There was no avoiding the sun, but in this position I wouldn't be looking right into it. Bobby reclined as much as he could in an upright chair and spread out his legs. He closed his eyes. I sipped my coffee and continued gazing at the nothing-green view.

After several minutes, Bobby cleared his throat. With his eyes still closed, he said, "I was thinking about dinner. I still have to check my schedule, but whenever it is, feel free to bring someone if you want. I can invite June to even the number." He peeked at me. "She said you two met."

"Thanks, but that's all right."

"There won't be any parents. And I certainly won't tell."

"It's not that. I don't have anyone I'd want to bring."

"No?" He opened his eyes and turned to me.

I didn't like his tone. His laugh with Ann at my expense came to mind. "I've got better things to do with my time."

"Like what?"

"My career," I said indignantly.

After a pause, he said, "That's a shame."

"Because Chantal thinks I'm wasting my time? She doesn't know me."

"She thinks you're the only one in your office with promise."

"She does?"

"Ann was just telling me last night."

Perhaps I should have eavesdropped longer. "Then what's the shame?" I blustered.

"The shame is that you think it's an either-or proposition, work or love."

"Not everyone wants both." I hated this conversation. Why was it so hard for people to believe that a woman of childbearing age didn't want a mate?

"You just haven't met Mr. Right yet."

"And you're just hopelessly in love."

He shifted in his chair. "Because you don't think my parents will ever come around?"

"No. I mean, I don't know about—"

"Ann's going to apologize to my mother. She's not used to having to restrain herself in front of family. She's used to speaking her mind. Her attitude is take what I have to say or shove it."

"It's a healthy attitude if you're not Korean. But what I meant before is that you're so hopelessly in love, you think everyone else should be."

"Oh. I'm not that much of a goner. I am thirty-one."

"Some people, though, don't need another person. Some people are self-sufficient in that regard. Some people, some women, actually want to be left alone."

"You don't ever want to get married?" He sat up.

"Marriage is an outdated relic of a patriarchal past. It's just a property contract now made palatable by some grand, romantic notion of love." The words came out by rote.

"Would you feel that way if you could marry anyone you wanted?"

I ignored his question. "If marriage wasn't about owning women, controlling them, it would be available to gay couples. I'll get married when they can."

"You may not be waiting long. Vermont's already got those civil unions."

"Well, I'm holding out for the whole country."

He leaned forward. "But, you know, being opposed to marriage doesn't mean you have to forfeit a love life. You can have long-term relationships. Gays do it."

"I'd rather invest the time and energy in something that'll last."

"Sounds like you've never been in love."

"Have I fallen to the point of losing my senses? No. But I don't believe romantic love is this transcendent, transforming thing." I didn't say it was instead destructive and selfish; look at the Montagues and Capulets.

Shading his eyes with his hands, he studied me. "You're really serious."

"I'm committed to me." I smiled, liking the sound of those words. "Someone has to be."

I was still grinning at him when his mother called out to us.

"Hey, you two," she sang, skipping toward us, my mother trailing behind. I straightened my face. She smiled at my mother.

"I tell Mrs. Lee we find you together. You two like each other when you little and you like each other when you big. You kids talk about what?" she asked, bouncing in her heels. Next to her, my mother looked subdued.

Mrs. Oh probably thought everything was going according to her plan: Put us together alone and he'd fall in love with me. She gave me too much credit. Or maybe it was too little. I looked to him to give an answer that would bring her down a notch. He was preoccupied looking at his cuticles.

He was probably afraid of encouraging her. Everything he said would. The only solution was flight. His—since he could take a bus home without raising any hackles. I didn't think it was too much to expect him to follow my thinking; he had been reading my mind earlier.

"Bobby was just telling me that he had to get back to the city," I said. "He didn't want to wake you and he was asking me to explain to you why he had to miss breakfast."

"Bobby has to go?" Mrs. Oh asked.

"I do?" Bobby looked confused and a little hurt.

"You said you did."

"Where you have to be?" Mrs. Oh asked.

"I don't know," Bobby said.

"You don't know?" my mother asked incredulously.

"It no important," Mrs. Oh said.

"I thought you said it had to do with work," I said.

"Work?" Bobby repeated.

"Bobby no work Sunday," Mrs. Oh said.

"Or your apartment?" I offered.

My mother put her hands on me and lightly ran her fingers across my shoulders and neck. I looked up at her. "Which it is?" she asked. "Work or the apartment?"

"The apartment?" Bobby said. It sounded too much like a question.

I touched my mother on her hand to get her attention. "How are you feeling today?" She knew that I knew it had all been a charade, but I couldn't think of anything else.

"I fine." She winked and rubbed her stomach. "Much better."

"I don't know what Ginger is talking about," Bobby said. He pushed his chair away from the table and folded his arms across his chest.

I turned back to my mother. "Mrs. Oh said it was a headache."

"She did?" My mother put her other hand on her forehead. "I did. I had a bellyache and headache. Also fever. It was food poisoning."

"Food poisoning!" Mrs. Oh exclaimed. "I no poison my guest. You had headache."

"Not food poisoning," my mother corrected herself. "I just eat too much too fast."

Mrs. Oh harrumphed. "I thought so."

"So we have to go now?" my mother asked, looking down at me and then at Bobby. "Where do I take you?"

"But why you go now?" Mrs. Oh asked. "Bobby say he no have to go."

"I don't," he confirmed. "I want to eat breakfast."

"So I do," my mother said. "I have big appetite now. Mrs. Oh is a great cook."

My mother jabbed her knuckle hard into my back. "Yes," I said. "A great cook. I was hoping to eat leftovers from last night."

Mrs. Oh smiled. "Then we decide. Everybody stay and eat breakfast."

CHAPTER 21

Mrs. Oh wanted Bobby to make his French chicken dish, pushing for it even when he pointed out that it made for an unusual breakfast. She finally settled for a frittata and fruit salad when Dr. Oh came down, saying he was starved. She suggested I help Bobby while the parents relaxed outside, and I agreed, happy for the chance to explain why I'd said he had to go back to the city. Since coming into the house and fetching a shirt, he had been acting noticeably cold to me, pointing to where the cutting board and knives were kept and speaking only to tell me I could slice the melon and bananas if I wanted to. But Mrs. Oh kept on returning to the kitchen—for more coffee, a spoon, to make orange juice—so I limited my comments to how good everything looked and smelled.

Finally, breakfast was ready and we carried it outside. Dr. Oh had a strong aversion to leftovers, didn't even like to see them, so I didn't get to eat any more Korean food. It was just as well; I had that photo shoot in four days.

Dr. Oh wasn't as unpleasant as I had expected. He simply didn't talk, reading his newspaper as he ate. The rest of us took our cues from him, refraining from speaking, silently pointing to the salt and pepper, even chewing as quietly as possible.

Dr. Oh scraped his chair back. He threw his napkin onto his plate and stood up. "Good meal, son. I'm going to the golf course." He said some polite pleasantries to my mother in Korean, nodded to his wife, then me, then left. Mrs. Oh got to her feet and rushed after him.

"Delicious eggs, Bobby," my mother said. "I wish I watched you make them."

Bobby turned back from looking at the house. "What? Oh, thanks. I'll give you the recipe."

"That be nice. Thank you."

He pointed in the direction his parents had gone. "Do you know what that was about?"

My mother frowned. "What do you mean?"

"He's not normally that rude around guests. Did they have a fight out here while I was cooking?"

"C'mon, Bobby. What do you think? They argue because you gonna marry Ann. Your father blames your mother."

Bobby started to rise from his chair. "He hasn't—"

"No, of course not." She pulled him down with her adamancy.

Suddenly, I realized why I remembered Mrs. Oh for talking loudly—and why she used to sleep occasionally at our house, arriving in the middle of the night, swollen-eyed and red-nosed. My mother would shoo me, drawn by the commotion, back to my room, but I could hear Mrs. Oh through the walls for hours.

"How do you know?" Bobby asked.

"I stayed here almost every night."

"You did?"

"I know your father."

Mrs. Oh came back with a platter of ribs, kimchi, eggrolls, and rice. She put them down in front of me. I was about to protest that I was full, but my mother signaled me to eat. Obediently, I filled my plate.

"Such nice day for play golf, Daddy no wait." She took her former seat and looked at all of us, smiling brightly. "What everyone talk about?"

Bobby was raptly interested in his fingernails again.

My mother said something rapidly in Korean. Mrs. Oh raised her eyebrows, then laughed nervously. She gave the air a dismissive wave. "It no big deal. He just mad the cake is ruin. Ginger shouldn't put so many candle."

I opened my mouth to defend myself, but my mother kicked me under the table.

Bobby looked up. "That's right," he said slowly. "I said that the candles were too close to each other."

"You do, Bobby. We should listen you." Mrs. Oh put a couple of ribs and eggrolls on his plate. He picked up his fork and started to eat. She reached over and smoothed his hair. He didn't shake her hand off.

Still smiling, Mrs. Oh turned to me. "Ginger, you remember you and Bobby are birds in church play together?"

Warily, I nodded. We had been ravens. It was just months after my father left, when I was almost five and Bobby was nine. We walked across the stage, flapping our arms—ordered on pain of expulsion not to swoop or caw—while a half-white girl named Sally pointed and exclaimed at us. Originally, Sally was cast as my fellow feathered friend and Bobby was the person who shouted that the prophet's words had come true.

"You remember? That American girl is your partner, but you cry so much, I go to Sunday-school teacher Miss Park and ask Bobby switch place."

Sally, pretty with brown hair and eyes, was always referred to as "that American girl," even by us kids, who went to school and played with Americans. We were just following our parents, who sometimes used even worse language when talking about Sally. None of the children liked her, but the reason I didn't want to be paired with her was that I wanted a bigger role, a speaking part. I had gone to Mrs. Oh because my mother, preparing for her broker's license at the time, was too busy to even listen.

"I say, 'Bobby, Ginger so upset. How we gonna help her?' Bobby say, 'Mommy, I be Ginger's partner.'"

"You talked to Miss Park?" my mother cut in. "All this time I thought it was that girl's mother, Mrs. Rogers."

"No, it was me. I help you. Bobby help Ginger." Mrs. Oh sounded annoyed at the interruption, though she might have just wanted to stop my mother from asking for the particulars of what she'd said to Miss Park.

I certainly wanted Mrs. Oh to change the subject. Just thinking of her talk with Miss Park filled me with shame for having instigated it—and gall for having understood it. Unlearning Korean hadn't been entirely unconscious.

Mrs. Oh had brought Bobby and me early to rehearsal in the church basement. Miss Park, as always, looked surprised. She'd had one of those surgeries where the fat was removed from above her eyes to make her eyes look bigger. But she looked practically petrified when she came to understand that Mrs. Oh didn't want more lines for Bobby; she wanted him to switch roles with Sally.

"I don't want Bobby with that American girl either," Mrs. Oh said in Korean.

"She's just a child," Miss Park said. "Jesus loves all the small   "

"Don't give me a Bible lesson."

"I was just saying that as a Christian woman—"

"I said not to lecture me, miss," Mrs. Oh said. "Yes or no, will you let Bobby and that girl trade?"

Miss Park raised her eyebrows at the tone of Mrs. Oh's voice. She looked at me while she was thinking. "No," she finally said. "Mrs. Rogers is a kind, good Christian. It'll hurt her feelings."

"What about Mrs. Lee's feelings? It's insulting and shameful to have her daughter put with that GI wife's daughter."

"Shameful?" Miss Park's laugh came out like a bark. "She should be used to shame, still showing her face in our church. At least Mrs. Rogers observes the sanctity of marriage. I told Reverend Kim that I didn't think he should let divorced women in our fold no matter how much money they *used* to have."

"You said that to Reverend Kim? What did he say?"

Miss Park smiled smugly. "He agreed with me. Thou shalt not commit adultery, and according to the Bible, divorce is adultery. He's going to talk to the deacons and elders about what to do. Also to the people up for a deaconship, like your husband. What kind of woman drives her husband away?"

"She . . . she didn't drive him away," Mrs. Oh sputtered. "She—"

"Yes?" Miss Park leaned over to hear the answer.

Mrs. Oh drummed her fingers on her lips, making up her mind. Slowly, she recounted the sordid details.

Miss Park gasped. She looked absolutely thrilled. "Really!"

"Yes." Mrs. Oh looked around. "But don't tell anyone. That's a secret."

"No, of course not. I won't tell anyone."

Mrs. Oh pulled me in front of her and put hands on both my shoulders. "So, you see this child, this poor bastard child, has enough problems."

"Yes, yes, of course. I understand. Of course Bobby can switch with Sally."

"Good, and I'll talk to Mrs. Lee about leaving this church."

"Bobby and Ginger get along so good, laugh and run around the house," Mrs. Oh was saying.

"That was a hard time when I first went to work," my mother said, reminiscing. "You helped me a lot."

"Ginger, you think about those days."

The Sunday of the performance was the last time I went to Korean church. I was never able to find out whether Mrs. Oh really felt contempt for my family, because the Ohs moved a month later. I'd assumed she did because of the way she'd cut off contact with my mother. But maybe she didn't. She was, after all, pushing Bobby and me together.

"You too, Bobby. You no stop the past."

Bobby's face remained blank.

"The Lees are good friends to us. We are family. We are . . . how you say?" She interlaced her fingers.

"Entwined," Bobby quietly said.

"We help them, they help us. We are guard angel each other." She screwed a finger at him, tightening the bolts. "They care about you, and they—not Ann—good for you, for us."

"We'll talk about that later." Bobby stood up and swayed a little. He waved his hands in the air as though he were batting away cobwebs.

"We do? What we talk about?" Mrs. Oh took a bite of an eggroll and chewed with her mouth open. I watched, transfixed. She gave my mother a triumphant smile, spinach stuck in her teeth like bugs on a windshield.

He started to clear the table. "About Ann. About how I'm not going to marry her."

I jerked up in my seat, banging my knee on the table.

"But later, *Oma*." Not looking at me or anyone, he said, "We should be getting back to the city."

"Ginger, help Bobby," my mother ordered. She waited for him to leave, then leaned toward Mrs. Oh and started to say something in Korean.

I remained where I was. I couldn't believe what had just happened. I could but I couldn't. Mrs. Oh must have been trying to reach Bobby all week to give him a guilt trip about his father and that was why he refused to take her calls. But if he cared so much about his mother, why had he gotten engaged to Ann in the first place?

My mother stopped talking and looked at me. "What wrong?"

Mrs. Oh looked at me too. "We have dishwasher," she said, misunderstanding my failure to move. She propped her feet on Bobby's empty chair. She said something in Korean. I understood the word for lazy.

My mother stacked the remaining plates and handed them to me. "Ginger just afraid she gonna drop them. I don't let her carry my dishes." To me: "Just be careful."

Mrs. Oh jumped up and took the plates from me. "Bobby cooked, my turn clean. Mrs. Lee, we talk in kitchen." She hurried away.

My mother opened her mouth, but nothing came out. She closed it, grabbed the silverware, and followed Mrs. Oh into the house.

Almost instantly Bobby came back outside. "There's been a change of plans. It's just the two of us going back now. Your mother is staying and my mom is going to give her a ride later. They probably want to celebrate."

I didn't say anything. I had nothing to say. I went into the house to retrieve my purse. When I came downstairs, the mothers were laughing as they tussled over the leftovers. Bobby and I stood to the side and watched their antics as my mother kept taking the tinfoil packages out of the bag and his mother kept putting them back in. I hadn't seen my mother act like that in years.

"Give some Bobby," she protested.

"Bobby like his father. He no eat leftover." Mrs. Oh finally grabbed the bag and ran to me. Fending my mother off with her back, she shoved it into my hands, laughing. "Go!"

My hands received the bag, but I stayed put.

"She don't need them," my mother said over Mrs. Oh's shoulder. "I here. I cook for her."

"My food better." She continued to guard my mother from the bag.

"I learned from you."

"So mine better."

My mother ran around the kitchen island and reached me from the other side. She took the shopping bag and dumped it on the counter before Mrs. Oh could stop her.

"She can't eat this much."

"Sure she can. She have healthy appetite."

"She have too healthy appetite. She eat too much already."

"What you talk about? She skinny."

"No. She fat. Look at her."

The two mothers stopped and looked at me.

"She fine," Mrs. Oh said after a lifetime. "Maybe I take out ribs."

"Okay. Also the eggrolls and jhapchae."

They sorted through the food, my mother taking out more left-overs than they'd agreed upon and Mrs. Oh putting everything back in the bag. When they finished, the bag was as full as it was before their skirmish, and we all walked outside.

Down the road, where my mother had parked, Mrs. Oh gave me another one of her rib-crunching embraces. Bobby bent down and she kissed him on the cheek. I held my hand out for the keys. My mother hesitated, then dropped them in my palm. Before I closed my fingers over them, Mrs. Oh plucked them up. "Bobby drive. He the man."

Wordlessly, Bobby took the keys and walked around to the driver's side. As we pulled away, I watched our mothers, now arm in arm, shrink in the side mirror. I watched until they were specks.

CHAPTER 22

"If you want to drive, I can pull over and we can switch," Bobby said after we'd turned the corner and traveled several blocks.

"That's all right. I don't care one way or the other."

Bobby fiddled with the radio, listening to just a note of music before switching to the next station. He worked his way up the spec-trum, then down, then hit the off button. After some time, he turned onto the highway and started weaving in and out of lanes as he sped past cars going the legal limit. We were coming up on car tails too quickly. I turned my head to the side window.

Bobby had just done the only thing he could do, the thing I had been thinking all along that he should do, and yet I felt nothing. Not happiness. Not satisfaction. I supposed it was because his renouncing of Ann didn't affect me, my family. I was just a bystander who knew the combatants.

But that wasn't true. Somewhere along the line, at some unnoted point, I had stopped thinking of him as another George, and I had started identifying him with myself. And a part of me had wanted him to stay the course, to steam ahead, to break free.

His relenting—his relinquishing—was mine. That was the problem with being around people of your own kind. If you don't like who you are or the position your life puts you in, you don't want to be looking in a mirror. That, I supposed, was why Korean Americans like Bobby and I tended to make friends with Americans and not each other. Misery doesn't want its own company.

At least Bobby wasn't madly in love with Ann. Or he claimed he wasn't. One wasn't really so far from the other when the heart is used to following the mind, when the mind is used to bridging disconnects, skipping over inconsistencies, going back and forth between two cultures, two value systems, two realities. I suspected his Ann was my Julian. Back then I, too, had high hopes for love, for its magical, transcendent power.

I met Julian my last year at Madison. I had heard of Dr. Brathwaite as soon as I arrived on campus to work on the dissertation I had no interest in writing. The English Department was abuzz over the handsome visiting professor from London who specialized in modern poetry with an emphasis on women poets. Reportedly, he even had good teeth. There had been sightings of a ring on his left hand, however, and speculation was heated over its significance. All the whispered theories floating over the silver ring with a black stone that was sometimes present and sometimes absent from either his middle or ring finger could have made for a paper on the semiotics of male rings that would have made Derrida proud.

At the first wine-and-cheese gathering of grad students and faculty, I saw what all the commotion was about. Julian was tall and thin, with black hair, blue eyes, and horn-rimmed glasses. I hadn't felt the stirrings, the lift, of attraction in a long time. My course work finished, my orals passed, I had been living with the emptiness, the void, for months. But here was someone who sparked something in me. Because I was the only person, male or female, to refrain from expressing any interest in him, I was nominated to talk to him and find out if he was single, and if he was, whether he was straight.

Fortified with a glass of cheap red wine and watched by six pairs of eager eyes, I joined him and Dr. Elizabeth Chambers standing in a corner of the department lounge. She was in her late fifties and a bit batty, and she posed no threat to the hopes of the Julian fan club.

"You must get a whiff of our original copy of *The Faerie Queene*," Dr. Chambers was saying. "It's got a very peculiar smell, lead maybe, and I'm wondering if it could have belonged to Queen Elizabeth. The book is in our special collection of rare and antique books on the top floor of the library." She held her arm out to me. "Ginger, here, could take you. Have you met?"

I stepped forward and Dr. Chambers made the introductions. Julian, who had been listening intently with pursed lips and a furrowed brow, relaxed his face into a smile. He looked genuinely pleased by my intrusion.

"I can take you to the eighth floor," I said, "but I can't promise I'll be able to accompany you past the glass doors. The last time I was there, the librarian caught me putting a book in the wrong place, and she may have suspended my visiting privileges."

"That doesn't sound like Irene. I'm sure she'll let you in." Dr. Chambers patted my arm. "Now, Julian, when you go, be sure to open the book in the middle and hold it up to your nose, like this." She demonstrated, bringing her hands, open like a book, to her face, covering her eyes. Julian took this opportunity to twitch his eyebrows at me like Groucho Marx, while darting his eyes at Dr. Chambers. "Breathe in deeply"—she inhaled—"and hold it for as long as you can." She exhaled slowly and smiled dreamily.

"Sort of like hashish, is it?" Julian asked.

I caught my breath. Dr. Chambers was friendly, but she wasn't one of the professors who went to Friday happy hour at the Owl, trying to be hipper than their years.

"Hashish?" Dr. Chambers frowned. "I'm not familiar with hashish. . . . But I suppose it's not unlike marijuana." She tittered at her admission.

"Enough said. I'm sold." He turned to me. "Shall we go then, you and I?"

I understood he wanted to get away from Dr. Chambers, and nodded. My friends had entrusted me with a mission, and I couldn't walk away from him without answers. I also wanted to go with him. "When the evening is spread out against the sky," I said, pointing to the drawn curtains.

In unison: "Like a patient etherized upon a table." He offered me his arm and I took it.

It turned out that Julian didn't have an ID card yet, and I didn't have enough pull at the library to get him past the security guards. So I took him to the Owl, thinking the crew would straggle in after the party. They never did, but we stayed until closing, discussing politics, the state of American poetry, the best place in town to get a pizza. He was articulate and smart, and he had a way of hanging on your words, making you feel like you knew what you were talking about. His ring was purely decorative and he was heterosexual.

I took him to the grocery store later that week and soon we were spending every minute out of the classroom together. Over the course of the following four months, I found out that his favorite poet was Elizabeth Bishop, his favorite male poet Hart Crane; his leanings were socialist; his father was an Anglican minister, his mother a schoolteacher; he listened to punk rock bands from the eighties; he favored light ales over dark ones; he poured Tabasco sauce on everything he ate, including French fries. I was being reckless for me, but not really. He was due to return to London at the end of the semester.

By tacit agreement, we never broached the subject of our feelings for each other—he because he was a typical Englishman, me because I didn't know how one started such a conversation. I was also confused. The time I was with him, I forgot myself. But when I was alone, in the library, in the shower, awake when he was asleep, I was poignantly aware of how much I preferred my own company, of how much lighter, relieved, I felt. He could transport me, but he couldn't transform me.

Matters came to a head two days before he left the country when he asked me to move to London. He popped the question while sitting on the floor of my apartment with his back up against the old orange couch. I sat on the opposite end of the sofa, my feet on the cushion, my arms wrapped around my knees. We had just gotten back from the library, where we'd finally gone to sniff the rare books, and were sitting in silence. Sad as I was that he was going, that my plunge into abandonment was ending, it was a struggle not to be a little elated. I didn't want to hurt his feelings, and the only way I could do this was by not speaking. After his question inquiring where I wanted to eat dinner went unanswered, he too stopped talking.

But then he broke the silence and asked me to come with him. He stretched his arm out to me, managing only to touch my toes—I had positioned myself out of reach. I sprung to my feet and paced the apartment, my nervous energy taking me down the hall and to the bedroom.

"Ginger?" Julian called out, laughing. "Where are you going? I didn't mean to come to London this minute."

I came back but remained standing. The Ginger who was usually ignored was pushing to say yes, to hell with everyone and everything. Get carried away, be carried away. Leave Madison, this apartment, this ragged, secondhand orange couch.

My eyes fell on a framed photograph. It was one of the few recent pictures I had of both my mother and me. We were on vacation in Hawaii. It had been hard finding someone to snap the photo; my mother didn't trust any of the strangers near us with her expensive camera. Finally, a Japanese couple had strolled by and taken the picture for us. All the other photos of the trip were either of her or me—alone.

"But the consequences," I blurted out. "Do you know what you're asking me to do?"

"You mean your dissertation? You can write it anywhere."

"No, what I would really be doing by going with you." I told him everything, my fears, my yearnings, the situation with my mother. As I spoke, I knew I was making a mistake. His face closed before my eyes.

He delicately licked his lips. "I think you misunderstood. I meant go to London for the winter break. Maybe some other time, then." He grabbed his sweater and coat. "I should get going. I've still got some packing to do." He missed my mouth and pecked me somewhere near my nose.

I watched the door close behind him and listened to it click. It sounded like the lid of a coffin snapping shut.

He called two days later from the airport to say good-bye, both of us eager to get off the phone, and we never spoke again. I wasn't the person he'd thought I was, just as he wasn't the person I'd thought he was. He was just another person. What folly to think I could live through, for, a man.

I left Madison for good five weeks later.

Bobby blasted the horn. I turned forward to see we were fast approaching the low end of a red sports car. We were boxed in on both sides, and I grabbed the handle of the door, bracing myself for a collision. Right when I thought we were going to crash, the driver ahead sped up just as Bobby jammed hard on the brakes. I felt my neck snap.

"Stupid, fucking woman driver," he said, emphasizing each word with a pound of the horn. "She must be driving forty-five miles an hour."

"How do you know it's a woman?" The back windows were black. I rubbed the back of my neck. It was fine but for the knot of tension.

"Because it's always a woman."

"You don't mean that, so I'm not going to comment."

"You don't mean that, so I'm not going to comment," he mimicked. He swerved into the left lane, raced past the Porsche, then swung in front of it. "Look behind you," he said, his eyes on the rearview mirror.

I didn't move. "I don't need to look. Her being a woman doesn't prove anything."

"Just look."

"No."

He switched back to the left lane and slowed down. The car behind him honked, but he continued to brake. The Porsche caught up to us, and Bobby matched its speed so we were driving side by side.

"What are you going to do? Bang into her?"

"Just look."

"Fine." I turned to see a middle-aged woman in sunglasses and chemically processed blond hair. She was holding the steering wheel with her arms and giving us the finger with both hands.

Bobby zoomed ahead, cackling like someone out of his mind. I scooted as far from him as the door would let me.

"Mr. Hyde comes out of the closet," I said.

Bobby stopped laughing and looked at me. He turned back to the road. "What's that supposed to mean?"

The suspicion in his tone surprised me. "I just meant that you're acting like a madman, Dr. Oh. And you're driving like a maniac."

"Oh." He decelerated.

"What did you think I meant?"

He didn't reply and I didn't feel like repeating my question, so we drove in silence. It was interesting how the story of Dr. Jekyll and Mr. Hyde had come to signify a particular construct of personality. I wondered what a Ginger Lee would represent if I were put into print for public edification—or amusement. The abiding daughter, no matter the personal cost, was already represented by Ruth, Andromeda, Cordelia, Catherine in *Washington Square*. By far, the good daughters

of fathers outnumbered the faithful daughters of mothers; unhappy
wives, reluctant brides, frustrated lovers, and resigned spinsters
swelled our ranks.

But all of the heroines I was thinking of lived in an earlier time,
when women had fewer options. They weren't surrounded by female
friends who were doing as they pleased.

I would be the anachronism, the daughter of immigrants who
couldn't fully live in her time or place.

Bobby maneuvered to the far right lane, looking in my direction
to see that the path was clear. The sign for the exit to Manhattan
loomed ahead. He held my gaze.

"Can you blame me?" he asked softly.

It took me a second to connect his question to what I had said
earlier about his acting like a madman. "For what?" I still asked to buy
time.

"For feeling angry, frustrated, sick of it all."

"You won't always feel that way. You did the right thing. You
wouldn't have been able to live with yourself."

"You call this living?"

He had a profession, but I wouldn't find pandering to rich people's
vanity fulfilling either. "Like you said, you can still have a love life.
At least you're a guy. You won't be breaking new ground. There's a
precedent for confirmed bachelors."

"You think our mothers will accept that forever? They won't. I
mean, mine did, but then I turned thirty."

"That still gives me three years."

"And then what are you going to do?"

"They can stop us from marrying people they don't approve of,
but they can't make us marry people we don't like. They're not that
backward."

Signs for the George Washington Bridge appeared, and he
became engrossed in following them. When we were on course again,
he said, "You need a better plan."

It wasn't as though I wanted children someday. Not having them was an act of kindness to my unborn descendents—mixed Korean Americans, real Korean Americans. I had seen how Sally was treated. Plus, if I had identity issues, what would they have? I didn't see why I couldn't hold out forever.

The bridge, magnificent in its size and structure, lay before us. I caught my breath. Large bridges always did that to me. Their sheer existence, spanning across air, connecting the unconnected and seemingly unconnectable, was testament to human ingenuity and filled me with awe in a way that skyscrapers didn't. Perhaps it was because you didn't naturally spend as much time on a bridge as you did in a building. Bridges weren't a destination or a place to stay. It was something to think about.

We reached the other side and immediately came upon Manhattan congestion. We headed east, moving inches at a time.

Bobby cleared his throat. "Since marriage means nothing to you"—we crawled a foot—"how about entering one of convenience? Marry me, Ginger. It's the only long-term solution."

"Are you serious?"

He took his eyes off the road and looked at me.

"It's crazy." I refused to even consider it.

"It's not crazy. It's sane and reasonable." We came to a red light. He turned to me excitedly. "It'd be the ultimate marriage based on friendship. It'd be a model marriage."

Cars honked behind us. He went forward.

"I like your company. You like mine. I've got an enormous place—you could stay for free."

"Ask someone else," I said, shaking my head. "Ask . . . ask June."

"I did already."

"You did?" I turned to him in surprise. "When?"

"Several months ago, when my parents really started putting on the pressure, setting me up on those dates with all those awful Korean-y women. June had been willing to pretend to be my girlfriend in med school, coming home with me on the weekends and holidays, but she drew the line at m—"

"So you would marry the woman you love," I finished for him.

Bobby made a face. "I asked Ann to marry me for the same reason I asked you and June."

"You don't love her?" My mother had been right. "But she's not Korean."

"I didn't know you two weeks ago."

"But why make a huge stand for someone your parents don't approve of and you don't even love?"

He pulled the car into a space in front of his building and shifted into park. He turned to me. "Because some stands are still compromises."

"What? How?"

"Think about it."

I stared at him, trying to make sense of it all. What compromise was he making? Why would he offer Ann when she wasn't at all acceptable?

He was a puzzling person. Just from the fact that he was what every Korean mother wanted her son to be, a medical doctor, I would have figured him to be one of those guys who'd joined the Korean association in college, dated its female members, and married one of them right after medical school to keep his house and start his family. True, when I had known him he hadn't traveled in the noisy pack of kids who probably did grow up to become officers of their college Korean club. But all the girls back then teased him so much because they thought he was cute. He would have had his pick of women to anoint his wife, and any family would have been happy to be joined with his.

Suddenly, I knew what it was. His charade with June, his proposals to her and Ann, his resignation to a loveless marriage, his knowledge about Vermont—even his cooking and impeccable taste in clothing.

"You're gay." His compromise was marrying a *woman*.

"I trust you won't tell your mother."

"That you're gay? Of course not." It was none of her business.

He smirked. "So marry me?"

Slowly, I shook my head. "Sorry, but no."

He nodded. "All your talk about not believing in love. I should have known better than to believe you." He got out of the car. "Call me if you change your mind."

CHAPTER 23

So Bobby was gay.

I admired him. His courage. His strength. His self-denial. The political climate encouraged gay people to come out of the closet, to shout that nameless love from the mountaintops. But Bobby knew he wasn't an individual. He wasn't free to be true to himself. Maybe I was making excuses for him, and maybe I was a coward, but he and I had responsibilities over and above the usual ones, a duty to our families, to who we were. That was our lot. That was what it was to be second-generation. When your parents move to America, leave everything and everyone they know and love, you have a bigger obligation to do right by them, to make their trans-Pacific journey worth it.

After parking my mother's car in the lot and running into the apartment to change clothes, I had taken the subway to work. I now rolled the last of the metal clothes racks into the conference room. The building turned off the air-conditioning on the weekends, and I wiped my face with my T-shirt.

Still, as much as I would have liked to help him, his proposal was preposterous. I wouldn't even entertain the idea. I certainly wouldn't tell my mother of it. Knowing her as well as I did, she would lean and lean on me until I changed my mind. Or worse, she would call Bobby and say yes for me, secretly arrange the wedding, then tell me we were going to church for a special evening service.

I could, however, understand his desperation, his willingness to use any means possible to get out from under the jackboot of Koreans.

I parked the rack next to the others along the length of one wall. Boxes of socks, scarves, and sweaters lined the opposite wall. On the table, I'd neatly arranged shoes, belts, purses, and miscellaneous jewelry. The plan was for people to come through one door and pay me on their way out the other. Everything was in order. I turned off the light, shut the door behind me, and headed back to my desk.

Was it because we were all uniform, with black hair and black eyes, that Koreans were so conscious of proper appearances, fearful and unaccepting of deviations?

I hadn't thought, really thought about, relived, that conversation between Miss Park and Mrs. Oh in years, but it had been lying below the surface of my consciousness like an underground stream feeding into my comprehension, feelings, outlook. I had always known my mother didn't flutter from church to church only because of her job, just as I'd always known her insistence on my acting like a lady didn't stem only from old-fashionedness. She clung to her respectability like a life preserver.

That was why she had so completely cut off George when he defied her and married an American. His choice was an embarrassment to her, another black mark. Good Korean families didn't join with outsiders. The announcement had also taken her by surprise; she hadn't even known he was dating. Her emphasis had been on academics. He was only twenty-two and headed for medical school; she must have thought she had more time. He, on the other hand, must have thought she was bluffing when she made her ultimatum. It was the only explanation I could come up with.

But after the deed was done, and he realized she was serious about her threat, the thing I couldn't make sense of was why he never tried to make peace. Why, in thirteen years, had he never tried to contact us—or at least me?

I bent over to get my purse from the bottom drawer of my desk. When I straightened, I saw the computer was on. I sat down and logged on to the Internet.

He was the one who left. It was for him to reach out to me. I typed his name into a search engine and clicked on the listing I knew would give me the eight George Lees in the area.

Would he be happy to hear from me? Or would he hang up? Maybe he would pretend not to be himself so I wouldn't call again. I wondered after all these years if I would recognize his voice.

I put the phone down, and it immediately rang, making me jump. The caller ID said it was my apartment.

"When you come home?"

I was about to say I was finished but thought better of it. "Why?"

"We gonna go to Korean church."

"Today? Why?" There wasn't any way she could have planned a wedding already. She couldn't know about the proposal; there was no way Bobby would have told her. Was there?

"Dr. Oh is church elder and—"

"You want to go to church with the Ohs?"

"No, they go already. I found a late service near here."

"You didn't get your fill?"

"I don't go with them. I don't have right clothes."

That was baloney. Her suit would have been fine. "Then what did you do while they were in church? You didn't sit in the parking lot, did you?"

"No, Mrs. Oh took me to bus stop."

"*Oma*, I could have waited for you."

"That all right. We forgot about church in all the—"

"Victory celebrating."

"Yeah, Mrs. Oh lucky lady. She has good son. But now that engagement over—"

"We're not respectable enough," I finished for her. We were good enough to help them but not to join their family despite what Mrs. Oh had said at lunch about our being entwined. I was completely off the hook, but now I felt like marrying Bobby just to spite his parents.

"That why we have to go to church."

"To appear religious?"

"No, to meet some men. How I raise such silly daughter?"

"Wait," I said. "Bobby *was* your only bachelor, wasn't he?" I remembered her instruction last night to try to meet the male guests.

"Boy, this couch discomfortable. How you sleep on it?"

"*Oma,*" I said sternly.

"And ugly. Ginger, have you looked at this couch?"

"You don't have any more men."

"Yeah . . . okay, you got me. But don't worry. We find them our-selves."

"You mean you can find them. I'm not participating." It was one thing to agree to meet these men, it was another to actually hunt them down. The escapade was close to being over; if I could only stand firm, it would be. Freedom was within reach. "I don't have the time."

"How much you got left?"

"I've got to—" I didn't feel like lying. "I'm not talking just about tonight. I mean in general."

"I here for a week. You don't have no work."

"But that's about to change."

"You mean the modeling? That nothing. You can practice smiling in the shower—and in church."

"Thanks for taking my job seriously. With support like that, it's no wonder I'm still a stupid flunky."

"You didn't tell me you flunked out of school. You said you dropped out."

"I did drop out."

"Then who flunked?"

"No one."

"But you—"

"I meant gofer, lackey, bottom of the totem pole."

"What?"

This was why we never talked about things that really mattered, things that I could use help figuring out. Even if I could somehow convey my feelings without redefining and simplifying each word to meaninglessness, she wouldn't have the vocabulary to respond. "Never mind," I said.

"No, tell me. What you mean?"

"That is an ugly couch."

"Ginger."

"You really want to know?"

"Yes! Tell me."

I took a deep breath. "I'm just feeling frustrated with my life. That I'm still an assistant, you know?"

"I told you don't go to grad school."

"You did and I made a mistake. But your constantly reminding me that my bloom is fading doesn't help."

"Time don't stop."

"You think I don't know that?"

The other line ringing broke the silence. It was Walker Prescott. I told my mother to hang on and clicked over. "Hello?"

"Sam?"

"No, it's Ginger."

"Oh, hi. Is Sam there?"

"No, it's Sunday. This is her office."

"I know. She said to try her here if I got her voice mail on her cell."

"She did?" Perhaps she was coming in to do something to Chantal's office.

"Can I call back and leave a message?"

"You can leave it with me."

"I'd rather not."

He probably didn't realize we were friends. I went back to my mother.

"Okay, maybe my words are wrong. But I only try to help. I come here to help."

"But a husband is not—"

"No, listen to me one time. I support you when you do the right thing. But studying English and modeling." She blew air through her lips. "Sometimes I think you don't know who you are. Maybe you are American inside, but you are still Korean outside."

"Things are different since you arrived. Korean models—Asian models—are in. But that's beside the point. I'm modeling for the visibility."

"Fine, so do it. I glad to hear you have goal and plan. I support you."

"Thanks, I guess."

"But spend time with your mother, with more your people. Come to church. Eat doughnuts."

I wouldn't have minded waiting for Sam and going out for a drink, hearing about Walker, what she had planned for Chantal. After the weekend I'd had, I felt the need to reconnect with my other self, the self that was Sam's hip, flip friend. But contrary to my mother's easy delineation, I was more Korean than just on the outside, and duty called.

CHAPTER 24

The address in the telephone book for the In God We Trust Korean Church of New York was a large dry-cleaning establishment a fifteen-minute walk away from my apartment.

"You wrote it down wrong," my mother complained after we'd

tramped up and down the same block, peering at the building numbers for the third time. I'd already come to that conclusion but kept it
to myself, thinking that if I pointed out my mistake, she'd think I'd
done it on purpose.

"Maybe it shut down." In Milwaukee, Korean churches were constantly springing up, only to disappear once the founding member
made peace with his or her former minister.

"No, the telephone message said they have sermon this afternoon." She wiped sweat off her face with a handkerchief.

"Mom, you must be dying in that suit jacket. Take it off," I said,
stepping behind her to help her.

She took several steps away from me and wrestled with the damp
jacket herself. She had sweated through her white blouse so that the
back was transparent. I scanned the block for a restaurant; we might
as well eat dinner. A dressed-up Korean woman walked into the dark-
ened dry-cleaning store that we were now standing across the street
from.

"Look over there," I said, nodding my head in the woman's direction. "The dry cleaner is opening now. She must have come straight
from church herself. Look at the way she's decked out."

My mother spun around to see. She grabbed my hand and started
to run across the empty street. The church must be in the store.
When we reached the door, she put her jacket back on and wiped her
face again with her handkerchief, then used it on my face before I
knew what she was doing and could squirm away.

An elderly Korean man stood inside the door. He gave us pro-
grams, then pointed down the stairs. He and my mother exchanged
bows. I shyly tilted my head down and in his general direction as I
hurried after my mother.

As we click-clacked down the stairs in our heels, the preacher's
voice grew loud and clear. A rotting stench also grew stronger.

Stepping off the bottom stair, I found myself at the back of a large
cellar-cool room. About fifty people sat in folding chairs, facing the
minister at a wooden pulpit. Though the lights were dim, probably to

keep the temperature down, the hundreds of cut flowers in big plastic containers that filled the sides and front of the room stood at attention. I slid into the chair next to my mother. She and the woman we had seen earlier were whispering to each other.

"What did she say?" I asked after they'd stopped talking. Before she could respond, a woman in front of us turned around and shushed us, holding her finger in front of her lips. My mother gave me a warning look and then turned her attention to the sermon.

The minister was speaking Korean, and I listened for biblical names and words I knew to guess the topic of his sermon. But he was one of those impassioned sermonizers, and I couldn't pick out anything recognizable from his heated rhetoric. Out of boredom, I looked at the backs of black-haired heads in front of me. From the many crew cuts, I noticed the men outnumbered the women by far. It would be my luck to find the one congregation that was mostly single men. I watched for left hands—the ring fingers—to scratch or feel their heads, but no one's scalp seemed to be giving them trouble.

I settled into my chair, expecting to be there for a while. The preacher was decidedly long-winded, and the regular rise and fall of his voice soon made me sleepy. I felt myself starting to doze off, when sudden silence jolted me awake. The entire room seemed to start and sit up. Amens filled the air.

During the last hymn, my mother leaned toward me and whispered we should leave immediately after the service was over. I raised my eyebrows at her, but she ignored me and went back to singing falsetto with the few other women. The room was so loud, I thought I could mimic her without anyone hearing me. A hard jab in the side stopped me after the first note. I opened my mouth again only for the last amen.

As all the hymnals clapped shut, my mother put hers back under the chair and grabbed my hand to leave. The woman next to her, however, wouldn't let us slip past her. She was as loud and insistent as the clashing patterns of her blouse and skirt. The woman in front of us, around my mother's age but as tastelessly dressed as the first woman, then turned around and greeted us. They clearly meant to strike up a conversation. After several polite attempts to get away failed, my mother dropped my hand. I couldn't understand what they were saying, so I wandered toward the flowers. They were still bundled with rubber bands around the stems. It looked to be the last day they would be more alive than dead. The tall plastic buckets they stood in were the kind in delis around the city.

A man around my age said something to me in Korean. He smelled strongly of stale mothballs. I looked at him, then beseechingly toward my mother, who was too immersed in her conversation to intercede for me.

"Pwetty wose," he said haltingly. "You take." He picked up a couple of dozen roses and handed them to me.

I stepped back and motioned with my hands that I didn't want them. "No thank you. I wouldn't want to take flowers from the church. God might strike me down or something." My laugh came out too loud. I turned bright red.

"No, leally. You take. I give." He pushed the flowers at me again. The stems dripped water onto my toes.

With the smile still on my face, I turned my head toward my mother. This time she and the other two women were looking at me. The other women returned to their conversation. My mother continued to stare with an expression that could be described only as distaste.

I doubted she would be bringing me to any more gatherings she found in the phone book. To make sure, I took the roses and exuberantly thanked the man. His collar was frayed and I couldn't even hazard a guess at the make of his jacket. I tucked the flowers under my left arm, then offered my right hand and introduced myself.

I couldn't pronounce his name, so I told him I would call him Mr. Han. I doubted he understood a word I said. As fluent as I was in broken English, I could only barely make out what he said. I gathered his sister owned a deli and he was working for her. We gestured a lot and laughed and smiled.

"Ginger, let's go," my mother said, coming toward us.

"But, Mom, I'm talking to Mr. Han here. He gave me these flowers. Wasn't that nice of him?"

My mother rapidly rattled off something in Korean to the man, slightly tilted her head, then pinched my arm hard as she steered me to the stairs.

She didn't let go until we'd put an entire block behind us.

"So much for doughnut hour," I said now that we'd slowed and I'd caught my breath. I tossed the roses in a trash can we passed.

"This not my city." She sighed. "I didn't know it gonna be all first-generation worker. They speak even worse English than the students last night."

Most of Dr. Oh's students were fresh from Korea too. She could cloak her class consciousness in talk about generations, but I didn't know why she was bothering with me. The pool of suitable suitors was decidedly small in my case. The ones who met her standards and came from good families would probably think they could do better than us. I was beginning to see the futility of searching for them.

"Let's face it, Mother. We're our own people. Our family is fine the size it is."

She stopped walking and cocked her head. "You don't wanna marry ever?"

"*You've* been single for most of your life."

"But I have you," she said.

"And I have you," I said.

She hugged my arm to her body and we started walking again. I sensed that the husband search was over and that she would be returning to Milwaukee soon. I was happy and I was sad. My thoughts turned to work and the career that would be my passion, my life.

CHAPTER 25

After a weekend of Koreans, Monday came as a relief. I couldn't wait to get to the office, but as I came out of the bathroom showered and dressed, the aroma of breakfast reached my nose. A plate of French toast and sausage, accompanied by my mother, awaited me in the kitchen.

I approached the counter warily. Was all her talk yesterday about taking my job seriously just lip service? "I can't go shopping today," I said. "I have to go to work."

"I know. Hurry up and eat. Don't be late."

I was running a little behind. I'd woken at a ridiculously early hour again but had misjudged the time and gone for a longer run than I should have. I just kept hearing Mrs. Oh's voice saying that she would take out the ribs.

I picked at my food. "What are you doing today?"

"I go shopping."

"For what?"

My mother put down her mug of coffee. "I just look and see."

She had nothing else to do. I expected she'd soon get bored and announce her departure date. I took one last bite of sausage, wiped my mouth with a napkin, and carried my plate to the sink.

"That is what you wear to work?" she asked, looking me up and down.

"Not this again," I groaned. I had on a pair of black pants and a black top.

"I help you. You wanna be a fashion editor, but you don't wear nothing special."

"This is how everyone in the department dresses."

"More reason to wear something different." She walked to my closet and rummaged through the hangers. "Here, put this on." She held up a multicolored, striped Donna Karan dress I'd bought at my first sample sale and never worn.

"It's from last year's collection. People will think I took it from the closet."

"And they see how good it look. They buy more clothes."

I shrugged and unbuttoned my shirt.

"That much better," she said after I'd put on the dress. "Now, what you have to do today?"

"You mean besides the sale?"

"You have meeting? You have presentation? You have project?"

I shook my head three times.

"You have phone calls?"

I shook my head again.

"No wonder you flunky. You don't do nothing."

"They don't give me anything," I said defensively.

"No one give you anything in this world. Show some initiation. What you learn in school?"

I looked at her blankly.

"Never mind. What you learn from me? Don't you watch Mommy? How I hustle and work hard to get clients and houses."

"I'm doing what you said. I'm looking out for opportunities, like the photo shoot on Thursday."

"That not enough. You have to ask. You have to take."

"What exactly?"

"I don't know what going on there. Everything. Anything."

"I can't just take other people's work."

"There way to do without stepping on toes. Find work. Come up with ideas, like the closet. Use your brain."

"Okay."

"And make you sure you get credit. Tell everyone what you do."

"I'll try my best."

"I mean it. Don't leave to Sam and Sharon to be your speakswoman."

"They're the ones who have the power to promote me."

"Open your eyes. The people above them have even more power."

"I'm too insignificant for them to waste their time on."

"Babble-oney. If Sam depend only on old fashion boss, she will be up for bigger job?"

"Okay," I said, gathering my keys and purse.

She followed me to the door, pulling the skirt of my dress straight. After tucking a strand of hair behind my ear, she took my face in both of her hands. She gazed at me.

"You so much prettier than me at your age."

"Mother."

"I just mean you have so much more. You can go more far."

"Not if you keep me here."

She let go of me. "Knock them down, my Ginger."

CHAPTER 26

❧

The closet sale was a smashing success. Word spread through the building to the other magazines, and the bargain hunters came in droves. Hell, who had declined Sam's invitation to browse first, saying she didn't need any old clothes, came running the second Sam reported to her that corporate people and other editors in chief were stopping by. They spent the morning standing next to me, happily chatting with the VIPs like the best-looking belles at a summer cotillion. Dakota had tried to join them, but Hell kept stepping in front of her, and when Chantal dropped in to check on how the sale was going, she told Dakota to stand at the other door to control the number of people coming in.

"Turnout's better than I expected," Chantal said loud enough for Hell, Sam, and the CEO they were talking to to hear. Mac Klempner's presence was a rare honor.

"Yes, someone should be congratulated," Hell said, beaming at us.

Grinning, I turned to the woman waiting for her change.

"Thanks," I heard Sam say. I spun my head to her.

"Hey!" The woman in front of me knelt to collect her bills. Chantal bent down to pick up the dollar that had landed near her foot.

"Sorry," I said, looking again at Sam.

Her eyes darted down to Chantal, then back to me. To Hell and Mr. Klempner she said, "It would have been a waste to donate the clothes to people who wouldn't appreciate their value."

"And so now we donate the money," Hell said, "and take the tax write-off."

"Like father, like daughter," Mr. Klempner said. "Speaking of which, Graham must be in the middle of another takeover. He hasn't been at the club recently."

"Sam." Chantal rose. "You're not really going to take the credit for this, are you?"

"Of course not," Sam said without even pausing. "I was about to say I didn't come up with the idea. Magazines at other companies have done this."

Hell gave Mr. Klempner a meaningful look. "But I'm sure they didn't raise as much money as we are. I'm sure designers make those editors return the borrowed clothes."

"Sammy, you'll have to be even more remiss about returning them," Mr. Klempner said.

A five-dollar bill was thrust in my face. As I took it, Hell laughed heartily, drowning out Sam, who probably was only smiling politely. Her father wasn't even permitted to call her that anymore.

"What I meant," Chantal said, "was that the praise should go to Ginger. She did all the work."

"Who?" Hell asked.

"Ginger," Sam repeated.

I turned to them and saw she was pointing at me. I took a step closer to them.

"My assistant."

"Who I've *also* recruited to model in that multi-culti story you loved so much, Hell," Chantal said. To me: "Your eyebrows look fine, by the way."

I smiled mutely. I knew what she meant by *also*, but it wasn't my place to clarify. I couldn't help her, but I wasn't about to stop her either. Sam gave me a quizzical look.

"Chantal, don't you think you're going a little too authentic again?" she said. "I mean, stories with real people rate high with readers only if we're making fun of what they're wearing."

"Yes, no real people in fashion pages," Hell said. "You know that Chantal."

"But—"

"Absolutely not."

"The story's a hard enough sell as it is," Sam said.

I probably would have looked stiff and awkward next to the professionals anyway. She was doing me a favor.

Mr. Klempner cleared his throat. "You don't think readers will like it, Sam?" he asked. "Why are we running it then?"

The sound of shouting drew my attention across the room. Two people were fighting over a pink Dolce & Gabbana blouse. I ran to them to break it up. The shirt was from when the deconstructed look was in, but it originally had both sleeves. The combatants still wanted it. I said it would go to the highest bidder and ended up selling it for seventy dollars to the young man who certainly didn't work for the company's sports magazine.

". . . all these other problems of abbreviated Americans that you never hear about," Sam was saying.

"That particular angle is fresh," Mr. Klempner said. "I like that."

Hell, who had been pursing her lips, nodded. "Yes, I like that much better also."

"Maybe for an article," Chantal interjected. "We can't really show it in a fashion spread."

Mr. Klempner stared at her, then slowly nodded his agreement.

"I've got it!" Sam snapped her fingers. "We can run personal essays along with the photos."

Hell looked cautiously at her boss. "In a fashion story?" she asked.

"They'll be short," Sam said. "Long captions, actually."

"Brilliant!" Mr. Klempner said.

"Done," Hell said.

"But who's going to write them?" Chantal asked. "The models certainly can't. And what are they going to be about?"

"I could interview the models and write up what they said," I blurted out.

Everyone looked at me in surprise.

"Or better yet," Sam said, finally ending the silence, "Ginger could write what I was just telling you about her mother's husband-hunt. She could do the Asian story."

She had told them about that? If I wanted the world to know my business, I would have penned a memoir. I would never presume to speak for all Asians, but at least if I wrote this essay, I could salvage Hell's and Mr. Klempner's opinion of me.

"She's never written for us before," Hell said.

"I can vouch for her," Sam persisted. "It would be a reward for all the great work she's done today."

Hell shook her head. "We don't have the time to chance it."

I tried, Sam said to me with her eyes.

"If she's looking for more work, she can assist on the photo shoot."

"Aerin and Dylan are already—"

"A third will make the work go faster." Sam smiled at Mr. Klempner. "Time is money."

"We pay the models and photographer by the day," Chantal said.

Mr. Klempner, who had been swiveling his head from one to the other as though he were watching a tennis match, looked at Sam, waiting for her return.

"I know. But you're shooting at three different sites. You could easily go into overtime." She crossed her arms over her chest. "And that's charged on an hourly basis."

"A third assistant who doesn't know what she's doing isn't going to make that much of a difference."

"Chantal, I said she was going," Hell said. "End of discussion."

"No, I think she has a point," Mr. Klempner said, nodding his head at Chantal. "If she has to tell her"—he glanced at me—"what to do, it may take up more time."

"It won't," I said, finally finding my voice. "I'm a quick study."

"And it's not as though styling is rocket science," Sam added. "Anyone who dresses themselves can do it."

"She'll just do what the other assistants are doing," Hell said.

"That's the last thing I need," Chantal mumbled under her breath.

Hell shot her a look. "Mac, please don't second-guess me on this, of all things."

Mr. Klempner took a step back. "You're right, there are bigger decisions to make." He shook his wrist to see the time. "Why don't we go to lunch? All our talk about ethnic culture has made me hungry for sushi."

Hell smiled. "That would be great."

Sam nodded.

"Chantal?" Mr. Klempner asked. "Are you free to join us?"

Chantal started but quickly recomposed herself. "I wish I were. But I've got arrangements to make for this shoot—find an Asian model, for one thing."

He nodded approvingly. "Perhaps another time."

From the look on Sam's and Hell's faces, I was sure they would change his mind by the end of their meal.

"I'll walk with you to the elevator though," Chantal said.

The four of them left, Mr. Klempner and Chantal leading the way. Sam looked over her back and gave me the thumbs-up. I returned to collecting money.

CHAPTER 27

"Not bad," my mother said. We were feasting on Mrs. Oh's leftovers and the triumphs of my day. She put her untouched ribs on my plate. Now that I wouldn't be modeling, I was making up for lost eating.

I finished chewing and swallowed. "It's better than that. Hell ordered that I go to the photo shoot. She stood up to her boss for me. She's vested in my future now."

"Only because she protects her territory. You gotta be careful. You gotta watch your feet."

"I know, I know." I dumped the last of the kimchi over my rice. "But it's like you said, her backing is the most valuable of all. Chantal can't push me aside whenever it's convenient or in her best interest."

"You still gotta do a good job for her Thursday." My mother handed me the sesame oil, which I poured over my kimchi-pob. "Not so much!" She held her palm out.

I capped the bottle. "I'll be the best assistant she ever had." Yesterday I would have put my money, little as it was, on Sam's getting the directorship. Now I wasn't so sure.

"Do that. But don't act higher than the other girls. Don't make them hate you."

"What do they matter?" I asked, mixing my food.

"Ginger, don't you know? They as important as the bosses. They your competitions. They have reason and ability to spoil things, keep you down."

"Okay." Her advice from the morning had been good.

"Make friend."

"They never made an effort with me." I put a forkful of rice in my mouth and made a face.

"I told you so."

I pushed my plate away.

"You overeat anyway. Don't eat like that in front of men. What you weigh? One hundred ten pounds? Five feet seven inches?"

"What men?" I asked, plucking up a rib with my fingers.

"So be bigger than the other girls," my mother answered. "Already you are since you close to Sam."

My friendship with Sam hadn't hindered Dakota's overtures. It had propelled them, if anything. I wasn't going to be used again.

"Go out to dinner with them. But not this Friday. You have a date."

I choked, spitting my mouthful across the counter.

"Don't do that either on your date," she said, wiping up my half-chewed food with her napkin.

"What date? With who? I thought church was your last attempt."

"That was dumb mistake. I have better ideas." She handed me a slip of paper with a time and name of a restaurant. "His name is Yeung-rok Yun."

"What kind of name is that?" I couldn't tell his first name from his surname. In Korean, you said the last name first, but my mother flipped them for me.

"Korean."

"I know that. I mean, if he has a Korean name, does he even speak English?"

"Of course. He grew up here. I don't bother with men from Korea anymore."

"Where did you find him?"

My mother shrugged.

"Forget it. I don't have the time." I flung my hands in the air. "We've got all this strategizing to do."

"Ginger, life can't be all work. That lopeyed."

"But it's what I have to do now to get ahead. I'll get balance later."

"When? How much later? Your bloom . . . I mean—"

"Mother, a husband isn't the only other thing in life."

"I know you think that. You said you had me. But Mommy don't live forever. I don't want to leave you alone."

I would have had George. I thought of the list I had almost called. "There are other people."

"You can't depend on friends. They get married, have children, and don't have time to fool around with you."

"So I'll make new friends."

"Over and over? Everyone eventually settle down. That human situation."

"Not everyone," I said, thinking of Bobby. And Ann and Chantal. I had a stitch of a thought. The two must have been more than roommates. It would explain why Ann was willing to marry Bobby.

"You don't even have hobby, other than shopping, run, and read book. Right?"

"So I'll find more." After her dinners and parties, my life did seem sort of empty. I would be sorry to see her go, though not inconsolable.

"Like what? What your interests? Tennis? Poker? Knicks?"

"What does it matter?"

She stood up and started to clear the plates. "I just say they should involve other people."

"I won't take up needlepoint and knitting. I'm not a total recluse."

"But you always pick solitary game. Even as child. Jigsaw puzzle, crossword puzzle . . . still you do them?"

"Occasionally, but that's just the way I am. You make it sound like I hate people."

"Then go on this date."

"But—"

"I know you prefer your own company. But that because you haven't found someone else you like as much. Give people a chance. Give him a chance."

"But you're mixing apples with oranges."

"What fruit gotta do with this?" She shook her head. "I just say you never have no boyfriend. And maybe that because the people you share interests with are like you and also like to be alone. So open yourself to new interest, new activity. Go on this date."

"Fine." My own mother thought I was a loser. Though I kept so much from her that it wasn't surprising that she thought I was so one-sided, or that I needed help finding a mate. I'd never looked at myself from her point of view. "I'll meet this guy Friday, but only to prove I'm not closed to new experiences and that I can be pleasant to be around. I can even attract the opposite sex."

"That all I ask." She handed me the stack of plates. "And also wash dish. I dry. You will see, two people nicer than one."

CHAPTER 28

Sam was already in when I arrived at the office. She shoved the papers she was working on into a desk drawer, but not before I glimpsed her doodles of bridal gowns.

"How's Walker?" I asked, taking a seat.

"Walker? How?" She nodded. "He said he spoke to you Sunday. He's fine. But look at you in your blue dress. You were wearing color yesterday too."

If she didn't want to talk about Walker, I supposed it was her prerogative. "Too bold a statement? It was my mother's suggestion."

Sam shrugged. "Plenty of aspiring editors go that route, then change to black once they've established they can have an opinion if they need one. But a word to the wise—if you're going to call attention to your fashion-forwardness, you shouldn't do it with last year's collection."

All of my colorful clothes were old, bought before I realized everyone at the magazine wore black. "I guess I'll have to go shopping." I smiled. "I have a feeling I'm going to like this career."

"It's fun as long as you don't take it seriously. It is just clothes." She shook a cigarette out from the pack that had been sitting on her desk. I was surprised to see three butts in the ashtray already; she must have come in even earlier than I'd thought. She offered the Marlboro lights to me, but I passed. She lit up, leaned back in her chair, and put her feet on the desk.

"So when did Chantal ask you to be a model? And more important, why didn't you tell me?"

"Last week. I was going to, but I didn't have the chance, what with the weekend and the closet sale."

"There are such things as phones."

"I was crazed." I filled her in on the party and Bobby's proposal. As nonromantic and insincere as the latter had been, I had to admit a small part of me was pleased, relieved really, that I had one offer before the age of thirty. Sam with her trust fund had at least five.

Sam's feet fell to the floor. "That's why you didn't come in Friday. I can't believe you've been holding back from me."

"I could say the same," I said, thinking of Walker.

Sam made a face. "This gay man sounds perfect. I can't believe you said no."

"Really?" Maybe I should reconsider.

"No, not really," Sam said, shaking her head. "I was being sarcastic."

"Right." I knew Bobby's proposal was ludicrous.

"But I am surprised you didn't jump on the offer. You're so afraid of disappointing your mother." She stubbed out her butt. "But it's like what Hell said. Parenthood is a bitter berry. That's why she doesn't have any kids."

"Which reminds me, I can't believe you told everyone my business yesterday."

"Don't get your knickers all knotted up. It's not like they even care." Sam lit another cigarette. "I had to say something." She blew out a long stream of smoke. "And I made it up to you, getting you on the shoot."

"Thanks, by the way."

"No problem. We're a team. You and me." She didn't need to say "not Chantal."

"How'd lunch go with Mr. Klempner?"

Sam smiled. But before she could answer, the phone rang. "I better take this in private," she said, looking at the caller ID panel.

As I stood to leave, I leaned over and saw it was Walker. Aside from the fact we were discussing work, whatever happened to valuing the conversation of female friends as much as any man's?

"Ginger!"

I turned around.

Her hand covered the phone mouthpiece. "You should check in with Chantal. Ask what you can do for the shoot."

"Can you spare me like that?" I joked.

She didn't hear me, her back turned already.

CHAPTER 29

The rest of the day and the following one were taken up with preparations for the photo shoot. I had to help the other assistants catalog the clothes that were going to be shot, pack them, and call in last-minute adds. We also had to confirm the vans, drivers, caterers, site

locales, makeup artist, hair stylist, and photographer and crew. Fortu-
nately Chantal did find a new Asian model, and whatever objections
she'd had to my going on the shoot had dissipated. I kept on meaning
to engage her in conversation about Ann and Bobby but never had
the opportunity.

Being busy like that made time go by unnoticed. Both nights I
took a car home, leaving the office well past midnight. I probably
could have come home earlier, but once the other assistants realized I
was going on the shoot, they stopped being so nice and helpful. They
even steered me wrong in a couple of time-consuming instances, mis-
informing me about how to have a guy from the mailroom pick up
the clothes trunks and having me steam the clothes unnecessarily.

Dakota was no help either, having never been on a shoot. She'd
actually been acting a bit frosty since finding out I was going.

I hadn't been busy like that in a long time, not since Madison.
The tasks weren't mentally challenging, but when I came home I was
physically exhausted, bone tired the way farm laborers must feel after
a long day of baling hay or whatever back-breaking, honest work they
did. I slept easily.

Because of the late hours I was pulling, I saw little of my mother. I
gathered from our drowsy, short exchanges in the mornings and evenings that she was passing her days sightseeing and shopping. I hoped
she was enjoying the sights; from the absence of store bags, she didn't
seem to be doing much shopping. She wanted me to rat to Chantal
about the other assistants, but I didn't want to get her involved. I was
older than them and thought I should be able to handle them myself.
I was going mention it to Sam, but I was seeing so little of her, and
when I did, she seemed so preoccupied, I never did.

Finally Thursday arrived. Conveniently for Chantal, the designated pick-up point for the production vans was right in front of her
building. Dressed back in black—I wanted to be comfortable—in a
calf-length pencil skirt and cotton sweater set I'd salvaged from the
bags meant for donation, I groggily flutter-stepped the ten or so

blocks to the meeting place. I'd forgotten that the narrowness of the skirt made walking difficult, and cursed my bad choice.

The just-dawning sky was gray and hazy, and I wondered if the first set of the photo shoot, which was outdoors by a pool, would have to be rescheduled. The four scenes of American life we were depicting were socializing, eating, shopping, and dating. I felt like I was walking through a black-and-white film of Depression-era city streets. The usual hustle and bustle and noise that I loved so much hadn't begun yet. It was five A.M., so early that the stores were still shuttered. An empty cab occasionally drove by, slowing to see if I needed a ride. The sidewalk was deserted save for the homeless people sleeping in their boxes and a woman watching her terrier pee.

As I nervously clicked down the sidewalk, I went over my objectives for the day. I wanted to look like I knew what I was doing. I wanted to fit in with the other assistants but stand out as being more competent. I wanted to impress Chantal with my panache and intelligence. I wanted not to be kicked off the shoot and sent home early.

I passed a Korean man opening the metal gate to his deli, and I remembered I wanted to buy cigarettes—to be correctly accessorized. All the assistants smoked; they spent more time riding the elevators to go outside than any other activity. Whenever I came or left, a small group of them would be in front of the building in a cloud of smoke.

I waited for the man to open for business, and after he motioned for me to come in, asked for a pack of Marlboro reds. Sam and the other assistants smoked lights, but I was trying to make a statement. The harsher cigarette said I was tough, defiant, renegade. I used to smoke the brand in school.

The elderly Korean man behind the counter shook his head.

"Do you want ID?" I asked, opening my purse. I got carded all the time.

He shook his head again. "Smoking no good for young lady like you," he said sternly. It was touching how this silver-haired man who didn't know me felt compelled to inform me of the health risks. I was sure he didn't warn all of his customers.

I probably reminded the old man of his granddaughter, so I decided to be nice. I thanked him for his concern, but assured him that I was well aware of the cancer risk.

He shook his head again. "Does your mother know you smoke?" He said it like a threat, like he was going to pick up the phone and call her.

For a split second I panicked that he knew my mother. But from the way she'd rushed us out of that church, I knew that was impossible. Even if she'd walked into the deli to buy a soda or sandwich—we weren't far from my building—she wouldn't have said more than a polite hello. As prosperous as he was from the look of the store, he probably wasn't in the market for a new house in Wisconsin.

He was denying me cigarettes just to exert his power over me, another Korean. To me, he wasn't another hardworking Asian immigrant struggling to make good—one of thousands of nobodies. He was more than a nameless cashier who took my money. He was also an elder who claimed my respect.

"Or does your husband know you smoke?"

He most definitely did not know my mother.

"May I please just have the cigarettes?"

The man stared at me and I stared back, refusing to blink. I could have gone to another store, but I couldn't let this man dictate whether or not I smoked. I was tired of other Koreans choosing when I was or wasn't a member of their community.

A person behind me cleared his throat. I turned to find a line had formed, and blushed to think they had all overheard our conversation.

"I'm not Korean," I said.

He squinted, pursing his lips. "You look Korean," he said suspiciously.

"I'm Chinese, fourth generation. My great-grandfather came to San Francisco and worked on the railroad." The lie sprang into my head and flowed out of my mouth.

He nodded and put the pack on the counter. Apparently, the Chinese could die if they wanted; he actually gave me a handful of matchbooks, as though to hasten my expiration. I held a ten-dollar bill out to him. I had read somewhere that to Koreans that was rude. I should have put it on the counter. He put my change also directly into my hands, and before I could say thank you, he was ringing up the next person in line.

I'd smoked three cigarettes by the time I reached Chantal's building. Several people—the makeup artist, hairstylist, and manicurist, I presumed—were already sitting in the production van, which was nothing more than a customized trailer with ten roomy seats. They were all dressed astonishingly sloppy, in jeans and sneakers.

I took a seat near a friendly looking Latina woman. She scooted away, waving the air in front of her nose. "Phew!" she said. "Did you come straight from a nightclub?"

"Sorry," I said. "It's been a rough morning."

"Smells like a rough life."

"That too." I moved over a couple of seats. Now I could look out the blackened window. The doorman from before, the Japanese-speaking Santa look-alike, was standing outside. He smiled and mouthed "good morning" as he held the door for a man in a pin-striped suit carrying a leather briefcase. The man swept out and down the sidewalk without returning the salutation. The doorman tipped his hat to the man's back.

I remembered the doorman's Irish lilt. You didn't have to be a Korean immigrant to be a nobody. His job, like the deli cashier's, was just a living, not a source of identity or pride. It was interesting, though, how he had chosen such a low-level position. From the way he spoke Japanese, he must have some education. And English was his first language. He had no barriers. What was his excuse?

Plus, he was white. He could associate with people at large, the way I did. Perhaps that was how Anglo immigrants differed from others. The first generation was like the Korean second generation; it could move freely among society.

As I understood it, that was why Koreans of my mother's generation were as clannish as they were in America. They kept to themselves for the most part because they looked different, their customs were different, they ate smelly food. They were uncomfortable and it was so much easier to stick to their own kind. Wanting Korean in-laws and grandchildren was just an offshoot of wanting to feel at ease in a life of feeling like a foreigner.

Still facing the window, I realized my eyes were resting on Bobby, walking through the door. Smiling, he stopped to chat to the doorman. Though the window was black, I slunk down.

It was a shame that I couldn't marry Bobby, that I couldn't do that for my mother, do that to the Ohs. But there were limits to what even I was willing to do. I didn't know how marrying a gay man was worse than not marrying at all, but it was. I felt it viscerally. Maybe Bobby and I could still be friends. I wouldn't have minded getting to know him and June better. She'd said to call her, but that was before I turned down Bobby. I wondered if the invitation still stood.

"Who you hiding from?"

I jerked in my seat and turned in the direction of the voice, to find Chantal standing in front of me, her hands cupped over her mouth like a megaphone. She must have come out of her building when I was lost in thought.

She bent down to look out the window. "Oh, it's Oh." She put her purse in the empty seat next to me, then walked to the front. "Eight people are in the first van, so there should be seven here." She counted, moving her lips, then gave both drivers the go-ahead to move out.

She came back to me and sat down. "He's not a bad guy, though I'm glad he and Ann aren't going through with that wedding."

I nodded. "You get to keep your roommate."

She started. "That's right, you called us." She shrugged. "She would have continued living with me. It was a platonic arrangement."

"I know she was just doing him a favor."

"Too big a favor, if you ask me."

It dawned on me that she was the friend in fashion June had mentioned. "Yeah, even June wasn't willing to make that kind of sacrifice for him."

"You know June?"

"Through Bobby. You?"

"We went to college together."

"So you went to college with June, June went to med school with Bobby, and Bobby went to college with Ann." I felt like I'd stumbled upon a nest of buddies. "That's cool how you and Ann wound up hitting it off and are living together," I said, hinting at her secret while fishing for its verification.

"Yes, it is cool." She mumbled something about wanting coffee and scrambled to her feet. She went to the little breakfast buffet in the back, but when she returned, she proceeded to walk by me, explaining she needed to think about how to rearrange the photo shoot if the Hamptons were as cloudy as Manhattan.

I could respect Chantal's close protection of her privacy, her desire to keep her sexuality a secret from work. It was none of my business.

Still, I wanted to talk more. I covered my disappointment with a smile of understanding.

CHAPTER 30

Chantal burst through the small crowd, heading for the van, as I climbed down. The sky was as overcast here as it was in Manhattan, and she'd decided to skip the set around the pool and shoot on the beach later in the day when the haze would have burned off, hopefully. We were moving on to the eating shots in Tatiana's kitchen.

"I knew this was a fricking mistake," Chantal muttered as she stormed past me and up the stairs. She slammed the door shut.

I looked around. On the edge of the tree-lined path leading to the house, Tatiana stood, dressed in a silk robe and slippers, her hands on her hips, watching us. I groaned. She was getting three thousand dollars for letting us use her place; I'd hoped she'd be out shopping. I turned to Aerin and Dylan, who were pulling out cigarettes and lighters. "What's going on?" I asked, fumbling in my purse for my pack.

One of the blond clones explained that Tatiana was upset that Lulu, the Asian model, had arrived an hour early and woken her. Lulu's boyfriend lived fifteen minutes away and she had gotten here by herself. On top of that outrage, we were several minutes late, and Tatiana was threatening to cancel the entire shoot.

The trailer door opened and Chantal came out. "Someone get me that bitch's friend on the phone," she said. No one moved, so I pulled out my cell phone. Sam's phone rang and rang; her voice mail must have been full. The receptionist wouldn't be in for another hour; maybe Sam would come in early again.

Chantal saw what I was doing and came to me, holding her hand out for the phone. I closed it. "She's not in the office yet," I said.

"Try her at home, then. You must know the number."

I did as I was told. Sam's machine picked up. I told Chantal.

"Shit," Chantal fumed. "She must be on her way to the office. Leave a message for her to call as soon as she gets in. Tell her it's a fricking emergency."

I was about to explain that Sam's voice mail wasn't working but thought better of it. I'd keep on calling until Rosie arrived. Chantal paced back and forth as I listened to the phone ring.

"Someone give me a cigarette," she said. With the phone cradled between my ear and shoulder, I hurriedly shook one out, beating the other assistants by half a second. She coughed as she took her first drag. "What is this shit?" I showed her the pack and she continued puffing. I'd never seen her angry like this, though I'd heard tales from Dakota.

"I can't get through," I said after the twelfth ring.

"Dammit." Chantal smoked her cigarette down to the filter and tossed the butt into her coffee. She gave me the cup. When she spoke, it was with considerable calm. "Everyone, unload the vans," she said. "Ginger, come with me."

Pleased to be singled out, I followed her into the trailer, tossing her garbage into the wastebasket near the driver. He went outside to give us privacy.

"We can't wait for Sam," Chantal said. "With the weather and change in schedule, it's really tight. You know Tatiana. Can you speak to her?"

"What do you want me to say?" I was starting to think I should be more clear about the extent of my acquaintance with Tatiana.

"You spoke to Sam, and she said to go through with the shoot."

I was confused. "You make it sound like Sam told her to call it off."

Chantal leaned forward, boring into me with her eyes. I stared back, trying to make sense of it all. Sam wouldn't ruin my first shoot. Would she? Of course she would. There were no friends in business. For a player, I had been played.

I strained to keep a blank expression. After several minutes, Chantal drew back and relinquished her gaze. She shrugged. "It was just a hunch. Maybe I guessed wrong."

"Or maybe you didn't. But it won't work to lie. Tatiana could call Sam to check on our story. We should offer her something. Something she can't resist. It can't take that much." She did come from Sam's set.

"Like what?"

I tried to think like my mother. "Money? Can we offer her more?"

Chantal shook her head. "We're already over budget. Sam gave her two thousand more than we normally pay."

I ransacked my brain, trying to think of the things I knew about Tatiana. The short-lived, badly concealed affair that had ruined her marriage had been with a film-star heartthrob of teen America. Tatiana was a snob, but she was also vain as hell. It had blown her away that he could have any gorgeous actress or model, and he wanted her, Sam had explained. I snapped my fingers. "I've got it. Let's offer to put her in the shoot."

"No way. She's not good-looking enough. And she's hardly ethnic."

"You don't have to use the photos she's in." Sam had once shown me the contact sheets from a shoot. Hundreds were taken for the six pictures that ran.

Chantal shook her head. "It's going to waste time we don't have."

Right then someone knocked, and opened the door without waiting for a response. He had two cameras slung around his neck, and he was ruggedly handsome, with tousled dark hair and a nose that looked like it had been broken more than once. Like everyone else on the crew except me, he was dressed in jeans, and he wore a soiled white T-shirt. He must have been in the other van coming here, because this was the first time I was setting eyes on him. I assumed he was the photographer, Tarn Friesch.

He took a drag from his cigarette, threw it down, and mashed it with his heel. "Hey, Chantal." He bowed hello to me. "What's our next move?" Even his voice was ruggedly handsome.

"I don't know yet. Ginger and I were just strategizing."

Chantal sat down and he walked over to her. He crouched to be at her eye level. "Do you want me to take light measurements now or should I hold off?"

"Do you think the bitch will let you into her house?"

"I was thinking I'd take measurements by the lagoon-style pool. It's starting to get bright and it's really gorgeous."

"Go ahead," Chantal said. "And scout the property for other shots. But remember, the story is to look all-American."

Tarn stood his full height. "In the Hamptons?"

"Prosperous all-American."

"Gotcha." Tarn pointed his index fingers like pistols and shot with his thumbs. He moseyed to the door, took hold of the knob, but swung back to us. He fixed his gaze on me. "Hey, beautiful," he said. "Want to come with me and take Polaroid test shots?"

"Me?"

"No, Tarn," Chantal said, waving him off. "I need Ginger. Use one of the other assistants." When the door closed behind him, she rolled her eyes.

"To meet Tarn is to be hit on by him."

"I bet he's rarely turned down," I said, hoping my cheeks weren't as red as they felt.

"Yes, well, most women aren't as discriminating and smart as you and I."

I had a genius moment. "You know what?" I said. "Tarn should talk to Tatiana. He's her type and she would totally respond to him."

Chantal jumped to her feet and wrenched the door open. "Tarn!" she shouted. "Come back."

He stepped into the trailer again and winked at me. Chantal socked him in the arm and told him to stop flirting with her assistant, that she needed him to save it for Tatiana. They agreed that he would ask her to be his test model, and while they were thus engaged, he would coax her into letting the shoot proceed.

While Tarn was working on Tatiana, Chantal ordered the makeup and hair people to prepare the models, and the staff to get the clothes ready. Dozens of outfits, with shoes, handbags, and jewelry, had been brought for each of the four models. The planned scenario was "eating" in the kitchen. I started to unpack a trunk and hang clothes on one of the metal racks.

"Anyone seen Lulu?" Chantal asked. No one had since we first arrived. "Ginger, go find her," Chantal commanded.

I started to pick my way around the house, following a foliage-covered dirt trail. I sank a heel every couple of feet. I'd never met or seen Lulu but assumed I would know her if I saw her. I made a complete circle without bumping into anyone, let alone a tall, rail-thin Chinese beauty.

Instead of reporting my failure and rejoining my toiling colleagues right away, I decided to take a short break. Though still cloudy, the sky was a brilliant blue, and it was calling me out from under the trees shading the house. Tatiana was lucky to live here. The silence was peaceful, like at the reservoir in Central Park. I felt I could stand here the entire day and just look and be.

My phone rang.

"How it go?"

"We're missing a model, but okay," I said, touched that my mother cared so much. It reminded me of my first day of school, when she wouldn't leave until the teacher made her. I told her how I had already been of help to Chantal.

"That good. I let you go back, but I have question. The things you look for in a man is what?"

"Mother! I'm working now."

"Okay, we talk later."

I turned off the phone and slid out of my mud-encrusted sandals. Could she have realized there was more to compatibility than having Korean parents? I walked barefoot in the grass along the path, back to the private road and toward the gate that led to the main road. Kindness, intelligence, a sense of humor, I supposed. Confidence but not to the point of arrogance, sensitivity but with an edge, understanding and patience. Bobby, sort of. A Bobby who looked like Tarn. A Tarn with depth and a receptive mind. Someone who didn't like me just for my looks, my "exotic" looks, who wasn't repelled by the things that come with being Asian, who cherished me despite my differences.

As I neared the closed white picket gate, I realized a car was on the other side, its engine idling. Still walking on the grass, I came up to the shiny black Rolls-Royce. Although Lulu had all the windows up, I could hear, or rather feel, the pounding bass of the stereo. She was jabbering on the phone, her free hand wildly gesticulating in the air. If she saw me, she didn't acknowledge it.

I took out my cell phone to tell Chantal I'd found her, then realized I didn't have a number to call. I was going to have to make the trek back to the vans, but I wanted to make contact with Lulu first. It wouldn't matter that I had thought of having Tarn talk to Tatiana if Lulu left. Were all shoots this troubled?

I walked to the driver's side of the car and knocked on the window. I had to knock several times to get Lulu's attention. She turned to me, said something in her phone, then rolled down the window. A blast of music hit me like I'd walked into a wall.

She looked at me expectantly. Her eyes were puffy and red. Still, she was the most beautiful Asian woman I'd ever seen. I felt the stirrings of jealousy.

"I was sent to get you," I said.

Lulu cupped her hands behind her ears. "What?" she shouted.

I pointed back at the house. "They're waiting for you," I yelled, enunciating every consonant. "They want to do your hair and makeup."

Lulu shook her head. "I no go," she shouted. "That bitch scream me because—"

"I know. For arriving early."

"What?"

"For arriving early," I boomed.

"What? No!" Lulu shook her head. "That bitch . . . bitch . . . fucking bitch . . ." I couldn't make out the words in between the curses. The music had reached a deafening crescendo. I shook my head and pointed to the general vicinity of the stereo controls. She turned down the sound.

"Thank you," I said. "What did you say?"

"That bitch. That fucking bitch. That shit-eating, cow-fucking bitch. *Dai hao gao.*" Though the music was down, she was still shouting.

I motioned for her to lower her voice. "Calm down," I said. Tatiana was a bitch, but these model types were hypersensitive.

It was the wrong thing to say. "I no calm down," she shrieked, her arms jumping. She smacked one hand against the steering wheel and screamed in pain. "I . . . I . . ." She gave up trying to find the words in English and broke into Chinese. A voice from her cell phone started squawking. We both jumped at the sound. Lulu brought the phone up to her ear with a jerk and continued her tirade.

I watched in silence as she worked herself up into a hysterical state. Tatiana must have really chewed her out. Or with the language barrier, maybe Lulu had misunderstood the cause of Tatiana's wrath.

Lulu interrupted my thoughts with the slam of her car door. She stood next to me and pushed the phone at me. "They want talk."

"Ginger, it's Chantal. I'm on with Bianca, Lulu's agent."

"Hi," Bianca said.

"Lulu's really upset," Chantal said.

"Tell me about it," I said, sneaking a peek. She was lighting a cigarette.

"Do you know Cantonese?" Bianca asked.

"No, I don't even speak Korean." I knew now wasn't the time to get prickly, but I hated it when people assumed the different Asian languages were alike.

"I told you she's Korean," Chantal said. She cleared her throat. "Well, from what we can gather, Lulu is upset because Tatiana mistook her for the new maid."

I choked on my outrage. "You're kidding me." All those times Tatiana had pretended not to remember me—had she been wondering why she was being introduced to the help?

"No, unfortunately, I'm not. And given the situation, I can't exactly ask Tatiana to apologize. So what I need you to do is calm Lulu down, assure her that Tatiana has nothing to do with the magazine, and bring her back to the house."

"How am I going to do that?" I asked. "She doesn't speak English."

"Be soothing, sympathetic. Relate to her as a fellow Asian. Tell her it's an understandable mistake, that if it had happened to you, you would be laughing."

"Yeah, tell her she's got to chill if she wants to make it in America," Bianca said. "And tell her she's beautiful. *Mei, mei, mei.* That's Cantonese for beautiful."

"But don't take too long," Chantal said. "Tarn's already in the house. Do you think you can do this?"

I looked at Lulu again. She was quietly smoking, looking at her nails. She'd chipped one when she hit her hand on the steering wheel. "I'll do my best."

"You'll do fine," Chantal said. "I have confidence in you."

I gave the phone back to Lulu, who was now watching me with a sullen look on her face. I took out a cigarette. After the third match went out, Lulu offered her lighter.

"Thanks," I said, closing the lighter. It was silver and from Tiffany's. Sam had the same one. "Nice."

"My boyfriend give," Lulu said, taking the lighter back. She wiped my fingerprint with the bottom of her black shirt. "You should get."

A boyfriend or a lighter? There wasn't time to ask. "Listen," I said. "I know what that woman in the house did, but . . ." I took a deep breath. "But these things happen here. You shouldn't take it personally."

Lulu looked at me blankly. I plodded forward. "I mean, I've had things like that happen my whole life. When I was a kid I had a friend whose mother would make rice and beans every time I stayed for dinner. Now that I'm an adult, I realize Mrs. Dummy, I mean Mrs. Denny, was trying to make me feel at home, but it just showed how racist she was. Mexicans, Koreans—we all ate rice and were the same to her. Plus, it defeated the whole purpose of my eating there. I wanted meat loaf and mashed potatoes and peas. I ended up telling her I didn't like Mexican food, and I was never invited over again."

Lulu continued to stare blankly.

"Or get this: In high school, I had a trigonometry teacher who would mock me when I answered a question incorrectly. He'd ask me if I was really Asian, or he'd caution the class that I wasn't typical of my people. And during the interview for candidates for the academic decathlon, he actually asked me why I, a Korean, thought I could represent my school. He asked this in front of three other teachers, and no one said anything, no one even shifted uncomfortably in his seat. I was completely stumped for an answer—and got such a low score on the interview that I didn't make the team."

I hadn't thought of Mr. Reed in years, and was surprised by the anger I still felt. "It sucks to have to deal with all the stupid racist bullshit. It's not fair and sometimes it's enough to make you want to poke out everyone's eyes, because if they couldn't see me, they wouldn't know I was Korean."

I threw down my cigarette and ground it under my foot. All these feelings nauseated me—and were counterproductive. With an effort I stamped them down and reminded myself of my purpose.

"But that was all a long time ago. Things are better now—that asshole teacher would be reprimanded today. I just told you about him and Mrs. Denny to show you that what happened with Tatiana was really nothing. At least you weren't a kid, a defenseless, dumb kid. Don't get me wrong. I'm not saying that what happened to you is good or understandable, because it's neither, not in this day and age. But on the bright side, I bet Tatiana will never make that mistake again."

I drew a deep breath, astonished by the length of my monologue. Lulu wasn't even listening. I was glad. I wished to God I had told Mr. Reed off. But I had been taught as a child that I had to be well behaved because I didn't represent just myself, or my family, but Koreans, and even all Asians. To this day, I tipped generously to incline waiters and cabdrivers to treat Asians civilly, if not kindly.

But why did I have this responsibility? And why didn't native-born Americans feel the same need to put their best foot forward? It was preposterous and unfair that to get along in this country we Asians had to be understanding of the whites. Since when did hospitable graciousness fall on the shoulders of newcomers?

I acted on behalf of the newcomers, but I wasn't even one of them—though I had been born in Korea, this was the only country I knew. That was what was so screwy about my position. I identified with the white point of view. I could see both sides of the coin at the same time.

Lulu started to pick at her chipped nail. She had no idea how lucky she was to have grown up in the land of her ancestry. I was as much a foreigner to her as Tatiana or Bianca. The other models had more in common with her than I did—and could probably relate more.

"You are beautiful, beautiful, beautiful," I heard myself saying. "Lulu is *mei*." She smiled brilliantly.

"Lulu is *mei*," I said again. I held my hand out for her to give me the hand with the chipped nail. I studied the one imperfection. "Come with me." I pointed to myself, then to the house. "Up there, the manicurist can fix your nail." I pantomimed polishing her nail. She bobbed her head eagerly, like a child agreeing to a chocolate ice cream cone. She freed her hand and I followed her back to the house.

She was immediately whisked into one of the vans; the other models were already in the house. Chantal was there too, so there was no one to congratulate me on my good work. Aerin and Dylan, smoking and picking at the lunch buffet set up by the caterer, weren't about to glad-hand me and acknowledge my indispensability. I started to head for the house—I was curious to see Tarn at work—but was stopped by the two indistinguishable assistants. "Tatiana is worried about her floors," Tweedledee smirked. "No extraneous people are being allowed in," Tweedledum added.

CHAPTER 31

By the time we left the second site, the main shopping drag in Southampton, the sun was near the horizon and we were three hours behind schedule. On the ride to the third and last location, a hotel with a dock in front and a sandy beach in back, Chantal instructed me to get the men we photographed in the hotel bar to sign release forms. But once we parked and saw how late it was, she changed her mind and decided to do the bar scene in the city and just shoot on the beach.

Tarn, however, felt different. The two of them were having a heated conversation in the parking lot. From what I could gather loitering near them, he thought we should proceed in the bar and reschedule the outdoor photos for another day; the sun was casting long shadows that would ruin the pictures.

"I hear where you're coming from," Chantal said, using the advice she'd given me earlier about relating to the person you're trying to manipulate. "But there are hundreds of bars in the city, while there are no beaches. I don't have the budget to come out again, so I'd rather risk taking the beach shots. If they don't come out, we'll redo them in the studio."

With his arms crossed tightly across his chest, Tarn shook his head. "I can tell you now they won't be any good. It's just going to be a waste of film and time and money. If you don't want to shoot in the hotel, let's go home." He flicked his wristwatch. "I gotta get my crew back."

Chantal also looked at her watch. "I understand you're concerned about paying your guys overtime. We'll work that out. I'll pay them. Let's get going with the shoot."

"You'll pay them?" he asked, relaxing his arms. "It'll be time and a half."

"Yeah, I'll pay them."

"For the whole day?"

Chantal scowled. "No, Tarn, not for the whole day. Just the overtime."

Tarn pondered the proposition on the table. He shook his head again. "No, this isn't just about money. It's also about artistic vision. You're asking me to violate mine."

Chantal stomped her foot and growled.

"Shooting on the beach in shadow!" Tarn threw up his arms. "Why don't you ask me to take pictures of the Taj Mahal with all the lights off? It's ludicrous!"

Chantal looked away from him and noticed me. I didn't stop walking until I reached the front of the hotel, where the docked boats were. On this side, the western side, the horizon was painted in streaks of red, violet, pink, and orange. It was what I imagined the sky looked like at the dawn of time.

The noxious smell of cigar smoke wafted to my nose. I turned my head in its direction, guided also by the sound of squeals and laughter. Down the quay, the four models and Acrin and Dylan were lounging on the upper deck of a yacht. A middle-aged, deeply bronzed man hovered over them, the offending cigar in one hand and a green champagne bottle in the other.

This was the first time I was seeing the four models together. I watched them raise their flutes and clink them against each other. I was struck by how much their looks approximated the Western standard of beauty. Lulu was tall for an Asian; she had round eyes and her hair was curled. Jacqueline, the black model from the Caribbean, had light skin and long, straight hair. Catalina, Argentinean, was blond and blue-eyed. And rounding up the hyphenated-American mix, Dinah, the token white, was from Latvia.

Fresh on the boat, I chuckled. That's what I would call this tableau.

Actually, that wasn't such a bad idea. At least, it would make a great caption to the scenario happening on board. It could be girls' night out, replacing girls having fun at the beach. The sun's position in the sky wouldn't matter.

I ran back to the parking lot. Chantal and Tarn were squatting now, smoking cigarettes. Their argument hadn't progressed far since I'd left them.

"I know you're an artist," Chantal was saying. "I'm your biggest fan. Who do you think chooses you for most of my shoots?"

"Guys!" I interrupted breathlessly. They looked up at me. "Guys," I said, lowering my voice. From the way Tarn was eyeing my calves, I was sorry my skirt was long. I crouched down to be at their level but lost my balance on my high-heeled shoes and tipped forward. I caught myself, putting my hands on the ground.

"Whoa, careful." Tarn reached out for me, but I waved his hands away.

"Ginger, we're in the middle of something," Chantal said.

"I know. That's what I wanted to tell you." I explained my idea.

"Fresh on the boat?" Chantal said after I was finished. "It could work."

"Let me see," Tarn said. He stood up and helped me to my feet.

When we reached the dock, the sky was flushed even redder. Tarn had his doubts, concerned that the backdrop would look apocalyptic. But he was willing to try it. Chantal was game for anything as long as pictures were taken.

This time, standing on the dock, I was able to watch the shoot. Tarn's camera sounded like a machine gun, he was taking so many pictures so quickly. At his direction, the models, quickly put in bikinis and sarongs, changed their pose every several minutes. Each time someone moved, Chantal ran into the frame and adjusted a strap or strand of hair. Most of the changes she made were imperceptible.

After a dozen rolls of film, Tarn came down to where I was standing to shoot the models from below. He had the foursome stand against the rail and wave. You couldn't see their lower halves, but with their colorful bikini tops, the stern of the yacht, and the brilliant sky, it was the money shot, to my mind.

"Beautiful," Tarn said under his breath, his camera shuttering away.

"It is a nice picture," I agreed.

He took his eye away from the camera and turned to me. "No, you. I was addressing you."

"Am I in the way?" I took several steps back.

He made up the distance I had just created between us. "No. I just wanted to tell you that you should be up there," he said, pointing his chin in the direction of the boat.

"Yeah, well, model-handler, clothes-steamer, scene-picker. I can't do everything," I said. Why was I cursed with such active capillaries? I fidgeted under his stare.

"Why not?" he finally asked. He turned back to the boat. "Hey, Chantal!" he hollered.

Chantal appeared next to the models. "Yeah? Is that a wrap?"

"No, I have one more idea." He grabbed my hand and dragged me to the yacht. He pushed me ahead of him. I tripped on a step and he steadied me, putting his hands on my waist. He kept them there. Chantal was waiting for us at the head of the stairs. "I want to do a party scene with more people on the deck. It could replace the bar scene."

Chantal looked at her watch. "It's getting late." She pointed up. "And dark."

Tarn let go of my waist and crossed his arms over his chest. "Who was just saying we should take all the pictures we can as long as we're here? Come on, I'm inspired." He looked at me. "Ginger was right. This boat is a great prop. We'll set up strobes."

Chantal stared at me and then looked around the deck. "But we don't have any extras."

"Sure we do. We've got Ginger here, and the other assistants, and my guys—and the owner of the boat."

"We don't have clothes for your guys."

"So we'll get guests from the hotel, as we were going to in the bar."

Chantal pursed her lips and pivoted toward the dock. When she turned back to us, the smile I had glimpsed was gone. "Okay, but I'm not paying overtime for your crew."

"As of right now." Grinning, Tarn looked at his watch again. "It's almost eight."

Chantal clapped her hands to get everyone's attention. She might have had something in her eye, but I thought she winked at me. Aerin and Dylan and the hair and makeup people gathered around us.

As what we were to do became clear, everyone began to titter with excitement. Apparently our being in the shots was unprecedented. While we got ready, Chantal helped the models into evening clothes. We could wear anything remaining on the racks that hadn't already been photographed. The last in line, I got stuck with a one-sleeved red dress with rumba ruffles. It was the best of my choices.

While we were getting ready, Tarn had his crew set up lights and round up men on the dock and in the hotel lounge. They even got a couple of tuxedoed waiters with silver serving trays. When I saw all the men on the deck, I went back into the van and retrieved the photo release forms. Everyone signed without reading the form except for the yacht owner. He was still going over it when Tarn called everyone to their places.

I wound up standing near the models, but one of the other assistants, either Rosencrantz or Guildenstern, pointed out that I would dilute the focus on the models' ethnicity. Chantal agreed and moved me to the back. Tarn had the assistant who made the suggestion go with me, to give me, he explained, a conversation partner in the shot.

As Hamlet said of the dastardly duo, their defeat did by their own insinuation grow.

Tarn told us to look like we were having fun. We extras tried. "Relax, beautiful, relax," Tarn kept on coaxing. I felt both frustrated and pleased at the special attention, but then I realized he called everyone beautiful, including the cigar-smoking owner of the yacht. After taking a roll, Tarn let go of his camera and it fell to his stomach, the neck strap catching it. He motioned for one of his guys and the owner of the yacht to come to him and they formed a huddle. When he was finished whispering, the two headed for the stairs, clambering noisily in their hurry. The owner went belowdecks and the photo assistant ran into the hotel.

The owner returned with a boom box and the photo crew member came back with a case of champagne. Tarn plugged in the radio and cranked the volume. "Let's have a real party," he shouted, popping a cork. He took a swig and gave the bottle to Catalina, who did the same and passed the bottle to the next model.

The popping of more corks followed in quick succession, accompanied by the sight and sound of the bubbly spraying and soaking its shrieking liberators. People started talking and laughing, loosening and swaying to the beat of the music. Someone switched the radio station to a mambo, lifting people to their feet. Arms and bottles aloft, the dancers herded to the middle of the floor.

Abandoned by my conversation partner the moment the champagne started to flow, I watched from my seat alone, until Tarn, jitterbugging, suddenly appeared and pulled me by the arms to my feet. Still holding one of my hands, he lifted his arm for me to thread under it and twirl into his chest, his arm wrapped around me. Deftly he spun me out and then pulled me close, putting one hand on my waist. He steered me toward the crowd. We danced face-to-face, his camera jabbing me in the gut.

Lulu tapped me on the shoulder, and Tarn and I broke apart. The other models and extras swarmed around us, separating us farther. An almost-full bottle of champagne materialized in my hand, and I lost track of Tarn. But he must have torn himself away from the professional beauty and gotten back to work, because at some point I was aware of his flashing bulb.

I was also aware of Chantal standing on the edge of the party, watching. Every now and then she would go up to a model and straighten the bodice of her dress or smooth her skirt. Under conditions like these, modeling was a cinch, I thought as I gave my almost empty bottle to either Goneril or Chlamydia, dancing next to me.

The photo session came to an abrupt end when the music was turned off. Chantal clapped her hands and shouted that the shoot was over. Tarn had run out of film.

"But there's still champagne!" one of the male extras shouted. Another case had been brought on board, compliments of the hotel.

"Too bad," Chantal said. "I'm not paying for another day of renting these vans. Assistants, help the models out of their clothes and pack up. You'll have to change when we're on the road. I want to be out of here in twenty minutes."

The van carrying the three models who lived in New York drove away while the last of the trunks and equipment were being loaded onto my van. I was happy to see that Tarn had stayed behind. My work done, including getting the release form from the boat owner, I boarded and took a seat next to a window. I watched Tarn, carrying the box of remaining champagne, head for the door I had just come through, and I removed my purse and stack of papers from the seat next to me. But when I looked out the window again, Chantal had intercepted him. I followed her finger as she pointed to Lulu standing several feet away, next to her Rolls-Royce. Listing a little to one side, she was engrossed in watching her car keys dangle on a finger. Tarn gave the champagne to Chantal and jogged to Lulu. He helped her into the passenger side of her car.

Chantal appeared at the front of the van, and the driver closed the doors behind her. Holding the box of champagne against a hip, she counted the passengers and then told the driver we were ready to

go. As the van started to roll, Chantal came down the aisle to where
I was sitting. She put the box where my purse had just been. "This is
Tarn's," she said. "Make sure we give it to him at the shoot in his stu-
dio Wednesday."

"I'll remind you to take it."

"No, you remember to take it. You're coming. Tarn requested you."

I swallowed hard. "Tarn?"

"It's up to me, but I agree with him. You did dynamite work
today." She took the forms from me and smiled.

CHAPTER 32

I was still floating, high from the bubbly and Chantal's compliment,
when I entered my apartment a little past midnight. The lights were
on and I was glad my mother was still awake. I took several steps forward and stopped. White lace curtains hung on the windows and a
spanking white sofa stood where my old orange couch had been. A
wing chair in canary-yellow leather was next to it. It was my apartment; there, out of the corner of my eye, were the boxes of books and
bags, now less full, of discarded clothes.

My mother, wearing pajamas, came out of the bathroom. "How
it go?"

"Good." I looked uncertainly at the new furniture. It was nice,
but where was the old couch? My mother was beaming at me, clearly
waiting to hear some appreciative noise over her purchases. The old
couch was just a beat-up, cumbersome memento. Still, I wished
she'd consulted me. "You shouldn't have spent so much," I heard
myself say.

"It nothing," my mother said, "for my successful daughter. You have to live who you are."

Or were about to become. If I lived at my real station or level of income, I'd be in a box on the street. Maybe if I didn't have my mother padding, dressing, burying me with expensive clothes and brand-new furniture, I'd have gotten to where I was sooner—and be further along. Yet, I would take where I was now over where I had been even two weeks earlier. There was nothing like accomplishing something to feel competent, capable, powerful. Action was exhilarating. Success, independence, future—here I came.

"You like?" It sounded more like a command than a question.

"It's really nice." I did appreciate her generosity. Cheap she wasn't. And Sam was rich *and* high on the masthead. I couldn't blame my mother for my late climbing start. "But let me tell you about my day."

I steered for the couch and kept on moving my feet, but I wasn't going anywhere. I turned around to see she'd grabbed me by the tail of my shirt. She pointed to my shoes. I went back to the door as she went into the living room. The first sandal I flung off hit the door, the other the row of shoes, sending them helter-skelter like bowling pins. I left them there.

My mother was sitting on the new couch, her arms draped over its back. I sank next to her into the down-filled cushions, resting my head on her soft shoulder. I closed my eyes and felt at peace.

"Hey, you not baby. Get off my lap."

I opened my eyes and moved over, giggling at my mistake. "Sorry, I'm tired."

She leaned over and sniffed. "Were you in a bar? You smell like alcohol and smoke."

"Yes. No. I mean, I came straight home. But we had a little champagne while we were working."

My mother made a face. "That a funny job that gives you drink."

"It was to loosen us up. All the assistants had to dress up and pretend to be at a party." I started to tell her about the shoot.

After five minutes, she cut in. "I glad you did good job, but I don't stay up to hear you boast." She yawned. "I want to show you the new furniture. I spended all week shopping."

"So that's what you've been up to." I wagged my finger at her. She smiled, pleased, and I leaned over and kissed her on the cheek. Grimacing, my mother wiped my kiss off with the back of her hand. "You smell terrible."

"I do?" I tested my breath, exhaling into my hand. "It must be from the cigarettes."

"You smoke?" my mother said, her eyes widening.

"Occasionally," I said weakly. I needed to shut up, or before I knew it I would be blabbing about Tarn.

She scowled. "That disgusting habit. Nice young lady don't behave that way."

"Everyone in the fashion department smokes. I was trying to fit in, like you said."

"They do?" She shook her head. "I don't know about this business. Maybe it not so good idea to work there."

"Don't say that," I said, suddenly alert and sober. "It's a fine, respectable career."

"But no one is good, smoking, lying to you, sneaking into other people's offices. I don't like that Sharon girl either. I think she a dyke."

"What?" I didn't even know my mother knew that word.

"Lesbian. Gay. She likes "

"I know what a dyke is." If my mother could tell Chantal was gay, did she know about Bobby? It was better to change the topic. "It has nothing to do with me."

"It shows she has no morals. I don't like her."

I bit my lip, waiting for my annoyance and frustration to wash over me. I couldn't argue in favor of non-Korean men and I'd lost the war over feminism with her; I wasn't about to try to open her mind to gays. She was a product of her time and generation. "Chantal's okay,"

I said. "Everyone at work is okay. It's just a competitive business. I can handle it."

My mother looked doubtful, nudging me over the edge.

"What? You think I can't?"

She put a soothing hand on my arm. "Of course you can. My daughter can do anything she tries. But I just wonder why you want this career. If it worth it."

"Of course it is," I huffed. Maybe I did just fall into fashion. But I liked clothes, and I was making headway.

"What about medical school? Be a doctor. Like June."

"I'm too old," I said. "As you like to say, my bloom is almost over. These brain cells are full."

"That ridiculous. You never go anywhere if you think like that."

"I don't understand why you're picking on my job again. I thought we'd made a turn."

My mother shrugged. "I help you because you my daughter. But it just a job. It just a paycheck. I would rather to stay home and be with my children." She sighed. "Sometimes I wish we never left Korea."

I'd never heard her say anything like that before, not even after George disobeyed her. She loved her job, her autonomy, her freedom. Here, she was the head of the family, answering to no one. Despite my struggles with identity, I was glad we came.

"You don't mean that."

"Yes, I do."

"Since when?"

"For long time. Maybe I raise you better."

"You raised us fine."

"Most is okay." She shifted in her seat. "But we don't talk so good, or as good as I do if I use my language."

"We talk fine." It was true.

"No, sometimes we don't, not as mother to daughter."

She looked so sad, her hair matted down on one side.

"Well, try again. What is it you want me to understand?"

She paused, searching for words. "I just say children are only reward in life. Everybody work, no big deal. Mrs. Kim's daughter Jenny is accountant, Mrs. Un's Gloria and Grace both lawyers. But then they marry, have children, and stop work, or work part-time. Marry, have children, stay home."

"But that's not what I want out of life."

"Ginger, you ask too much of your job. Maybe it gives some feeling of confidence and pride if you successful, but it not enough to fill a whole life. Single is lonely life, trust me, I know."

I reached over and fluffed her hair.

"And the right person . . . there not many. Maybe there one. But he don't appear when you ready. He appear when he appear."

"I said I would meet this guy tomorrow."

"I know," she said. "Also, don't forget Bobby."

She had my head spinning. "I thought he was over. His parents don't want me."

"They get over themselves." She smiled sheepishly. "He called tonight. He invites you to his dinner party."

"We're just friends, Mom."

"If you say so." She yawned and stood up. "I told him you date nice Korean man tomorrow, so he knows you not easy catch. Men don't like easy catch. No chase, no fun."

I laughed, embarrassed by her Cosmorality and that she had used it on Bobby. On the bright side, at least she didn't suspect he was gay. "There's no chase if there's no one doing any pursuing."

"Exactly." She creased her forehead. "Matchmake is too old fashioned for young people today." She relaxed her face into a smile. "So don't call him back until Sunday. Don't be too eager."

"I won't," I said truthfully.

She started walking to her bed and stopped, turning back around. "Also, please stop drinking and smoking."

CHAPTER 33

"Cranley meeting," Nina, Hell's assistant, shouted, walking down the hall. I was helping Dakota—she was talking to me again—dislodge the teeth of a stapler from the back of her skirt. I handed the stapler to her with the suggestion that she go back to making her staple jewelry if she was intent on wearing office supplies.

Sam and Chantal appeared in their doorways, last month's issue and a grease pencil in hand. The Cranley meeting was when someone from the eponymous market research firm went through the magazine page by page, reciting how the focus group rated each photo and story. Sam said it was a waste of time, but Hell insisted that all the editors hear the numbers. Sam, who'd been on the phone all morning, waved and hustled for the corridor, wanting to get a good seat. Chantal started to follow her but stopped and turned to me.

"Aren't you coming?"

"Me?" I asked.

Sam spun around.

"Nina was supposed to tell you you're invited. I suggested it to Hell in the elevator this morning."

I suppressed my smile, feeling Dakota's glare, and grabbed an issue. My hand hovered over a pen.

"Here," Chantal said, breaking her grease pencil and holding out a half to me.

Together we joined Sam and continued down the hall. Positioned between them, I didn't know what to say. Neither one said a word.

Hell's corner office was already packed. Sam took a folding chair from the stack and put it down in the first row, blocking the aisle. Chantal and I started a new row in the back. Paige, the fashion copy-writer, planted a chair next to me.

I'd been in Hell's office only once before, to deliver a new kind of padded bra, compliments of Sam. A year's worth of magazines lined one wall, each month's newsstand sales written in red grease pencil over the cover model's face. Competing magazine covers hung either above or below our issue, depending on their sales. À la Mode was at the top of each column except for the last three, where we were in the middle. The top seller for those three months, Vogue, had mus-taches and thick eyebrows drawn on it.

An oak desk, remarkable for the absence of a computer, stood in the corner in the front of the room, near the windows, and a large round table was next to it. Hell, the executive editor, art director, and managing editor—the top echelon of the masthead—sat at the table, along with a woman in a purple suit and burgundy-framed glasses. There was one empty seat. Sam, who was remonstrating with Nina, suddenly stood up and took it. Nina folded the chair Sam had just vacated and carried it back to the stack.

I glanced sidelong at Chantal, but she was bent forward, immersed in a conversation with the woman sitting in front of her. From what I gathered, she was telling Chantal we were in for a com-mand performance. Hell was in an especially bad mood; the meeting was starting later than scheduled because Mr. Klempner had sum-moned her upstairs, according to Nina, who would know.

"Would the last person to arrive please close the door," Hell announced.

The soft chatter came to a stop. Everyone looked around as though to say it wasn't her. Paige didn't budge.

Hell sighed. "Chantal?" She was sitting closest to the door. Hell motioned at it. When Chantal took her seat again, the meeting started.

Last month's issue had done even worse than the month before, though its cover had rated high. Hell sat with her arms crossed over her chest, frowning, while the marketing consultant gave the bad news and the staff wrote down the numbers with their grease pencils. For each photo or story, the researcher, Judith, in a voice stronger and deeper than I would have expected, said the percentages of people who found it very interesting, interesting, somewhat interesting, and not interesting. It didn't sound very scientific.

As Judith droned on, a dark cloud seemed to descend upon the room. Paige, who had brought a layout and was working on its copy, was commended for a story on women who found love after death—of their husband or boyfriend, I assumed—but for the most part people were singled out for humiliation. Whenever something got less than fifty percent in the very-interesting category, Hell would interrupt Judith and demand to know what went wrong from whoever worked on the noxious piece. Each exchange would end with Hell saying something like "No more incurable-disease stories" or "I don't want to see another damn freckle." The responsible editor or art designer would nod and furiously scribble down the mandate.

I looked over at Chantal to see she was defacing a model in a perfume ad. I recognized the handiwork. She and Paige seemed to be only half listening. They put aside their work, though, once we got to the fashion pages.

I had been thinking our numbers would be in the eighties or nineties; we were primarily a fashion book, after all. But I was wrong. They slipped down to the twenties and teens. That seemed to be normal, though, since Hell didn't stop Judith—until we came to a story declaring white and black checks to be the new black, called "Dare to Be Square." It rated a nine.

"Nan, what is the meaning of this?"

The room was quiet. Hell looked up from her copy of Judith's fat report and threw it across the table, where Nan would have been, where Sam was now.

Sam cleared her throat. "It looks like our readers don't like chess."

"It is a boy's game," someone piped in.

"Yeah, I could never beat my brother."

"I prefer checkers."

"Or Scrabble," Paige added.

"So then why did we run this story?" Hell asked, stabbing the table with her finger. "Whose idea was it?"

Sam cleared her throat again. "Checks were a hit at the shows. Everyone was falling out of their seats." She shrugged. "There's no accounting for taste."

"If that's the case, what am I paying you for?"

Everyone seemed to inhale en masse. Sam's back stiffened. After an eternity, she said, "I thought you were paying me for my taste. I thought our job was to tell the reader what she should like."

"No!" Hell threw the executive editor's pen at Sam, nearly hitting her. "That's the elitist, trickle-down attitude that I absolutely detest."

I looked down at the magazine on my lap, not being able to bear witnessing Sam's dressing-down, would-be saboteur of my first shoot that she was. The print on the page they were discussing came into focus. I'd never bothered to read the captions to fashion stories—like most readers, I suspected. This one was almost verbatim what I'd written for Paige, as were the ones on the following two spreads. And Hell didn't trust me to write.

"I liked the clothes," Sam said. "What more do you want from me?"

"Then maybe you're the wrong person for your job. I need someone with more common taste. I need someone from Topeka." Hell looked around the room, her eyes stopping on me. "Your assistant is from the Midwest." She pointed at me. "Would you wear these clothes?"

Everyone turned in her seat. I opened my mouth without an answer. The patterns were too busy, too attention-getting, but I couldn't make Sam look bad. I closed my mouth, then opened it again. "I think maybe instead of analyzing the clothes, we should question the method of rating here."

People were shooting me don't-go-there looks, but it was too late.

"I mean, Judith said that nine percent of people found this partic-ular dress very interesting. But what does 'very interesting' mean?

Couldn't the other ninety-one percent have been thinking, 'I'm already planning on buying this dress because I love it, so I'm skipping to the next page'?"

"It's possible," Judith said.

"Hmm," Hell said.

Chantal patted me on the arm.

Hell turned to Judith. "Then why are we asking this question? It's useless."

"It's generic, relevant to everything. No one is going to say they loved the story about liposuction or the latest date-rape drug. We can custom-tailor the wording to each story, though that's going to cost you more."

"Fine. Let's do it. Now, with all the department heads here." Hell pulled her chair closer to the table. She waved her hand at the rest of us. "You're all dismissed."

"I knew you'd do me proud," Chantal said before rushing out ahead of the crowd.

Paige, slipping past me, said, "Nice save."

"Nice copy," I said pointedly. She smiled, not comprehending my meaning.

I stood in the aisle, waiting for Sam, in the meantime getting several thumbs-up and hearty thank-yous for cutting the meeting short.

"Let's order lunch first thing," Sam said, sailing up to me, pulling up the rear. "I'm famished."

"You feel like eating?"

We stopped in Nina's outer office. "You mean that?" Sam asked, jerking her thumb back at Hell. "That was nothing." She put an arm around my shoulders. "It's how she weeds the weak from the strong."

"Ugh."

"You'd better get used to it, right, Nina?"

"You got that right," Nina said. She flipped open a date book. "You still want to meet with her this afternoon or do you want to give it a day?"

Sam sighed. "This afternoon. I want to clear the air before the weekend."

"The Southampton Animal Shelter fund-raiser," Nina said, nodding, licking her finger, and turning the page.

"Is that the big shindig you invited me to?" I asked. I hadn't realized it was tomorrow already. More face time with Hell.

Sam frowned. "Sorry, I thought you'd be busy with your mom, and so I asked Hell to go with me. I can't exactly withdraw the invite now. Next one, I promise."

"Sure," I said. She was right about my mother. Plus, despite her dismissal of Hell's scathing words, I didn't know that I wanted to be linked to her any further in Hell's mind.

We ambled down the hall, her arm still around me, heavy like a harness.

CHAPTER 34

I went straight to the restaurant from the office, the rest of the day having been taken up with returning the clothes from the shoot. An hour early, I passed the time pleasantly, talking to a recently retired pro football player. Flirting was fun when you felt like someone. He was rather old, though, and so fifteen minutes past the time what's-his-name was supposed to arrive, I started to think about leaving. But then I noticed a short Korean man in a sport jacket a size too big peering around the coatrack. How goofy. He had to be my man. I considered slipping out and telling my mother he stood me up, but I was in a festive mood—up for a night out.

I got his attention and he, looking embarrassed, waved back. As he walked to me, I told my conversation partner that my date had arrived. The burly man in a black turtleneck tried to get me to stay, and it took several minutes of maybe-next-timing to get my hand back. My date was standing next to me, grinning, by the time I did. With heels on, I had at least five inches on him. I would have to tell my mother I liked them tall.

"You must be Yeung-rok Yun . . . or Rok-yun Yeung," I said, offering my just-released hand.

He crushed it, not taking his eyes off the big man. "My friends call me Rock." It was a ridiculously macho nickname, but at least it was based on his real one. He leaned over and into my ear whispered, "Is that who I think it is?"

I thought the man had been giving me a line, but maybe he really was a football player. "You mean John John—?"

"Oh, my God!" Rock clapped a hand on the man. "John Johnson! I'm your biggest fan! I love you, man!"

Mr. Johnson looked put out by Rock's familiarity but softened as Rock reeled off a description of every game-saving catch the man had made in his long, long career. I fiddled with my purse and looked around the restaurant, waiting for the one-sided love fest to end. This was my first time at the four-star Michel Gerard. Majestic marble pillars, elaborate crystal chandeliers, white linen tablecloths. It was the kind of place meant for fur stoles and diamonds, the kind of place I could get used to.

"You're with her?" Mr. Johnson asked, tilting his head at me.

Rock looked confused. "Yeah, but let's pull up stools and talk some—"

"Man, are you crazy? What are you doing wasting your time shooting the shit with me? Get a table, and wine-and-dine this lady."

"Right." Rock smiled broadly, his chest filling out. "She is fine."

I rolled my eyes. Did he think I couldn't hear him?

They did some fraternity-brother-like handshake.

The maître d', who'd been nervously watching Rock, ready to step in at the slightest signal from Mr. Johnson, motioned for us to follow him.

"John Johnson. I can't believe this hand shook the hand of the all-time greatest pass receiver in the history of the NFL." Rock held his hand up, admiring it.

"You look like you're never going to wash it." I laughed. It was refreshing to see someone passionate about something. I wondered if I would be that way if I ever met Donna Karan or Muiccia Prada—or Gloria Steinem.

Rock grinned, looking very much like a little boy. "Nah, that would be silly." Still, when we reached our table, he used his other hand to pull my chair out for me.

Normally, I hated it when men did things like that—and I knew protesting put them off. But this time I kept my mouth shut and graciously sat down.

"Whoa, look at the prices!" Rock exclaimed, his nose in the menu. Faced with his bent head, I noticed his hair was thinning at the crown. He probably wore it buzzed for that reason. "You could feed a family of eight for the cost of one dish."

"Do you want to go somewhere else?" I asked, looking uneasily at the other tables. No one was paying attention to him.

"Nah, we're here. We might as well try it. It's said to be the best French in town, and that supposedly is saying a lot."

"So you're a connoisseur of French cuisine," I said, admiring the quality of the menu's black leather as I opened it. There was just one page, and it was in French. My foreign language skills were limited to German and Latin. We were in trouble.

"Do I give off that impression?" He sat up and straightened his jacket and tie. "Actually, I'm more of a steak-and-potatoes kind of guy. The lady behind the counter recommended this joint."

"The counter?"

"At Tiffany's, where I met your mom. She helped me pick out a brooch for my mom. She turned sixty last week."

"That's nice." I smiled, thinking mine would be lucky if she made it to that age. I should have insisted she tell me where she found him.

"Tell your ma she liked it a lot."

The waiter walked by and Rock put his thumb and index finger in his mouth to whistle. I lunged over the glasses and silverware and grabbed his sleeve.

"Why don't we wait for him to come back."

He eyed my hand, still on his wrist. I let go and settled back in my chair, blushing.

The sommelier arrived with the wine list. Rock selected the cheapest bottle.

"So what do you do?" I asked once we were alone again.

"Your ma didn't tell you I'm an analyst? She grilled me like the KGB."

"She's charming that way. But she didn't share the info with me."

"She showed me a picture of you. I thought it was a scam at first, but then I thought, what the hell? If you're a dog, I'll just go to the bathroom and not come back."

"So if you're gone for a long time, I'll know to get the check."

"Nah, you're all right." He patted my hand. "But what's your story? Why is your ma getting you dates? I'd think a chick like you could get her own."

"You know how it is. My mom wants me to marry a Korean."

Rock jerked back, holding his hands up in the air. "Hey, she never said the M word to me. I agreed to just a date."

"That's okay," I said, laughing. He looked terrified. "I'm not looking to get married either. I'm just doing this for my mother."

He put his hands down, looking relieved. "Broads are always trying to tie me down, but the Rock has got to roll."

A skinny, raven-haired waiter came to take our order. "It's about time, *mon frère*," Rock said. He leaned over and explained behind his hand that that meant "my brother." Back to the waiter: "What's your name?"

"My name?" the waiter asked.

"Right. Your name," Rock said.

"My name. Is it necessary for you to have it? Is there a problem? I will get the maître d'."

"There's no problem. I'm just trying to get to know you. Anyone who handles my food, I like to be on a first-name basis. I'm Rock and she's Ginger."

I attempted a smile. As embarrassing as he was, I had to hand it to him. He was the most American Korean I'd ever met.

"Okay, you want to be friends. I am Jacques."

Rock stuck his hand out and Jacques shook it with a limp wrist.

"I suspect this is your first experience of fine French cuisine. I will recom—"

"Jack, the lady and I will have two of your juiciest steaks."

"I will?" I asked.

"But we have so many delightful specials." The waiter flipped the menu open, clearly irritated by the interruption.

"We'll stick to the steak. Well done. I don't want to see any red."

"Actually—"

"No red?" Jacques cut me off. He looked as though he'd just been asked if he was British. "Would you like catsup with that?"

"You mean ketchup? On steak?" Rock shrugged. "Okay, I'll give it a try." He winked at me. "When in Rome."

"Sir, I cannot insult my chef with your order. Perhaps you would be happier at the steak house down the street." He put his hands on his hips and struck a defiant pose.

Rock threw his napkin on the table and started to rise. Hastily, I put a hand on his arm and turned to Jacques. "On second thought, we'll have whatever you recommend." I wanted nothing more than to leave, but it would be too embarrassing to decamp now. The other tables would see us as a couple of Asians out of our element.

Jacques stole a look at Rock, then bowed to me. "Very good, mademoiselle." He went over his suggestions and I nodded without listening. He rapidly walked away.

"What an asshole." Rock replaced his napkin on his lap. "You
know he's just going to bring the most expensive dishes on the
menu."

"It's a pricey place." I took a sip of wine. "I'm sure whatever he
brings will be fine." I drained my glass. The sommelier magically
appeared at my elbow and refilled it.

"If it's not, I'm not leaving a tip."

Soon a pumpkin soup with chestnut ravioli arrived and occupied
us for a good ten minutes. I ate quickly, almost compulsively, trying to
hurry the meal along. At first Rock only dipped his spoon in his soup,
but once he got his first taste, he picked up speed. We ate in appreciative silence.

The first course was followed by a beet, frisee, and Roquefort
cheese salad. Slowed down by the unwieldiness of the frisee, we took
stabs at talking. We discussed New York, the heat, and his summer
share on Shelter Island. By the time the busboy took away our plates,
the conversation was on an even keel.

"Have you been living here long?" I asked, impressed by his
insider knowledge.

"About ten years in Manhattan. But I'm from Long Island."

"Third generation?"

"Me? I came here when I was six."

"That's right, your name. Why didn't you change it?"

"What's wrong with it?"

"Nothing. I would just think you got teased for it."

He thumped his fist like it was a football. "No one made fun of me
twice."

"But doesn't it give you trouble at work?"

"These days people don't have a problem with Asian names, especially in business. Yeung-rok, Rock, Rocky. I like my name. You must
have a Korean one."

"My middle name." I didn't even like to say it.

"It was once your first name."

"Not since becoming a cognitive person." Me-sook was the baby who had come on the plane in her father's arms. She was disconnected from me.

"What is it?" he asked.

I shook my head.

"C'mon. You know mine."

"That's because it's your name."

"Okay, then tell me what it rhymes with."

I started to run through the alphabet, just to know the answer. But I stopped when I realized I was coming up with gibberish. "In English? Nothing."

"No, not in English. In Korean." He looked at me like I was stupid.

Funny, I had never thought of Korean words as rhyming. They were just a stream of sounds. I didn't even know when one word ended and the next began. "I don't know."

"You just don't want to tell me because then I'll guess it."

"No, I really don't know."

"Right." His refusal to believe me made me feel weird about myself. What was wrong with me that I didn't even know what Korean words rhymed with my name? It was a child's game. I certainly knew what words rhymed with Ginger—or half rhymed. Finger, linger, ringer, singer.

The foie-gras-stuffed chicken arrived. Rock dug in. I admired the expert way he handled his utensils, deftly cutting the meat, then pushing a little chicken, cranberry, and spinach onto his fork with his knife. Though I'd grown up using a fork, it wasn't until college that I realized Americans didn't bite food off it. I'd made my mother buy a set of steak knives, but like Sam's smoke rings, I'd come too late to them.

Rock looked up and smiled. Still munching, he put his utensils down and took a swig of wine.

"Did you say it was your mom's birthday last week?"

He nodded, his mouth full of food again. "We rented one of those boats that circle the entire island of Manhattan. We had like two hundred people on board."

"That sounds nice."

"Mom's worth it." He continued chewing. "My sister and brother-in-law kicked in five hundred, but I paid the rest."

"You have a sister?" I asked before he could tell me how much he'd paid. "Older or younger?"

"Farrah." He nodded. "Younger."

"She has an American name."

"She couldn't take the teasing," he said, shrugging. "After her favorite Charlie's angel."

"She got to name herself?"

"You didn't?"

"It's not exactly normal to pick your own name." I would have chosen something less feminine, less exotic-sounding, for myself. Robin, Chris, or even Keith. I knew a female Keith at Madison; no one ever questioned or challenged her.

"It is if your parents barely speak English."

I nodded in understanding, remembering how, as a teenager, I'd had to deal with the car mechanic and do my mother's taxes. Maybe it wasn't so cool to name yourself. At least I hadn't had to do that.

"So your sister's married. Does she have kids?"

"Yep." His eyes brightened. "Wanna see them?" Before I could answer, he whipped out his wallet.

"That's Madonna. She's three. And that's Simon. He's one."

They looked like that Sally girl from the church play, with light brown hair and eyes. I politely smiled at the photograph. The children were cute, but I couldn't help but feel for them, knowing what identity confusion and struggles lay ahead. To be so thoroughly split to the core. "Their dad's white. Your parents must have been unhappy."

"My parents? No. They like Brendan. His parents? Yes, but they came around."

"Your folks are unusual."

"Just realistic. They brought us here. What can they expect?"

Maybe they didn't care what Farrah did. She didn't continue the family line. It was sexist, the one double standard my mother wasn't guilty of.

I wondered if George had kids, and if they looked like Farrah's.

"Don't you like your food?" Rock pointed to my barely touched chicken breast. His plate was empty.

"I'm not really hungry." I'd managed to down only half my sandwich at lunch, but I was too intrigued to eat.

Rock eyed me. "Are you one of those girls who are scared to death of being fat?"

"Me?" I asked, astonished. "No."

Rock twisted his mouth as he wiped his plate with bread. "I suppose you wouldn't tell me if you were."

"I'm really not." I'd tried to diet for only a weekend and it was for a specific purpose. I hadn't even gotten on a scale.

"You know, most guys don't think bony is sexy." He pointed his glass at me. "We like something to squeeze."

"You don't have to lecture me." I laughed. "I'm well aware that fat is a feminist issue."

"And still you don't eat."

"I eat. Trust me, I eat." I grabbed the heel of the baguette and slathered it with what was left of the butter. I took a big bite.

"Much better." He smiled. "Let's get you dessert."

I didn't want something sweet and rich, but when the waiter came back, I ordered chocolate mousse just to prove Rock wrong. He requested the apple tart.

"So, how did you get to be so enlightened?" I asked after the waiter left.

"I'm just a twenty-first-century kind of guy."

"You are unusual." I thought football fans were, by definition, lugheads.

"You're really hung up on this Korean thing."

"I'm not."

"We're not all old-fashioned sexist pigs."

"I know," I said, taken aback.

"Do you? I've only just met you, and don't take this the wrong way, but you're kind of prejudiced against us Koreans."

"I am not prejudiced against Koreans." How could I not take that the wrong way?

Rock shrugged. "You remind me of women I knew in college."

Dessert arrived and I waited for Jacques to leave. "How so?"

Rock cut into the pastry, ignoring my question. "This is one good apple pie." He offered me a forkful, but I shook my head.

"Rock, how?"

"Hmm? Oh, right." He wiped his mouth. "The way you're self-loathing." He picked up his fork again and pointed it at me. "I bet you wish you were white."

"What! I don't. I'm proud to be Korean." I'd never voiced or even thought that sentiment, but in that instant, my back up against the wall, I felt it deeply was true.

"Could've fooled me."

I tossed my napkin onto the table. I didn't like my middle name and I didn't know what Korean words rhymed with it and I didn't like Korean men and I steered clear of Koreans, but that didn't mean I wanted to be white, that I wanted to be someone else.

"If I hated Koreans, would I be here having dinner with you?"

"You said you're doing this for your mother."

"I did?" I was getting all mixed up. I wasn't used to having to defend my ethnic pride. "Well, she adamantly wants me to marry a Korean, while, I might add, your parents don't. Maybe you and your family are self-loathing."

"No, we're open-minded. The Rock is an equal opportunity lover."

"Or an all-around self-hater. If you loved yourself, wouldn't you want to be with someone like you? To have children who looked like you?"

Rock held his last piece of pie midway to his mouth, his eyebrow arched. "What's that supposed to mean? You got something against my niece and nephew?"

"No," I faltered. "I'm just saying that I'm glad to be a full-blooded Korean."

"I don't believe what I'm hearing. You know the old prejudice against mixed marriages doesn't apply to our generation—and shouldn't to anyone's."

"I know."

"But you look down on Madonna and Simon."

"Not down. I feel for them. You and I are split culturally. But they're split physically, genetically."

"What difference does it make?"

"At least we can pass for Koreans."

"You've clearly never been to Korea. Over there, they'd treat you just as badly as they'd treat my niece and nephew. Or worse. My niece and nephew are bilingual."

"Well, I'm not talking about there. I'm talking about here."

"Here my niece and nephew are happy, normal kids with two heritages. They're not split. They're blended. And if you ask me, they're better off for it. At least their parents speak English and grew up here."

I'd never thought of it that way.

"Man, do you have issues."

"And you don't?"

He pushed away his empty plate and leaned back in his chair. "Do I look like I do?"

No, he didn't. He was a happily adjusted second-generation Korean American. He was like a revelation to me.

"So tell me how you wound up so healthy." I scooted my chair around the table, closer to him.

Rock watched me with an amused expression. He shrugged. "I've never thought about it."

"Think about it now."

"No, I mean I've never agonized over my Korean-ness or American-ness. I am who I am."

"Never? Not even when you were getting into fights at school?"

"Sure, when I was a little punk. But then I got older and more important things came up."

"What could be more important?"

He looked down at his zipper and then grinned at me. "That came up."

I pushed my chair away from him. The uncontemplated life was hardly the answer. I looked around the room for the waiter.

"And football tryouts, then practice, then games. Did I tell you I was all-state wide receiver and won a full scholarship to Florida State?"

"No, you didn't. I've never known a Korean to play football, but I'm not surprised." I got Jacques's attention and signaled for the check. "You seem the type."

"Thanks. Football made me the man I am." He pointed his finger at me. "Maybe that's the answer to your question. A team sport is how I came to be so well grounded. Do you play one?"

"Me? No."

"I didn't think so. But you should try one. I have a friend— Korean, by the way—who plays field hockey in Prospect Park every Saturday. She could hook you up."

"No thanks."

He nodded knowingly. "You don't want muscles."

"No, it's just not me. I'm not a field hockey kind of person."

"What kind of person are you?"

He was also a second-generation Korean American. It didn't define him or what he could or couldn't do. "Busy," I finally said.

The bill was handed to Rock. While he studied it, I got ready to leave, putting my purse on my lap. The evening had been eye-opening, entertaining even, but not one I wanted to repeat. Rock slammed the black book shut and leaned over conspiratorially.

"You know, this isn't going to work between the two of us," he said.

"No?"

"Nah, you're not athletic. And you're too traditional for me—the way you order expensive meals and hardly eat, and let your mom arrange your dates and everything."

"Hmm." I took the check. "Let me get this."

His eyes widened. "Are you sure?"

"I insist." I put my mother's credit card down.

CHAPTER 35

When I came back from my run late Saturday morning, my mother was hanging up the phone—in her haste, missing the cradle at first. I lifted an inquiring eyebrow, but she ignored me. She was probably booking her flight home. I leaned toward her to give her a kiss. I had woken with a headache, but the run had done me good. I felt limber, loose, energized.

While pounding the dirt path, circling glistening water, I, my mind, had ranged over what Rock had said. Perhaps I was more con-flicted about my ancestry than I'd admitted. Perhaps the childhood perception that what was American was cool and what was Korean wasn't still lingered in my beliefs. Perhaps there were things about being second-generation that I disliked. But that did not mean I secretly hated myself or my mother. Everyone had things about them-selves they didn't like. Everyone had ambivalences, inconsistencies. People who didn't were either self-deluded or bores. Surrounded by still air and silent tall buildings, I realized that I was actually pretty together. For all my feelings of dividedness, I was fundamentally whole.

My mother held off my kiss with a straight arm. "You sweaty. You shouldn't go out look like that."

"I was running," I said, wiping my face with the bottom of my T-shirt.

"You can't run more like a lady? Why you have to exercise? Your leg get bigger."

"And stronger."

"That why you exercise?"

She was right to be incredulous. "No, actually. I run because I like to. It makes me feel good. It clears my head."

My mother weighed my answer, her lips turned down. Slowly, she nodded her acceptance. She smiled. "How was your date?"

I pulled up a stool at the kitchen counter. "It was a no-go. We didn't see eye to eye on a lot of things."

"So sit down. I know he short, but you only notice when you stand."

"He was too short." I laughed. "But that's not what I meant. I was too Korean in some ways, and not enough in others. We're just too different from each other."

"But you both raised here. You have same background."

"Even brothers and sisters turn out differently."

"I know," my mother said, casting her eyes down. "But I don't understand. He spoke perfect English. He bought a present for his mom."

"Yeah, he told me how he met you," I said wryly. "No more of that."

"No more," she agreed, shaking her head. "That don't work with young people." She sighed as though the end of civilization were at hand. "Young people so fussy." She picked up a Korean newspaper from the counter and opened it to the classifieds. "They want Knicks fan, they want soft heart, they want soul mate. It miracle anybody get together."

"What—are—you—doing—reading personal ads?"

"That next stage." She busied herself with the paper. "Mrs. Min's daughter met her husband that—"

"I am not answering any personal ads! I'm not that desperate."

My mother peered over the paper, giving me a who-are-you-kidding look. She put the paper down slowly. "Of course we don't call them. We put ad in. They chase us."

"Mother!"

"What?"

"It's not going to work. I . . . can't read Korean." I just barely stopped myself from saying I wasn't attracted to Koreans.

"I translate."

"But if they read Korean, they're going to be just like—"

"Their mom translate for them too. Now, how I should describe you? I already started." She reached for her pad of paper.

"Instead of looking for a son-in-law, maybe you should put your energy into looking for your true son."

She looked up. "George? He has nothing to do. He long ago lost."

Not if I could help it. The rift was a consequence of our being Korean, but the continuing separation wasn't. Running my last lap around the reservoir, I'd pictured her cuddling her grandkids as she'd done with me, washing their kimchi, and crooning the refrain to "Old MacDonald" with a puzzled look on her face. I assumed George had children; he'd been married for thirteen years.

She sat in silence, musing. "Why you say George? He call you?"

"No," I said carefully. "But we could call him." I knew why she'd never tried; she didn't want me to think it was okay to follow his example. But I was an adult now.

"Bad idea," she said at last.

"I'm not going to do what he did."

She stood up straight. "Brother is not the same as husband. You need husband." She put her hand on her forehead. "I don't know. Maybe I should said yes to Mr. Quong." She frowned. "Then you don't think single is so good."

"Mr. Quong asked you to marry him!" I didn't know who he was, but the very idea of someone liking my mother in that way astonished—mortified—me. "When?"

My mother blushed, realizing her slip. "Long time ago. You were in second grade. I didn't take seriously. George didn't like him."

Thank God George was around to put a stop to that. The idea of a stepfather, even a would-be stepfather, appalled me. Apparently, control over spouses went both ways.

"It wasn't a mistake," I said to reassure her, wanting to stamp it in her brain that it would never be a mistake. Maybe I was reacting like a child, but my pact, my resolve, depended upon her being single too. "I would still be the way I am—except I'd probably like Korean men less."

My mother jerked up. "You don't like Korean men?"

I swallowed hard. In all of the morning's deep reflecting, I hadn't come to terms with that.

"Aha! I thought so. You don't like Korean men. You rejected Bobby and Yeung-rok first."

"That's not true. The lack of interest was mutual with both."

"He called though."

"Rock?"

"No, Bobby. He called again this morning." She wagged her finger at me. "He likes you."

"It's not what you think. He wants to be friends."

"Friends first. Boyfriend later. It better that way. That the way young people do it." She smiled at her wisdom.

If she'd only tried to be this hip, tried to understand young people, with George. "Mother, you need to accept the fact that Bobby and I are never going to happen. He doesn't like me. He never will."

"How do you know?"

"Because he's—" The disclosures were getting out of hand.

Bobby's secret was his to tell. "Because like you said the other day, I'm odd."

"Him too."

"What do you mean?" I asked, wondering if she suspected the truth.

She shrugged. "I just say put two single socks together. They make a pair."

"A mismatched pair."

"But at least a pair. Give him a chance. I don't live forever." She said it like a threat. "Don't do like me." Her voice cracked.

"I won't," I said, thinking of George again. "I have to go to the office."

CHAPTER 36

"Ginger?" A baby wailed in the background. "George isn't here, and I can't talk right now. I'm glad you called though. Really really glad."

I didn't know what to say and regretted my haste. This was the seventh number I'd tried, and I'd thought out only my introduction, that I was Ginger looking for my brother, George. A couple of men had offered to be my brother and one woman had grilled me suspiciously, but overall they'd all quickly informed me I had the wrong George Lee. When I'd dialed the number in Chappaqua, I'd half given up. But I'd found him, and the realization overwhelmed me. I sunk back in my office chair.

"But I hate to let you go. I can't believe you called. I've been begging George to try to find you, especially since the baby came.

But he was afraid you wouldn't want to talk to him, that he'd waited too long. I told him he was wrong. That even though I'd never met you, I knew you'd want to reconnect. I've seen pictures of you—when you were a kid, of course. I can't wait to meet you."

The baby interrupted her nervous rambling, shrieking now. "Shhh, Ginger, shhh."

I knew I was stunned by the enormity of what I'd just done, but I was confused. "I didn't say anything."

She laughed, making the baby scream even louder. "No, I wasn't talking to you. The baby's name is Ginger. We named her after you."

I felt my body go slack and gripped the armrest with one hand to stop myself from sliding out of my chair. All these years I'd thought George had forgotten me, but he'd named his daughter after me. It was just so sad I'd taken until now to reach out to him, that it had taken a bad date, a failed search for a husband, to put me on the phone.

"She's not normally like this. I don't know what's gotten into her," George's wife said. I was loath to ask her name.

"I . . . I have a niece," I finally croaked.

"Two, actually. We have another daughter, Betty, named after your mom. We thought it would be a peace offering, but she never responded to the birth announcement. Beth's twelve, going on thirteen. We call her Beth."

"She's a teenager!" She was nearly as old as I was when I last saw George. It dawned on me that they must have gotten pregnant their senior year. I felt somewhat jealous, resentful, of the girl.

"You didn't know?"

My mother must have thought I was too young at the time to tell me. It would have been nice to know why George got married when he did.

The baby was really screaming her lungs out now. "I better go. But give me your number. I'll have George call you as soon as he gets back. He just went to the grocery store to get snacks for the baby-sitter tonight. He won't be more than half an hour. He's going to be so excited when he hears you called."

I gave her the number at work.

"You're in New York? Oh my God! We're only a fifty-minute train ride away. You could come here now! But wait, we're going over to the Russells for dinner. George will have to sort this out."

We hung up. I didn't know what to do with myself. I went into Sam's office to soothe my nerves with a cigarette.

There were five butts in the ashtray when the sound of people talking and laughing drew me out of my trance and toward the voices.

It was Ann and June.

"What . . . what are you doing here?" I asked.

June seemed surprised but happy to see me. Ann looked wary.

"Hi, Ginger," June said. "We're . . . ah . . . waiting for Chantal. She went to show Bob where the men's room is."

"Bobby's here?"

"We're going to a rug sample sale, but Chantal left the address here," June said. "Do you want to come?" Ann nudged her, snorting.

"Thanks, but no thanks," I said. "I'm waiting for a phone call." There was no need to be cryptic. "From my brother."

"George?"

I turned around to find Bobby and Chantal behind me. I gave them both a big smile and said hello.

"I thought you and your mother weren't talking to him."

"Why not?" June asked.

"He married an American." Given the people I was with, I added, "Woman."

June nodded in understanding.

"Good for him," Ann said. "Score one for the Americans!" She lifted her arms as though her team had just made a touchdown. She was clearly acting out whatever resentment she still felt for the treatment she'd received at the hands of the Ohs. Chantal, who was now standing next to her, stepped on her toes.

"Don't mind her," June said. "She's been drinking."

"I heard that," Ann said. "It was just two bloody Marys."

"And my mimosa," Bobby reminded her.

"Oh, yeah." Ann grinned.

"We should get going," Chantal said, putting her arm around Ann and trying to steer her toward the hall. Over her shoulder, she tossed, "As long as you're here, there's a pile of magazines on Dakota's desk that needs photocopying."

I was willing to be her drudge on shoots but not in the office—and certainly not on weekends.

"But I'm talking to Ginger," said Ann, refusing to move. "I want to congratulate her on stealing Bobby. You are more woman than me." Giggling, she cupped a breast and puckered her lips in a kiss at me.

I made a face.

"Ignore her," Bobby said.

"I didn't steal him. It's not like you two were a real couple."

"So he claims to relieve his conscience," Ann said, throwing Bobby a pout. She stomped her foot like a sullen child. "I was looking forward to walking down the aisle in a beautiful white dress and having kimchi thrown at me."

"All right. It's time to go," Chantal tried again.

"But you're still going to do it," June interjected. "Wear a white dress. With Chantal."

Chantal angrily bit her lip. Ann stopped playing with her breast. Bobby just stared at the calendar on the wall.

"Oh, come on, guys," June said. "Ginger knows you're together. She caught you looking at wedding dresses, she knows you live together, you're both single. Why else would Ann do Bob that big a favor?"

I had been right.

"Well, if she didn't know before, she knows now," Ann mumbled. Chantal's wrath was palpable and sobering. June stared at them both.

"You don't have to worry, Chantal. I'm not going to tell anyone, not even Sam."

Chantal's eyes narrowed to slits. I hoped she didn't think I was making a veiled threat.

"Chantal, let up on her," Bobby said. "She doesn't know you well enough to know you're just being an idiot."

I gave him a look of thanks, adding, "I've suspected for a while and haven't said anything. My mother guessed too."

"She did?" Bobby asked, alarmed. "Does she know about—?"

"No, no," I said. "She doesn't have a clue. She still thinks there's hope for us." June elbowed him.

"Oh, what's the big deal?" Ann asked. "You should come out to your parents. And you too, Chantal, to your office. I'm tired of being a secret."

"I'm going to Vermont, aren't I?" Chantal retorted.

"My parents would never understand," Bobby said almost at the same time. "They're not American."

"Only after I agreed to marry Bob," Ann said to Chantal. "You said yes only to stop me from marrying another person." She held her palm out to silence Chantal before she could respond. She turned to Bob. "You make it sound like there are no gay men in Korea. You know, living in America didn't do this to you. You're not the only Korean queer out there."

"Yeah, I bet there are even more gays in your family," added June.

"If there are, they've been disowned."

"So be disowned," Ann said. "Fuck 'em if they won't accept you."

"It's not that simple. We've had this conversation hundreds of times."

"Why not?"

"It just isn't."

I was surprised that they didn't know what I knew—that Bobby was afraid his father would blame his mother.

"At least try," Ann persisted. "Look at Chantal's parents. They came around."

"What's that supposed to mean? My parents have always liked you," Chantal said.

"Only because they thought for years that I was just a friend."

"But they know the truth now, and they said they'd come to the wedding."

"I don't want to discuss this now." She jerked away from Chantal, losing her balance for a second. To Bobby: "So you're going to continue living a lie and get Ginger to be your beard?"

My eyes widened. I thought I'd made it clear that I wasn't interested.

"I was willing to help you at first," Ann continued, "but now that I've met your folks . . . It's time for them to have a rude awakening. They could use some cold water, along with boiling oil, tar, and feathers, thrown at them."

"Leave him alone," June said. I agreed but remained quiet. I got the sense they were just bickering like four old married people, eternally going over the same disagreements. It took real confidence in each other's friendship; I'd never interacted with Sam like that.

"I thought you wanted him to come out to his parents," Ann said.

"I do, but he's not going to do it," June said. "His mother is going to continue trying to set him up and he's eventually going to give in and marry someone none of us can stand. I'd rather he marry Ginger. She'd benefit as much as him."

"I'm touched," I said.

"I like you. We all like you." June put her arms around Bobby and Chantal. "Don't you want to join our little family?"

"Don't do it," Ann said. "Don't be fooled by her sweetness."

"Hey!"

"And don't let your guard down around him—or before you know it, you'll find yourself a married woman."

"He has a really nice apartment," cooed June.

"Sorry, I haven't changed my mind," I said. "The answer is still no."

"Bob here doesn't understand that when a woman says no, she doesn't mean maybe," Chantal said.

Bobby grinned. "I haven't exactly been in the situation where I'd find out."

"Well, this woman is saying no and means it," I said. "But thanks for asking. You may be the only one to ever ask."

"Then don't say no," said June. "Say you'll think about it."

"Think about how happy you'll make your mother," Bobby said. "She likes me."

"I've got other plans for her," I said. Bobby gave me an inquiring look. "My brother. I'm waiting for him to call to set up a surprise reunion." That reminded me why I was there. I took a couple of steps back to listen better for the phone.

"Are you sure you want to do that?" June asked. "Surprise her?"

"Yeah, maybe you should consult her," Bobby said. "Make sure she wants to see George."

I didn't want to give her the chance to say no. "She'll want to see him."

Bobby nodded. "Yeah, Korean mothers love their sons more than life itself."

"Not just Korean," Chantal said ruefully.

"So how are you going to surprise her?" Ann asked, rubbing her hands together.

"I'm just going to bring her to a restaurant and have George there."

"Taking a page out of her own book," Ann said. "I love it."

"But she's pretty sharp," Bobby interjected. "Won't she suspect something's up?"

I had stupidly already suggested calling George. "I suppose I could lead her to believe we're having dinner with you." I looked at Bobby. "Is that okay?"

"Sure," he said. "But how are you going to do that?"

"You could call when I'm not home and leave a message confirming for whatever night we're going to dinner."

"You're craftier than I thought," Chantal said. I took it as a compliment.

Bobby nodded. "I can do that. Just let me know what night."

"I'll call you tonight. It'll be sometime this week, I hope."

"Sounds like a plan," June said. "I'd love to know how it plays out." She smiled. "You can tell us when you come to Bob's for dinner."

"I called you and left a message"—Bobby smiled—"with your mom."

"Ooh, are you going to make bouillabaisse?" Ann asked.

"Sure," I said. My phone rang. "I've got to get this." I ran for it, wondering how I was going to talk to my brother for the first time in thirteen years with them there.

"Guys, we should get going to that rug sale," Bobby said, herding them toward the hall.

"How's Friday?" June shouted.

"Great. I should have a happy story to tell by then." I brought the phone up to my ear.

CHAPTER 37

❧

"I got into Harvard and I beat you by sixty points on the SATs," I blurted out. After an initial burst of each of us rushing to exclaim how great it was to hear the other's voice and not believing how many years had passed, the conversation had dwindled to a series of little bursts with the intervening lulls growing longer and longer.

This wasn't the deliriously happy reunion I'd always imagined. I was nervous like I was on a first date.

"Really? That's great. We were two for two, after all. I tried calling the switchboard there the year you'd be a freshman. They didn't have you listed."

"That's because I went to Madison. Mom wouldn't let me go out of state."

"Oh."

I wanted to kick myself. The time for recriminations was over. "You tried to reach me?"

"Well, I was trying to find out if you'd gone to Harvard. I don't know that I was actually going to call. You were still under Mom's wing."

My turn to say "Oh." I didn't tell him I still was—or point out that I'd been out of college for six years.

After a pause he said, "But you made it out. What are you doing in New York?"

I briefly told him about my magazine career, explaining that I was still only entry level because I'd loitered in academia for five years.

"She didn't insist you go to law or medical school?" He sounded angry.

"She tried, but she eventually gave in."

"That doesn't sound like her."

"Well, you know, she's changed in some ways."

Another long pause, then: "I'm sorry for everything, Ginger."

It was what I had longed to hear, and yet the words took me off guard. The old hurt surged in my chest and licked the back of my throat. I waited for it to subside so I could speak.

"For what? You did what you had to do." I kind of felt that way now that I knew the circumstances. They weren't star-crossed lovers, just badly protected ones.

"Still, my fight was with her, not with you. I shouldn't have cut you off. But you were just a kid, and I still had to go to med school, and Karen was pretty freaked out—Beth was on the way."

"It's all in the past. But thanks." I cleared my throat. "I did always wonder why you never called me even just to say good-bye."

"It was an insane time, and I guess I didn't think the break would be permanent. But then time kept on passing, and contacting you seemed harder and harder to do. But I never stopped thinking about you. We named our second daughter after you."

"Yeah, your wife . . . Karen . . . told me."

"She reminds me of you when you were a baby. She's ticklish and she giggles a lot. You have to meet her—and everyone else."

"Yes. Yes. We have to get together." I was glad we were moving on to my plan. "I know you can't do tonight. But how about tomorrow night?"

"Hmm, I think we have plans. Let me ask." I heard him consult Karen, who must have been standing next to him. "How about Wednesday?" he asked, returning to me.

"You can't do sooner?"

More muffled whispers. "No, I'm afraid we can't."

After thirteen years, I supposed four days weren't long to wait.

"I can't believe I'm going to see you," he said. "What do you look like?"

"Sort of the same, but, you know, taller." He laughed. I tried to give him a better picture. "I guess I look like Mom. That's what people say, at least."

"That's too bad."

"What do you mean? Mom's good-looking."

"I know, but that woman is . . . well, as long as it's just your appearance that resembles her."

This was not good. I'd assumed that the mere act of contacting him would dissolve all hard feelings between everyone, but clearly, he was still angry with her. Well, I was planning a surprise for her; I could make the surprise for both of them.

"You can decide how little or how much I am like Mom on Wednesday. When and where?" I needed to firm up these details now, so he wouldn't call the apartment.

He suggested some overpriced tourist trap; he was a typical suburbanite who rarely came into the city.

"Ew, no," I said. Besides, our mother would feel more comfortable in a Korean place. Because I knew so few, I suggested the Secret Garden, the Ohs' favorite restaurant. After a long silence, during which I guessed Karen was shaking her head no and George was nodding his head yes, George said it was fine with them—that he couldn't remember the last time he'd had kimchi. I told him I'd make the reservation and we said good-bye.

I stared at the phone for a long time before picking it up again to call the restaurant and then to leave a message for Bobby. The plan was under way.

CHAPTER 38

Monday finally arrived. I was never so happy to go to the office, walk past the sentry of smokers in front of the building, see the photos of half-naked women in suggestive poses along the hall walls. It had been hard spending the rest of the weekend with my mother without telling her I had spoken to George. She'd even wanted to go to the Secret Garden on Sunday night. Immersed in a copy of *Washington Square* I'd dug out of one of the boxes—now that my life was back on track, I found I could read novels again—I'd slipped and said we were going Wednesday.

"Why? What Wednesday?" she'd asked.

"I can't say. It's a surprise."

"Ginger." My mother had stood in between me and the light, her hands on her hips. "You should know better. I find everything out."

Not everything, I hoped.

Now I stepped off the elevator and greeted Rosie. Talking on the phone, she put her pen down and shoved a handful of messages at me. She pointed to her phone; Sam's and my lines were flashing.

I ran down the hall to my desk. The phones were ringing like church bells gone mad. My mother couldn't have possibly placed an ad already. I grabbed the phone. The other lines continued to ring.

A man cleared his throat. "Uh, Ginger?"

I looked down at the phone. I didn't recognize the number on the caller ID. "Yes?" Dakota's phone, several feet away from me, was also ringing now. She was nowhere in sight, Sam wasn't in yet, and Chantal's door was closed.

"It's Tarn. I gather I'm calling at a bad time."

I sat down. "It's okay. I can talk." I swiveled in my chair, turning my back to the phone. The other callers could phone back. I waited for him to speak.

"I just wanted to tell you I enjoyed meeting you the other day."

"Me too. I mean, I enjoyed meeting you. I've already met myself, of course." I could feel my cheeks heating up.

Tarn laughed. "I told Chantal I wanted you at the studio Wednesday. You did great work, though that's not the only reason."

I inhaled sharply.

"Do you know if you're coming?"

"Chantal said I was."

"Excellent. Maybe we can go out for a drink afterward."

"To discuss photography?" I asked, recovering myself.

After a beat: "Sure. And magazines. The magazine world. I know a lot of fashion directors I can put you in touch with."

I turned back to my desk and the phone. Another of Sam's callers had hung up, but the line that had gone dark was lit again. What was going on? "That sounds great. I'll see you Wednesday." As soon as he said bye, I switched to one of Sam's lines—to hear the caller hang up. I answered the other line.

"Is this Sam Starre's office?" a familiar man's voice asked.

"Yes." I tapped a pen on a pink message pad.

"You should say so when you answer. You sound like you're at home."

"She's not in yet," I said, ignoring his unsolicited advice.

"Then please tell her that Walker called. Walker Prescott."

He had some nerve, lecturing me about my professionalism when he was making a personal call to her office.

"Will she know what the call is regarding?" I asked pointedly.

"Yes."

The other two lines continued to ring. I didn't have time for this. "I'll give her the message." He started to say something, but I hung up on him. It was rude of me, but if he told Sam, and he seemed like the kind of jerk who would, she would understand.

I picked up another line.

"Hello?" a woman said. "Sam?"

"Sam's not here. Can I take a message?"

"Yes, tell her Ella Pritchard called."

I had chatted with Ella at several of Sam's parties, but I didn't acknowledge that we knew each other. Like Tatiana, the editor in chief of *Beautiful Bride* never remembered having met me. She probably wanted to discuss another fund-raising event.

I wrote down the message and put it and Walker's on Sam's desk. I was finished taking messages for the morning.

When I came back to my desk, Dakota was bent over at it, scribbling something. She turned, hearing me move my chair.

"Ginger! I've been looking for you all morning. I'm going nuts setting up for this brunch bash. Can you get the cake from downstairs? The delivery guy has been waiting for fifteen minutes."

I sighed. I was really ready for that promotion. Associate editors didn't have to answer other people's phones—or help set up for the monthly party.

"Hurry. We don't have a lot of time." She grabbed my hand and stuffed a wad of cash in it. "That's two hundred thirty for the cake and tip. Take the freight elevator so no one sees you. It's supposed to be a surprise."

I looked down at the money in my hand. The cakes at our parties weren't usually this extravagant. "What's the special occasion? Who's the surprise for?"

Dakota's eyes bugged out. "Sam didn't call you at home?"

"Why? What's happened to Sam?"

Right then Nina knocked on the glass wall and pointed to her watch. "Sam's coming! She just got on the elevator downstairs."

"I've got to go," Dakota said. "Get the cake!" She and Nina ran down the hall.

I decided not to wait for the arthritic freight elevator and ran down three flights of stairs to the room where I usually picked up lunch. Delivery guys slouched against the wall, shoulder to shoulder, morosely waiting to hand off their packages and be paid. I identified my man right away from his tall white cake box. He gave me attitude about how long he'd been there, and I deducted half his tip.

While waiting for the elevator, I peeked at the three-tiered white cake with "Congratulations" in marzipan. It looked like a wedding cake. Was Sam getting married? To Walker? Those doodles of wedding dresses leapt to mind. But this was implausible. As little as Sam and I were talking, getting married was too big a thing to have not told me. Maybe she was going to be in the wedding of one of her society friends—a princess or daughter of a duchess. The office had, after all, thrown parties for sillier reasons.

I reached our floor and entered the conference room by way of the connecting kitchen, leaving the cake on the counter. I found myself behind two banquet tables draped in white linen. Large silver serving dishes with Sterno burning underneath them stood on one table; a tray of fresh fruit, a basket overflowing with breakfast pastries, coffee and tea dispensers, china plates, cups, and silverware were laid out on the other.

The sound of applause drew my eyes to the front of the flower- and balloon-festooned room, where everyone was standing. They were facing a beaming Sam, who was flanked by Hell, the depart- ment heads, and Chantal. Had Hell cut the contest short and named Sam the director? But then Chantal wouldn't be up there. A banner covered with the staff's signatures hung on the wall above them. In big Magic Marker letters, it read CONGRATULATIONS, SAM! WE'LL MISS YOU!

Had Sam finally quit to live the life of leisure she was born to? I wondered if anyone in the room had won the secret pool that had been going on for years. At five dollars a shot, you could try to pick the month and year Sam would get tired of working and decide to fol- low beautiful weather around the globe. Dakota said Sam's first boss started the pool after Sam took her job.

I shook my head. That didn't make sense. People wouldn't be congratulating her.

"I am moved beyond words," Sam said. "Really, guys, this is all so wonderful of you." She waved her arm, encompassing the decorations and food. I looked for Dakota to see how she took Sam's giving the credit for her and Nina's frantic activity to everyone on staff. Dakota, on the edge of the crowd, stood sideways, so all I could see was her profile. She was grinning, her eyes locked on Sam.

"I'll never forget this," Sam continued. "I'll never forget any of you."

I couldn't believe Sam was leaving and she hadn't told me. Per- haps she had tried to force Hell's hand over the weekend, claiming to have another offer, and Hell had called her bluff. I felt like a medi- cine ball had been spiked into my chest.

"Take us with you!" Aerin or Dylan shouted. The women stand- ing near her simultaneously took a step away from her. There was a smattering of nervous laughter.

"I wish I could. I'd snatch all of you away, but Hell would never forgive me." Hell nodded her agreement.

"So take only some of us!" the very blond and very young assistant persisted.

Sam gave a wry smile in response. She had gotten another job. If she took anyone, it would be me.

Hell cleared her throat. "It seems time for me to take over the floor before my whole staff throws itself at you, Sam. This is a bitter-sweet moment for me. I'm thrilled that you're getting your own com-mand, but I'm also heartbroken that you have to leave to do it. You're not just a great fashion editor to me."

Her own command? I threaded my way through the crowd and sidled up to Dakota.

"You're a wonderful editor," Hell continued, "a delightful conver-sationalist, and a good friend. I don't know who's going to sit next to me during all those boring fashion shows and luncheons now."

Chantal, with her arms clasped behind her back, looked down at her feet.

"Where is she going?" I whispered.

"Like the banner says, I'm really going to miss you."

Sam and Hell hugged. Dakota leaned toward me without taking her eyes off them.

"That said, I want to present this gift as a token of our undying affection for you." Hell bent down and picked up a large Barney's shopping bag. She gave the black bag to Sam. "I apologize that it's not wrapped. Nina claims there wasn't enough time."

"She was named editor in chief," Dakota said out of the corner of her mouth.

"This is from all of us. We hope it will come in"—cough—"handy."

Sam reached into the bag. Everyone teetered on their toes to see what they had given her.

"I gathered that much," I said. "But editor in chief of what?"

Oohs and aahs drowned out Dakota's answer. Sam held up a large Louis Vuitton doctor's bag, the season's handbag of choice. She already owned one.

"Skye only got a Filofax," an associate editor loudly whispered near us. She had been Skye's assistant—I knew who she was because she had red hair. She had done her boss's job so well while Nan was conducting interviews that she was promoted.

"Unlike Skye, Sam isn't going to the competition," Dakota said loud enough for the grumbler to hear. The two had started around the same time. "Plus, Skye was just a fashion editor."

"Who cares about Skye," I said. "Tell me where Sam is going."

"Let's eat!" Sam said, prompting the room to burst into chatter. Like noisy schoolchildren dismissed for recess, people headed for the banquet tables.

Without answering my question, Dakota made a beeline for Sam, surrounded by staffers wanting to give her their personal congratulations—and their résumés, I was sure. I watched Dakota push and nudge her way into the center of the blondly ambitious knot.

"You must be psyched," said Aerin or Dylan. I needed to learn who was who. "Have you given notice yet?"

I frowned.

"Don't tell me you're trying to keep it a secret," she laughed. "Everyone knows Sam's taking you. She hired you." She tapped the shoulder of the associate editor, who then spun around toward us. "Gwen, do you think Sam is taking Ginger with her?"

"Of course. They're best friends."

"Ginger isn't talking. She's being coy or, excuse me, discreet."

"Why bother? The only surprise would be if she didn't take you."

"What's your new title? Associate editor or editor?" someone I'd never seen before asked.

"It can't be editor," Gwen scoffed. "She hasn't even made associate."

"Yeah, but we're talking about a bridal book. How hard can it be to cover wedding and bridesmaid dresses?"

Ella's phone call came to mind. Even she had known before me.

"So what is it? Associate or editor?" Gwen persisted.

Everyone was looking at me. I couldn't admit I had yet to speak to Sam.

"You're going as her *assistant?*" the woman I'd never seen before asked incredulously. She was wearing bright lipstick and blue eye shadow—probably beauty-department discards. She must have been a freelance copy editor. They sat closest to the beauty department.

Even if Sam offered me a job, I wouldn't take it. Fashion was one thing, but a bridal magazine—there was just no defense. I couldn't devote my life energy to helping women make their wedding as dreamy as possible. Maybe I could do what Gwen had done, and so impress Chantal while she was looking for Sam's replacement that she promoted me before hiring someone new. Chantal must be the new director.

I looked for an escape beyond the group encircling me. Chantal, standing nearby, caught my eye. She smiled and joined our group.

"Guys, you'll find out soon enough." She leaned over and took my arm. "I have to steal her away."

They parted, clearing a path for me, looking like junkyard dogs who've had their quarry snatched from them. I followed her out to the hall.

"Congratulations! On your promotion." Could she be pulling me aside to tell me I was moving up as well?

We stood just outside the conference room door. People were trickling out, loaded down with bottles of water and napkins full of pastries. Chantal moved us farther down the hall, toward the elevators.

"Thanks, Hell's going to make the announcement tomorrow," she said, waving her hand impatiently. "More important, at the shoot, did you get the boat owner to sign a location release form? It wasn't with the others."

CHAPTER 39

"Dammit!" Chantal slammed her fist into the wall I was leaning against. "I was counting on you."

"But . . . you . . . you never mentioned—"

"Do I need to tell you everything? This is why I don't bring new people to shoots. We'll never find him."

"We have his name on the other—"

She waved me off. "It's illegible. Now all those photos on the boat are useless. Luckily I have Tarn reserved for Wednesday. I'll use the male models for that shoot. I'm going to have to forget the girls-having-fun shots."

As much trouble as I was in, I hated to see that happen. Time for female friends was always the first to go—in life and in its dramatization. "But if we're shooting at the studio anyway, can't we do both?"

Chantal shook her head. "You returned the swimsuits, remember? And there isn't time to get them back."

"Then couldn't we do the friends in party clothes instead of dating? It just seems to me—"

"I need the mix." She worried her lip. "Actually, the studio isn't going to do anymore." She flung her hands in the air. "Great, now I need a bar."

"That can't be too hard. I can start making calls."

"No, I'll do it. You go tell Annabelle to alert the models that they'll have to report to a different, as yet to be determined, location. Then come back to my office pronto."

She started to walk away but stopped when she realized I hadn't moved. Scowling, she said, "What are you waiting for? You're still an employee of this magazine."

"It's not that. It's just that I don't know where Annabelle sits."

"How long have you been here, for crying out loud?" She stabbed the air with her finger. "Down that way, the third office on your left."

I ran down the hall and gave Annabelle Chantal's order. She frowned at the extra work of making a couple of phone calls but said she would get to it. I came back to my office and found Chantal's door closed. I could hear her shouting and decided not to knock until she was finished. With my ear pressed against her door, I looked over at my area. In my absence, it had been converted to a greenhouse. Expensive bouquets covered the desk, two were on my chair, and three more were squished onto the shelf above the desk. Someone had even moved stuff around to make room for them.

"Ginger?" Sam called out.

I hesitated, unsure what to do. Chantal had said to come immediately back to her, and I didn't want to piss her off anymore. But she was on the phone and I wanted to talk to Sam. Jumping to a bridal magazine suddenly seemed more appealing.

"Ginger?" Sam called out again.

I stepped into her office. There were even more bouquets—crammed on the ledge along the windows, on the couch, on her desk. Dakota sat in my place, directly across from Sam. She didn't move when she saw me.

"What took you so long?"

"I was waiting to talk to Chantal. We have to find a bar to shoot in." I explained what had gone wrong.

Amusement flashed across Sam's face.

"It's not funny," I said. "Chantal blames me."

"It'll be fine." She twisted her mouth, thinking. "I know, my friend Darren is the silent partner in a place in the meatpacking district. Decadence. They just opened and could use the publicity. Hang

on." She picked up the phone and motioned for me to sit. "Wednesday, you said?"

I nodded, moving a wooden box of white orchids from the couch
to the floor, and sat down. I waited while she spoke into the phone,
not taking my eyes off her, not even to glance at Dakota.

"Done. It's all set. Here's the number and contact person. Call
him once Chantal approves it." She scribbled on a piece of paper and
gave it to me.

"Thanks. I don't know what to say."

"Nothing to it. Consider it my going-away present to the
magazine."

"That's right. You're leaving, and I haven't even congratulated
you." I jumped up and moved toward her with my arms open. "Editor
in chief. You said you were going to do it and you did," I said, hugging
her. She squeezed back and we started bouncing up and down. It was
like old times, like when Sam found out she got a D and not an F in
calculus or when her dad gave her a BMW convertible for her
twenty-first birthday.

Dakota cleared her throat.

We dropped our arms and separated.

"But I don't even know where you're going," I said, pulling my
shirt down.

"It's a new spin-off of Beautiful Bride called Sexy Bride. The title is
still being test-marketed. What do you think?"

I mustered as much enthusiasm as I could. "It sounds great."

"Excellent. I'll tell Walker we have another subscriber."

"Walker?"

"He's the publisher," Dakota answered for Sam.

Oh, yeah. Sam had said he was in the same business. I couldn't
believe I'd assumed he was a love interest. All this thinking about
husbands and marriage was affecting my brain.

"He called this morning," I said to let Dakota know I wasn't completely in the dark.

Sam licked her lips. "Yeah, I know, we talked already. He was a little annoyed that I leaked news of the launch to O'Henry already."

"You had to give notice to Hell. Someone here would've told him."

"Actually, I'm out of here after tomorrow. Company policy, so I don't steal any secrets."

I had no idea things would move so fast. I wished Dakota would leave so we could talk more openly.

Sam read my mind. She looked at Dakota and cleared her throat. "Could you check on the car?" Dakota reluctantly got to her feet. "Please close the door." She left it open a crack, so Sam got up and closed it herself.

"I hope I don't regret making her an associate editor." Sam resettled in her chair. "It's already getting to Ms. West's head."

"You're taking her?" I supposed I knew that already.

She frowned. "I owe her."

"For taking the blame for contacting that designer?"

"That, and other things." Sam worried her lip. "I know this is hard to believe, but I'm actually doing you a favor not taking you."

"You're not taking me?"

"I have room for only one associate and you're not experienced enough for anything higher."

"Couldn't I go as your assistant?"

"You don't want that. Walker says I need a career secretary." Sam leaned over her desk. "Listen, bridal books are the pink ghetto of magazines."

"The other assistants didn't seem to think so."

"They're just desperate for a promotion. Trust me, if you went with me, you would have a hard time getting back into fashion."

"You're going."

"It's different with me. At the editor-in-chief level, the category doesn't matter so much as the top-dog experience. I wouldn't go to be fashion director."

I ran my fingers through my hair. "But why didn't you even tell me you were up for the job?"

"You know my policy about—"

"But we're friends!"

We stared at each other. She made a sad face.

"Maybe hiring you wasn't the best thing for our friendship." She stretched her arms across the desk toward me. "I made a conscious effort not to treat you the way I treated my other assistants, who all quit on me. But I guess that wasn't enough." She turned the undersides of her arms up.

"I suppose I could've accepted more of your invitations to go out on the weekend."

"And I could've insisted harder." She picked up a pen and started spinning it over the knuckle of her thumb. That was a trick I had taught her first with a chopstick. "But you know, to be honest, it was weird for me to see you with my old friends. To you they must seem dumb and superficial."

"They're New Yorkers."

"Like me. I guess that was it. I felt like a fraud in front of you. Even with this bridal book. You knew me as Dr. Griswold's star student." Dr. Griswold had been head of the women's studies department.

"You're moving up. You shot straight to the top. I'm proud of you."

Sam made a scoffing sound. "I didn't exactly shatter any glass ceilings. Dad's putting up the money for the magazine. Walker had no choice."

"So what? You were about to be named fashion director here, and your dad doesn't own Hell."

"Not exactly. She told me over the weekend that Mac wanted Chantal. He didn't think the little Sammy who used to steal olives from his martinis could handle the job." She smiled ruefully. "Sometimes contacts can hurt you."

"This move is bigger anyway."

"Yeah, you're right." She shook her head. "Enough about me. We have to talk about you. I think you should move with Chantal to the fashion director's office along the corridor of power."

"And be her assistant?"

"It'll be better than staying here with whoever replaces me or takes Chantal's old job. Chantal knows her shit. You'll learn a lot from her."

I exhaled softly.

"She won't be that bad. Just stay on her good side."

I nodded. "Speaking of which, I should probably tell her we have a bar." I held up the scrap of paper I'd been twisting. "Thanks for this."

"No problem."

I started for the door.

"Ginger?"

I turned around.

"Dad's throwing me a party at the Rainbow Room. Starts at nine." She smiled. "I won't take no for answer."

CHAPTER 40

Chantal had heard of Decadence. I didn't tell her how I'd found it, afraid she would nix it out of distrust for Sam—and wanting the credit for myself. The quick save seemed to placate her; she switched back to using "we" instead of "I." Amid the continuous ringing of Sam's phone and arrival of flowers, I spent the next several hours doing Chantal's bidding, calling in more clothes, confirming the makeup and hair people, checking in with Annabelle, and making all the other arrangements. I was also answering Chantal's line; Sam and Dakota left at lunch, saying they wouldn't be back.

At the end of the day, Chantal threw a file of handwritten notes and pages torn from magazines on my desk.

"More photocopying?" I asked, rising from my chair.

"No," she said, swinging her purse onto her shoulder. "I've got to do a TV appearance next week, now that I'm director."

My phone rang. I ignored it, seeing it was my mother. It stopped finally, then started again.

"Are you going to get that?"

"Yeah." In the phone, I said, "Fashion department."

"Ginger, I heard about a date service for Koreans and—"

"I don't think so."

"But—"

"I'm working now." I hung up with more force than I meant to use. "You were saying?" I said.

Chantal paused. "I was saying that I hate this part of the job."

"I could go for you." I was serious. It was probably an early segment on a local morning talk show, six-thirty-A.M. early, but TV was TV.

"Yeah, right. You can type up these notes instead, and dig up slides of these clothes from the last shows. I want it all on my desk first thing in the morning."

"Maybe next time," I mumbled to her departing back.

I didn't know how long I'd been toiling, when Gwen, Aerin, and Dylan walked by. I'd thought I was the only person left, and waved. They passed without waving back, immersed in their conversation, then came back.

"Hey there," Gwen said. "I heard you're not going with Sam. That really sucks."

Word certainly traveled fast.

"Dakota said you're going to be Chantal's assistant," she said with sympathy in her voice.

Granted, I was still officially Sam's assistant today, but Chantal hadn't been as monstrous to me as she had been to Dakota. I was optimistic. "It'll be good for my career. Sam didn't go on shoots. I want to be a stylist."

"Is that why you're not going with Sam?"

I nodded slightly. It wasn't a total lie.

"Then you shouldn't stay here either," said Aerin or Dylan, the one with the chipped front tooth.

I didn't respond.

"Listen," Gwen said, "we're going to an FD meeting. Wanna come?"

"What's FD? Fashion department? Feminist dissenters?"

"No, fucking disgruntled," the one without the chip said. "It's a club for anyone who works in magazines and hates their boss."

"It's not just that," Gwen said. "It's a professional association for networking, career advice, and moral support."

"Emphasis on the moral support. All we do is get drunk and bitch about how sick we are of being assistants."

"And get hit on by losers at the bar who ask us to buy them drinks."

"Are things so bad?"

"When did your spaceship land? Dylan and I have been assistants for more than two years," said Aerin. "You have to be connected to be promoted, or get really lucky and have a nice boss."

"Gee, guys. If you keep on putting it that way, everyone will want to join." Gwen turned to me. "We need to branch out to other magazines so we can find out about other opportunities."

"It's just the three of you?"

"Right now we're focusing on how to get the most out of our jobs so that when there is an opening we're qualified for it."

"But you're already an associate," I said.

"I'm a glorified assistant who still reports to an editor who can't tie her own shoelaces. I swear, if it weren't for cabs, she'd never find her way to the office, which, come to think of it, wouldn't be such a bad thing."

"Can't your old boss Skye help you?" I asked.

"No, didn't you hear? She got married and moved to London."

"That's what I want to do," said Dylan. "Marry someone rich and move to Europe. She met her husband through a designer."

"That's where you come in," said Aerin. "You must know all sorts of great guys through Sam."

"Aerin, you make it sound like we want Ginger only for her contacts."

"You said—"

"Never mind what I said," Gwen said between her teeth. She turned the corners of her mouth up and looked at me. "So, Ginger, want to join us for a drink?"

I wanted to hang out with them like I wanted a lobotomy. It was better before, when I didn't know who was who. "I'd love to, but I can't."

Gwen shot Aerin a dirty look. "How about just the two of us going off to talk? I could tell you more about the club."

"Sorry, I've got to finish up here."

"So come when you're done."

I looked at my watch. "I've got plans afterward."

"Sam's party."

I was surprised they knew of it. "Are you all going?"

"We wish," Gwen said.

"Can we go with you?" Aerin asked.

"Aerin!" the other two shouted in unison.

CHAPTER 41

The party was sedate for a party thrown by Sam. Despite the pulsing music, people were just standing or sitting in circles. Feeling like I'd pulled an all-nighter—tired and yet wound up—I made a tour of the dark private room, sticking to the outskirts, looking for Sam. She wasn't anywhere, which explained why no one was dancing. At least Dakota wasn't there.

I headed for the open bar and knocked back a glass of wine. I held my glass out to the bartender for a refill before diving into the thick of the crowd. People made way for me to walk, some with dirty looks, but no one gave me an entry into their group. As I squeezed past backs and through conversations, I was reminded of the Ohs' party, where I'd at least had the excuse that people were speaking Korean.

At the edge of the crowd again, I stood, nursing my drink. A balding man in a navy blazer and sockless loafers was watching me. What the hell, I thought. I made eye contact with him and he strolled over.

It turned out he wasn't friends with Sam or anyone else at the party. He'd been in the main bar and come at his thirst's own invitation. He'd had too much free alcohol, but even sober and coherent he was probably still a bore. I let him ramble about his three tours in 'Nam—he wasn't the first Vietnam vet to tell me how he'd fought for "my country"—as I scoped the crowd for a more interesting conversation partner.

I was on the verge of giving up and leaving, when I heard my name shouted. A tall, silver-haired man with a perennial tan, Sam's dad, Graham, was waving from across the room.

"Ginger, so glad you could make it," he boomed, giving me a kiss on the cheek. "Come with me. I have some people I'd like you to meet." He bowed slightly to the vet. "Excuse us."

"Thank you," I murmured as we walked away. I liked Graham and always felt comfortable around him despite his predilection for young women. Unlike my mother, he treated me like an adult.

"I was derelict for not seeing you come in. I promised Sam I'd keep an eye out for you until she got back."

"She left?"

"Only for an hour or so. She was feeling faint from not eating dinner, and I made her go to the restaurant. You can go join her if you like, though she's probably on her way back."

"I'll stay here, thanks." I didn't want to cramp his style, but chasing after Sam seemed a little too schoolgirlish. I took a sip of wine, waiting for him to speak. That was the thing about the Starres, you could always depend on them to make conversation.

"So, how are you, Ginger? How's Betty? Sam tells me she's in town."

It took me a moment to realize he meant my mother. She was as much Betty as I was my Korean name. "We're both fine."

"Sam said she's having you date up a storm."

"I wouldn't call it a storm," I said, blushing. I shouldn't have been surprised Sam had told him.

"Nothing to be embarrassed about. Lord knows I could use help in that department."

"Sam must not have fully explained the—"

"You don't have to explain."

"But—"

"I set up Sam all the time. She, unfortunately, thinks I'm too old for her—"

"Yeah, I heard how she met Walker," I said loudly, making him stop short. "You probably thought he was going to romance her, not recruit her."

Graham paused, then chuckled. "Yes, I have to say I don't get your generation. You've taken all the fun out of dating."

"Exactly what you've done to my party!" Sam hugged her father from behind. Dressed in a halter top and black leather pants, she bumped him with her hip to move over, and squeezed between the two of us. "Dad, what happened?" she asked, nudging me to sway with the music. "I leave for an hour and I come back to a wake."

Graham shrugged, bringing his hands up in half-surrender.

"I'm so glad you came," she said in my ear. To him: "Were you hitting on Ginger?" She motioned for me to finish my drink. I obeyed, and she gave the empty glass to her dad. "Excuse us, we have some partying to do."

As we made for the center of the dance floor, Sam, sashaying, pulled a dozen or so people along with us. The deejay put on a disco song and more rose to their feet.

"Don't mind Dad. He just broke up with another girlfriend."

"It's fine."

"What?" Sam asked, putting a hand up to her ear. I repeated what I'd said, but she shook her head, mouthing she was the dancing queen. After the next song, a man grabbed her by the hand and she spun away.

I took a couple of steps back and closed my eyes, still stepping in time to the music. Free of the gaze of other people, I let go, shaking and shimmying. The beat of the music seemed to emanate from deep inside and I danced to it, the feeling of uncontrolled movement wonderful. My arms went up, my head waved from side to side, pulsing lights flickered through my eyelids.

The sound of someone whooping opened my eyes just as a heavy body tumbled into me. Feeling my feet go out from under me, I reached out blindly to stop my fall, pulling down with me the man who had knocked into me.

Ugh, I thought, squirming and conscious of how sweaty I was.

"Ginger?" He lifted his upper body, his hands on either side of me holding his weight, so I could turn and see him.

"Tarn?" My body relaxed.

"I was hoping to bump into you here, though not literally."

"You found me all right." I waited for him to get off.

"I'm quite comfortable." His breath was warm and heavy with alcohol. "What if we just stayed this way?"

I gazed into his dark brown eyes, aware only of the pounding beat and the urge to move to it. I strained upward, and he, sensing what I wanted, started easing toward me. I closed my eyes and waited.

His lips pressed against mine. It'd been a long time since I'd come in contact with someone's mouth.

"Get a room!" someone shouted.

I finally managed to wrest my lips away from his, but Tarn continued to kiss my neck. I squirmed until he got the picture and heaved himself off me. I scrambled to my feet. People, smirking, turned away.

"Somewhere more private, beautiful?"

Before I could answer, a blur of red hair streaked toward us and launched onto Tarn.

"There you are," Tatiana shouted, clinging to Tarn's T-shirt to steady herself and causing him to lose his footing. They teetered like timid dance partners. "You were here, then you were gone. I thought you went to get me another vodka tonic." She turned to see who he was looking at. Her eyes scraped me up and down.

"You're with her?" The volume of my voice astonished myself. A long-forgotten memory, feeling, popped into my head. Standing with a friend on a field, as far from the gym teacher as we could, swinging a golf club at balls, bellowing curses until we were hoarse.

"What the hell's the matter with you?" I didn't know whether I was angrier that he was kissing me when he was with someone else or that he could have such unselective taste.

Tarn stood dumbly, his mouth flapping open and shut. Tatiana looked at him, then at me.

"What's going on?" she asked. "Tarn"—she wagged her finger at him—"have you been flirting with the help?"

I waited for what she'd said to replay in my head. I had heard correctly. "You!" I gathered my breath and rage. "You stupid, shallow, racist, vain, insulting, pathetic, cow fucking, dog-eating bitch. I have more education in my little finger than you have in your pea brain. I certainly have more manners. I should have said this last week, but I'll say it now. Lulu is not a maid. I am not a maid. Asians in general are not servants."

My heart was pounding when I finished. Tatiana and Tarn were stunned into silence. The entire room seemed quiet, though the music continued to blare. Everyone was staring, too shocked even to be smirking. Sam looked away.

I couldn't see the vet to tell him this was my country, and so I left.

CHAPTER 42

"Ginger, wake up." My mother's hoarse pleading penetrated through my dreams. The ringing I was hearing wasn't a school bell but the alarm clock. I flung my arm out and slapped it off.

I lay still, waiting for the fog to clear. I hadn't missed a test. But I had screamed at Tatiana. I pulled the pillow over my head.

"Ginger, you get up? Ginger?"

"Yeah, okay." I willed myself out of bed, my muscles groaning and my head pounding. The shower helped, as did the two aspirin. Somehow I dragged myself to the office.

So this was what it was like to have a career, I thought, stowing my purse in my bottom desk drawer.

Sam appeared, carrying a cup of coffee. She was dressed down, wearing Cavalli jeans and a plain white blouse, the tails knotted. Her hair was pulled back in a ponytail.

I wasn't sorry for what I'd said to Tatiana; she needed to be told off. But I did regret how out of proportion my outburst had been to the offense and that I'd made such a scene. In the light of sobriety I knew that her comment hadn't so much set me off as tipped me over the edge, for which I was embarrassed. I cautiously greeted Sam.

"Is it nine o'clock already? I was hoping to be further along." She headed for her office and motioned for me to follow.

If she didn't want to talk about last night, I was happy to oblige. I picked my way through the clutter of already-dying flowers joined by cardboard boxes and bubble wrap. Her wastepaper basket overflowed with files and old issues of the magazine. I removed a box filled with shoes and purses from my chair.

Sam sat down heavily and brushed away an errant strand of hair. "I hate packing. I'm tempted to throw everything away. Really, when am I ever going to use this?" She picked up a dictionary and threw it at the trash can, making it topple over.

I leaned over to pick up the spilled garbage. "I can help," I said.

"Would you? Thank you."

"It's the least I can do the last day as your assistant."

Sam fumbled with her lighter, striking the flint three times before finally lighting her cigarette. She offered me the pack, but I shook my head.

"Do you remember when Muffin the Fourth died and my mother wanted me to come to Scottsdale, but I had that paper for my psychology of women class to write?"

"Sure, I wrote the paper so you could go," I said, relieved. Our friendship was too old to be undone by one drunken night. "You got an A and Dr. Griswold was so impressed, she wanted you to go on to grad school."

"Right." She took a long drag from her cigarette. "She also wanted me to submit the paper to *The Journal of Feminist Studies*, and you didn't think that was right. But instead of telling me, you just clammed up and slammed drawers and books and doors."

"Did I?" I primarily remembered the incident for the favor I'd done her and Dr. Griswold's high opinion of my work. We had laughed because the course had been grad level and I hadn't even taken a women's studies class at the time.

"You did and it was pretty ironic, since the paper was about women's silence."

I reached across the desk for her silver lighter from Tiffany's. She saw what I wanted and handed it to me. "But we talked when your father left a message wanting to know where he could order copies of the journal." If it hadn't been for him, I never would have known she'd gone through with publishing my paper under her name.

"We made a pact back then—remember? We agreed to tell each other when we saw morally reprehensible behavior in the other."

I scratched my head, trying to figure out what she was talking about. "Oh, you mean the Hamptons shoot. How you tried to use Tatiana to sabotage it." I waved my hand. "I never brought it up because it didn't matter."

"What?" She looked at me incredulously.

"As far as I'm concerned—"

"What are you talking about? Sure, I hired away that model before you were involved. But I relinquished the one you used when you did become involved."

"I'm talking about telling Tatiana to call it off."

"I did no such thing." She tossed her ponytail. "It's your behavior that needs discussing."

"Last night? I lost my temper, but I'd hardly call it a lapse of—"

"Sleeping with a man is not the way to advance your career."

"What?"

"I know what you were trying to do with Tarn."

"I wasn't attracted to him for his connections."

"Please, Ginger. I've never seen you get so worked up over a man before. The stakes had to be higher than just liking the guy."

"Really Sam, I—"

"Now, don't get defensive on me. It's a hard call when the guy's our age and flirty and hot. But take it from someone who knows, you'll regret it."

"You slept with a photographer?"

"No, a PR guy for a designer. But he didn't do anything for me, which is the point I'm trying to make. Tarn may be Chantal's favorite photographer, but he can't help you."

I sat speechless, waiting for my nausea to subside. No wonder she'd been so tight-lipped about her ascent at the magazine.

"If anything, he'll hurt you." She shook out another cigarette from the pack and held her palm out for the lighter. I didn't relinquish it, holding out a flame instead. She settled back in her chair. "What with Chantal on the lookout for grounds to fire you."

"Fire me?"

"She wanted to let you go. She said you weren't eager and energetic like someone fresh out of college would be."

"She said I was too old?" The sterling silver lighter was hot in my tight fist.

"I had to push for you. If it weren't for me, Hell wouldn't have ordered Chantal to take you as her assistant." Sam stubbed out her cigarette, rising to her feet. "I should finish packing. My plane for Bora Bora is this afternoon." Sam opened and closed the cabinets behind her, standing on her toes, peering at the top empty shelves.

"Now, when I come back"—she turned to me—"I think you, Tatiana, and I should all get together for a drink and make nice."

"I'm not taking anything I said back."

"I'm not asking you to."

"Someone had to set her racist butt straight, tell her that Asians weren't put on this earth to serve her."

"She knows that. Her high-priced divorce lawyer is Filipino."

"He still serves her. I hope he's overpriced and incompetent."

Sam smiled faintly. "Don't say that. I loaned her the money for his retainer." She dropped a handful of pens in the box at her feet. "Listen, I was as appalled as you were that she mistook you for the help. But she's going through a hard time right now, with the divorce and having no money. It's messing with her head."

"Her head is always messed up."

"That's true. But she's not all that bad. She does have some redeeming qualities. If she didn't, she wouldn't be my friend—or Gloria Steinem's."

"She's friends with Steinem?"

"She was invited to her wedding."

"Steinem's getting married?"

"There's a blurb in today's paper." Sam pushed the *Post* at me, opened to the gossip page.

Gloria's partner choice wasn't even iconoclastic. He was richer, he was older, and from the old paparazzi photo, he wasn't even shorter than Steinem.

First Sam, then Chantal, now Steinem. It was raining role models.

"So what exactly did Tatiana do at the shoot?" Sam asked, rolling her chair closer to the cabinets and climbing onto it. She wobbled and grabbed the back of the chair to steady herself. Someone should hold the chair, I thought.

I got up and walked out the door.

CHAPTER 43

I sailed out the building, down the street, for blocks, stopping when I reached the bottom edge of the park. A newspaper lay abandoned on the steps of the fountain; I sat on it and stared, absorbing the sights and sounds of continuing life.

Tourists with cameras and maps, and black and West Indian nannies with white babies were out in full force. A gang of teenage boys rolled by on skateboards, laughing and carefree. I watched a horse attached to a buggy snort and stomp its front feet as its driver bought a cup of coffee from a vendor. A homeless man climbed past me and started to wash his clothes in the dirty-water fountain. He was singing a show tune.

A pigeon landed near my feet and pounced on a pizza crust. Three more filthy gray birds arrived and the first one grabbed his find and tried to walk away. But the others wouldn't let him escape, chasing him and pecking at the bread but mostly at his neck. In his panic, he ran toward me, bringing the squalid trio with him. I kicked in their direction and they all flew away in a burst of flapping wings.

If only it were so easy to send my thoughts scurrying away. I shook my head like a dog shedding water. My mind still felt harried, jumbled.

I wasn't any better than Sam or Chantal, who obviously was trying to get rid of me not because I was too old but because I knew she was gay. I had been playing both sides of the fence, loyal to whoever was helping me at the time. I had pandered to Tatiana's vanity, gone along with the prevailing sentiment that Lulu was just being hypersensitive instead of making a stand for her—all so the shoot could proceed. I hadn't shared the credit for the closet sale success. Sleeping with Tarn hadn't entered my mind, but his mentioning he had magazine contacts certainly hadn't repelled me. In my heart of hearts, I had been willing to do whatever it took to advance my career.

But wasn't that what everyone did? Wasn't I just looking out for number one? Trying to forge an identity? Become someone?

Maybe Rock had had it right. I should think less and just be. Maybe Graham had been right that I took dating too seriously. Maybe my mother was right that I expected too much from a career. I seemed to be struggling far more than anyone I knew. Was I making life harder than it was?

But thought was the seat of being. Thought, which included want, was who I was. And the me who wanted to be someone in her own right, who craved success and applause, whose company I preferred, would not exist without my particular deliberations and navigations.

I didn't know what I meant. But I did. I was founded in my dualities, my differences, my splits. I didn't need to resolve all the inconsistencies and contradictions. Sometimes it was enough to know they were there, because the core, uncharted, invisible-but-felt part of me was unchangeable. At my age, I was already me. Wanting to be some-one was to want to be someone more, not someone else.

It was all nonsense, but it was startling, obvious, thrilling, boring, comforting—and freeing.

"Everything's coming up roses!" the man behind me warbled full-throttle.

I turned and saw he was now stark naked and bathing in the shal-low brown waters. His aged body was still beautiful, toned with mus-cle, kinetic.

Flowers that were fading, I realized, were in full bloom.

CHAPTER 44

"What's all this?" I asked, coming into the apartment. Bags from the Korean grocery store covered the floor and kitchen counter. "There's enough food here to feed all of North Korea."

I'd had a long afternoon. Sam had already left when I returned to the office, and that afternoon marked the first five hours of my official servitude to Chantal. Even though Dakota was still there, Chantal had me packing her files for her move to Nan's old office—the announcement had been made—getting her shoes from the repair shop, and scheduling a dental appointment. She hadn't appreciated the improvements I made to her TV notes and had made me retype them. I knew she was purposefully being horrid. I could take it as long as I was still going on shoots.

My mother stopped humming and turned around from the sink, smiling. "Go wash your hands. Mommy gonna teach you how to cook!"

It was a standing joke between us, and a point of pride on my part, that I cooked like a bachelor. From the time I'd put in in her kitchen, slicing, dicing, and sautéing, I knew only simple dishes like fried tofu and soybean sprouts with kochujang sauce. I didn't know how to make anything that involved more than three ingredients. It occurred to me that it was strange that she hadn't tried to train me sooner in this most basic of wifely duties. She'd always been busy and I'd never wanted to learn, but if she wanted me to marry a Korean, she could have tried harder, made the time.

The old resistance bubbled like stomach acid; as long as there were restaurants and she was alive, I didn't need to cook. But the new, enlightened me thought it was a good idea. Cooking wasn't antifeminist, it was pro-independent.

"Okay," I said, putting down the Louis Vuitton bag Sam had left for me, along with a note apologizing for the casual way she'd broken the news of Steinem's nuptials. She hadn't expected me to take it so personally.

"You go shopping today?" my mother asked, eyeing the purse. She came around the counter, wiping her hands on a dish towel. She picked it up. "Louis Vuitton. Expensive." She put it back down. "It nice though."

I could see her mind calculating what crazy thing she could push me to do as back payment for her largesse. "It's a present from Sam," I said, heading for the bathroom. I normally would have felt self-conscious having a Louis Vuitton bag, knowing that even when I saw a Korean with one I assumed it was fake. But now I didn't care. Plus, Sam's giving it to me had clearly irritated Dakota.

My mother said something I couldn't hear over the water splashing in the tub. I was washing the city grime from my feet. "What?" I shouted. I came back to the kitchen.

"I ask if it apology present." She was picking onions out of the bag. "For not giving you job." She gave me five onions and a knife.

"Maybe a little bit. But we're cool. Now that we won't be working together, we'll see more of each other socially." I started peeling the smallest onion.

"That nice. You never know when you need bridesmaid."

The onion had many dried-out layers. I kept on taking them off. At the center was a little green bulb. I held it up, smiling. Ibsen's metaphor had been off.

"*Aigoo*, what you do? Peel only the skin."

"Sorry," I said sheepishly. I pushed the onion hulls into a pile on the counter and reached for another onion.

My mother cleared her throat. "Bobby called today." She looked down at the package of sliced beef she was unwrapping.

Maybe it was for him that she suddenly wanted to teach me how to cook. The plan was proceeding; it wouldn't be long before she would be making George's favorite dishes. "Yeah?" I tried to sound nervous. "What did he say?"

"I didn't pick up. I was in the bathroom." Too nonchalantly, she pointed at the answering machine with her knife. "He left a message."

"Thanks. I'll listen to it later."

"Korean should stick together."

"Then what are we doing in this country?"

"I didn't know before I come American are funny people. They nice to your face only."

"And Koreans aren't?"

"They prejudice. They never will see you like one of them. They put the Japanese citizen in camp during World War Two."

"That was a long time ago! That wouldn't happen now." I picked up another onion. "What's with this anti-America kick you're on?"

"Ann was horrible to Mrs. Oh." She was scraping the skin off a claw of ginger root as big as her hand.

"Because she deserved it—not because Ann's white."

My mother's knife slipped, but it didn't cut her. She got a better grip on it.

"She lesbian too."

"Her sexuality has nothing to do with her character—or nationality."

My mother put the ginger down and wiped her hands on the towel. "Where your blender?"

I picked up the second-to-last onion. "I don't have one."

"You don't have one? How we make bulgogi sauce without a blender?"

"I've never needed one before." I pointed to the onions. "Should I stop?"

She shook her head. "No, I just gonna have to chop up everything." She made space on the counter for the cutting board, moving the bags of food to the floor and sink. "This kitchen too small for Korean chef."

"Finished!" I said, putting the last onion down. "Now what should I do?"

She looked at the pile of onions and onion parts. "Peel two more."

"More? What are we making?"

"Today we make bulgogi, mandu, and pajun."

"That sounds like a lot of work." I nosed around the bags, looking for the onions.

"You have a lot to learn. I leave Saturday."

"So soon?" I hoped her ticket was changeable. I was sure she'd want to stay longer to become reacquainted with George and to get to know his family.

"I here for three weeks." She sighed. "I have to go back before Mrs. Un steals all my clients."

I looked up from the plastic bags. "Sounds like Koreans aren't as nice and noble as you've been making them out to be."

"That different. That business."

"Mrs. Un was your friend before she decided to copy you and get into real estate."

My mother stared at me, pushing her lower lip out in thought. She cracked a smile. "Korean worse."

I found a bag of rice crackers. My mother looked up from her chopping at the sound of the bag bursting open. She opened her mouth and I popped a cracker into it.

"It's going to be weird not having you here. I've gotten used to coming home to you."

My mother buried her pleasure in her chopping. "I only phone call away. And Mrs. Oh in New Jersey. Visit her."

"She's a poor substitute."

My mother opened her mouth for another cracker. She chewed and swallowed. "She good enough for Bobby."

"She's his mother," I said, munching. "Her English is hard to follow. It's not as good as yours."

She scooped up the ginger bits onto the edge of her knife and slid them into a big bowl. "You just used to me. Bobby probably say same thing about me." She rooted around the shopping bags and tossed me a bulb of garlic.

I crammed one more handful of crackers into my mouth and dusted off my palms. "Should I finish with the onions first?"

"No, do the garlic. We just make bulgogi. I hungry." I felt her eyes on me as I struggled with the garlic, picking at the skin with my fingernail. "Here, do it this way." She broke off another clove and cut off the ends. "It easier." She quickly broke apart the bulb and sliced off the tails of all the cloves before returning her knife to the onions.

"You think Mrs. Oh English so bad?"

"It's pretty broken."

My mother nodded. "We took class together, but she never thought she stay here so long. They go back when Dr. Oh retires."

"Really? Does Bobby know that?"

"Probably."

Bobby had only five years to go.

"They would just desert him like that? Alone in this country?" I wiped my eyes against the outside of my hand. The onion and garlic fumes were getting to me.

"If he would marry Korean, he won't be alone."

"That's why they opposed Ann? Because if he married her, they wouldn't be able to abandon him? Seems sort of selfish."

The onions my mother was adding to the ginger were affecting

her eyes too. She started mincing the garlic. Watching her, I suddenly felt the urge to hug her. She would never go back to Korea. I
was lucky she would never leave me alone.

"Mrs. Oh gave up her country to give Bobby life here." She put
the last of the garlic in the bowl and picked up a wooden spoon. "But
maybe she made mistake. Maybe we all made mistake."

"I don't agree. Bobby probably disagrees." I finished skinning the
last clove. "Done! Now what?"

"Take out the soy sauce and sesame oil," she mumbled.

I walked around to my mother's side of the counter to reach the
cupboard. She swung her head out of the way so I could open and
close it. I handed her the bottles she wanted and returned to my
place, facing her.

She uncapped the soy sauce and then slammed it down. "If I don't
bring you here, then you don't have such a hard time to match up."

Maybe it wasn't the onion and garlic bothering her eyes. "*Oma,*"
I said softly. I reached over for her shoulder, but she shrugged my
hand off.

"Nobody tell me raising children here so difficult, so complicated.
Nobody tell me about all the problems. And nobody know how to
manage."

"You've managed pretty well."

She took a couple of chops at nothing on the cutting board, then
started scraping it with the dull side of her knife. "No, I didn't," she
finally said. "Something wrong, you never date. I came here to help
you but I can't. I failed you."

"I've dated."

"Yeung-rok don't count. It didn't work."

"No, I mean I've dated."

She looked at me in surprise. "When? Who?"

She could handle the truth. When had I started to think she
couldn't? I knew. When George told me I had to look out for her, protect her.

"In college, at grad school."

"Why you never tell me? What a revolution!" Her tears were now from laughing. She wiped them on the backs of her hands.

"Because they weren't Korean. You wouldn't approve."

"How you know? I never met them."

"But George—"

"I made mistake. I didn't expect it. I didn't know what to do. I didn't know nothing."

"So American guys are now okay?"

"You not getting younger." She stuck out her elbows and shifted a little to nudge me out of her space. "Peel the green onions. Two bunches. Wash them first."

I retrieved the scallions but put them down. "Is that a yes or no?"

"That depend on who he is."

I walked around the counter to face her. She looked up from pouring soy sauce into the bowl.

"I'm seeing how much you're using. How much is that?"

"Don't you see? This much."

"But how much is that? A cup?"

"I don't know," she said, barely suppressing a smile. "This much." She poured a little more, then reached for the sesame oil.

I stopped her with a hand on her arm. "Can we pour this in a measuring cup so I can see?"

"That too much trouble. Just look." She dribbled sesame oil into the bowl, maybe about a teaspoon, and started to mix everything. Dipping her finger into the sauce, she tasted it. She added more sesame oil and tasted again. "Something missing." Her eyes flashed. "Sugar. Get me sugar. And water."

I walked back around the counter. I handed her the sugar and went to the sink. "How much water?"

"A glass."

"A cup?" I started searching for the measuring cup in the cabinet.

"Sure. Make it cold."

I let the tap run, then filled the glass up to the line marking one cup. When I turned to hand it to her, she was putting the sugar bowl down.

"How much sugar did you just add?" I asked, eyeing the sugar as it dissolved in the black pool of soy sauce.

She shrugged, taking the water. She made a face at the glass, rotated it, and drank from a spoutless side. "Those crackers are salty."

I gave her an exasperated look.

"What wrong?" she asked, putting down the empty glass.

"This isn't much of a cooking lesson."

My mother started stirring with the spoon. "Just taste until you have enough." She took my finger and pushed it to the bottom of the bowl. When she brought it up, it was covered with bits of garlic, ginger, and onion. She put my finger in my mouth.

I made a face. "That's really strong."

She tasted the sauce herself. "Hmm. Too much garlic." She poured more soy sauce and sugar.

"You don't really know what you're doing, do you?" I reached for the rice crackers.

"Sure I do." She grinned, taking a handful of crackers. "I know the ingredients, that the important part."

"Maybe we should call Mrs. Oh."

"Not necessary."

She wiped her hands again and returned to sloshing soy sauce and spooning sugar into her concoction. Slapdash was how she cooked, how she lived here, improvising and customizing to taste. Perhaps she didn't always get things perfect, but I'd been a fool for never taking her example or turning to her for advice. I'd been sweating over my Korean and American halves, trying to keep them in balance, when they all got mixed up anyway.

"I don't make bulgogi in a while. I rusted." She tasted again. "Maybe too much ginger."

"What do you mean, you're rusty? You just made bulgogi last Christmas."

The sugar hit the counter with a thud. "Oh, yeah." She put her hand on her forehead, frowning.

"You're getting old," I teased. "They say the mind is the first thing to go."

She twisted her mouth and squinted, regarding me. Whatever she was pondering, she made up her mind and relaxed her face. "My turn for revolution."

"What?" I asked cautiously.

"I didn't make the bulgogi."

"Sure you did. I saw you. You made kalbi too."

My mother smiled sheepishly. "I put in sauce and fry. But I don't make sauce. I buy from Mrs. Bak."

"But it tasted the same."

"I always buy from her. She good cook."

I looked at her, laughing in half-amazement, half-surprise. I couldn't believe she'd tricked me all these years—or that she'd bothered to.

"No time. And I don't really like to cook—all the peeling and cutting. I hate to cook." She looked happy, relieved, to be getting this off her chest.

"You didn't have to go to all that trouble."

"I knew you missed Korean food."

"We could've gone to a restaurant. What else do you buy from Mrs. Bak?"

She put her finger in the air as though she had an idea and motioned for me to move out of her way. She came back to the counter with her arms full of peanut butter, jelly, and bread.

I repeated my question, opening the jars for her.

"Just little things. Her mandu, pajun, jhapchae, ojingo-juk—"

"Basically everything I don't know how to make," I said, shaking my head.

"Except kimchi. I get that at the grocery store." She covered a slice of bread with peanut butter and jelly, folded it over, and held it out to me.

We were both doing the best we could for each other. That was what ultimately mattered to both of us.

"You in shock?"

"No, I'm fine," I said, really meaning it. I accepted the proffered sandwich and took a bite. "What a revolution."

"Both ways, *mang-nae*. Both ways."

CHAPTER 45

My stomach had been churning since the subway ride downtown to the shoot at Decadence. I'd drunk nearly a pot of coffee and smoked half a pack of cigarettes throughout the morning, but they were the treatment, not the cause, of my nerves. I was jittery about the reunion dinner, but it was still hours away. The bar owner had forgotten to tell his manager to come early, and we had to wait two hours for her to be roused out of bed to unlock the door, but Chantal had used the time to ready the models in the vans, and now we were well under way. We were in the process of changing the models for the third time already. Tarn was keeping his distance, but that was fine by me.

The reason I was having trouble unbuttoning one of the male models' shirts was that Lulu had just been put into an embroidered Chinese silk dress with a princess collar, and I wanted to tell Chantal that it was a bad idea. Lulu looked great, especially in the bright red, and I knew chinoiserie was hot—I'd seen the runway pictures from Paris. But no matter how trendy and flattering the dress was, it just seemed wrong and contradictory to put it on a Chinese woman in a story about assimilation. With scarlet lips and her hair pulled into a bun, she looked like the West's stereotypical image of a Chinese woman.

"For crying out loud, I've known fifteen-year-olds who could take my shirt off faster than this." The blond slapped my hands away from his chest.

"I'll bet you do, little man," said Jacqueline, her hand on her hip, waiting for her turn. With heels on, she towered over him.

"You should know, Jackie. You were one of them."

"You wish."

I gave him an apologetic upturn of my lips and took a couple of steps back. In the front of the van, Chantal was on her knees, shortening the bottom of another male model's pants. Her mouth was full of pins; now was probably not a good time to start an involved discussion.

"Here." My model shoved his shirt into my hands. "Now what do I put on?"

I helped him into a white Helmut Lang T-shirt, then started undoing his pants. He covered my hands with his. "I can do that myself, thank you."

"Sorry, I wasn't thinking," I said, blushing.

Jacqueline cackled. "You go, girl."

Chantal joined us, the door closing behind her model. "What's the holdup?"

"Ginger was trying to get into Brad's pants."

"I wasn't. I was just trying to help him get them off."

"Honey, that's how it always starts." Brad shook his head like he'd seen it all.

Jacqueline screamed, pointing at his underwear. "Man, don't you change them in the morning? Those tighties aren't so whitey."

"They're clean. They just got washed with the colors."

"In hot water, clearly. They look like they shrunk too."

"Let's see *your* panties, missy." Brad reached out to grab the skirt of Jacqueline's dress, but Chantal intercepted his hand.

"Let's not and say we did." She sized him with her eyes and threw him a pair of jeans. "Put those on and go back to the bar. We've got to get moving, people."

He stood back to shake the pants out and started climbing into them.

"Now, what are we going to put on you, Jackie." Chantal quickly sorted through the clothes rack. "Ginger, help her out of that shift."

Now probably still wasn't a good time to raise my objection to Lulu's dress. Jacqueline lifted her left arm; the zipper went down her side. The dress was still too tight to hike above her hips.

"It's pinned in the back, love." She spun around and lifted the long hair of her wig. "Brad, still have trouble opening doors?" she asked on seeing he hadn't left yet.

He gave her a wry look and held up the brown shoes he'd last been wearing. "Chan, do you want me in these again?"

I was going to wait for him to leave before taking off Jacqueline's dress, but she raised her arms, so I pulled it over her head. She let her hands fall back down to her sides, leaving her bare breasts uncovered. Brad didn't even blink.

"No, not the brown shoes," Chantal said. "The cowboy boots, over there." She pointed to them on the floor near him.

He gathered them and sat down heavily on one of the black leather seats. He turned his head and looked at Jacqueline, grinning. "Your panties are purple."

She shifted her weight to one foot and rested a hand on jutting hip. "At least they're clean."

Chantal came up to us, holding a sheer white Prada dress with yellow horizontal stripes that looked like ribbons. She held the hanger up to Jacqueline. "This will look beautiful on you."

"It's lovely," Jacqueline said, fingering the gauzelike material.

"Yes, it—" Chantal frowned. "You're wearing purple underwear."

Jacqueline teetered on her heels. "Yeah, I couldn't find a skin-toned thong this morning."

"Your panties are purple," Brad sang like a little boy.

"You!" Chantal stabbed a finger at him. "What are you still doing here?"

"I'm waiting for someone to help me with my boots."

Chantal snapped her fingers at me. "Ginger, what are you waiting for?"

"I thought he could do it," I said, rushing over to him. I shoved his foot as far into the zipperless boot as I could and motioned for him to stand. He stupidly put his weight on the foot only halfway in the tall boot and, losing his balance, grabbed my head.

"Slide your foot forward," I said, trying to remove his finger from my eye with one hand while holding the boot in place with the other.

"I can't," he grunted. "They're too small."

"They're not small," Chantal said. "All the shoes are size twelve."

"But—" He thought better of arguing with her and sat down, kicking the boot off. To me, he grumbled, "I have wide feet."

"So I'll go al fresco," Jacqueline said. "I don't mind."

"You can't. The dress is see-through."

"Point your toes this time." His foot still wouldn't go deeper than the instep.

"What choice do we have?"

"Stand up and step down hard," I said. He pushed off my back as he got to his feet.

"Ginger!" I turned to Chantal just as Brad stomped down, catching the tips of my fingers.

"Shit!" I screamed, stuffing my fingers into my mouth to stop the throbbing.

"Such language," Jacqueline said.

"Sorry. I didn't see your fingers. Are you okay?"

"I'll be fine," I muttered. I turned back to Chantal and Jacqueline before they could wipe the amusement off their faces.

Chantal cleared her throat. "Ginger, what color underwear are you wearing?"

I pulled my waistband down to look. "Beige."

Chantal held her hand out. "Hand them over."

"What?" This was above and beyond horridness.

"You heard the woman, drop trou, baby," Brad said, clapping his hands.

I spun around and gave him a dirty look, putting my smarting fingers back into my mouth. Sheepishly, he reached for the other boot and started to put it on.

"Stop being so uptight," Chantal said. "You're holding us up."

"I promise not to pee in them."

"It's not that. It's . . . it's just . . ."

"What an assistant has to do," Chantal finished for me. She had a hard look on her face.

"Fine," I said, walking to the bathroom. I wanted to ask why it wasn't what a fashion director had to do but kept the thought to myself.

"Aw, c'mon, you get to see us naked," Brad said as I shut the door.

"Brad, what are you still doing here? Get out. Scram."

I could hear him protest as I took off my jeans and underwear and put the jeans back on. Not a comfortable feeling, but I would live. I would even be a sport; Chantal wasn't going to run me out of my job over a pair of underwear. I heard a door slam as I came out. Jacqueline was already wearing the dress.

"Where'd he go?" I feigned disappointment. "I was going to throw these at his face." I held up the required undergarment in a bunched-up ball.

Jacqueline smiled, reaching out for them. "It's just as well. He would have stuffed them in his mouth or something." She slipped into them.

"That'll do," Chantal said, pulling the dress straight. The beige was a tad lighter than Jacqueline's skin. "Let's get back to the bar." She held the door open.

I watched Jacqueline run across the sidewalk and disappear behind the bar door as I waited for Chantal to come down the stairs.

"Thanks for your contribution." She patted me on the shoulder. "I would have given her my underwear, but I'm on the rag."

"No problem," I said, strangely pleased by this bit of personal information. "Whatever it takes, right?" I scooched my jeans down so the hard inseam wouldn't be touching my skin.

"That's the spirit." She started to walk.

It was now or never. "Chantal." I reached out and stopped her. "There's something I wanted to talk to you about."

She looked at her watch. "Can it wait? We have to be out of here by four, in two hours, and for once in my life I'd like to finish on time."

"Actually, it can't." I took a deep breath. "It's about Lulu. The dress she's wearing. I don't think she should wear it."

"Lulu's dress?" She looked up, mentally summoning the outfit in question. "The red cheongsam? It looks gorgeous on her. What are you talking about?"

"It does look great. But she doesn't look assimilated in it."

Chantal shook her head dismissively. "It's very au courant, very stylish. You don't know what you're talking about."

"I know it's very trendy—for white people. But it doesn't look it on her."

Chantal shook her head again. "It's a Vivienne Tam. She's wearing it ironically."

Ironically? You couldn't argue with irony. It was the academic equivalent of a crazy eight. It could be anything any person said it was. I should let it go, but I'd gone this far.

"It's like me wearing a T-shirt that says queer," Chantal continued to explain.

"Only to people who know you're gay. To people who don't know, it's offensive."

"Are you saying the dress is offensive? What's offensive about it? I'd think you'd be happy to see the East influencing the West for once."

"I'm just saying that no real Asian woman would wear it. I wouldn't."

"Vivienne wears them. She wore one to her show, and she was in the Sunday Style section wearing one at some fund-raiser, for some animal shelter. Did you see Helena and Sam? They looked like twins in practically the same outfits."

I would definitely stop declining Sam's invitations. Being in the *Times* was an accomplishment a fashion maven could put on her résumé.

"I'm sure that'll all stop now," Chantal said with a smirk.

On the other hand, if I started appearing on the page, Chantal and Helena would hate me. But what were we talking about? "Vivienne can wear her dresses. They're her dresses. Everyone gets her irony."

"I don't think she's being ironic. She's just getting them publicized."

"Exactly! That's exactly my point."

"What is? You lost me." She was irritated now.

"That you can't assume irony, because people get it when it's not there and they don't when it is."

"It's just a dress," Chantal said. "And it stays on Lulu. End of discussion. Let's get back to the shoot."

"I think you're making a mistake."

She turned back to look at me. "I said end of discussion."

"It would look just as good on Jacqueline, and they'd take only minutes to swap."

"Is this a ploy to get your underwear back?"

"No, of course not!" I said, taken aback. I wouldn't put the pair back on even if they were returned that minute.

"You didn't make a peep about the rumba ruffles last week."

"That's because you didn't put them on Catalina. I wore them. Listen, I'm just trying to voice my concern, trying to make a real contribution. I mean, what's the use of having an Asian perspective on your staff if I don't tell you when things bother me?"

Chantal folded her arms across her chest. "I didn't know you felt that way."

Maybe I'd gone too far. It was just a dress. "I don't . . . I mean, I didn't before because I didn't have an issue before."

"It bothers you that much, huh." She let her arms drop. "All right. We'll leave it to Lulu. If she doesn't like the dress, we'll change it."

I put my hands together in a silent clap, smiling.

Chantal pointed at me. "Only if she has a problem. Stay here. I'm going to get her."

She came back with Lulu, Tarn, and a ham sandwich.

"Tarn, this doesn't concern you," Chantal said on seeing he'd followed her out. "Go back in and eat lunch."

"I've been nibbling all afternoon."

Lulu giggled, covering her mouth with her hand. I supposed nibble was a funny-sounding word. Or perhaps something was going on between the two of them. I doubted he came out to see me.

He glanced at her, then looked back at Chantal. "I've had enough to eat. I just came out to have a cigarette." He fished a pack out of his front jeans pocket. I wondered that they didn't get crushed when he sat.

"It's a bar. You can smoke inside."

"Yeah, but I wanted some fresh air."

"To smoke?" Chantal raised her eyebrows but let them drop. "Suit yourself." She turned to Lulu, taking a bite of her sandwich. Once she'd chewed and swallowed, she slowly enunciated, "I have a question to ask you."

"Yes," Lulu said excitedly.

"Yes?" Chantal threw me a look. I shook my head to say I hadn't already mentioned the dress to her.

"Yes," Lulu repeated. "I go to studio and take more picture."

Tarn choked on his smoke. "No, beautiful, that's for something else." He collected himself and looked casually at Chantal. "Another job."

"Yeesh," I said before I could stop myself. A shift of his weight was the only sign that Tarn had heard me.

"I don't want to know what that's about, but whatever it is, Lulu, you should probably check with your agent."

Lulu just smiled blankly at Chantal, playing with her hair.

"The reason I brought you here is to ask you about your dress. Do you like it?"

Lulu looked at Tarn, then at me, for help. I held my head stiffly to stop it from shaking no. Tarn looked puzzled.

"Yes," she said cautiously.

"Great. That's all I wanted to know." Chantal smiled nicely at me. "Let's get back to the shoot." She put the last of her sandwich in her mouth.

"It cloth my grandmama wear. It old style, very old style." She plucked at her stomach. "I look my grandmama." She sighed prettily.

Chantal gulped down her mouthful. I stepped forward. "Would you rather wear something else? A different dress?"

Lulu blinked several times before slowly nodding. "If I do."

I looked at Chantal, who was pressing her lips together.

"Okay, let's change her. Ginger, get Jackie."

Tarn quickly tossed his cigarette and rushing ahead of me, grabbed the door. "I don't get it," he said, his curiosity winning over his need to pretend I didn't exist. "What's wrong with the dress? She looks like a perfect China doll."

"Precisely," I said, stepping past him.

I immediately spotted Jackie next to the buffet table with Brad. They were throwing grapes in the air and trying to catch them with their mouths. Jackie was having a harder time of it, having to keep her wig from falling off.

I helped myself to an untouched stack of brownies. "Jackie, you're wanted back in the van."

"For what?" She lobbed another grape in the air. Brad pushed her aside to nab it, but she foiled him, batting it down in midair. She grinned, looking very proud of herself.

I decided to give her the short answer. "Lulu doesn't like her dress. You have to swap."

Jackie looked at Brad. "I don't blame her. It's ugly. I don't want to wear it either."

"Take it up with Chantal. She's waiting for you."

"Can you believe this shit?" she asked Brad before storming off.

He shook his grapes like they were dice. "Since when do we have a say in what we wear?"

"It's a special situation," I said, thinking I should have taken the time to explain the whole matter.

"Well, my feet hurt. Do you think Chantal would consider me special enough to change these boots?"

I looked at him. It was true that most pictures in the magazine were cropped mid-calf, above the feet. "Are they cutting off circulation?"

Brad continued to play with his grapes, now bouncing them up and down in his open hand as though he were weighing them. "I'm going to talk to Chantal."

Despite his pinched feet, he was halfway across the room before I could stop him. With a sinking feeling I watched him grab all the other models and herd them out the door. Tarn slipped out with them. The makeup and hair stylists soon followed. I was alone with the photo crew and plates of pastries. I grabbed a few more brownies, though I knew they wouldn't temper the tempest in my stomach, and went back outside.

"I'm just saying orange is not my best color."

"These pants are itchy."

"I want my hair down. I hate my ears."

Chantal stood in the doorway of the van above the mini mutiny. Lulu peered over her shoulder. Tarn stood off to the side with his hands in his pockets, watching the spectacle, along with a growing snowball of pedestrians and store clerks.

All of this for a little red dress. I was mortified and scared out of my mind about what Chantal would do when she got me alone, but I was also astounded, a little pleased with myself. I had started this rebellion, me, a latter-day Paul Revere.

Or was it Ben Franklin? John Adams? Johnny Tremaine? Well, whoever had led the Boston Tea Party, that was me. And though I could have and should have contained this uprising, it was, in the end, for a good cause. I had spoken up.

Chantal saw me, and using the full length of her arm, she waved me to her.

CHAPTER 46

I washed my face in the ladies' room at the restaurant. I had enough time to reapply my makeup before my mother or George and his family arrived—though regrettably, not enough to go home and shower and change, as I'd originally planned. I'd called my mother two hours ago when the shoot ended and arranged for her to come here, resisting the urge to ask her to bring a pair of underwear. She'd have asked why and I didn't want to have to explain.

Chantal had fairly quickly regained control over the models with firm words and by refusing even to hear their demands. But we'd still run an hour over, and so in a doubly foul mood, she'd kept me at the bar. She had managed to hold in her rage for the duration of the shoot and had even sent everyone and the vans on their way. But Tarn was taking a long time packing his cameras, and she'd burst, ripping into me in front of him.

"You stupid shit," she'd spat out. "What the fuck did you say to Jackie?"

I had known for hours that this was coming and was prepared to apologize. It was my fault, unlike the mistake with the location release form. But the insult to my intelligence, her curses, Tarn's presence, changed my mind. Now I was angry. The damage had been contained, and she was overreacting, probably homing in on an excuse to fire me.

But I wasn't going to be sucked into this scene and I turned away from her. Tarn had finally finished putting away his gear and stood tensely still, watching from a couple of feet away.

Chantal grabbed my shoulder and roughly spun me to her. "Who the fuck do you think you are, turning your back on me. I'm talking to you."

I coolly looked her in the eye. "Were you? I was looking for a stupid shit." I glanced at her hand on my shoulder. "Kindly de-hand me."

She reared back, her mouth opening to roar some obscenity, I was sure.

Instead, she burst into laughter. Maniacal, head-thrown-back laughter. Tarn and I exchanged looks.

"You said you were looking for a stupid shit," she said between gasps, "and you looked at Tarn."

I tried to smile with her. Maybe it was funny.

"Hey," Tarn said, taking several steps forward.

Chantal halted him with her hand, still laughing. We waited. Just when she seemed able to speak, she lost control again. "The models" was all she could say.

Tarn joined in first. It had been an absurd spectacle, models revolting. I started to giggle. Chantal snorted, making me, then Tarn, laugh harder, which in turn made Chantal start up again. "De-hand me," Tarn mimicked, starting another wave. We were swept into a continuous eddy of laughter. Finally, all we could do was whimper, looking at one another while trying to regain our breath.

"Of course," Chantal said, holding her stomach, "you're never going on another shoot."

I'd thought I was drained, but now I felt faint.

"Chantal," Tarn said.

She shook her head. To me: "Consider yourself lucky I'm not firing you." To Tarn: "Contact sheets first thing tomorrow. Ginger will send a messenger." She pivoted on her heel and strode out the door.

Tarn took her place on the stool. He ordered two gin gimlets, mumbling they were in tribute to my name, at last it was time for our visit, and sipped his drink in silence while I digested what had just come down.

Time passed—the clock on the wall was permanently frozen at three, but it still ticked. I finally took a long draft, thinking, inexplicably, of the bags of clothes and boxes of books at home that I had to unpack. Tarn took that as a cue to start talking. He said he would talk to Chantal, assured me he could change her mind.

I was grateful to him for sticking around; without his presence, who knew where the conversation with Chantal would have gone. Yet I hadn't forgotten his earlier overture, the kiss, Sam's warning. "Thanks, but that's okay."

"Really, I would be happy to say something to her."

I shook my head. "I'm a big girl. I can speak for myself."

"You certainly can."

I peered at him over the rim of my glass. "You mean the other night with Tatiana? It wasn't—"

"Please, don't make excuses or apologize. I like spitfires." He slapped the counter and signaled the bartender for another round.

His impression of me pleased me, off as it was. Maybe I could become a spitfire, or at least be known as someone who spoke her mind. "Tarn, I have to level with you."

"You don't date white guys," he said, accepting his fresh drink with a nod. "You kiss them but you don't date them."

"What makes you think that?"

"Why else would you be turning me down?" He leaned toward me. "I bet it bothered you that all the male models were white too."

I put my drink down. "You know? I didn't even notice. But you're right. To assimilate isn't to date whites only."

"To my eternal disappointment," he said, sighing. "You'd think I'd learn by now. But I can't help being attracted to Asian women, your elusive, exotic mystique. I must have a complex or something."

"Or maybe you should stop hitting on women you meet through work."

He looked at me, not comprehending.

"I was going to say before that I don't date professional contacts. I do date whites."

"You do? Then we need to get you another profession!"

"Tarn."

"Okay," he said, grinning. "But if you ever switch careers, you let me know."

"I wouldn't hold my breath."

"You never know." He pocketed his change and gave me another grin. "Indeed there will be time. And time—" He stopped, scratching his head as though to bring his thought to the surface.

"And time yet for a hundred indecisions. And for a hundred visions and revisions," I said, realizing why his earlier mumbling had sounded familiar. Did all men know Prufrock's love song by heart?

He pointed at the clock. "Especially according to this clock."

I became aware of my reflection in the mirror again. My makeup was done; I looked presentable. My mother and George would be arriving any second. I zipped my cosmetic bag closed with a flourish. It was time to go and make our visit.

CHAPTER 47

I spotted George standing next to the hostess podium. He was tall and handsome and resembled our father as he looked in the yellowing photographs stashed in the back of our mother's closet. But the way I first identified him was by his wife and daughters. Karen was pretty, tall, and with short straw-blond hair, wearing a Ralph Lauren plaid skirt and pink button-down shirt. His preteen, Beth, had light brown hair and eyes, colored as though her Korean and white genes had been mixed like paint. From what I could see of the baby, squirming in her mother's arms, her hair was even lighter than her sister's.

"George." I meant to speak above the din, but my voice failed me. I suddenly felt my legs shake as I walked closer. "George!" I managed to say louder. I waved a limp arm. Karen, looking at all the faces around them, saw me first and elbowed George. Smiling brightly, she pointed to me with her chin. She lowered the baby to her hip and tapped Beth on the shoulder.

George bounded across the several feet separating us and swooped me up in his arms, lifting me off the floor. "Ginger, Ginger, Ginger!" he said hoarsely into my hair, squeezing me so hard, my ribs hurt. I didn't try to get more comfortable. I didn't move.

He put me down. My brother—he was still as open with his feelings as he was when we were kids. He wiped his tears with the palms of his hands, then with his sleeve. Speechless and filled with wonder at the sight of my brother in front of me, I brought my hands up to cover my mouth. I realized then that my face, too, was as slippery wet as a stepping-stone in a rainstorm. And just realizing I was crying made the tears come pouring out even more. I was a damn gusher.

Sadly shaking my head, thinking of everything that had led me to this moment, I used my palms and the backs of my hands and the collar of my shirt to dry my face.

"Ginger, it is *so* good to see you. I can't believe it's you, it's us."

I vigorously nodded my agreement.

"You're so tall and grown-up—and pretty."

I smiled through the tears that were trickling down again. "I told you I looked like Mom."

George shrugged. "And you don't have braces. I can't call you railroad mouth anymore. What am I going to call you?"

I sniffled loudly. "Crybaby still seems to apply."

"You were never a crybaby. Come and meet Karen and the girls." He put an arm around my waist and we walked over to his family.

I offered Karen my hand, but she ignored it, instead throwing an arm around me and holding me tight against her plump breasts. The baby on the other side started to fidget, and she released me.

"This is just so wonderful. I'm sorry it's taken this long for us to meet. For years I've been telling George—"

"Honey—"

"But the important thing is that here we are, at last."

"Yes," I said, glancing at my brother. She'd been that woman, that intruder, all these years, and yet now I felt like the stranger, the interloper.

Beth squeezed between her mother and father and popped up in front of them. She stared boldly, her mouth open, her braces glinting. I couldn't get over how big she was.

"This is Beth," Karen said. "Beth, this is your aunt Ginger."

"Hi, Beth." I waved, not sure what else to do.

She blinked at me and turned to her mother. "She speaks American!"

Karen chuckled. "You mean English. And of course she does."

"But she's Korean."

"She's Korean like me," George said.

"But I thought you said she lived in Korea and that's why we never—"

"She lives in New York now." George looked uncomfortably at me.

"Yes, I live in New York now," I said haltingly, not sure whether I should fake an accent. It hadn't occurred to me that he'd have to make up a reason to explain why this was the first time she was meeting me.

"Do you like Korean food?" I asked Beth, to be saying something. She shrugged.

"She's never had it," Karen spoke for her. "This is an adventure."

I looked at George, surprised. I couldn't imagine him eating anything but Korean food.

We stood and smiled uncomfortably at each other.

Karen broke the silence. "And, Ginger, this is your namesake." She shifted the struggling baby, cradling her in her arms. The baby resembled her sister more than either her mother or father. The two girls didn't look Korean—and yet they did. Both had the same shape of face as my mother had. I took one of the baby's little hands and started to shake it. She stared at me, frightened, then let loose a bone-rattling scream. She frantically shook her hand free and buried her face in her mother's chest.

"I'm so sorry," Karen said, swinging the baby up to her shoulder. "She's normally not this cranky around strangers. She's tired and it's past her dinnertime." She felt the baby's diaper to see if there was anything else.

"Let's get our table so you can feed her." George reached out for the baby. "Honey, let me carry her. Your arms must be tired." They exchanged her and a quick kiss. He gently rocked the baby, who quieted down to a whimper. "Did you make a reservation?"

I looked away from his hands and up to his eyes. "Yes, under

Ginger." He started to turn in search of the hostess. "But another person is, er, joining us." Where was she? I looked at my watch.

He arched an eyebrow.

I couldn't decide whether to tell him now or wait for her to arrive. In my plan, she was supposed to be here when they arrived.

"Dad." Beth was tugging on her father's hand. "I'm hungry."

"I know, sweetie. It won't be much longer."

She made a face and stepped away from our little gathering.

Feeling sorry for children like her, thinking they would have my problems magnified, had been wrong, I realized, watching her test the leaf of a plant for its realness. Beth was a typical, healthy, sullen preteen. George and Karen would help her through whatever lay ahead. Rock had been right. I had been practicing the same kind of uninformed prejudice that my mother had against gays and Americans.

"Ginger!" someone called out behind me.

George looked up and smiled. I spun toward the door.

"Bobby!" I said. Had he misunderstood he was only to pretend he was coming? Still, and strangely, I was glad for his presence, I supposed for the distraction he provided. He pecked me on the cheek and smiled expectantly at the others. "You know George, my brother. And this is his wife, Karen, and their girls."

Bobby pumped the adults' hands.

"Did Ginger just say we knew each other?" George asked.

"As kids. In Milwaukee. Our parents were friends. The Ohs. I'm Bob Oh."

George slowly nodded. "Sure, I remember. Bob Oh." He smiled and looked at me, probably remembering our joke about Bob's name. "That's great that you kept in touch all these years."

"Actually, we just recently became reacquainted," Bobby said, "through our mothers."

"It's a long story," I cut in.

"Dad." Beth was back. "Is this my uncle?"

Her too? Did everyone want us to get married? Several seconds passed before I realized George was waiting for me to answer.

"No, we're just friends." I laughed, looking at Bobby.

"At this point," Karen said, nodding knowingly.

They must have thought he was the unexpected person joining us. And to be invited to this momentous event, he must be a fiancé. I wanted to clarify the situation.

But my mother came rushing through the door.

"Bobby, Ginger. I so sorry I late. I couldn't get a c—" She froze, staring at George. The wallet she was putting in her purse fell to the floor.

George stared back, frowning.

"Surprise!" I said. I raised my arms but immediately pulled them down. They were supposed to be exclaiming and jumping into each other's arms—not standing stiffly in growing silence. "George, it's Mom," I said, worried that as impossible as it seemed, he didn't recognize her. I knew she knew who he was.

"Karen, grab Beth," George said harshly. "We have to go." He held the baby close to him and marched past my mother, who stepped into Bobby to give him plenty of room. He headed for the door.

"Wait! Where are you going?" I turned to Karen for help. "Where is he going?"

She took Beth's hand and shook her head, sighing. "You shouldn't have done it this way. You should have asked first."

"But . . . but I thought he wanted to patch things up, become a family again."

"With you." Her eyes darted to my mother. "Not with her."

"Why not?"

"What she did was . . ." Her eyes welled up. "I have to go. Come on, Beth." She took a step, but I grabbed her free hand.

"Don't," I pleaded.

She turned back to me. "I'll talk to him, for the girls' sakes. But I doubt it'll do any good."

Helplessly, I watched her quickly walk away, dragging Beth by the hand. Beth turned around and stared at us, bewildered.

"Let them go," my mother said quietly. She was white and leaning heavily against Bobby.

"How can you say that?" I asked. "That's your family." I pointed to the door. "That's your family," I repeated.

"They don't want. Let them go."

"That's what I did last time." I felt tears spill down my face and brushed them away with my hands. "Not again. Not without a fight."

I ran past her, through the door, and out onto the sidewalk. I caught a glimpse of Beth's pale green skirt before it disappeared half a block down. I followed it through the revolving door and found myself in a diner.

"A table for three and a baby chair if you have one," George was saying to the host.

Beth saw me first and got her mother's attention.

"Ginger!" Karen said, surprised.

"George!" I said. This was between him and me.

He turned around and looked at me.

"What are you doing?" I asked him.

He continued to stare coldly, the muscle in his jaw twitching.

"We, ah, decided to eat dinner here," Karen explained. "Beth's hungry, we're all hungry, and the next train to Chappaqua isn't for another hour. You're welcome to join us if you like." She massaged George's upper arm. "Right, honey? Ginger is welcome to eat with us."

George's cheek finally stopped twitching. "Sure, you can join us."

"What about Mom?"

"She's your mother, and she's not invited."

"But she's just next door. I'll go get—"

"My family will never have anything to do with that—"

"She's not—"

"She is. The things she said—"

"George," Karen said. "The children."

"I'm not a child," Beth morosely interjected.

George looked at her, then longer at Karen. "She made her decision and she has to live with it. Our lives were really difficult when she could have made them easier. If it weren't for Karen's parents, I don't know how we would have survived. How I would have gotten through med school."

"You're holding a grudge because she didn't give you money?"

"It's more than money. She completely cut us off, refused to accept my choice, which you wouldn't think she'd do after what happened to her."

"I would think, after what happened to her, you would be more understanding. You caught her off guard. She regrets what she did. She loves you. You weren't there after you left. You don't know what it was like living in that house."

"And you don't know what it's like to be written off by your own mother. After all the ways . . . after everything." In a lower, calmer voice: "She did it with Dad, she did it with me, it's a miracle she hasn't done it with you. I won't ever expose my girls to—"

"But she's—"

"It doesn't matter. I have my own family now. I would like you to be a part of it, but if you are, I don't want to hear about that woman ever again."

"But Mom and I are a package deal," I persisted. "You can't have one without the other."

George shrugged. "It's your choice."

His hard heart hurt me as though my own were ramming against it. Perhaps he loved the girl I had once been, but there was no chance for the adult me. He would never understand me, the part that was inseparable from our mother. I looked at my brother George and his wife and his children and I didn't know who he was. The boy I had known had cut off more than his mother to become a man.

"I'm hungry," Beth whined.

"You should eat," I said. George was making a mistake. I was probably making another one walking away. Still, I said, "I'll let you go."

CHAPTER 48

I pushed through the revolving glass door and walked a full circle, ending up inside again. George and Karen were arguing. They halted on seeing me.

"This is stupid," I said, planting my feet in front of them. "Your daughters need their grandmother and aunt." I offered Beth my hand, and after a moment's consideration, she took it. I pulled her to me.

"No, they don't," George said, taking Beth's other hand, tugging her to him. She took a couple of steps, then stopped. We stood, with her in between us, linked by her.

"Yes, they do."

"For what?"

"For . . . so they can know the other half of their family, their heritage. So they can be whole."

"They'll hardly learn it from you. You speak only Korean food."

"So we'll learn together." A glimpse of the future flashed in my mind. Beth, an older Ginger, my mother, and I shopping in Seoul. It would be fun.

"They don't need that useless clutter taking up space in their brains. They're being raised American."

"With no appreciation of their other half? Even adopted Korean children get cultural field trips to folk fairs and restaurants."

Karen cleared her throat. "Given the circumstances, we decided it was for the best," she explained in an apologetic tone.

"They'll want to know eventually," I persisted. "They'll need to know why they should be proud of who they are when they get teased for looking different."

"They're my daughters. They'll have reason enough to be proud." Cut off from his father, and then his mother, George probably considered himself a self-created man, his belly button a deformity instead of a scar from birth. His arrogance was maddening.

"All right, then the girls need their grandmother and me so they'll know that all Koreans aren't assholes."

Beth loudly inhaled, not in a prudish way, but in an excited-the-adults-are-using-bad-language way. Certainly she was old enough to have used the word herself when with her friends.

"Ginger," Karen said sharply.

"Pardon my French," I said. "I mean, so the girls will know that all Koreans aren't as stubborn and unforgiving as their father."

"They'll hardly learn that from being around Mom," George fired back.

"Yes, they will. I told you, she's not the same." I'd always thought of her the way he did, as the roadblock, the sign that pointed you in a direction you didn't want to go, but it occurred to me then that the barriers she'd put up were only sawhorses that were easily blown through, her signs only cautionary. George and I had always done as we wanted.

"She may have let you choose your major and study a useless subject, but she hasn't changed her stance on the important things, like who you can marry."

"How do you know she—?"

"If she had," he spoke over me, "you wouldn't be with that fairy Bobby."

"Fairy?" When had he become a homophobe? Or maybe he'd always been one. After all, no one took on the prejudices and bigotry of the patriarchal establishment as its wanna-be members.

George misunderstood my question. "C'mon, Ginger. Bobby was a sissy playing with dolls back in Milwaukee. It's obvious."

"That doesn't prove anything. You played with my dolls too."

"Once, and it was just to look"—he glanced at Beth—"to see if they were anatomically correct."

"You were molesting my dolls! I'd say that's worse." I folded my arms across my chest and looked at Karen, who was frowning, probably thinking of the times she'd left her daughters' toys alone with him.

"It was in the pursuit of medical knowledge," George said to his wife, having followed my eyes.

"Pursuit, my foot," I said, taking old pleasure out of needling him. "You were just a horny teenager taking advantage of your little sister's dolls."

"Shut up," he barked.

I took a step back, surprised he didn't know I was trying to lighten the mood.

"George," Karen warned, "the childre—"

"I'm not—" Beth started again.

"—girls, I mean."

George nodded without taking his eyes off me. "Go back," he said in disgust, waving his hand toward the street. "We were fine without you, and we'll continue to be fine once the memory of this evening has faded. Go back to your mother," he said derisively, "and your pansy boyfriend."

Now I was sorry for him. Sorry because I was glad he had left my life when he did, that he stopped being my role model when I was young enough to correct his influence.

"Dad," Beth said. "If he's a pansy, how can he be her boyfriend?"

Karen cleared her throat, sounding like a sputtering engine. "Beth, not—"

"Good point," I said, talking over her.

"He's in denial," George said to me, "like you and your mother are."

"Mother?" I said. "Mother doesn't know—"

"Please," George cut me off. "She used to call him a girl-boy. She used to joke that Mrs. Oh was raising her son to be the daughter she always wanted."

"His mother made him gay?" Beth asked incredulously. "I didn't know—"

"Not now," George said sternly. He took her by the shoulders and ushered her to his side. She looked up at him, then cautiously sidled closer to her mother.

"I'll explain later," Karen half whispered.

I gave her a pitying look. "Why wait?" I threw my arms up in frustration. "Why not tell her now? Let her know now that her father is a pompous, self-loathing, homophobic ass."

"Ginger," Karen said, now in a threatening tone. She put her free hand on one of Beth's ears.

"Sorry," I said at first automatically, then really meaning it on seeing Beth turn her eyes away. As old as she was trying to be, she was an innocent. I had been barely older than her when George fought with our mother and I first realized our mother wasn't always reasonable. But at least I'd been spared from hearing George's insults.

"I'm sorry," I said to Beth, then Karen. This time I would leave properly. I kissed the girl good-bye.

"You're going?" Beth sounded genuinely disappointed.

"Things don't always go the way you want and you can't do anything about it," I said. "But then you grow up and realize you wouldn't want it any other way." I turned to Karen. She hugged back more than I was expecting, squashing the baby between us. Her hand slid down my arm and covered my hand. She gave it three quick squeezes before letting go.

As I walked away, I heard Ginger, who had been strangely mute all this time, come back to shrieking life.

CHAPTER 49

❧

My mother and Bobby were sitting in red chairs, murmuring in Korean. He was holding her hand in both of his.

"So much for surprises." I took the empty seat next to Bobby and watched a waiter carry a tray of mostly red food.

It was funny how it wasn't family but friends who were most giving, colleagues forgiving, non-kin kind. I knew the stakes were higher with relatives. But why was that? Why did I expect more of people who did not choose to be in my life than people who did?

"I knew they don't come back," my mother said. She exhaled loudly.

I looked at her until she looked away. "I'm sorry," I said.

"I sorry too."

I reached across Bobby and put my hand on top of theirs, breathing in the smells of grilling bulgogi. Three outcasts, each in our own way.

But membership in the Korean community wasn't by choice; it, too, was by virtue of blood, of extended blood. Non-Koreans saw us as a clan. I had seen us as one. And I had expected more of it, of them. But if I were in Korea, I wouldn't expect understanding from, or accept responsibility for, strangers because I looked like them. Americans didn't go to parties with other Americans and feel their identity unravel if they didn't click with someone. If an American wasn't attracted to another, no one thought she was racist against her own people.

That was the thing about being Korean in America, or any minority who stuck out. We were lumped together and we accepted the lumps.

Perhaps my wanting to be with non-Koreans wasn't a form of self-loathing but an unconscious desire to be appreciated for who I was, despite my differences, for my differences.

The special status given to the bond between two unrelated people was starting to make sense. To be chosen, to choose—that was something.

"At least Bobby here," my mother said. "Good thing I call and remind him to come, even though he not meant to come."

Bobby turned to me. "I knew the plan wasn't for me to be here, but she said it would be the last time before she left and I thought I'd just pop in to say good-bye."

"I'm glad you're here." George had derided him for being less than a man, but Bobby was more of a man. He didn't think he had to leave the bosom of his family to be a man. He wasn't willing to abandon his duty. He was willing to try to juggle it with his duty to himself. As was I.

That wasn't selflessness. That was selfishness. That was wanting it all. I had thought I was half an American, half a Korean, and that to forge a distinct, a distinguished, identity I had to choose. I had to abnegate part of myself. But integration wasn't a compromise of the self, it was a triumph of the self.

To be fulfilled wasn't to be free to do as you pleased. It was to be free of regrets. To make your dash, negotiate the rocks, span the gaps without ever jettisoning the things, people, values, that were important.

Bobby stood up, rubbing his stomach. "Should we make the best of things?" he asked.

I stood too, pulling down my creeping-up jeans. I knew he meant eat dinner, but I said yes, thinking of my life to come.

CHAPTER 50

"To the chef," Bobby said, raising his crystal wineglass.

"To the chef," Chantal, Ann, and June echoed, lifting theirs.

I had set out Bobby's fine china for the special occasion, my first dinner party since moving in with him. The table was laden with all of my favorite Korean dishes: A3, A7, S5, S10, S12, T2, V1, and V11. I'd taken a page from my mother's recipe book.

"Whoever he or she may be," I said, clinking glasses.

"Everything looks beautiful," Chantal said, eyeing the colorful food, silver candlestick holders, and yellow-rose centerpiece. She moved her fork to the left of her plate and the knife and spoon to the right.

I was always getting that wrong. I motioned for everyone to dig in.

"Where to start?" Ann said, her tie-dyed butterfly sleeve dipping into the kochujang sauce, or koch-up, as Bobby called the condiment. She took particular pains in choosing her clothes, I'd learned, delighting in tweaking her partner's fashion sensibilities.

It had been two months since my mother left. I was still Chantal's assistant, still banned from photo shoots, but I had been promised the next editorial-assistant spot that opened in features. Paige, assigned the task of writing the hyphenated-American personal essays, had turned to me for help. I had agreed to write them on the condition I get credit for my contribution. They weren't anything Pulitzer, but the experience of going over the edit and copyedit and cutting the copy to fit the allotted space made me realize I was in the wrong department, and I had requested a transfer with Chantal's backing. The executive editor, also an English-lit grad-school dropout, though many years ago, had cautioned me that I may not move for months, even a year, and Sam, who wasn't too busy to talk on the phone, had suggested I send my résumé to other magazines. It was good advice, but I was staying put for now, having heard through the grapevine that an assistant was pondering joining her banker boyfriend in Hong Kong.

Sam's test issue was shipping tonight, which was the reason we were an odd number. Just last week Chantal had shot Sam's cover. Walker had been insisting Sam use the photos of Asian models she had commissioned—they had cost so much—and she had finally convinced him that the inaugural cover needed to be more mainstream. Her choice of freelance stylist had surprised me, but she had said that Chantal was the best. Business was business. Chantal apparently agreed.

Chantal and I rode the subway to work together most mornings, but the second we stepped into the building, she was all briskness and commands. She did remember, though, to say thank you and please. When we were outside the office, like here at the apartment, with the crew, she was still grouchy, but that, I discovered, was her way. From watching Ann, June, and Bobby, I'd learned that the best way to deal with her was to rib her. I didn't have the ammunition yet, or the years of history to pad the pokes, but I was working on all that.

Ann wasn't a drunk. She just drank a lot. She said we would, too, if we saw the things she saw in the emergency room. That didn't hold muster with June, who was urging Chantal every chance she got her alone to do an intervention.

June was constantly telling people what she thought they should do. She was on my case to stop smoking. She had also prodded me to return Karen's call. Now that I was getting to know her, I thought she was more like my mother than me.

I didn't mind her nosybossiness. It was her suggestion, after all,

that I move in with Bobby, whose large mortgage and monthly main-
tenance fees were prohibiting him from taking on more pro-bono
work. Now I had a bedroom separate from the living room and
kitchen, as well as a dining room, terrace, and doorman, and I was
just minutes away from the reservoir; Bobby spent every other Friday
at a clinic in an underserved area in the Bronx. His parents and my
mother had objected to the platonic arrangement, protesting that it
would dampen both our love lives. "You're living with me forever,"
Bobby had said, hanging up with his mother, who had threatened to
stop fixing him up.

Unfortunately, she hadn't kept her word, and Bobby, at his wit's
end, had just the other night turned to my mother, who had promised
to explain young people to Mrs. Oh. He had yet to come out to my
mother, and I didn't know whether she suspected Bobby was gay, as
George had claimed. I hardly had the chance to speak to her. *Cha-
gun Oma*, or Little Mother, his name for her, still called regularly, but
usually to talk to Bobby-*ya*, her affectionate name for him. She did
understand, finally, that he and I were just friends. I'd joked once that
it was a good thing I wasn't near marrying anyone, as she wouldn't
have the time to get to know him, and she'd very sternly informed me
that while Bobby-*ya* was her son-out-law, she still expected a son-in-
law from me.

On the dating front, June had set me up with a couple of doctors
she knew from med school. They'd both been drips, as Bobby had
warned me they would be, and I'd told her to hold off on arranging
any more until Bobby and I had finished planning for my mother's
sixtieth birthday. We were going to surprise her with a trip to Europe;
he wasn't coming but he was loaning me his credit card.

When Bobby and I weren't going over travel brochures, we were
watching kung-fu movies—he'd introduced me to them—or playing
board games. We made great roommates. He believed that a home
wasn't a home if it didn't have kimchi in the fridge and chocolate ice
cream in the freezer.

"Ginger, you're not eating," June said. "Do you not feel well?"

The conversation stopped and everyone looked at me.

Flowers, food, friends. It was the tableau missing from my fashion story. I picked up my chopsticks.

This was a happy ending without a wedding.

ACKNOWLEDGMENTS

I have been lucky in family, friends, colleagues, and teachers. In particular, I would like to thank my parents, Susan Hwang and David Hwang, the strongest and bravest people I know; my brothers, Kelley Hwang and Charles Hwang, and sister, Christiana Hwang, whose generosity enabled me to pursue the very non-second-generation occupation of novel-writing; Sandra Dijkstra, agent extraordinaire and driving force behind this dream; ace editor Trena Keating, whose enthusiasm, insight, and sagacity illuminated the way; Maureen Brady, Chuck Wachtel, and E. L. Doctorow for their invaluable encouragement and advice; Melissa Hammerle for the grant and all of her kindness; my dear friends, Vincent Santillo and Mark Manjoney, who buoyed me with pasta, weekends on Fire Island, and tech support; my beach buddy, Sabrina Weberstetter, for her many acts of help; freelance swami MP Dunleavey, who was never too busy to talk; and my official photographer, John Smock, for his patience and constancy.

I would also like to send shout-outs to the following, who supported, helped, and/or employed me over the course of the writing of this book: Jennifer Zahn, Helen Eaton, Christopher Hemblade, Jill Kurland, Toni Olasewere, Sonia Nikore, Samira Franklin, Kevin Delgado, Alyssa Colton-Heins, Neeti Madan, Paula Derrow, Jill Herzig, Cindi Leive, Judy Coyne, Dana Points, Ellen Seidman, Faye Haun, Val Frankel, Mary Hickey, Toni Hope, Jessica Branch, Laurel Touby, Emma Segal, Russell Carmony, and the CWP crew.

Finally, a special thanks must go to Julie Kramer, my first reader, second brain bank, and best friend. Her humor and heart emboldened me to chase after my butterflies.

ABOUT THE AUTHOR

Caroline Hwang is a magazine editor and writer whose work has appeared in *Glamour, Redbook, Self, Newsweek, Mademoiselle, CosmoGirl,* and *YM.* A graduate of the University of Pennsylvania with an M.F.A. from New York University, she lives in New York.